FELDY'S
GIRL

This is a work of fiction. Every character and incident in this book is imaginary, with the exception of historical characters referred to by their actual names, used fictitiously. All other names, characters, places, and incidents are the product of the author's imagination, or used fictitiously. Resemblance to real persons living or dead, business establishments, events, or locales is coincidental. Mona and Mike Shapen, and a couple of walk-ons, previously appeared in the novel *Now Playing At Canterbury*, by Vance Bourjaily, and have stepped into this book with the permission of Mr. Bourjaily's literary heirs. Thanks to them, and thanks to Mary Jo Joyce for her editing.

EAN-13: 978-0-9835572-0-3
Library of Congress Control Number: 2019937733
Rex Imperator, USA

FELDY'S GIRL

a novel by
Joseph Dobrian

REX IMPERATOR, New York, N.Y.

BOOKS BY JOSEPH DOBRIAN

FICTION
Willie Wilden (2011)
Ambitions (2014)
Hard-Wired (2016)
Feldy's Girl (2019)

NON-FICTION
Seldom Right But Never In Doubt (2012)

TRANSLATION
The Butcher of Paris, by Jean-François Dominique (2015)

Before I can tell my life what I want to do with it,
I must listen to my life telling me who I am.

—Parker J. Palmer

This book is dedicated to two ragin' Cajuns, who gave me invaluable encouragement and advice throughout the process: Katherine Perkins and Beth Ann Mock.

FELDY'S GIRL
by Joseph Dobrian

TABLE OF CONTENTS

BOOK I

FELDY'S GIRL

The first word I ever spoke was "Feldy," according to family tra-
dition. Not "mama," or "dada," or even "no," which I understand is the first word for a lot of babies. Mine was "Feldy," or
so my parents have told me. I think they're kidding, but that's
what they say. Anyway, I never called them anything but "Birdy"
and "Feldy," instead of "Mom" and "Pop" like my big brothers
Lou, Jack, and Jerry do. My next-older brother, Win, picked it up
from me. My younger brothers, Duffy and Sander, took it for
granted.

I remember an incident from the spring of 1956, when I still
hadn't quite turned six years old, that may have been the only
time I ever hurt my father's feelings. I'm pretty sure I never did,
after that. Maybe I didn't then, either; I just sensed that I did. It's
a funny memory; I laugh when I recall it—but I still feel guilty
about it to this day. I'm 17 now, so it has been a while. It wasn't
a sin. It wasn't up to the level of dishonoring my father. But I
would be mortified to ask Feldy if he remembers.

This would have been a few days after it had been announced
that Feldy would be the new Head Football Coach of the State
University Rivercats, in State City, Iowa. He had been Head
Coach of the Paiutes, of Winnemucca University, and we were
still living in Winnemucca, Nevada.

Feldy came home from his office that evening grinning all over his face—which didn't happen too often, because he always had lots on his mind. Plus, he is not a smiley person, as a general thing. He has these small, slightly squinty blue eyes, and some people think he looks like he's sneering, most of the time. I've never seen that, but it's what I've been told that people have said. I've seen reporters say it in the papers. Maybe because he's big and husky, and tough-looking, which also makes him seem intimidating.

People love Feldy when the going is good. They find ways to blame him, and put him down, when it isn't. That's human nature.

On this evening, Feldy came in the front door carrying one of those cardboard cylinders that you store maps or pictures in. Birdy was working on getting dinner ready, but Feldy called us all to the dining room table to see what he had brought home. I'm pretty sure Sander was not involved. He wouldn't even have been two years old, then. But the rest of us—Birdy and my brothers and I—we all gathered round. Even Duffy, who was only three and could barely see over the top of the table. I was wondering what this could be about, because I hardly ever saw Feldy all excited and happy like that. He hadn't even taken his hat and raincoat off.

"Okay, so you've all seen pictures of the Rivercat uniforms, right? What color are they?"

"Brown," said Lou. Lou would have been not quite twelve, then. He looked puzzled. "Brown and white. White numbers and white pants."

"That's right," said Feldy. "The way it was explained to me, they wear brown for the 'good earth of Iowa.' Only their uniforms are brown like the brown in a box of Crayolas. We all know what else that's the color of, right?"

I shouted, *"POOP!"* much louder than was needed to fill up that dining room. I fell apart giggling; my brothers laughed; Birdy gasped and then laughed; Feldy laughed the hardest of all.

"That's right!" Feldy gave me a quick little finger-point. "So I went and talked with Dr. Deger, over in the art department, about how maybe he could come up with a new design that would adjust the colors, and maybe re-design the team's logo, while he was at it. He's still working on the logo. But here's what he came up with for the uniform."

Feldy reached a finger into the cardboard cylinder and coaxed out a big sheet of thin white paper, rolled up. He carefully spread this out on the dining table. It was a mock-up of a football jersey—front and back—knee pants, and helmet. The brown of the jersey and the helmet was much darker than "the brown in a box of Crayolas." It was the color of unsweetened chocolate, almost black. The numbers on the jersey, and the pants, were a light camel color. The sleeves of the jerseys had two narrow stripes of camel, separated by a stripe of bright red.

"See, it's still brown, but it's a more impressive brown."

"Cat poop!" I screamed. Feldy looked taken aback for an instant, then laughed and looked like he was pretending to be horrified.

"And the pants are squishy baby poop!" Still screaming. I cracked me up, at that age. It's funny how I don't have much of a sense of humor anymore, now that I'm older, and I'm well aware of it. I wonder how that happened.

"Oh, my God!" said Feldy. It's anyone's guess whether or not Feldy was disappointed at my reaction—I can't help but think that he must have been—but he just looked back at me and laughed like he really thought it was funny. Maybe he did.

"Oh, Terri, that's awful," said Birdy. She was smiling at me, but the smile had a little warning in it. Birdy is small and thin—like a bird, a sparrow maybe—and she is a smiler, but she hardly ever laughs loudly. She has so many different smiles, and each smile means something different. I can always tell what each of her smiles means. So can other people, I bet.

"It's very nice, Dear," she said to Feldy. "Terri's kidding. Those are very pleasing colors. I especially like that red stripe on the sleeves. Just that touch of red really makes it jump."

"Yeah, I thought so too," said Feldy. But he looked slightly deflated, like I'd taken the edge off his mood.

"I was kidding," I told him. "It's nice." I really did think it was nice, but I was afraid Feldy wouldn't believe me.

"Yeah, Pop, it's great," said Lou. Jack and Jerry kind of grunted, to show they agreed.

"It's great 'cause it looks exciting," said Win. "Like what a good team would wear."

Win was almost seven; He was already learning diplomacy at that age, which I have never quite done.

That remark obviously lifted Feldy's spirits back up.

"I'm going to have these uniforms made, out of my own pocket," he told us. "I'll introduce them as soon as we move to State City. I'll hold a press conference when spring practice starts, and do it then. Maybe the athletic department will like it, and maybe not, but it's always easier to ask forgiveness than to ask permission. I'll worry about the athletic department reimbursing me later."

He grinned again.

"It'll be all new poop, right, Terri?"

§

Some of my happiest times, all through my growing up, have been when I'm sitting with Feldy, talking—mostly about sports, but about plenty of other stuff too. By the time I was nine or ten, I knew way more about football than any boy my age. I probably could have coached a college football team myself. I loved, more than just about anything, to have Feldy tell me about being a football coach. When I was 14, Feldy stepped down from his job as Head Coach at State University, to become Athletic Director. Okay, technically it was a promotion. Ever since then, I've learned about how to run an entire athletic program, from him— but that's a less interesting job.

It's the night of February 1, 1968. Feldy and I are sitting in the den of our house in State City, watching the ten o'clock news.

Feldy has a modern-looking black leather lounge chair, which is officially his chair. He'll sit with his feet up on a matching stool, in the evening, and usually he'll have one of his black Tabacalera cigars in his mouth. Feldy can work on the same cigar for as much as two weeks. He might take a few puffs on it after dinner, then let it go dead and mouth it, you might say, for the rest of the evening.

I'm sitting across the room, on the green velveteen sofa, with my legs tucked under my Black Stewart plaid school skirt. My legs are too long. All of me is too long. I may have stopped growing, at last, but it's too late: the damage is done. I'm only an inch or so shorter than Feldy, who is six-one and a half. I've been told I have nice hair, but otherwise I'm not much to look at. You know that "awkward age" that a girl goes through, when she knows darn well that she's as graceful as a hippopotamus and pretty like an iguana? For me, that stage started at about age ten, and I'm still in it.

It's just me and Feldy, watching TV. Birdy is upstairs, in bed. Duffy and Sander—the last two of my brothers still living at home—are up in their rooms too.

The sports report starts at 10:15. It leads with coverage of the press conference that took place earlier this evening, up in Green Bay, Wisconsin. Vince Lombardi has announced that he's stepping down as Head Coach of the Green Bay Packers but remaining as General Manager. He said something like, "It's impractical for me to try to do both jobs, and I feel I must relinquish one of them." He then introduced his successor as Head Coach: Phil Bengtson, who has been his defensive coordinator for the past few years.

I don't want to look over at Feldy. I keep staring at the screen, trying to think of something I can say that might be useful, but nothing is coming, so I wait till the commercial break, then I ask Feldy, "Are you okay?"

Feldy starts a little, like he had been in his own thoughts till he heard my voice.

"Oh. Sure."

As usual, he's half-lying in that chair, with his shoes and jacket off and his tie loosened, and superficially he doesn't look any different from any other night, but I can sense that he's just trying not to show how down he feels.

"It was a long shot to begin with," he says. "Bengston was always the guy I thought would get it. He's who I would have gone with, if I were Lombardi."

(People switch the "t" and the "s" in their minds, and call him "Bengston." Even though it's Bengtson.)

"Well, play the Glad Game."

Feldy smiles a tiny bit.

"Okay. It would have been a thankless job. That's an old team. They were old, last season, and they're getting older. They might win their division this fall, but I doubt it. You know how I feel about Lombardi, but I wonder how comfortable I would have been with him looking over my shoulder, maybe even undercutting me. Good enough?"

"There you go," I say. "But, do you really think he would do that? Do you think he'll do that to this new guy?"

"Hard to say. He'll miss coaching. He'll notice how Bengston isn't doing it the way he would have done it, and he'll get frustrated. He might not give a damn if Bengston screws it up. He might even secretly hope that's how it'll turn out."

"You've still got, what, 25 other pro teams to choose from?"

"Oh, sure. Pro football is all grown up now, and it'll get even bigger. It'll get really, really big. I'm still talking with people, here and there. But this one's done now. Realistically, it wasn't going to be anybody but Bengston. He's going to have a lousy time of it. The players won't respond to him like they responded to Lombardi; the fans won't like him because he's not Lombardi."

Ordinarily, I would go up to bed as soon as the sports are over—I don't care about the weather report—but on this evening, I feel I have to sit there in case Feldy needs to talk more, or to keep him company if he doesn't. But Feldy stays focused on the TV as though this were any other night. When the weather report is over, he gets up from the sofa, says, "Goodnight, Terri," as he always does if I'm still in the room, and goes upstairs.

I sit there for a couple of minutes more, before I go up to my room and to bed, and I play the Glad Game, too. I'm glad we won't have to sell this house and move to Green Bay.

I love our house. We've lived here since we got to State City. Hilltop Street is one of the nicest neighborhoods in town, with huge oak trees and big old houses. Some of them are pretty fancy, with little details on the outside, so you can tell they were built a long time ago, back when they built fancy houses. Hilltop Street runs north to south for about five blocks, and our house stands at about the mid-point. It's probably the biggest on the whole street. Almost a castle. Red brick with two white columns, one on either side of the front door, which hold up a little balcony.

Mine is the smallest of the five upstairs bedrooms, but it's the only one, other than the master bedroom, that has a private bath. My brothers don't care much about the look of their rooms, but when I was confirmed, in seventh grade, Feldy and Birdy let me redecorate my room to celebrate the occasion. I chose the wallpaper, the bedclothes, the dresser, the throw rug, everything.

I love all kinds of light blue—maybe because you see light blues so much in church. The wallpaper in my room is this bright, cheery sky blue, with dusty rose and light green accents. The sheets and blankets on my bed are mostly light blue too. The dresser is a light pine, and on it sits a framed portrait of St. Teresa of Ávila, in her cell. I've got another small painting, a reproduction of Rubens' *Assumption of Mary*, on my writing desk. I got the desk from a junk shop, and it's dark wood, which doesn't quite go with the rest of the room, but it's such a nice piece.

Next to the Rubens painting are my Douay-Rheims Bible and a Missal, which is one of my favorite possessions, only it's not as useful now that they've made so many changes in the Mass, and switched to English. Feldy and Birdy gave it to me for my first communion. The St. Joseph Continual Missal, bound in dark brown leather, with gold leaf and illuminated letters. It's such a beautiful book.

I have an ivory-colored crucifix, just maybe four inches long, on the wall above my bed. A bedroom isn't a bedroom without a crucifix. It's comforting, if you understand why it's there.

I have grey teeth. I can't help thinking about that, every time I brush them. Birdy took tetracycline for an infection while she was pregnant with me. Nobody knew at the time that if your mother took tetracycline while she was expecting you, your permanent teeth would come in grey. Birdy was all apologetic, when she saw what was happening. She explained that nobody had known about that side effect—so I understood that it wasn't her fault. I never held it against her. Birdy promised me that when I was older, I could get my teeth capped if I wanted to, but then right around my eleventh birthday, I saw the movie *Pollyanna*, and I read the book—and it sounds silly, but *Pollyanna* may have had more of an impact on me than any other book I have ever read in my life, except the Bible.

I learned to play the Glad Game, as Pollyanna did. In the movie it was called "The Glad Game," but in the book it was just called "The Game." Whenever something bad happened to Pollyanna, or if she got a result that wasn't what she wanted, she would force herself to find the silver lining, and be glad about it. I found a way to be glad that I had grey teeth.

I told myself to be glad that my teeth were something I could offer up to God, as redemptive suffering. But then as soon as I had that thought, I told myself that that was absurd, and shameful. To think that having grey teeth was suffering, really? I told myself, instead, that my teeth were a gift from God—to keep me humble, not vain. I even went through a phase of a few days when I included a thanks to God for my teeth, in my nightly prayers. Which I suppose might have meant that I was substituting Pride for Vanity. I laugh about that, but we all have one favorite sin, and Pride is mine.

Some people say that Vanity and Pride are the same sin, but I believe there's a slight difference. Vanity is petty. Pride is the mother of all sins.

Anyway, my grey teeth are a part of who I am. I keep a little sand timer on my bathroom sink to make sure I brush for a full three minutes. I use Listerine before I brush, to kill any germs; then I brush to get rid of the medicinal smell.

I brush my hair, 100 strokes, every night. I know I shouldn't be vain of my hair, but I am.

When I turn out my bedside light and kneel by my bed, in the dark, I usually know what my prayers will be, because they're pretty simple, and the Church has so many good prayers for every occasion, so you hardly ever have to make up a prayer yourself. But tonight I have to think for a few seconds, about how, exactly, I can ask St. Teresa to pray for Feldy.

"*Querida Santa Teresa*, I ask that you think about what's right for my father, and pray for him in the way you think best, and look after my mother and brothers too." I make no sound.

Then I say a Hail Mary, silently, and an Our Father. Finally, "Dear God, thank you for today. Let me remember the good parts, and learn from the bad parts. Forgive me for the things I did wrong and help me to be better tomorrow. Please help me to be the person you mean me to be. Amen."

That last line has always been the one most important part of my prayers, all my life long. "Please help me to be the person you mean me to be."

Then I get into bed. I remind myself that I get to practice my cello, first thing in the morning, and that makes me feel happy, lying there in bed with the light out.

My bedroom is where I practice my cello, usually—and I usually practice first thing in the morning after I'm washed and dressed, before breakfast. Birdy taught me and each of my brothers to play the piano, starting at age eight—except for Win and me. We both asked to start when Win was seven and I was six—and Birdy insisted that each of us learn some other instrument as we got older, or study voice, unless we wanted to really focus on the piano. I chose the cello because it sounds more like a human voice than any other instrument.

I see different colors, sometimes, when I play or hear music. Or sometimes noises—non-musical noises—will bring various colors into my head. Not every sound, or every note, but some of them will cause colors to flash in front of me, so that sometimes everything I'm seeing is shaded—like a tint being laid over a photograph. Or sometimes it's a sort of visual explosion, like if an electrical transformer had burst outside the house.

I sensed, even as a girl, that this was unusual: that most people didn't experience sounds as colors. Because I didn't, all the time. When I told Birdy about these colors, after our first-ever piano lesson, Birdy gave me a big smile.

"I've heard of that. It's called chromesthesia. That's a big long word, isn't it? I learned about it in college, in one of my psychology classes. It means you're going to be a wonderful musician one day—if you work very hard."

Sometimes I'll see colors when I'm praying, too. When I was older—14 or so—I started telling myself that these colors were God revealing Himself to me as the Holy Spirit. But it would have been prideful of me to have said that to anyone else, so I never have.

OVERACHIEVER

I'm one of those insufferable overachieving girls. Straight A's in everything. I do speech and drama; serve on the Student Council; play my cello; participate in Sodality. But I have never felt that I didn't have time for everything I wanted to do.

I understand that some people love doing nothing, but I can't understand why anyone *would* love doing nothing. I'm always doing something, and it's almost always something constructive. Okay: I'm a model teenager.

I grew up famous. There's no getting around that. In State City, I have always been "Feldy's Girl." When we got to State City, my two younger brothers weren't really verbal yet, but I was kind of talkative—and I was the only girl in Coach Feldevert's adorable family. While Feldy was coaching the Rivercats, at least once every football season—sometimes more often—there would be a photo of me in *The State City Examiner*, *The Cedar Rapids Gazette*, *The University Statesman*, *The Des Moines Register*, or various other Iowa newspapers. I would be cheering from the stands at Rivercat Stadium, or standing on the sidelines, watching the football team practicing.

The Feldevert family as a whole might have been adorable, but I don't think I ever was. I'm not a warm person. I'm almost always polite, but I'm never an extrovert—which is funny, because Feldy certainly is, and Birdy is quiet but she likes being around people.

On my first day in first grade, the teacher, Sister Mary Jane Patricia, knew who I was—although obviously she had only ever seen the name in the newspapers. When she called the roll, not even five minutes into that first day, when she came to my name, and said "Teresa fell-DEE-vert?" I gave her my politest smile and said "Here, Sister, but it's FELD-e-vert. Like ROZ-e-velt." Sister Mary Jane Patricia smiled back and said, "You're Feldy's Girl, aren't you? I'm so looking forward to the football season."

None of my teachers, or any of the kids I have grown up with, have ever made an obvious thing of it, but I couldn't help noticing, even at that age, that I always got treated as though being Feldy's Girl made me important. Because of that, I've always felt like I have something to live up to. I have to be better-behaved than the other kids; I have to work harder; I have to be neater and cleaner; I have to be at the top of my class every time.

I'm thankful for this. I couldn't have asked for a more wonderful childhood. There was never a better father than Feldy, or a better mother than Birdy. My parents always expected me to do whatever I did as well as I could possibly do it—and I'm glad.

I didn't fit the model of Little Miss Perfect, though, when I was growing up. For one thing, I was never little for my age. I'm pretty strong. I could do girl-stuff if I had to—dolls and playing house—but I hardly ever did, if I could do boy-stuff instead.

I love sports, even if I'm not very good at them. When I was a kid—from six up to about eleven—it was wiffle ball or kickball on the school playground in the spring and summer; football in somebody's yard (usually ours) in summer and fall and into the winter; basketball in somebody's driveway all year round.

I played football with the boys. Because I was Feldy's Girl, I usually got to be quarterback. When my hands got big enough, I could throw a hard, tight spiral, tighter than any boy in the neighborhood. Feldy taught me. He's a patient teacher, but he's a perfectionist. He would say, "There's wrong ways to do it, and the right way. Which way are you going to do it?"

Even as a girl, I could punt a football a long way. I'm slow on my feet, so I was never much good as a receiver or running back, but I could block when I wasn't playing quarterback. On defense I was as good a tackler as any boy, if I say it myself. Not because

I was stronger than the boys, but because Feldy had taught me how to hit the ballcarrier right, to bring him down.

When there weren't enough kids around to form two teams, we would play "smear the queer"—where one kid picks up the ball and runs, in whatever direction, till he's gang-tackled—and I was one of the toughest kids in the neighborhood to haul down. "Smear the queer" is my very favorite game of all time, and it's too bad you can't play it when you get bigger.

Feldy taught me how to use my fists, too, when I was eight or so, in case I ever had to. He told me, "Don't start with anyone, but if someone starts with you, it's okay for you to finish it."

Then he told me about the one time he had ever punched someone really intending to hurt him. He told me that when he had been playing football at University of Wisconsin, one of the assistant coaches had called him, "You dumb bohunk."

"I didn't even think to do it. It was like my right hand was leaving my body on its own. And there was the coach on the ground, out cold. It wasn't the 'bohunk' that did it. It was the 'dumb.' For some reason, nothing has ever made me so angry as someone making fun of my intelligence.

"Anyway, once that guy had come to, the Head Coach told me maybe I'd better apologize to him. I said, 'Let him apologize first, then we can talk about it.' Coach dropped it right there, and it never got mentioned ever again."

So I probably could have punched out most of the kids in the neighborhood, only I never did, because nobody ever started with me. Of course, boys are handicapped because everyone knows you can't hit a girl—but if they had wanted to, you know what? I bet most of them were afraid of me.

I had to win. If you and I were spitting at a crack in the sidewalk just for bragging rights, I had to win. Always within the rules. I would never have cheated. But if I lost at anything, I wouldn't forgive myself easily. I could throw the tightest spiral because I had to throw the tightest spiral. I have always set higher standards for myself than my parents ever set for me.

Birdy was maybe a tiny bit put out, when I was younger, that I wasn't quiet and dainty the way girls are supposed to be—the way Birdy herself is—but probably she never minded very much. During school and our religious activities—Mass and so on—I *was* quiet and dainty, and of course I have learned to be a little more genteel, now that I'm older.

Even in first grade, I could read well enough to read the sports pages. I read the news parts, too, but I especially read the sports section, because that was where Feldy was. It took me a while to learn the difference between reporting, and opinion. The opinion articles were my favorites—when they said nice things about Feldy. Sometimes they didn't, and I would want to rip the paper up—only I couldn't, if the rest of the family hadn't read it yet.

Birdy used to take us kids to the State City Public Library pretty often, because she wanted us to read. Not all seven of us at once, of course. I must have been about nine years old when I discovered that in the adult reading room, they had at least the Sunday edition of newspapers from all over the country, plus a few from Europe. That was what I wanted to read.

Birdy was frustrated, at first, because that was all I wanted to do in the library: read newspapers. But she got used to it. She told Feldy about it—like she was impressed by it, after all—and I guess Feldy was impressed too. He said, "Terri, we ought to take you to the State University library. It's way bigger than the public library and I'll bet they have even more newspapers there."

The next Saturday morning—it must have been spring, if Feldy didn't have a game to coach—Feldy took me there. He said if I wanted to read newspapers for a couple of hours, he would go to his office for a while, then come get me. That was fine with me. I still remember reading *The Sunday Express* that day, and *The Milwaukee Journal*, among others.

From then on, every few weeks, I would ask to spend time at the University library. Feldy would drop me outside the building and come get me later. Technically, only State University students, faculty, and staff were supposed to use the library. But Feldy told me, "If anybody asks, tell them you're Feldy's Girl."

Nobody ever asked.

Sometimes, I would read the sports pages of newspapers that covered other Big Ten teams, the teams the Rivercats played against. Once, that September right before the football season started, when Feldy came to pick me up—Birdy was in the car with him that day, for some reason—I got into the back seat and asked, "Feldy, what's a thug?"

"It's a hoodlum, a bully, a bad guy," Feldy said. "Somebody who beats people up, or even kills them."

"Thugs were bandits, weren't they?" Birdy said. "In India, long ago. Where did you see the word?"

I told Feldy and Birdy that I had guessed that the sports columnist in the Columbus, Ohio paper hadn't meant it as a compliment when he referred to Feldy as "the Thug in Chief, at Thug University." But I hadn't been sure.

Feldy said, "Honey, you have to learn to let that stuff roll off you. That's what I do."

Birdy said, "I wonder if it's good for you, reading all those awful stories about Feldy."

"She's learning how the world works," Feldy said. "She's learning that newspapers aren't always honest."

Feldy turned around to glance at me, and he said, "Maybe you'll be the world's first honest journalist, one day."

In the fall of 1963, when I was in eighth grade, after President Kennedy was assassinated, I started thinking more about that.

During those few days in late November, our family was practically camping out in front of the TV in the den, or in the rec room in the basement, flipping back and forth between CBS, NBC, and ABC, depending on which network seemed to be offering the most interesting coverage or analysis at the moment. It was then that I became aware of Nancy Dickerson, who was one of the correspondents covering the events for NBC.

I had seen lady reporters on TV before, but they had all been covering women's stuff, like how the White House was being redecorated, or what a certain movie star's favorite recipes were. This was the first time I had seen a woman covering a hard news event. I didn't say anything to anyone about it, at the time, but that was when I first had the idea: "That's something I could do."

In the summer of 1964, I saw Nancy Dickerson covering the political conventions on TV. I started borrowing anthologies of journalism from the public library. That fall, I got on the staff of *The Visitor*, the school newspaper at St. Mary of the Visitation High School—although, as a freshman, I mostly handled the dull production work: proofreading and so on. I rarely had the opportunity to work on a story, and Visitation High is not the environment where exciting journalism is much called for.

It was a Sunday afternoon, in 1968, two weeks after Feldy and I found out that he wouldn't be the next Head Coach of the Packers. Feldy and I and Duffy and Sander were watching basketball on TV. I must have made an insightful comment, because Feldy said to me, "Terri, if you're going to be a journalist, you maybe ought to be a sportswriter. At least you would know something about what you were covering, which would be a leg up on about 99 percent of your colleagues. I could even see you calling games on radio or TV. Doing the play-by-play. Or maybe with your own show."

I didn't think much more about the subject that day, but for the rest of that winter, the idea kept creeping back into my head. One night at the dinner table I said, "Feldy, if I wanted to be a sportscaster, how would I go about it? I suppose I would major in Journalism, then try to focus more on TV and radio reporting... but that isn't what girls do, is it? Calling football games."

"Never heard of a girl doing it," said Feldy, "but no reason why you couldn't."

"I want to try all kinds of journalism. I might not go into sports at all, but it's fun to daydream about."

Birdy said, "You'd be good. Just in general, you'd be a good TV or radio journalist. You've got the voice and the presence."

"You know what you ought to do?" said Feldy. "Write a letter to Joe Barnett and Sonny Bell." Mr. Barnett and Mr. Bell are the "Voice of the Rivercats" for football and basketball games on State City's main radio station, KSCR. "Tell them you'd like to work for them this fall. You know, maybe not even for pay, as a gopher, sort of. So you can see how the whole business works. It'd be a great experience."

I composed the letter that very night.

Dear Mr. Barnett and Mr. Bell:

My name is Teresa Feldevert. I am the daughter of Leo and Bernadette Feldevert. I am graduating from St. Mary of the Visitation High School this spring, and I will be entering State University in the fall—possibly as a Journalism major. I don't know yet whether my focus will be on broadcast or newspapers, and I don't know whether I will concentrate on sports or on other subjects, but as you might imagine, on account of my family background, I am generally interested in sports. All sports, but especially football. I am on my high school paper, <u>The</u> <u>Visitor</u>; I play the cello (I might take a double major, in Journalism and Music); and I am interested in drama and forensics.

I thought it would be a tremendous experience to work with the sports department of a radio station this fall, especially on the days when you broadcast Rivercat football games. I would be happy to be one of the people who works behind the scenes, so I can learn how a football broadcast gets put together. I don't expect to be paid and I hope you don't think I expect any special privilege because of who my father is. (Excuse me for mentioning that at all, but it's an inescapable fact, isn't it?)

May I come and see you sometime in the next few days to discuss how I might be able to help you during the football season? I would be glad to provide you with references. Many thanks in advance for any consideration you can give me in this matter.

Sincerely,

Teresa M. Feldevert

Three days after I posted the letter, in the early evening, Birdy called me to the phone, and it was Mr. Barnett. He told me that KSCR would love to have me come into the station for an interview, maybe closer to the start of the football season, to talk about putting in a few hours as a production assistant.

"It's nice to know you're interested in journalism," he said. "You know, we've all watched you and your brothers grow up, over—what's it been? Ten, eleven, twelve years? But we still don't know much about any of you, do we?"

"I think that's how our parents want it," I said. "They've always told us that they don't want any of us kids to be inconvenienced because of who we are. They don't want us to have any special privileges, either. That's why I hesitated to contact you."

"I understand, but at the same time, you have certain advantages that you've gained from being your father's daughter. Like being so knowledgeable about sports. It wouldn't make sense not to take advantage of that. Anyway, it's not a sure thing. Come see us, right around the end of your summer vacation."

INTERVIEWING BIRDY

I came home from school on March 21 to find Birdy sitting on the sofa in the den, in her house-dress and apron, smoking one of her Kents and reading the *Examiner*. She didn't look up; she just said, "Rockefeller announced he's not going to run. So I guess it'll be Nixon against Johnson after all. I don't see Nixon winning that one, thank heavens."

Feldy and Birdy are Democrats, and some of their interest has rubbed off on me. I asked Birdy, "You don't think McCarthy or Kennedy will knock Johnson off?"

"That'll never happen. McCarthy certainly won't. He looks a lot stronger than he is. He's got a few noisy radicals on his side. Bobby, *maaaaaybe*, has an outside chance, but Johnson's got the whole party machinery behind him. I might prefer Bobby, but I won't get my hopes up."

All of a sudden, I got an idea for a story for *The Visitor*. I sat down next to Birdy and asked, "Would it be okay if I interviewed you? You could talk about what it's like to be the wife of the Athletic Director, about the political stuff you do— plus anything else you want to talk about."

"That would be fun for me. Maybe not for you: trying to make a feature article out of me. But sure, if you think you could do that. When would you want to do the interview?"

"How's now?"

The interview wasn't just conducted in the next few minutes. It went on, over several days, as Birdy and I found time to talk in private. Lots of it consisted of going over information that I had already learned, while I was growing up, but I had to get Birdy to elaborate on it. I knew, for example, that both sides of Birdy's family had come to the United States in the middle of the 19th century. I knew that Birdy's father, John Allen Duffy, made his fortune in real estate development and was one of the wealthiest men in Wisconsin—but I was not going to use that information in an article about Birdy.

I also already knew that my parents met in a psychology class at the University of Wisconsin, in the fall of their junior year.

"But I need you to say it," I told Birdy. "For the story."

"Well, I was sitting near the back of the classroom, that first day," Birdy said. "This young man walked in behind me, walked right past my desk, straight up to the front like he owned the room, and he sat down front and center.

"He wasn't the best-looking young man I had ever seen, but he was so big and well-built. So... *imposing*! He had this tight red-trimmed white sweater over a plain white dress shirt, and, you know, he's older now, but he was shaped like a V, almost, from his waist to his shoulders. Power just radiated off him. I know that sounds *cliché*, and I wish I knew a better way to describe it, but that'll have to do. It was almost a physical force. I felt like a tuning fork, vibrating. I hadn't been introduced yet, hadn't heard him speak, hadn't so much as made eye contact with him."

"Do you remember your first conversation?"

"Not really, but I remember the first thing he ever said to me. It was the second day of that class, and I was deliberately slow getting out of my chair at the end of it, so that he might notice me, so I was still sitting when he walked past me, and he said, 'You're going to strain your eyes, sitting back here.' Then he was out the door before I could say anything.

"The next session, I sat next to him, up at the front. And that's where I stayed. Then a few days later, when the football season started, Feldy told me to bring my friends to the game—so I did.

"I knew hardly anything about football, at the time. I just kept my eye on number 14. He seemed to be all over the field, mostly bumping into people and knocking them over.

"From then on, we were inseparable. He never proposed to me; we just understood, after a few weeks, that we would be married. We knew it by the end of that semester, at the latest."

In all, Birdy gave me way more information than would fit into one article.

Hardly anybody in State City knows that Leo Feldevert's wife's full name is Bernadette Eithne Duffy Feldevert, let alone that Eithne is pronounced "EN-ya." She's Birdy, or Mrs. Feldevert, to those who know her. Since moving here in 1956, Birdy has stayed in the background as the quiet, retiring wife of State University's legendary football coach, and now Athletic Director.

She has always been interested in politics (she's a precinct committeewoman for the State County Democratic Party, and looks forward to this fall's Presidential campaign) and she might want to get more involved in the political system once her children are all grown, but she is not much interested in a career at this point.

"I wanted to be a lawyer, when I was younger," Birdy says. "I did complete one year of law school, but then I started having children, and I realized early on that my true vocation lay in marriage and family. I never thought of not being a wife and mother, no matter what else I did. My husband's job has always forced him to travel quite a lot, so most of the responsibility of bringing up our seven children fell on me, but that's the way it should be. I believe there is such a thing as a man's sphere and a woman's sphere, and I consider myself extremely lucky to have seven healthy children, and to have participated in the life of one of the nation's most successful football coaches.

"There has to be one person in a family who is in charge, who is the leader. If my husband is busy and involved, and happy in his work, it's my duty as a wife to fit in with his plans. I understood that, going into our marriage. One thing I knew was not my duty, was to be an annoyance or a hindrance to my husband.

"It's not easy for any woman to be a football coach's wife, especially at the higher levels of college football. But I've been lucky that I never had to suffer the worst of it. I never had to go through what a coach's wife and family have to go through if the team is doing really badly. Still, we would get our share of crank phone calls, and so on, when the Rivercats weren't having a great season."

When her husband was Head Coach, Birdy seldom traveled with him to road games, or on recruiting trips.

"A couple times I went on a road trip with him and the team, but Feldy found it distracted him to have me there," she says. "He was happier to have me at home."

Now that her family is older, Birdy has become more involved in politics, which she says have fascinated her "since I was in sixth grade and Franklin Roosevelt was running for President." Recently, she says, she has gotten her husband more interested in her work with local and state Democrats.

"Feldy always tells me that I'm the politician in the family, that I should run for office. I've always thought that he should be the one to do that. He could be the Governor of Iowa, or maybe even President of the United States. He's so magnetic, and he likes to help people. We both felt that he was doing that, as coach. Now that he's Athletic Director, I wonder if he isn't frustrated, at times: not working directly with young men, being a model for them."

When Birdy told me that—when we did that part of the interview—we were down in the basement; she was taking clothes out of the dryer and folding them, and I was standing there taking notes, overcome with guilt, of course, because I was doing that instead of helping Birdy. I said, "But you should run for something. State Legislature, maybe."

"It has occurred to me," Birdy said. "But for one thing, people would say that I'm not qualified, that I'm only running because of whom I'm married to—and some people would say it's a conflict of interest, since the State Legislature has something to say about how the universities are funded. I wouldn't have a prayer. Not while your father is doing what he's doing."

"Tell him to retire," I said. "Tell him it's your turn."

Birdy laughed.

"Just imagine how that would go over! No, I'm happy to be right where I am. If Feldy is happy in his work, I'm happy. The only thing—and please don't publish this, this is off the record, okay?—I wonder how happy he is now. He never complains, but you know how he can get, when he talks about what he'd do if he were still coaching. He enjoys being challenged in his job, but maybe Athletic Director isn't the kind of challenge he wants."

"Would you want him to coach again?"

"Hard to say yes or no to that. The practice, the recruiting, he enjoyed all that. But what happened on the field would wear him out. You know how he could get."

I did. That's not to say that Feldy ever behaved badly to any of us, when he was a coach. But he would get migraine headaches. He had bleeding ulcers that he was afraid might get out of control one day. Before a game, Feldy would get so wound up that he couldn't even keep oatmeal on his stomach. After an easy win he would be fine—and oddly enough, he would usually be more or less okay after a loss. But after a close win he would usually shut himself in his study—and sometimes instead of brooding, he would cry. The rest of us could hear him, but we knew to leave him alone.

"It's hard for me to believe he really wants to go back to coaching, even if he talks about it," Birdy said. "He doesn't feel that he's ever gotten the respect he deserves as an intellectual. He wants to be respected for his smarts. I think that's what drives him, more than anything else in the world."

§

I'm staying after school for a few minutes to discuss the article with Sister Timothy, the faculty adviser to *The Visitor*. She and Monsignor Koudelka, who teaches Religion, are my two favorite teachers of my whole high school career.

We're in the "press room," where Sister Timothy has her desk. It's an ordinary classroom, with very little production equipment, since Visitation High isn't a big enough school to justify a newspaper that requires an actual printing press. *The Visitor* consists of sheets of heavy eight-and-a-half by 14-inch paper, Xeroxed and stapled together.

Nobody else is in the room. It's a beautiful afternoon. I can see out the window that the snow is melting fast. I want to get outside and take a roundabout route home—but I enjoy talking with Sister Timothy, too, and I do it every chance I get. I sit down next to her desk to wait while she reads the article.

Sister Timothy is somewhere in her 50s, probably closer to 60. Always stern-looking, although she's usually pretty good-humored without smiling. She has exceptionally upright posture—so her habit, coif, and veil make her look almost military. I bet even most priests are scared of her.

When she's done reading, she places the paper on the desk in front of her—ceremonially, almost—and raises her eyes to the upper half of her glasses to focus on me.

"This is almost perfect." She pauses to let me absorb that. "You give your mother the substance she deserves. I had no idea that she had gone to law school. It's an interesting picture of a marriage, too, whether you know it or not."

"I wonder if she has any regrets," I say. "About not finishing law school and having a career. I didn't feel right about asking that."

"No life is without regrets. But I would be surprised if she isn't doing what she wanted to do with her life—as she said."

"Well, she didn't have any choice, did she? She got pregnant, gosh, would have been just three months after they got married. And again, right after the first one: twins, that time."

Sister Timothy chuckles without smiling.

"Yes, that would get in the way of a law practice. But your mother evidently felt she had a vocation to the family. Stronger than any other. Or she would have postponed getting married. You know the old saying: 'If you didn't want to go to Chicago, why did you get on the train?'"

"Did you ever think you had some other vocation?" I ask. "Or did you always know?"

"Oh, no, Dear, I certainly didn't always know. When I was your age, I assumed I would get married and have a family. But as I went through college, as I learned more, I started to realize that I was too independent. I could tell that God didn't want that for me. I didn't actually hear it, but I felt God telling me, 'A husband would make you crazy; you have to be your own person.'"

That surprises me.

"You're too independent, but you joined an order?"

"Doing what I want to do, and doing it for God. Taking my vows... it was a freeing experience. I have never been so grateful for anything, as I have been that I got the call. Only a very few people truly have a religious vocation. I feel extremely lucky. It has opened doors into worlds that I couldn't have imagined."

Which shocks me, because that last sentence is almost word-for-word what Feldy told me once, years ago, about football.

Sister Timothy hands the story back to me.

"I want you to show this to Monsignor, before we publish it in the paper," she says. "You know how interested he is in the subject of vocation."

Monsignor Koudelka is a big, burly man—60 or so—who looks like he might have played football once, himself. He has thick, wavy iron-grey hair and a rugged-looking face—red, with a big mouth and a big nose. He talks with a slight European accent, like Lawrence Welk. He was born and brought up in a Moravian community in Nebraska. Some of the kids call him "Monsignor Wunnerful."

Monsignor has kind of a gruff way about him, so some of the parishioners at Our Lady think he's not bright or scholarly. But if you pay attention when he gives the homily at Mass, you can tell that he thinks his ideas through pretty well. In the classroom, sometimes he gets downright legalistic.

He's strict, but he's kind. Like Sister Timothy. I pay special attention in his classes. Monsignor told me once, when we were talking in the hall one day, "I don't think I ever had a girl more innerested in the Church than you are. One or two boys, but never a girl."

I handed my article to Monsignor the next day, before Religion class, and today he hands it back to me and asks me, "Do you think you would like to write your final term paper on your father's career? It will be a little unconventional for a Religion class, but I know you know the catechism—you don't have to prove that to me—and a piece about your father might be a good example of how a person hears a vocation, and follows it. You know, I'm sure my students get tired of hearing me talking about saving souls—and I would love to know how God brought your father to his work."

I'm amazed—and thrilled—that Monsignor has suggested this. It's going to be absolutely no trouble, since I knew most of the information already, and it will be easy to get Feldy to talk about his career. And so much fun to write it down for someone outside our family to read.

A VOCATION IN FOOTBALL

By Teresa Feldevert

The object of football, to Leo "Feldy" Feldevert, is to put the other team on their behinds. If you do that, you win— and winning is fun. Building character might be a by-product of winning, Feldy says, but it's not the point. Neither is sportsmanship. If you're not focused on winning, Feldy warns, you lose. Losing is not fun.

"It makes me furious," Feldy says, "whenever someone brings up that old Grantland Rice bromide: 'For when the One Great Scorer comes, to mark against your name, He writes, not that you won or lost, but how you played the game.' That is horse [manure]. That slogan would look great in a mutual fund manager's office, wouldn't it? I would get the [heck] out of there and find a manager who cared about making money."

Feldy doesn't discount the idea that football builds character—but only if you're doing your best to win.

"If you can teach a young man to leave everything he has out there on the field, win or lose, and then get ready for the next Saturday," he says, "he will carry that with him for the rest of his life, and he will be a winner in the world, whether he's a surgeon or a car salesman or a big-game hunter. He will be a better citizen, a better man, if he has learned to win at football."

Feldy studied psychology in his undergraduate years at the University of Wisconsin, and he says it taught him that every football player—or anyone in any walk of life—is motivated by something different.

"Football is the oldest sport in history. Cave-men would test their skills and strengths against each other. Then they started doing it in groups. First it was for real, for survival. Then later on, it was to establish a pecking order. Can one group of X number of men beat up another group of the same number of men? Then someone got the idea of introducing a ball. Or maybe it was a human skull, at first. At that point, it became a game; it became fun. More fun for the winners."

"Football is underemphasized in our educational system," Feldy insists. "We need more of it. People who don't know any better, complain that football players are coddled at colleges and universities. Nonsense."

Feldy, who coached the State University Rivercats football team for nine seasons, gave up coaching and became State University's Athletic Director in 1965.

"Football is a young man's game," he explains. "I didn't want to grow old in coaching, hanging on like that guy in that novel that I read in high school: Mr. Chips. That would have been pathetic."

But, Feldy admits, he can't imagine a life outside of football. He was born in 1921 on a tobacco farm near the town of Brailsford Junction, in Rock County, Wisconsin.

"I was good at all sports," he recalls. "Football was what I lived and breathed, though, and I almost didn't ever play it again, after my last game in high school.

"What happened was, in that last game, I had just punted the football to the other team, and ordinarily the play is over before the punter can get involved in it, but in this case, the kid on the other team had gotten through the tacklers and I was the one guy left who could stop him. I remember him coming toward me, then... nothing. I remember that I lost my sight. I was still conscious for a second or two, but everything was black, and all I can remember is thinking, 'Oh my God, I'm blind!'"

I had known that story before I started working on this paper for Monsignor. It had been right after my 13th birthday, when Feldy told it to me. He was still coaching the Rivercats and I had come with him to watch the team practice, early one morning in August before the school year started. We were headed home, driving through State City in Feldy's Pontiac Bonneville—we don't have it anymore, but I loved it because it was such a big, important-looking red car; always smelled of cigar smoke—and I asked Feldy whether he had ever liked any other sport as much as football, when he was younger. When he told me about getting knocked out like that, I was too horrified to say anything.

"The taste in my mouth. I can't describe it, but I'll never forget it. Somehow... hell, I was 17, I didn't know much about anatomy, but somehow I knew I was tasting my own spinal fluid."

"Eew."

"Yeah. The next thing I remember is waking up in a hospital bed. I remember someone telling me that I had been unconscious for four days, but I don't remember who it was that told me. One of my parents, or a doctor or nurse, could have been anybody. They had had to drill my skull open to relieve the pressure. I was damn lucky I didn't end up a vegetable.

"I remember at some point in the next few days, when I was at least conscious for most of the day and able to sit up in bed, a doctor said to me, 'I'm afraid there's not going to be any more football for you, son. Ever.' Right then and there was when I said to myself, 'I am not going to let anybody take football away from me.' It's funny, but the doctor telling me I couldn't have it, made me want it more than I ever had before."

"That's how it works," I said. "If somebody tells you 'you can't,' you've got to go and 'can,' right? So, did you decide right then that you were going to make a career out of football?"

Feldy was keeping his eyes on the road, but clearly thinking for a few seconds about my question.

"I've forgotten, now, what the clinical term for that is, but it's a thing," Feldy said. "Even if you would have had the good sense *not* to do it, if they hadn't said anything. Anyway, I was telling myself, for the longest time, that I was going to get a doctorate in psychology, and maybe I'd get to be the president of a university one day. I was going to be a great educator—like Booker T. Washington, or Woodrow Wilson, or Nicholas Murray Butler. But maybe subconsciously, that was when I decided on football. When the doctor said that. Even if I didn't admit it."

At the University of Wisconsin, Feldy defied doctor's orders and went out for the freshman football team. In his sophomore year, he joined the varsity squad, playing quarterback in a single-wing formation, in which the quarterback is more of a blocking back than a passer or runner. Some of the sports reporters were hard on him. One of them called him "the Badgers' enforcer." Another one called him a "goon." One of them called him a "cheap-shot artist."

I never believed that. Feldy always taught me to play tough but fair. Sometimes, if an athlete is really good, he'll be criticized for trying too hard. I'm pretty sure that was what was going on in this case. Feldy's record speaks for itself. In his junior and senior years, he was a first-team All-American, and dirty players don't get rewarded like that.

Feldy graduated magna cum laude with the Class of 1943, and went right to midshipman's school at Northwestern University. That fall, he became an Ensign in the U.S. Naval Reserve—and came back to Madison (where Birdy's family lived) in his naval uniform to get married. Feldy served on a destroyer/mine-sweeper in the Pacific, and was discharged as a full Lieutenant in the Naval Reserve in October, 1945. He spent the next few years as an assistant football coach: first at Wisconsin, then at the University of Michigan—and I was born on August 15, 1950, when he was an assistant coach for the Detroit Lions.

FELDY IS A LEGEND

That paper I wrote for Monsignor turned into an inspirational story, I have to admit, and now that I read it again, it embarrasses me a little. I put in some references to Feldy's religious beliefs, partly because I truly admire Feldy for them—but mostly to please Monsignor. I wrote, "Our whole family goes to Mass every Sunday, but you have probably seen my father at Mass by himself, occasionally, on weekday mornings on his way to work. We all make confession once a month—but my father goes oftener, because he says he needs it."

Anyway, the paper is sitting on my desk in front of me, with a big A in red ink on the top of the front page, and Monsignor has written, "What a remarkable story. You might have a vocation to journalism, indeed. You are an excellent writer!"

What I feel disappointed about, and guilty about—and a little relieved about—was that I didn't come close to telling Monsignor the whole story. Sure, I wrote about Feldy's "legendary career" as coach here at State University, but I remember so much more about his time as Head Coach of the Rivercats than what I wrote in that paper. It would make a book. It would take me a year to write it. They are not one hundred percent happy memories. Some of them are painful. But, gosh, what an exciting time, when Feldy was coaching the Rivercats. What a ride. Life with Feldy is never boring.

By 1954, when Feldy got his chance to be Head Coach at Winnemucca University, I had a vague idea of what football was, although I didn't understand how it was played. I didn't completely understand that the Head Coach of a college football team is famous, at least in the town where he coaches—but I understood that everyone knew Feldy. Every so often (for example if I were with Birdy at the supermarket), some stranger would crouch down to me and say something like, "Your dad's doing great. We all think the world of him."

The Paiutes had been the patsy of the Old West Conference for years. The previous year, their record had been 0-8-1. Feldy brought them in at 3-4-2 in 1954, and 7-2 in 1955. Then, in December 1955, Feldy got two phone calls within one day of each other. The first was from State University in State City, Iowa; the second was from Purdue University in Lafayette, Indiana. Both schools wanted him to coach their football team.

Purdue was and is a much bigger, more prestigious school than State. But when Feldy contacted the head coaches he had worked under—at Wisconsin and Michigan, and with the Lions—they all advised him to choose State.

Ben Oosterbaan, Feldy's former boss at Michigan, told him. "At State, you'd be a presence all over Iowa. They're the only game in town except for U. Des Moines—which hardly has an athletic program—plus a few little bitty land-grant colleges. You'd be a big, big man in Iowa—if you produce. At Purdue, no matter how good you are, you'll be competing for attention with Notre Dame, U. of Indiana, Ball State, Northwestern, and University of Chicago. So you won't be in the spotlight as much. If you want to be noticed, State's your choice."

Oosterbaan had recommended Feldy to State University's Athletic Director, Victor Enslowe. Years later, Feldy told me that story. He repeated to me what Oosterbaan had told him that he had said to Enslowe:

"Feldy will get results; he'll be great if you can deal with him. You might not like him; you might not like how he gets things done. Feldy is one stubborn bohunk. He's the original clogged toilet. Takes no shit from anybody."

Sorry about the language, but that's what Oosterbaan said.

Feldy got to State City in April, 1956; the rest of us stayed behind in Winnemucca. At his first press conference, on the day before the start of spring practice, he said, "I'm not going to pretend that State's football program hasn't been in trouble for a long time. I know it can be resurrected, and I know I can do it. The Cats will have a consistently winning team. I will not, cannot, be associated with a team that doesn't win and won't learn how to win. Are we going to the Rose Bowl this year? Probably not. Are we going to the Rose Bowl by the end of my five-year contract? Count on it."

Feldy then held up one of the new football jerseys, that he and the art professor at Winnemucca had designed.

"This will show the Big Ten that we mean business," he said.

Next, he rolled out a banner that showed an all-new version of the team's mascot: Muddy the Rivercat. Muddy had originally been a swimming catfish, white, with its features drawn in brown. Goofy-looking. I gather he had been regarded as a bit of an embarrassment as a mascot; he was almost never used to promote the team or the university.

On this new banner, Muddy was a menacing chocolate-brown monster of a catfish, with a camel-colored underside and red lips, standing on its forked tail, with its fins on its hips and a fighting expression behind its whiskers. Feldy explained to the reporters that while he couldn't force State University to adopt this new Muddy, it would at least represent the football team.

"I'm hoping that these new colors, and the new Muddy, will catch on for all our sports teams. Even as I speak, I've got students at work painting our team's football helmets in the new colors. I'm paying them myself, as my donation to the football program. This is going to be a year of re-dedication."

Okay, but here was the secret: Birdy's parents were funding a company that would manufacture sweatshirts and pens and coffee cups—anything, you name it—in those new colors, with the new Muddy on them. They would let some of that stuff trickle into State City—at gift shops, book stores, and so on—without letting State University know about it. Then when the football season began, in the fall of 1956, they would flood the school and the town with all this merchandise. Once it started selling, Feldy could offer to let the university buy into the company, so that the school could get some of the royalties.

I know that sounds sneaky, but Feldy thought it was going to be a big win for everybody. It was—and it would not have happened without him. It took a few months—like, the whole 1956-7 school year—for the new Muddy to be completely accepted, but he was.

That was a nice payoff for that art professor back at Winnemucca. The new Muddy made serious money for Grandpa and Grandma Duffy, too, and huge money for State University. Muddy transformed the image of all the State University sports teams. That was Feldy's doing—his vision—and he has never gotten anywhere near the credit he deserves for it.

That was also the start of all the problems Feldy had with Vic Enslowe, the Athletic Director. Enslowe had once been the Rivercats' head football coach—through three losing seasons, before being kicked upstairs. He had been A.D. for three years, before Feldy took over as Head Coach. (The guy who coached the three years between him and Feldy had won a total of four games.) Naturally, Enslowe was going to resent any coach who looked likely to outperform his own lousy record. Oh, that guy. "Petty tyrant" doesn't begin to cover it. Feldy called him a *Sitzpinkler*, which I'm not going to reveal what that means.

Enslowe could have pretended that he had been on board with the new uniforms and logo from the very start, and Feldy wouldn't have contradicted him; why would he? That would have made Enslowe look smart, I would think. But Enslowe wasn't smart enough to see that.

Rivercat fans didn't expect much from Feldy that first year. Everyone thought he was just another nobody. And at the beginning of the 1956 football season, people kept thinking that. Even with the new uniforms, the Rivercats started off at 0-4. They lost those games by an average score of 32-17, never by less than a touchdown. I didn't know this at the time, but I found out later that a lot of the players really hated Feldy. They thought he was harsh, too demanding. They feared him.

I know that Feldy didn't have much patience with athletes who weren't as talented as he was. He wasn't like that when he was coaching us kids—he was never unreasonable with us, at all, when he was teaching us—but I could tell, even when I was little, that he was holding it in: he was making a special effort to be patient with us, and he wished he could holler at us and rip on us like he did with the football team.

Maybe it would have been different, maybe his players would have liked him more, if his personality had been winning them any games.

The rest of our family took those four losses way worse than Feldy did. Lou, Jack, and Jerry would be almost in tears—although they tried to hide it, being big tough boys. Win was more stoic, and I didn't quite know what was going on. Birdy would look so sad, for the rest of the weekend. But Feldy would always cheer us up.

He would come home from the stadium, early on Saturday evening—or later, if it were a road game—and he would say, "Look, it's early; we all knew this was gonna be a rough season. Don't get so down. I'm not! Birdy, I'll get the coals going!"

Then, for the week before the Homecoming game, against Ohio State, Feldy ran closed practice sessions. On game day, the Cats never used their single-wing offense. They went with a slightly modified T formation, which the Buckeyes hadn't expected to see. The Cats rattled off four touchdowns in the first half. Ohio State couldn't get unstuck. The final score was Rivercats 42, Buckeyes 14, and I understand that three Buckeye players were carried off the field with injuries that put them out of the following week's game.

Feldy told the press, "I warned the State University administration, prior to the season, that this was not going to be a weak, passive team. I warned them that some of our opponents wouldn't like us. Now that we've shown that we can win, they are really not going to like us. But they're going to know we've come to play. They're going to know we're part of the Big Ten."

That one game turned it around. That one win made the newspapers write nice things about Feldy, made people smile at us when we were out in public. And maybe that press conference statement helped, more than a little. It sure made our family happier, and way more optimistic.

The following week, at Minnesota, the Cats lost another, but it was a nail-biter: The Gophers only won 10-7. Again, several of the Gophers had to leave the field with injuries. At one point, several spectators—presumably Minnesota students—who were standing near the visitors' bench, charged at Feldy in a body. They actually went for the visiting team's Head Coach, can you imagine? But several of the Cats were able to get in their way.

The next game, at home against Illinois, was way worse. Illinois already had a reputation as a rough team. This time, the officials were calling penalties against both teams for holding, clipping, roughing the kicker, you name it—but that didn't calm the players down. Halfway through the third quarter, a scramble for a loose ball turned into a brawl that cleared both benches, with even the coaches on both sides running onto the field. At the end of the game—which ended in a 13-13 tie—some State fans ran onto the field and tried to mix it with the Illinois players. This time, a few of the Rivercats had to get in *their* way, and protect their opponents!

Feldy told reporters at his Monday press conference that he wasn't going to suspend any of his players. "They were punished with penalties during the game," *The State City Examiner* quoted him. "I told them what I thought of their conduct."

In the context of the article, you could tell that the reporter was spinning it to make it look like Feldy was applauding the players' conduct, which I don't believe he was. Well, the *Examiner* didn't like Feldy. Oh, they liked him all right when he was winning, but that's another thing entirely.

There were three games left in the season, and the Rivercats played rough and tough in each of them, but within the rules. They won one of them; lost the other two by pretty close margins; their record at season's end was 2-7-1.

Nobody thought that the Cats had had a good season. But it was the best bad season State University had ever seen.

By the time the next school year started, in September of 1957, the old crayon-brown had disappeared from the State University campus. You'd see only the dark chocolate-brown, and the new Muddy—not just on merchandise, but on official campus signs.

I was in second grade, and learning about the Civil War, Lincoln, slavery, all of which I had only vaguely known about before. My parents had always taught me that you had to be extra-fair to Negroes, or "colored people," which was the polite term up to a few years ago: not treat them better than anyone else, but be sure you're treating them the same.

If you downgrade people for their race, you're downgrading God, who made man in His image. You can be discerning; you can have good or bad opinions of people, but you have to base those opinions on what people say or do, not on what color they are. That's what my parents brought me up to believe.

Feldy got a reputation as a social crusader. He recruited from Negro high schools in cities like Chicago and Detroit, and from southern Negro high schools, junior colleges, industrial schools. Some coaches and athletic directors from other Big Ten colleges criticized him. Not for recruiting Negroes, but for going all over the country to do it. I guess they felt it wasn't good form: like he was poaching.

Feldy would say, "Iowa is the smallest state in the Big Ten, by far. It's thinly populated, and State University is remote, compared to schools like Northwestern, Minnesota, Michigan, Ohio State. If we're going to be competitive, we have to work at least twice as hard to recruit, and travel at least three times as much and as far."

In practice sessions, Feldy focused on the "two Fs": fitness and fundamentals. His players blocked and tackled, blocked and tackled; ran the same plays over and over and over again. They would do grass drills and wind sprints till some of the players were barfing on the field.

Feldy would tell them, "The harder you work in practice, the harder it will be to surrender on Saturday. You can't leave the field knowing that you've given less than your best—knowing that you didn't do everything you could have done to win.

"If you never settle for less than your best, you'll be amazed at what you can accomplish. That goes for all of life."

He told his players, and reporters, that he subscribed to the K.I.S.S. principle: Keep It Simple, Stupid. He had the thinnest offensive playbook of any coach in the Big Ten. His teams hardly ever ran more than six or seven different plays in a given game— but Feldy's goal was to run those few plays to perfection. The other team could be pretty certain of which play was coming next, but if it were perfectly executed, it would work, no matter how well the defense was prepared for it.

If I am ever left with one mental picture of Feldy, it will be of seeing him from a distance, down there on the sidelines, during a game, with his long polo coat and his black fedora, and the cigar in his mouth, pacing back and forth, sometimes hollering at his players, sometimes glowering out across the field, while I'm hearing the crowd noise.

Even at that distance, and even when I was just toddling, I could feel the power radiating off of Feldy. I didn't know the word "charisma" then, but I have never sensed it from anyone the way I always have from Feldy.

The Cats improved to 6-4 in 1957, their first winning season since 1941. I remember walking around downtown with Feldy during that season, or being in a store with him, and people looking at him like he was God. I don't mean to blaspheme. That's what it was like. It was wonderful to see the looks in their eyes.

The following year, 1958, was a disappointment. It was a young team, since the 1957 squad had included so many seniors. Plus, we had a lot of injuries. We went 3-6-1.

But, oh, that next year. The Cats won their first five games in 1959, lost the sixth one in a heartbreaker against Michigan State, and went undefeated the rest of the way. The final AP poll had us ranked second in the nation—only because the Syracuse Orangemen had had a perfect 10-0 record.

Feldy has never been a jubilant person. But he was glowing, all through that season. In the Rose Bowl on January 1, 1960, the Cats demolished the Washington Huskies, 35-12. In his fourth year as coach. Not in five years, but in four. Feldy made the cover of *Sports Illustrated*, on account of that Rose Bowl. State University renewed his contract a year early, with a big raise.

It was at about this time that the Governor of Iowa, Herschel Loveless, speaking at a Democratic Party fundraising banquet at which Feldy and Birdy were sitting on the dais, referred to Feldy as "Iowa's First Citizen."

"Feldy has defined Iowa to the rest of the nation," Loveless said. "He has become our unofficial goodwill ambassador. He has shown America that Iowa isn't just the Potato State."

The Rivercats were almost as good in 1960 as they had been in 1959. They closed it out at 8-1-1, were ranked fifth in the nation by the AP, and would have gone to the Rose Bowl again, except that the Big Ten has a rule against any team playing in two consecutive Rose Bowls.

In the 1961 season, the Rivercats ended up second in the nation again in the AP poll (behind undefeated Alabama). They beat UCLA in the Rose Bowl, 31-7. And Feldy made the cover of *TIME*.

§

Feldy would talk a lot about his work, at home: the coaching part. The only time he brought home any part of his job that didn't have to do with coaching was when he was having tough times with Vic Enslowe. For the first few years we were in State City, to me, Enslowe existed as this sort of evil spirit: maybe not even human. I never actually met him: only ever saw him now and then, at games and special athletic events. I just knew he was my father's tormentor. If I hadn't known that his first name was Victor, I would have thought it was "Thatdamn."

Feldy thought he should be made Athletic Director, as well as Head Football Coach. It rankled Feldy that after two Rose Bowl wins, he wasn't given both jobs.

In the spring of 1962, at the end of the academic year, three starting players who were expected to return that fall as seniors were declared academically ineligible. Two others, who would have returned as juniors, got arrested for taking part in a brawl outside a bar in downtown State City, and State University suspended them "indefinitely." Feldy did what he could to get the administration to reinstate them, but he wasn't able to change any minds. When he asked Enslowe to support him, Enslowe gave him a telling off, instead: saying that Feldy was responsible for bringing "animals" onto the football team.

"I've taken a down-and-out program and turned it around," Feldy told us when he got home that night, "and that *Sitzpinkler* is still living in some fantasy world that he read about in those Frank Merriwell books."

We all agreed—all of us Feldeverts—that Enslowe resented Feldy for being a better coach than he had been. Anyway, that was only the beginning.

The Cats started the 1962 season by losing to Oregon State and Notre Dame. After the second game, Feldy told a *Cedar Rapids Gazette* reporter that it was too bad that several key players had been stripped away from the team before the season even got started, or we might have been 2-0.

"It's unfortunate that people who were in a position to do so, couldn't have found some way to discipline those young men in ways that wouldn't have destroyed their football careers—here, and maybe professionally later on."

The next day, the press published a statement from Enslowe:

"For too many years, the Athletic Director at State University has been lax and remiss in ensuring that the high school students recruited for our athletic programs are the type that will not only excel athletically, but will live up to the best traditions of the student athlete. For that, I accept full responsibility. I do not assign blame to anyone else. But our recruiters must become more vigilant in ensuring that we bring in student-athletes who have a sense of responsibility in their everyday conduct, who are not inclined to unacceptable behavior."

Feldy held his weekly press briefings on Monday mornings in the big conference room next to his office at the State University Fieldhouse. On the day that that statement of Enslowe's hit the papers, Feldy went on for some time, to the reporters: about the ticks that infested the practice field; the bad management of the team's road trips; the troubles that players and coaches had experienced getting game tickets for their families.

He said the student-athletes felt that the Department of Athletics was not standing by them, if they were fighting to retain their eligibility.

"As for my own performance," he said, "if the Board in Control of Athletics wants to get rid of me, they can buy out my contract. I'm not worried. I've got a wealthy father-in-law.

"I still have two years left on my current contract, after this one. I hope I can stay through this season and those next two. At the same time, my wife has told me that she wishes I would get out of coaching, or at least find a program where there's less aggravation. She feels that the current situation is affecting my health, and whether it is or not, I don't want to spend any more time in a program where some other coach might be happier."

A reporter from the *Gazette* asked, "Would you be more likely to stay on under a different Athletic Director?"

"I'd say it's obvious that Vic Enslowe and I are going to find it hard to figure out a way to work together. But it's not my province, who the University hires as their Athletic Director."

"Are you saying that one of you has to go: you or Enslowe?"

"I'm not saying it."

This was not a matter of the press creating a feud, and everyone knew it.

I had never seen Feldy as pumped for a game as he was for those few days before we played Indiana, the next Saturday. I didn't know, at the time, that he and Enslowe both had feelers out, looking for other opportunities, because they both realized that State City wasn't big enough for both of them, that they couldn't even pretend to work together for the rest of that season.

The Rivercats beat the Hoosiers 29-0. Birdy and my brothers and I were all sitting together in the VIP box, high up at the top of the stadium—but we went home without Feldy, as usual, because he would be occupied for a couple of hours after the game.

We heard him coming into the house, though, that evening. We could hear him singing the "Rivercat Rouser" at the top of his voice, from the garage, and when he walked into the house, we all mobbed him; he was hugging all of us and laughing; I'd never seen him like that. Never. I mean, Feldy is not a hugger. Not even with me.

But, boy, you should have seen the mood that Feldy was in, the following Friday, when Enslowe announced that he had accepted an offer to become executive director of the Sun Bowl, down in El Paso. I'm sure Feldy would have been tickled to death about that—but he came home that evening scowling. Right before *The CBS Evening News* started, he told us the good news first, and then the bad news: The President of State University, Lawrence Esterhart, had announced that the new A.D. would be the track coach, Ed Kuechenberg, who was scheduled to retire at the end of the 1964-65 academic year. (State University forces all faculty and administration to go on Emeritus status at 68.)

"He's a cypher," Feldy told us. I didn't know that word, at the time, but I could figure out what Feldy meant by it. "There's nothing to coaching track. All you have to do is tell the kids, 'Keep turning left, and get back here as soon as you can.' Oh, Kootch is a nice guy; he's not going to make any waves; he'll be gone in a couple of years—but damn it, this makes me mad." He switched on the TV, then sat in his official chair, glowering.

"This was arranged," he snarled to all of us in the room, while the TV warmed up. "They got it done to pre-empt me from demanding that job. I'll tell you more after the news."

He couldn't wait that long. He started up again at the first commercial break.

"It might be time for me to quit right here and now. At this point, maybe I've had enough of State University."

But saying that, quieted him down. It must have dawned on him that he couldn't quit then. You're only as good as the year you're having now, if you're a football coach. And we had only won that one game, so far that season.

If Enslowe had waited, he might have been the one to stay on, and Feldy might have been out. We got beat the next day—our Homecoming game—so almost before we knew what was going on, the Rose Bowl champs were 1-3.

We finally got it together, midway through the season, and finished 5-5. But all through that fall and winter, Feldy would mention to us that he felt he had done what he could for the Cats; that maybe it was time for him to do something else. But finally, he decided that he would wait for Kootch to retire.

Long story short, in 1963, we came back. We were 8-0-1 going into our final game, at South Bend against Notre Dame, which almost certainly would have been another easy win—but President Kennedy was assassinated the day before, and all football games were cancelled on November 23.

The Cats went to the Rose Bowl again, and beat Washington 24-14, which gave Feldy an undefeated season and three Rose Bowl championships in five years. He was named Coach of the Year by *Sports Illustrated*, *Playboy*, and the Associated Press.

But the 1964 Rivercats didn't have the talent. We won the first two games of the season, then lost three in a row—all of them conference games—and tied the next. We were 2-3-1, and Feldy was obviously sick. His clothes hung on him; he lost a lot of weight because his ulcers were so bad. Midway through that season, he accepted President Esterhart's offer to make him Athletic Director, when Kootch retired in the spring—without continuing as Head Coach. I thought Feldy sounded relieved, when he told Birdy and us kids how it was going to be, over the dinner table one night.

"Both jobs would have been too much, I have to admit."

The Cats did seem to gel, finally, starting with the seventh week. We played better; Feldy looked healthier; we won three of our last four to finish at 5-4-1.

At his final press conference as Head Coach, one reporter asked Feldy whether he might reconsider. Feldy repeated his standard line: "No, I've had a wonderful run. I have nothing but good memories of the past nine years, but I'm ready to try something else. I have no desire to grow old in coaching."

Over those nine years, Feldy went 54-29-6 in regular season play, with four Big Ten titles, plus a 3-0 record in Rose Bowls. I'd say that's enough by anyone's standards to make him State University's greatest football coach ever.

Now he has been Athletic Director for three years, and it may be more relaxing for him, but it's a lot less exciting for me.

NO ROMANCE YET

My senior prom is tonight. I'll probably be out till nearly dawn tomorrow morning, which is why Feldy, Birdy, Duffy, Sander and I are all at Saturday afternoon Mass, which Feldy calls the "cop-out Mass," because he says it's for people who don't want to get up on Sunday morning. Which of course it is, but we're making an exception in this case.

Our Lady is the biggest of the four Catholic churches in State City. (The smaller churches are St. Stephen, St. Boniface, and the campus chapel, St. Loy—which is where you worship if you're embarrassed to be Catholic, and trying to live it down. My brother Win sometimes goes to Mass at St. Loy because it's near the dorm he lives in, but he tells me he prefers Our Lady, too.)

I love going to Mass at Our Lady. It's as close to a cathedral as a parish church can be, with three altars and this enormous vaulted ceiling; the walls are mostly painted rose and cream and light blue on the inside; lots of dark wood. It's almost gaudy. So old-fashioned, with this wonderful statuary that dates back, I think, to the late 1840s. Along the walls are painted life-size statues of the Apostles, each of them holding the instrument of his martyrdom—except for St. John, who holds a chalice since he wasn't martyred. And smaller statues of various other saints, up at the altar. The Stations of the Cross in bas-relief. Just a wonderful church.

It horrified me when the parish adopted all those post-Vatican II reforms three or four years ago: starting the Mass with hymns, like Protestants; switching to English, with the priest facing the congregation. Those three amazingly beautiful altars—and the priest now has to celebrate Mass standing behind what might as well be an ironing board. But obviously Monsignor Koudelka didn't have any choice.

I'm disappointed at myself right now, that I'm not paying attention to the Mass as much as usual. Because the prom is just a couple of hours off. Which is no excuse, but there it is.

Not that there's going to be anything storybook-romantic about this prom. Not for me. But a girl's senior prom is supposed to be such a big thing, so I'm almost conscientiously willing myself to be excited about it. It should be fun. There'll be a fancy dinner at the Hilton Hotel, downtown, and dancing in the ballroom there; then at midnight there'll be the Party After the Party, back at the Visitation gym.

My date will be Jim Wagner, who is almost always my date for dances or for going to movies or plays. He's pretty sure he has a vocation to the priesthood. He'll be off to Holy Cross University, this fall. He's a good dancer and actor; he can talk about serious stuff. He's way more outgoing than I am, and that helps me to be more sociable too. When he walks me to my front door and says goodnight at the end of a date, he always thanks me and shakes my hand. Feldy and Birdy both like him. But maybe he's the last boy I'll ever date. I wouldn't be surprised.

On the day I told him and Birdy that Jim would be taking me to the prom, Feldy said, "It's almost a shame that Jim thinks he has a vocation. He might have been a perfect husband for you."

I said, "Being perfect is apt to be uninteresting." That got a big laugh out of Feldy and Birdy.

Maybe that's another reason why I've hardly dated any other boys besides Jim. Because he never tries anything and I know he never will. I wonder how I'll handle that business when I'm married—if I ever do meet someone who would marry me, and whom I would want to marry.

I'm sure that will be fine. But talk about sex has always made me uncomfortable. If other kids refer to it around me, I'll try to change the subject. Not because I'm any more of a prude than other girls, I don't think. It's not something I care to talk or think about at this point in my life. I don't know: maybe I'm not allowing myself to think about it, because of a feeling that I'm not supposed to.

When I was eleven or so and it was clear that I was becoming a woman, Birdy sat me down in her and Feldy's bedroom when nobody else was around, and asked me how much I knew about the "facts of life." I knew the basics. Birdy had told me herself, years before when I first asked, how babies grew in the mother's tummy. I grew up in a houseful of boys, so the anatomy was no mystery to me. Birdy and Feldy never kept information from me, and I had done a little research on my own. I told Birdy what I knew, and she corrected a few details that I had gotten wrong.

I asked her, "Is it fun?"

She said, "It's very nice. But it's not something that I can describe. You'll find out about it when you're married."

And why am I remembering all this, while I'm kneeling for the Consecration? I can't control what pops into my head, but I should at least try to get the thought to go away.

The only thing that I feel like I might have missed out on, growing up, is that I have never had a "best friend," like you read about in books. I don't think I'm disliked; I have no enemies that I know of. I have never had a friend I could spill my guts to, though—maybe because I have never been in a situation where I needed to spill my guts to anyone. I speak my mind but I generally keep my emotions to myself, because I figure nobody else would be interested in hearing about them.

The clique I have hung out with all through high school is the *élite* group, the "leaders," the student government crowd. I fit in with them fine. I laugh at their jokes, I have some pretty adult-sounding discussions with them—but I don't feel attached to any of them.

I have never had a boyfriend, either. Probably because I'm not much to look at. When I was little, like lots of girls, I had fantasies of meeting a Prince Charming. I loved the fairy tales about Sleeping Beauty, Rapunzel, and so on, even though I knew they didn't have a thing to do with reality.

When I read the novel *Johnny Tremain*, at age 12, I disliked Johnny. He was arrogant and rude, and I don't care for that. But I longed for poor Pumpkin: the British soldier who gets executed for desertion. I had about a week of dreams (the sort of dream that you have consciously, right before you fall asleep) of meeting a boy like Pumpkin: quiet, not too bright, but kind, with red hair, who might bring me wildflowers and be shy around me.

I would not care that he was not all that impressive, because he would be so sweet to me, and I still worry, now, that I might not be the kind of person who could ever be attractive to a boy like that.

Probably my complexion will clear up. I know my height will be less of a handicap as I get older. But if I ever do meet Mr. Right—which I'm not counting on—it won't be for a few years: I'm guessing not till after I've finished at State University.

Now it's almost time for Holy Communion and I'm still not paying enough attention to the Mass; I almost feel like I've put myself out of a State of Grace.

I can't wait to be all the way grown up. I want to be free to travel the world and be a citizen of it, rather than being Feldy's Girl in State City, Iowa. I want to be a concert cellist and a star TV reporter. I want to have eight or nine children. I want to achieve world peace, and convert a large percentage of the non-Catholic world to the One True Church. I might always be Feldy's Girl when I'm in State City—but once I'm gone from here, I'm going to be Teresa Feldevert to the world. And there is my Pride talking, again.

§

One house that I love almost as much as our big brick house is Grandma and Grandpa Duffy's summer home in Door County, Wisconsin. It's a gathering spot for the whole family. I don't think it has ever held all the Duffys and the Feldeverts at once, unless it happened when I was a baby, but I suppose it could. In any case, both of Feldy's parents died a few years ago, and his sisters were married and scattered around the United States before I was born.

Our family spends part of every summer in that house. Sometimes Grandma and Grandpa Duffy are there with us, but more usually they and my folks arrange to use it at different times, so it won't be such a crowd. It's a two-story white frame house, with lots of big picture windows so it's always so full of light and air. It's in a wooded area in a village called Ephraim, close to fishing and the Ephraim Yacht Club, on Lake Michigan, where we keep a couple of sailboats. It's smaller than our place in State City—although not much smaller—and the sitting room is cozier.

That's where we are this evening: Wednesday, August 28, 1968. It's the last week of our vacation: we drive back to State City on Monday. Duffy and Sander start school the next day; my first day at State University is September 9. The football season will start a couple weeks after that. When he was Head Coach, Feldy was never able to take time off in August.

Lou isn't here. He's about to start his second year of law school at Fordham University—and when he graduates, he'll be going into the army and joining the Judge Advocate General Corps. He's planning to get married this winter between Christmas and New Year's Day, and he's spending most of the summer with his fiancée and her family, in upstate New York.

Jack and Jerry graduated from the University of Kansas and the University of Oregon, respectively, this spring. (They were so twinny, all the time they were growing up. In their last year of high school, when they were being recruited by various college football programs, they told Feldy, "Splitting up is something we've got to do." Feldy said they were absolutely right.) They have both found jobs as assistant football coaches—at Rice University and the University of New Mexico—so they're busy with summer practice in Houston and Albuquerque. (I bet they're thanking Feldy, for insisting that they take ROTC. It's unlikely that they'll be sent to Vietnam, now.)

Win will be a sophomore at State University, this fall. Duffy is in eleventh grade, Sander in ninth.

It's pretty late at night. Feldy, Birdy, and I are watching the Democratic National Convention on TV. Feldy and Birdy sit together on the living room sofa; he's got a cigar going. Birdy is obviously agitated, because she's smoking one cigarette after another. Win, Duffy, and Sander are outside, talking.

The TV networks are partly showing what's going on on the convention floor, at the Chicago International Amphitheater, but mostly they're focusing on what's happening outside, where police seem to be going crazy on the antiwar demonstrators.

The cops are using mace, and their nightsticks. The demonstrators are chanting, "The whole world is watching! The whole world is watching!"

On TV, it looks like something you might see in Iran, or Tsarist Russia: cops breaking heads, assaulting anyone who's out on the street. It's carrying over into the convention hall. At least two TV reporters have been caught on camera being roughed up by cops or guards inside the hall.

Feldy, Birdy, and I are just staring. We hardly move, or say a word, for 20 minutes, till Feldy finally says, "This will kill the Democratic party. That damn stupid war might destroy this whole country. But we have to watch this. It's history. God help us all."

When Feldy says that, I have a flash of color in front of my eyes, a sort of shimmery purplish grey, not very pleasant. Maybe because when he says that, it hits me that I'm moving into a whole different part of my life. Sure, our family will still have summers together like this, but in about ten days I'll be moving into a girls' dorm at State University, spending most of my time with people about the same age as these demonstrators—and maybe a lot of them with those same views. Not that I necessarily disagree with the demonstrators. I think I agree with them. About the war, at least. But I hate what I'm seeing on the TV. I'm afraid it's where society is going: toward more of this.

I can't think of anything to say about it to Feldy and Birdy that would make any sense.

§

We're back in State City. It's a Thursday afternoon. I walk from our house, a little less than a mile, to the studios of KSCR, to talk with Joe Barnett and Nelson Bell about working there as an intern during the school year. I've never met either of them, although I've heard them on the radio many times. Mr. Barnett lives on a soybean farm, outside of State City, and farming is his family's main occupation, but he mostly leaves that work to the hired

46

hands. He's a disc jockey. He handles the "afternoon drive" shift at KSCR, and reads the news, plus he announces the play-by-play during the football and basketball seasons. I can see that he's well-built, in his mid-30s, with a flat-top haircut. He's wearing khaki chinos and a yellow polo shirt.

Mr. Bell is a tall Negro guy, except I guess you're supposed to say "black," now, according to some people, or "Afro-American." It's confusing. Mr. Bell is about ten years older than Mr. Barnett. He was a star basketball player at State University, in the late 1940s, and he's in real estate now. He's Mr. Barnett's second banana for the football games, but he's the lead announcer for basketball. Mr. Bell is dressed more like a man who works in town: dark blue suit, white shirt, maroon tie with white pin-dots.

They walk me around the studio; then we sit together in a conference room—each of us with a bottle of Coke from a machine in the hallway—and talk about how the football team looks, and how the basketball and wrestling teams might do later in the year.

Rivercat football fans have not found much to be happy about, the last three seasons. Bob Brosnan, who used to coach the offensive backfield under Feldy, took over as Head Coach in 1965. He was only 33, then, but most people thought he was the brightest of Feldy's assistants. Feldy used to say that Brosnan's main job was to play "nice cop" to Feldy's "mean cop."

"Nice cops" make great assistants. They usually don't make good head coaches. The Rivercats went 3-7 in 1965; 3-5-2 in 1966; 3-7 in 1967—adding up to 9-19-2. In 1967, they won three of their first four games, so the fans thought maybe Brosnan had finally turned the corner—then they lost their last six.

I have heard several people (and read several articles in the papers) suggesting that Brosnan would do a lot better, because he might feel more confident, if he weren't being constantly compared to Feldy. If people would stop saying, after a loss, "Feldy would have won that one."

Maybe. But Feldy *would have* won some of those games that Brosnan lost.

More than once, since Brosnan took over, Feldy has said to me something like, "I'm trying my best to keep my hands off, and not interfere, or kibitz. Believe that or not. Sometimes I have to question him, though. Sometimes I have to ask him, 'What was on your mind, when you made that decision?'"

The way Feldy explains these situations to me, I can see he's right, every time.

Anyway, Mr. Barnett is telling me he expects a stronger season in 1968.

"I have a feeling we might win six or even seven this fall," he says. "Brosnan's finally going to get it together."

Mr. Bell laughs. "You do the hoping for both of us, Joe," he says. "No, seriously," he turns to me, "Joe might be right, but I'd feel a lot more confident if your old man were still in charge."

I suppose "Thank you" is the proper response, so I say it, but I add, "Feldy thinks we'll do a lot better this year."

No, he doesn't. I try to remember anything positive Feldy might have said recently about the team, or Brosnan.

"He's optimistic," I say. "He'd love to see us go back to the Rose Bowl." (Probably he'd love to fly through the air like Superman, too, but that's about as likely.)

"You've got a real clear voice," Mr. Barnett says. He sounds surprised. "Lots of energy. I want to hear how you sound in front of a mike. Care to do a test, right now? We've got a few minutes before my show goes on. We'll set up in the studio, get you talking, then I'll interview you and Sonny on-air, for a few minutes, before we send you on your way." (Sonny, apparently, is what Mr. Bell is called for short.)

I'm floored. Sure, I've been secretly daydreaming that one day, maybe after I've been working at KSCR for a year or so, I might be offered some kind of a mike test—or maybe some disc jockey or other will have a bad cold and be unable to go on, and I'll be pressed into service at the last moment as an emergency substitute, just like in the movies. From that one broadcast, I'll be "discovered" by a major network, and go on to be the anchor of *The NFL Today*—or I might even be Walter Cronkite's successor. I can't believe I'm getting this opportunity, on the day when I'm in for a casual interview.

"Seriously? Yes, please." I'm trying not to panic. "But let's keep it about football. I hate talking about myself."

"Remember, high energy," Mr. Barnett whispers. We're sitting at a long desk in KSCR's main studio. I'm at his left; Sonny Bell is at his right. The Doors' "Hello, I Love You" is fading down.

A female chorus sings, "Joe Bar-nett! Radio Eight-Oh! Kay-essssssss, cee-ar!" That's the station promo. On the wall, under the window that lets onto the engineer's booth, a red "on air" sign lights up. Mr. Barnett's eyes open wide and he almost lurches forward in his chair, toward the microphone.

"And another beautiful afternoon in State City," he shouts into the mike. I've never seen such a quick physical transformation. One second, he's this calm, lazy-looking guy, and one second later it's like he's galvanized; I might have gotten a fatal electrical shock if I had touched him. I can't believe how fast he's talking. "Seventy-six degrees, bright and sunny; the kids should be getting out of school in the next few minutes to enjoy it. State University classes don't start till Monday, and that means another football season is just around the corner."

Now I'm scared. If that's "high energy," I have no idea how to match it. And I'm "on" in about five seconds.

"Here to discuss that with me for the next few minutes is my old friend Sonny Bell, who's going to be sitting next to me in the broadcast booth in a couple of weeks, and a special guest is with us this afternoon, too: Teresa Feldevert, whose father of course is State University's Athletic Director. Terri, I suppose you've had some opportunity to observe the Rivercat football team up close and with an insider's knowledge. Can we be optimistic, going into this season?"

"It always pays to be optimistic," I say into the mike. I tried to match Mr. Barnett's volume, anyway, and instinctively I know I have to keep talking, keep talking, not allow any "dead air," even for a second. "I can't help feeling confident in Coach Brosnan, from what we've seen in the spring and summer practices. It looks to me like we have a better than even chance of a .500 season this year, and we could contend for the conference championship. But we have to be realistic in our expectations. The Big Ten is so full of talent."

"At this time of year, Terri, does your father miss not being Head Coach?"

"Gosh, Joe, I don't know what's in my father's mind, but I would guess that this is one time of the year when he *doesn't* miss it, if he ever does. Just imagine the pressure the Head Coach must feel, at the start of the season. I have a feeling that maybe Coach Brosnan is looking forward more to the end of the season than the beginning, although I'm sure he's excited and eager to play that first game. I know I would be, if I were coach."

Joe chuckles. "Is that something you think about, Terri? Coaching the Rivercats one day?"

I laugh, too, maybe from surprise at myself, for the direction in which I'm driving the conversation.

"Ask me again in ten years, Joe. For now, we've got a great coach and a lot of star players returning from last year. I don't see how the Cats don't have a strong season. We have a great passing combination in Kenny Beebe and Beverley Bay, and our defense looks really solid."

Joe then brings Sonny into the conversation, and they talk about the team's overall prospects for a couple of minutes before we cut away to "Grazing in the Grass."

I love Hugh Masekela. He's my brand-new favorite. I mean, aside from religious music, and classical. For pop music, for right now, I love Hugh Masekela more than anybody, and hearing "Grazing in the Grass" is a good omen, I know it.

Joe whoops, and claps me on the shoulder. "You did great! This might be where you ought to have a career."

I notice that I'm breathing hard, as though I've just run a race. I can feel that my face is flushed.

"Thank you. I was scared to death!"

"You sure didn't sound it. Listen, we've got to get you back on the air this fall. I'm thinking, for the opening game, do you suppose you could join me and Sonny in the booth, maybe do a little color commentating, to see if you take to it? You've got a terrific presence on-air, and it might be fun to have the A.D.'s daughter as a guest."

My immediate reaction is to say "no way." I wouldn't be up to the job. I've got no experience whatever. But to say anything but "yes" would be crazy.

"I'm so grateful. And flattered! Are you sure I can handle it?"

"If Sonny and I can do this job, anybody can. You'll love it."

I get home, late in the afternoon, and Birdy is out—working at the State County Democratic headquarters—but Feldy is there, in his office, with the door open. I almost float into the room and tell him what happened. Feldy laughs: he's surprised, but obviously happy for me. He reaches out his left hand and gives my right hand a squeeze—which, for him, is a pretty strong display of affection.

"Honey, that's great! Be careful what you say on the air, though. We don't want people saying you're just there to be Feldy's mouthpiece, or anything like that. Whatever you do, don't go criticizing Brosnan, okay? If you can't say anything nice about him, don't say anything. There's already plenty of talk about how he and I aren't getting along."

That dismays me. I hadn't thought about that.

I say to Feldy, "You're right. Would you rather I told Mr. Barnett it wouldn't be a good idea, if I…?"

"No, no. You go right ahead. You know how to be tactful, and I'm sure you will be. Just always ask yourself, 'What would Birdy say if she were in front of the mike?' You do *not* want to think about what *I* would say, not when you're on the air. That would cause all kinds of trouble."

I have to laugh at that. I'm noticing how my mood has gone from top-of-the-world, to way down, to way back up again, in less than a minute.

I ask Feldy, "Maybe before the game, could you and I go over it? You know, you could tell me about the lineups, and what our game plan is probably going to be, and what theirs is going to be. That way I'll be prepared, and maybe I won't sound silly."

"That's exactly what we'll do," Feldy says, and if it's possible to feel even better than I felt a few seconds ago, that does it: seeing how happy Feldy looks when I suggest that.

BOOK II

FRESHMAN YEAR AT STATE

I've moved out of the house and into Radcliffe Hall, which is the freshman girls' dorm, on campus. I could have lived at home, and part of me hated to leave our house, but Feldy and Birdy have always encouraged my brothers and me to get out there in the world and live on our own as soon as we could. On principle.

I considered going to some other university, to make a clean break, like Jack and Jerry did. But in view of what I want to study, it makes so much more sense to pay in-state tuition and go to State University. I'll live in the dorms for at least my first year, and I hope I'll be invited to pledge Iota Delta Theta, since it attracts mainly music and art students.

Birdy told me, "I lived at home all through college, and I felt like I was missing out. You're welcome to live here as long as you want, but you're at an age where maybe you should be on your own."

In terms of comfort, it's a big step down from what I've been used to all my life. I'm in a triple room, the way most freshmen girls are, with one bunk bed, one twin, and three plain plywood-topped desk/dressers. I was the first of the three girls to move into the room, so I took the top bunk without anyone asking me to, which has immediately put me on the right side of the other two girls—which of course is why I did it.

Not that I interact with my roommates a lot, aside from when we're getting dressed in the morning. Even then, we don't have much conversation. We usually sit together at breakfast or at dinner in the dining hall, but we hardly ever discuss anything important. We don't have much in common.

Karen Whittlesey is a pre-med student. She's thin, on the tall side but shorter than I am. I think she's pretty. She has a slightly horsy, toothy face, with light freckles, and black hair that she wears tied back with a center part. I like Karen; she's always pleasant and polite to Andrea and I—Andrea and me, I mean—but she keeps pretty much to herself, as I do.

Andrea Schedl is little and skinny. She laughs a lot, and smokes Salems. Andrea has very straight hair, halfway down her back, dishwater-brown. She's more freckled than Karen. She dresses any old way, in plain skirts and peasant blouses or men's shirts, which swim on her. Andrea is an art major. She has covered the wall next to her twin bed (which she and Karen flipped a coin for, me doing the flipping) with pastel sketches of me and Karen, and imaginary animals.

Neither Karen nor Andrea seem to have a boyfriend, or a "home-town honey." The three of us talked about that, on our first night together, when we were all lounging on our beds before turning out the lights. Karen said, when we were discussing our schedules, "It sure doesn't look like I'm going to have any time to date, even if anybody asks me." Andrea said boys her own age were too immature to interest her. "Maybe I'll meet a cute T.A.; you never know."

"I'm in the same boat," I said. "I won't have time for that sort of thing, and I don't know any guys who are halfway grown-up. Anyway, I'm not interested in dating. Except maybe to be friends with someone. I'm waiting for Mr. Right. I'm sure I'll know him when see him."

Andrea said, "You're so old-fashioned. That's refreshing."

I hope God and St. Teresa aren't disappointed in me. I thought about going to Woolworth's and buying a little rug to pray on, before bed, but I'm afraid my roommates will think I'm showing off. So, I'm getting into bed every night and then praying. I feel guilty, but my family "just thinks" Grace if we're in a restaurant, so I suppose this is okay.

§

At the State University School of Music, cello performance students aren't admitted to a studio in their freshman year. They study with a graduate student, then test into Professor Giulio Meregaglia's studio at the end of the freshman year. He's got a reputation as a wonderful teacher, although people tell me he can be pretty mean if you don't come up to his standards. This fall, I'm working with a first-year masters student, Mona Shapen. Mona gives me a lesson once a week, and I take group instruction from Professor Meregaglia.

I had to like Mona as soon as we met, in a practice room in the Music Building. She might be the most beautiful woman or girl I've ever seen.

She's too dark to be a fairy princess. She looks like Joan Baez might look, if Joan Baez were twice as good-looking as she actually is. It isn't just her physical features, though. It's her presence. Mona has an aura. You can't see it, but you feel it. She almost shimmers. It's a kind of intensity, and serenity, both.

She's a little under average height—keeping in mind that almost any girl looks short to me—and slender, with nearly-straight black hair that flows loose halfway down her back; black eyebrows that are very high-arched and unplucked; almond-shaped dark brown eyes—Rivercat-color eyes, I said to myself, the first time I saw them—and a light brown complexion. She usually wears a black skirt and a plain white blouse with a small black and white peace-sign pin on one lapel—and a gold band on her left ring finger.

She was sitting on a metal folding chair, with her cello between her knees. She stood up, with this enormous, happy smile—she has perfect white teeth, not too big or too small; I'm envious—and held out her hand.

"Teresa?" She has such a light, soft voice.

"That's me." We shook; I sat opposite Mona in another folding chair, and opened my cello case.

Mona wanted to know about my background: where I had gone to high school; how long I had been studying cello; what my family was like. She clearly didn't recognize the name Feldevert, because when I mentioned that my father was State University's Athletic Director, Mona simpered and said, "Oh, you know, I remember, now, that I've heard that name or seen it in the papers. I guess I was halfway aware that he had something to do with sports, but I don't follow that at all, I'm afraid."

That made me like Mona even more, or at least made me feel more comfortable—knowing that with her, I was starting with a clean slate, with no assumptions being made about me because I was Feldy's Girl.

Mona doesn't have a noticeable accent of any kind, but the timbre of her voice is not Iowa; her presence is not Iowa; I couldn't have put her finger on how I knew, but I said, "You're not from around here, are you?"

"You can tell, right? New York. Manhattan. My father's a diamond cutter, which is probably about as different as it gets from what your father does."

"How did you end up here?"

"Well, I went to the High School of Performing Arts, then I got offered an orchestra scholarship here at State, and this is one of the best music schools in the world, so I didn't think about *not* coming here. Then I met my husband, or husband-to-be, in my sophomore year. We got married this summer—and now we're both working on our Masters degrees. He's in voice."

"Congratulations. On your marriage… and on your career, both."

"Thanks. You said you were first chair in high school? I'm sure you're better than I am already; what do you need me for?"

Mona laughed—uncertainly, I gather, since she had been trying to make a joke but it hadn't sounded as funny as she must have meant it to be when she said it. "No, I'm kidding, but I'm sure you're very talented. Do you have a favorite piece to play?"

"I love anything by Dvorák," I said. "And Elgar. I know I'm supposed to love Bach but I just don't. When you've heard one Bach suite you've heard them all."

Mona threw her head back and gave a huge laugh: it was bigger than Mona was. It almost made me jump, since she had been speaking so softly. The laugh gave me a quick flash of bright yellow light that faded into a sort of lavender color: really sweet and pretty, like her laugh.

"You've got to be the only cellist who feels that way," she said. "But it's brave of you to say it. It's practically heresy. Like condemning motherhood, isn't it? But maybe I can change your mind. Working on Bach certainly helps your musicianship."

Now that we've had a couple of lessons, I can tell that Mona is already a professional-level cellist. She hasn't decided whether she wants a career as a performer, or in academia. She'll get her Master's degree in two years, and then go for a Doctor of Musical Arts degree, either at State University or someplace else. She and her husband are on the same track, so they'll probably stay at State for their doctorates, if they can.

"I always knew I wanted a career in music," Mona says. Our lesson is over and we're casing our instruments. "Since I was maybe three years old. Mike was double-majoring in music and political science, but when we decided to get married he said it would make more sense if we were both in the same field, so we could help each other. I thought that was so romantic."

Mona and I are walking out of the practice room, each of us headed to another class.

"You'll have to meet Mike one day. He was going to be a journalist too, at one time." She laughs again. "Then he was going to be a public interest lawyer. Now I've dragged him down to wanting to sing opera."

This afternoon, coming out of the Music Building following my group lesson, I see Mona and her husband sitting together, studying, under one of the big elms next to the building. I assume it's her husband. Sure enough, it is *the* Mike Shapen. He stands up to shake hands.

Mike looks about Mona's age. He's on the short side, too: not a lot taller than Mona. He's well-built but squatty. He has black hair and a full short black beard. He's wearing jeans and a dark blue short-sleeved knit shirt. He doesn't make much impression on me for the minute or so that the three of us spend chatting—except I can tell, from the way they're looking at each other, that the honeymoon hasn't worn off. I'm wondering, while I walk the few blocks to my dorm, what it might be like, to want to look at a man that way. I can't imagine what romantic love might feel like. Seeing Mona and Mike together makes me curious, rather than wistful. I have no idea what to feel wistful for.

§

If I'm old-fashioned, Andrea has turned out to be new-fashioned. It's only a couple of weeks into the school year, and this fine morning Karen and I woke up to observe that Andrea didn't sleep in her bed last night. I've come back to the room after classes this afternoon and here she is. I tell her, "We were worried about you, this morning."

"Apparently I won't be spending every night here." She gives me a little smirk.

I must look shocked, because Andrea laughs.

"It was just a matter of time. I wonder why people wait."

I should keep my mouth shut. But that's not in my nature. Sometimes I could use a pre-emptive backhand.

"Because it's a sin," I tell her. "Outside of Holy Matrimony, it's adultery. It's breaking the Sixth Commandment."

"The Seventh, no?"

"If you're a heretic. Catholics and Protestants number them differently. Anyway, it's none of my business."

Andrea laughs again. "Don't knock it till you've tried it."

"Oh, I'll try it one day. When I'm married." I'm afraid I'm looking all serious. "But who's going to want to marry you, now? People are going to find out, and if you have that reputation…"

"Oh, please." Andrea looks annoyed. "Who thinks that way?"

I want to say, "Plenty of people," but I don't. Instead, I say, "It's not my business. Is this a guy you might want to marry?"

Andrea laughs. "At my age? No. He's just a nice guy."

I almost say, "Be careful," but I don't want to say anything that might sound like I'm advising contraception.

I know it's rude to ask, but I have to. Andrea and I aren't friends, really, but we share a room, so I consider Andrea a teammate, kind of—there's my football background—which means I have a duty to look out for her.

"But what if a baby comes out of all this? And what if this guy won't marry you?"

"He pulled out. And I'm going to go on the pill."

I see there's no point in continuing, but I have to force myself to stop composing a big long speech in my head.

"Judge not, lest ye be judged," Andrea half-sings, and she giggles. I can't tell if she's mocking me, or if she's nervous.

"Wouldn't dream of it."

§

The Rivercat Booster Brat Brekker is a morning event, always held on the Saturday one week before the first football game of the season: a bratwurst and hamburger feed, under an enormous canvas canopy set up on one of the practice fields near the football stadium, for members of the Rivercat Booster Club. It's a chance to hear speeches from the Athletic Director and the coaches of various sports, and to meet the athletes, especially the footballers, although only a few of those ever show up.

I've gone to the Brat Brekker every year since we came to State. People would notice if I weren't there. Not that I would think of missing it. It gets you pumped for the season. No matter how good or bad the team's prospects look, the Brat Brekker will make you feel optimistic for an hour or so.

Every year, it's pretty much the same format—and mostly the same people. They always used to exclaim at how much I had grown since the previous year—or, nowadays, how much prettier I've become, which makes me uncomfortable, because I don't think I'm pretty at all.

I invited Karen and Andrea to this one. Andrea is otherwise occupied, but Karen is walking with me, the mile and a half from our dorm to the event. We're both dressed down, in blue jeans, sneakers, and Rivercat sweatshirts.

"It's one of her art professors," Karen tells me, while we're walking. "His name is Bembo, or Bumbles, or something goofy-sounding like that."

"She's the goofy one," I say. "Aside from what she's doing to her soul. A professor isn't going to marry her. But I suppose if she's going to be doing that, at least she's not handing it out to every guy on campus."

"She will be," Karen says. "You know what'll happen. He'll get tired of her, and next fall he'll dump her for another dumb freshman. Then she'll be rebounding all over the place. Not that we're likely to be roommates when that happens."

We smell sauerkraut when we're still about a nine-iron shot from the canopy, and the other cooking smells start mixing in, the closer we get. The canopy is the Rivercats' secondary color—light camel—and the cords holding it up have those little triangular plastic pennants hanging from them: red, white, and black.

The crowd—like every year—is mostly older folks, plus some kids. More of them are townies, than are connected with the university. The Booster Club isn't just for the rich contributors to the athletic department. It's cheap to join, so it attracts fans from all different types of people. They're walking around, mingling, getting food from the steam tables, sitting and eating at the long folding tables that have been set up under the canopy.

The Rivercat Marching Band—240 students, in uniform—is standing easy, outside the canopy, along with the band's drum major and the baton-twirler. The baton girl is known at State University as the Lady In Red, and she receives the only full-ride scholarship for baton-twirling in the United States. The athletes are in street clothes, but they're recognizable. And there's Muddy: a student (presumably) dressed head-to-toe as Muddy the Rivercat. His job, during the festivities, is to caper around, among the visitors, clapping his hands or shaking his fist, without speaking to anyone. Coach Brosnan is here. Feldy and Birdy are here, naturally, and I introduce Karen to them.

If you've had any experience with college football events like the Brat Brekker, you know how they run. They're all pretty much alike, I gather, all over the country. At this one, we hear short speeches from the President of the Booster Club, and

Feldy, then Coach Brosnan makes a speech in which he says, "Our team is hungry for victory this year, and so am I. Realistically, looking over our schedule, I don't think there's a team we can't beat. At the same time, there's not a team on our schedule that can't beat us. Every game this year is going to be a struggle. But I'm confident that we'll have a winning season."

Karen half-whispers, "Is that true, or is he just saying it?"

"It's true, as far as he went. That's pretty non-committal. We should have a winning team. Maybe not the best in the Big Ten, but we should win more than we lose."

That's the general opinion, pre-season, but privately I'm less optimistic than I'm letting on. Sure, I try to sound positive, whenever I talk with anyone else about the team, but Feldy has been warning me not to get my hopes up.

HERE GOES NOTHING

Saturday, September 21, 1968. My début as a sportscaster. Or a sportscastrix. I walk from Radcliffe Hall to the stadium, by myself, feeling like I'm about to burst because I'm so happy and excited. This could not be a better example of the best of Iowa fall weather. I actually stop, for about five seconds, and silently say "Thank you, God. Thank you for this." The leaves are starting to turn; the sun is brilliant, the temperature is cool—it probably won't get much over 60 by game-time—with a light breeze, so that I practically would have to be dead, not to be all pumped up with energy, even if I weren't about to sit in the press box and comment on the game to… I don't know how many. Hundreds of thousands of people, all over eastern Iowa?

Just for extra, we're playing Feldy's old team, the Winnemucca Paiutes. Rivercat Stadium's seating capacity is slightly over 60,000, and it should be nearly full, this afternoon.

Inside the stadium, the crowd is like a single huge life form; it's like each fan is an individual cell. But so far in my life, I've

never been part of the crowd. I've been going to Rivercat football games since I was little, but Birdy and my brothers always
arrived early and got ushered to our seats in the VIP box. And
now I'm even more removed from the fans: in the press box, up
at the top of the stadium, sitting at a table in KSCR's booth,
watching the action through a big open window. I'm not complaining!

I'm wearing headphones; I have a microphone in front of me.
Sonny Bell sits on my left and Joe Barnett on my right. It's half
an hour to kickoff.

"It's a beautiful football afternoon here in State City, and the
State University Rivercats are on the air!" Joe is all jazzed up like
he was a few days ago, in the studio. A recording of the Rivercat
Marching Band playing the "Rivercat Rouser" starts up, and Joe
relaxes for those few seconds.

"Welcome once again to another great year of Rivercat football!" Joe is "on" again, as the music fades down. "I'm Joe Barnett, with Sonny Bell, and joining us for today's game is our special guest commentator, Teresa Feldevert. Welcome aboard,
Terri! We're going to count on you for some expert insights into
today's game against the Paiutes of Winnemucca University."

"Thanks, Joe." I speak good and loud into my microphone,
right on cue.

I remember what Joe told me a few minutes ago: "Smile when
you talk, smile really big. It'll go out over the airwaves, believe
me."

"It's great to be here," I say. "This is going to be a winning
year for the Rivercats; I can feel it!"

I glance over at the other side of the stadium, and catch sight
of the visitors' cheering section.

"Over on the other side of the stadium, I see some people in
red and blue who look like they must be Winnemucca fans, and
they're holding up a banner that reads, 'Feldy: Winnemucca
Loves Ya—But Not Today!' It's nice to know that they remember my father!"

Joe and Sonny are great to work with. They're not putting any
pressure on me to say anything. They only occasionally lob me
an easy comment or question to play off of. I feel a lot more

relaxed, now. I'm not believing this. This is exactly where I want to be, doing exactly what I want to do.

The Rivercats kick off to the Paiutes. The Winnemucca returner fumbles the kickoff, and State recovers it, deep in Winnemucca territory: first and ten at the Winnemucca 13. Not a bad way to start.

A running play loses a yard. Two passes go incomplete. I'm starting to get a nasty feeling about this, and in my mind, I can hear Feldy saying, "Toldja so."

Winnemucca blocks our field goal attempt, and takes over near where they would have been if they hadn't fumbled.

Winnemucca can't move the ball; they have to punt.

The Rivercats can only advance the ball to midfield; we have to punt too.

Our quarterback, Beebe, is also our punter. He can get tremendous distance sometimes, but he's erratic. This one isn't a good punt: it comes down into the returner's arms at about the 15-yard-line...

"And he muffed it!" Sonny cries, over the airwaves. The crowd roars. "The ball's rolling free, toward the Winnemucca goal line—and Abiatha Turner falls on it for the Rivercats!" (An even louder roar from the crowd.) "It's Rivercat ball! On the Winnemucca five-yard-line!"

The crowd is pumped. This time, we're going to score.

A "sweep" is a running play in which the two guards don't block forward—as they would, on an ordinary running play—but instead, they "pull." They both step back, out of their positions, then run toward one end of the offensive line. Their job is to clear a path for the ballcarrier around that end. The interior linemen—the center, guards, and tackles—have the least glamourous positions on the offensive unit. On a sweep, a fast, strong guard gets the chance to show his stuff. The center and the tackles never get to do that.

A sweep can be a devastating play—but in this case, Winnemucca reads it, knocks those two guards aside, and smears the queer with the ball. Second and goal, back at the 11. Beebe tries a dump pass on the next play, and completes it—but once again, the receiver gets trapped inside the line of scrimmage. Third and goal, now at the 14.

"It's these situations that are the test of an offense," I say into the mike. It's my first uninvited comment, and I immediately wonder whether I just said something insightful, or fatuous—or utterly inconsequential.

Beebe's next pass, into the end zone, gets batted away by a Winnemucca defensive back.

"And that's one test the Rivercats didn't pass—this time," Joe says. "Once again, the Rivercats will have to try for three."

Our placekicker, Roberto Abúi, comes from Vigo, Spain. He's a soccer player, so he kicks his placements with the side of his foot. That's a new thing, lately. Pro and college teams have been bringing in these European "sidewinders."

"They're lining up with Beebe to hold," says Joe. "Abúi ready to kick... there's the snap..." (A groan from the crowd.) "... and it's wide to the left! Once again, the Rivercats come up empty in a scoring situation. But it's still only the first quarter, folks, and good things are sure to happen!"

"Good things for Winnemucca, I'm afraid," Joe mutters to me and Sonny, when we go to a commercial break.

"I'm appalled," I reply, in a near-whisper, although I know I can't be heard on the air.

"Still not time to worry yet," says Sonny, "but it does not look good so far."

Again, on its next possession, Winnemucca has to punt, without having made a first down. This time, the Rivercats get the ball on our own 40. We start moving it. We get to midfield, and another first down, on two running plays. Another run, and a short pass, and we have another first down, on the Winnemucca 36. The crowd is with the team, now. I'm with them. I'm starting to hope. Winnemucca's defense doesn't look nearly as strong as it did on our first three possessions.

Our fullback, Baumhauer, picks up three yards on a power play. Beebe hits his favorite receiver, Beverley Bay, on a play-action pass. Bay runs it to the Winnemucca 12-yard-line for another first down.

"The Cats seem to be hitting their stride," Joe says into the mike. "There's a slant off right tackle, Baumhauer bulling forward, and he's finally hauled down at the six-yard-line. Second and four, deep in Winnemucca territory."

Beebe tries a rollout pass on the next play, sees all his receivers covered, and finally has to keep the ball himself. He does well to gain three yards on the ground, but it still leaves us with third and one, on the Winnemucca three.

"They're lining up tight," Joe announces. "Beebe might try to sneak it through for a first down; he's got Keenan, Baumhauer, and Miscowicz in the backfield. Beebe asks the crowd to quiet down…

"He takes it into the line himself and FUMBLE!" (The noise from the crowd is more of a howl of outrage, than a groan.) "The ball pops forward and Winnemucca recovers in the end zone! They're signaling a touchback… and it'll be Winnemucca's ball, on their own 20-yard-line, when we come back. Oh, my goodness, Rivercats!"

Joe, once he's off-mike, puts his face in his hands and rocks back and forth in his swivel chair.

I say, "This has got to be some kind of practical joke."

"Maybe they're getting all the bad luck out of their system," Sonny says. I shake my head, and nobody says much else till we're back on-air.

Winnemucca, from its 20, makes a first down—its first of the afternoon—but that's all they can do. They punt again. It's our ball, on our own 25.

The second quarter is more than half over. I figure, if we can eat up a lot of clock, while we drive for a touchdown, we can go into the locker room at halftime leading 7-0, which will give us a morale boost, even if we should be leading by a lot more.

The Rivercats pick up another first down, near midfield. Joe says, "Now we're driving. Still 4:13 left in the half. State U. has all its time-outs left. Bay is lined up wide left, Miscowicz is flanked out right. Beebe is fading back… the throw is to Bay… and he has it at the 30! He picks up another three yards, and it's first and ten for the Rivercats at the Winnemucca 27! Four minutes and two seconds left in the half. Let's go, Cats!"

"Nice and easy does it," I say. "Beebe is mixing up his plays intelligently now, and he's got plenty of time."

The Rivercats pick up another first down, at the Winnemucca 16, using up the clock by keeping the ball on the ground. Three plays after that, they make first and goal, at the Winnemucca four, with just over a minute left in the half.

"You can feel the confidence, now, in the Rivercat offense," I say.

"Beebe breaks the huddle and leads his team up to the line of scrimmage," says Joe. They're in a split T, with Baumhauer and Keenan behind him. The give is to Baumhauer, in a sweep to the left… and fumble again! Fumble again! It's Winnemucca's ball, on their own two-yard-line! I am not believing this!"

The first half ends—and we're scoreless. During the halftime analysis, Joe and Sonny stick to statistics as much as possible. They barely mention the fumbles. I chime in with a comment about how Beebe and Bay seemed to be connecting well.

How I wish I could say what's on my mind: I have seen better football played in our front yard on Hilltop Street.

"You're doing great," Joe tells me during a commercial break. "You're a natural. We're going to see about bringing you in for a few more games this year, if you're up for it."

"What do you mean, 'if'? Although it doesn't look like I'm bringing the team much luck, so far."

"Oh, that's not you," Sonny says. "They don't need any help from you. They stink on their own. Brosnan must be having a stroke, right about now."

"Brosnan wasn't making those errors," I say, "but you *have* to have ball-security. If you don't, it reflects on the coaching."

Joe smiles. Maybe he's thinking, "You would say that, wouldn't you?" but he doesn't say it.

Instead, when we're back on the air, Joe says, "It might be nerves, at the start of the season, or they haven't acquired the smoothness they'll have after a game or two. You often see that."

"You didn't used to," I reply. Then I gasp and clap a hand over my mouth. Judas, that went out to the listeners. Joe and Sonny both grin at me.

The Rivercats receive the opening kickoff in the second half, but can't move the ball, and have to punt.

The Paiutes stall out; they have to punt too.

This time, the Rivercats take over at about their own 20, and start moving the ball. Miscowicz gains 15 yards on an end-around. Beebe flips a pass to the tight end, Mankiller, that gains another 12. Baumhauer runs up the middle for five more yards. We're in Winnemucca territory again. Another play-action pass to Bay, and we have a first down on the Winnemucca 41.

"Let's go, Cats!" Joe exclaims again, into the mike.

Now it's getting tougher. We get another first down, and another. We're down to the Winnemucca 17. But then two running plays get us only three yards. On third down a couple of Winnemucca tacklers flush Beebe out of the pocket and sack him—the first time that has happened that day—at the Winnemucca 21.

"The Cats will have to try to settle for three," Joe says, "but we've got to get something on the board, and a three-point lead might be enough to do it. They're lined up in field goal formation, Beebe to hold; Abúi is ready... there's the snap, the kick... and he shanked it! Way off to the right; the kick is no good. Oh, brother!"

On the last play of the third quarter, the Winnemucca quarterback throws a pass that gets picked off by one of our defensive backs, Vanderdender, who is tackled before he can run it back. State takes possession once again, on the Winnemucca 29.

"Now the Rivercats have a minute or two to re-group between quarters," Joe tells the listeners. "The Winnemucca defense has got to be tired by this time."

"Our offense is doing a lot of things right," I say. "And our defense has been the big surprise of the afternoon. If we can put together a drive here, that could decide the game."

If. What an "if" that is. Baumhauer gets thrown for a two-yard loss, on a play that just didn't develop. On second down, Beebe can't find a receiver. He has to scramble, and ends up getting sacked, losing another ten yards.

"The pocket can only hold up for so long," I say. "There comes a point where the quarterback has to get rid of the ball, or that's what'll happen."

On third and 22, from the Winnemucca 41, it almost happens again. Beebe sends all his eligible receivers downfield, but can't find anyone open for a few seconds. Finally, Miscowicz gets free of his coverage; Beebe seems to see him; he's set to pass—and he loses his footing. He seems to trip over nothing; he goes sprawling to the turf, eight yards behind the line of scrimmage.

"Right on his keester," Joe cries. "A fitting end to that possession, we have to admit. Fourth down, now, and 30 yards to go, on the Winnemucca 49, and I don't see how Abúi can try a field goal from there."

Beebe at least delivers a decent punt: the Paiutes are starting at their own 10.

"Let's see if we can get a fumble or an interception here," says Sonny. We're on defense, so he takes over the play-by-play.

No such luck. This time, Winnemucca is able to move the ball, if laboriously. They eat up a lot of clock before they have to punt. We've got the ball back, but deep in our own territory, with only 2:30 to play.

"This could be the Rivercats' last possession," says Joe. "Still no score in today's game, folks, and the fans here at Rivercat Stadium are getting restless. Beebe breaks the huddle and leads the team up to the line of scrimmage..."

Slowly, we move the ball upfield. With one minute to play, we've got a first and ten at our own 35. With half a minute to play, we gain another first down, almost at midfield.

"If we can pick up another 20 yards, we might be within field goal range," Joe says. "The Rivercats still have one time out left. They're at the line, Bay wide left, Miscowicz wide right..."

I want to say into the mike, "Let's go, you guys!" but I'm afraid of sounding like a whining girl, so I keep still.

Beebe throws an incompletion. Then another. Twelve seconds left on the clock.

"We could be looking at a scoreless tie in our season opener," Joe says. "Third and ten for the Rivercats on their own 49, but they still have two plays left, as Beebe prepares to take the snap from Berggren..."

"Beebe fading back... he's looking for Bay, running a fly downfield... he throws... and it's INTERCEPTED! That's

Tetzlaff, the right corner for Winnemucca, and he's got a clear field in front of him! He just stepped in front of Bay, and picked the ball off! He's running down the sideline, at the 40, the 30… there's nobody to tackle him… TOUCHDOWN! Touchdown, Winnemucca! And the gun has sounded! The gun sounded, just before Tetzlaff crossed the goal line! The game is OVER! The game is OVER! On a 70-yard interception runback by Charlie Tetzlaff, the Winnemucca Paiutes have prevailed, over the State University Rivercats! Final score, Winnemucca six, State nothing!"

I heard a huge groan from the crowd when Tetzlaff intercepted that pass, but the noise had faded to almost nothing by the time he crossed the goal line. The Winnemucca players are jumping up and down, now, pounding each other on the back, on their side of the field. Our offensive unit is walking slowly toward the tunnel; their teammates on the sidelines are hardly moving at all.

Coach Brosnan trots toward the Winnemucca bench; he and the Winnemucca coach meet at mid-field and shake hands. Only now are some of the Rivercats moving toward the Winnemucca side to congratulate the other team. Most of them are heading straight to the locker room.

The Rivercat Marching Band, which usually plays the "Rivercat Rouser" at the end of a game, win or lose, hasn't started to play. The crowd is still making hardly a sound. I'm too far away to see facial expressions, but they must be feeling complete disgust. And shock. That's what I feel.

"The Paiutes didn't win that game," I say into my mike. "The Rivercats lost it. We were 17-point favorites; we should have won by four touchdowns at least. I'm just… at a loss for words. This wasn't any one player's fault; it wasn't Coach Brosnan's fault. It was a team effort."

I wonder if I've overstepped a boundary, saying something as blunt as that over the radio—on my first day as a commentator, at that. I put the fingertips of my right hand over my mouth and glance over at Joe, then at Sonny, half-apologizing with my eyes.

"You might say that," Sonny says, quickly, to prevent dead air.

Joe and Sonny begin relaying some of the statistics to the audience: first downs; yards gained passing and rushing; the two quarterbacks' passing statistics, and so on. I stay quiet till we go to a commercial.

"I didn't say too much, did I?"

"It was the truth," Joe says. "Not a very nice truth, but someone had to say it. I'm afraid we're looking at a long season."

"Gotta think positive," says Sonny, "but it's hard to, after a mess like that. Terri, you did great, for your first time."

"You sure did," says Joe. "We're on the road the next two weeks, but we'll have you back up here for Homecoming, if that's okay with you. Unless you're going to be participating in the ceremonies with your family."

"They'll have to go through it without me. I'll be here."

§

I still go to Mass with the rest of my family, every Sunday morning, although now that I'm living in the dorms, I walk to Our Lady—it's about ten minutes from Radcliffe Hall—and we meet up there. After Mass, we all pile into the family hauler, which is a Chevy Suburban, and go to lunch at the Coffin, as we have done on most Sundays since we moved to State City.

The Coffin is a men's dorm. It's officially called Riverview. It sits on a hill overlooking the State River and most of the State University campus. Win lives there, now. It's a huge red brick hexagon with four short sides and two long sides, like a coffin—hence the nickname—built around the turn of the century in what I understand was called "Collegiate Gothic" style.

Besides the student dining hall, the Coffin has a public cafeteria that looks out on a beautiful lazy grassy courtyard within the hexagon. This cafeteria is called the Coffin Corner, although it's actually a pretty big space; I bet it can seat 150 people. Faculty and townies eat there in the evening. It's especially popular at mid-day on Sundays. Where else can you get prime rib for a dollar-fifty?

We're driving to Riverview after mass, and we're discussing this new batch of hymns that we just heard. Feldy is driving; Birdy is beside him; Sander, Duffy, and I are in back. Win probably went to Mass at St. Loy. We'll meet him at the cafeteria.

Birdy says, "I wish they had warned us. They're not going to have that kind of music at every Mass, now, are they?"

"Pretty lame," Duffy says. "The tunes don't make any sense, musically, and they don't care about sticking too many syllables into a line. It doesn't sound like church music."

Win is waiting for us in the main entrance hallway of the Coffin. Win is the only boy in our family who never played much football. He played it in our front yard as a kid, but he never took to it. Lou is medium-sized, not big enough to have played football after high school, but he played hockey and lacrosse. Jack and Jerry are bigger than Feldy, now. Duffy and Sander are both going to be monsters. Win isn't built like any of them. He's as tall as Feldy, but not husky. The only sport he's good at is golf. He plays the guitar pretty well, too. He's a year ahead of me—a sophomore at State University—majoring in philosophy.

My brothers are all nice-looking enough, but I wouldn't call any of them handsome, except Win. He's handsome like a movie star, the movie star who would play the stereotypical clean-cut all-American college boy who *doesn't* get the girl in the end, but congratulates the boy who does and wishes them well. Win usually dresses casually like any other guy, but neater, so that he looks more formal. He wears his hair slightly shorter than most guys on campus. He's wearing his church outfit today, of course: slacks, tweed sport jacket, white shirt, knit tie.

Duffy and Sander are leading us down the hall to the cafeteria; Birdy and Win are behind them; Feldy and I at the rear. I can hear Birdy saying to Win, "I'm afraid Our Lady has caught the St. Loy virus." She's telling him about the new lineup of hymns.

"That's a good way to describe those hymns," Win says. He has such a soft voice. The Professor on *Gilligan's Island* talked just like Win. "A virus. Or they're symptoms of a virus. Maybe I just have to get used to it. But it seems to me that that's not music for Mass. It's... it's Protestant, almost."

Birdy and Feldy both laugh, and we all get on the chow line, which on Sundays at noon consists of old couples, young marrieds, and families with children, mostly dressed for church. Prime rib is always on the menu, which is displayed in white letters on a black letter-board on a wall behind the steam tables. So is fried chicken, Swiss steak, baked ham, and beef stroganoff.

I go for the prime rib, mashed potatoes and gravy, a tossed salad, banana cream pie, and coffee.

Feldy hasn't mentioned the game, so far, and none of the kids are going to bring it up till he does. We're seated in the Coffin Corner's dining room at a round table for six, and starting to eat—we don't say Grace if we're in a restaurant; we just think it, because we're not supposed to make a display of our religion—when Feldy says, "Birdy and I each brought transistor radios to the stadium yesterday, Terri. To hear you. You made us proud. I've been listening to football on the radio since I was a little boy, and you were as good as any announcer I've ever heard."

"And your first time out," Birdy says. "You have a very nice radio voice. You came across as ladylike, but like a lady who knows her football."

"That's how to put it," Feldy says. "You should have been coaching the team, though."

Well, that makes my whole week, right there: hearing that from my parents. But I just say, "That was sad, wasn't it? You could tell they were doing their best. They should have won."

Feldy says, "They should have, but they didn't. End of story. Maybe they were doing their best, in the sense of trying hard. Everybody makes mistakes. But a well-coached team doesn't make that many mistakes. If they had been doing the best they could have done, they would have held onto the ball. They would have shown more grace under pressure. They weren't even under that much pressure, till the last few minutes."

"Plus, they obviously underestimated Winnemucca." Feldy is now addressing the whole table, holding forth. "You notice nobody got hurt yesterday? Nobody got shaken up? They weren't hitting as hard as they should have. They didn't intimidate the other team. Now, that is something I need to talk to Brosnan about. I've been saying this all along: he's too nice a guy. Football players aren't naturally hard-nosed, at least not most of them. You've got to teach them to be mean. Brosnan knows football, but he doesn't understand that part of it."

"Gotta be mean," Sander says. Sander is 14. He's on the freshman football team at Visitation High. For the time being, his favorite position is defensive end.

"You're the meanest, for sure," Win says to Sander. "You're the one that's going to the NFL."

"We can still have a good year," I say.

"This is our best chance for one, the best chance we've had since '63," Feldy says. He's looking stern. "We've got a lot going for us. I'm going to be seriously disappointed in Brosnan if he lets this year get away from us. I'm running out of patience."

He pauses for a couple of seconds.

"I'd also like to give old Hubert Humphrey a talking-to," he says. "There's another guy who isn't mean enough. He's going to have to learn, fast."

"Feldy, maybe that's your new vocation," I say. "It might be time to get out of the university entirely, and get into politics."

Birdy and Feldy both look sort of in between amused and bemused. Hard to describe how they look.

"I mean it," I say. "Ray's going to beat Franzenburg for Governor in November; you can run against Ray in 1970—then for President in '72 if Humphrey loses this time, or you'll still be young enough in '76 or '80."

Feldy laughs. "That's tempting. Kind of a long shot, wouldn't you say? But tempting. Anyway, Win, I'm curious. I didn't care much for those hymns this morning, either, but how do you mean they're Protestant?"

"Because," Win says, "the Roman Catholic Church is God, so to speak. The Mass is God. It's called the Sacrifice of the Mass because it re-enacts the Last Supper and Christ's sacrifice. Protestant services are *people*. They're people coming together to worship God—presumably. And that's fine for them. But the Sacrifice of the Mass is not people. Sure, people are involved, but the Church is God's gift to us; the Mass is the Sacrifice. People come to Mass to be with God, to witness the Sacrifice and take part in the last supper."

Feldy, Birdy, and I are all paying attention to Win.

"The Mass *can't* be about people. That's not its purpose. It's supposed to *not* be about people. It's supposed to... It's supposed to be *above* people. That's maybe the purpose of traditional liturgical music. To remind you of where you are, and why you're there. Liturgical music helps you rise out of the world. It helps you get closer to God. This goody-goody feel-happy music, it doesn't do that. It does the opposite."

Both Feldy and Birdy nod. Duffy and Sander are involved in a conversation of their own.

"You know, that kind of music has been around for a while, now, outside of Mass," Win says. "Us kids used to hear it at school, all the time. I don't know about you, Terri, or you young'uns" (he indicates Duffy and Sander, who aren't listening), "but I always hated it. These 'praise songs.' They try *soooo* hard to be modern, to be 'with it,' and they *aren't*. They embarrass me. They come across so... forced. I mean, don't they? Like they were written by some 'youth pastor' trying to be 'hep to the jive,' and coming across silly and condescending the way every youth pastor has ever done in the whole history of the world."

That makes me laugh out loud.

"It's even worse when you hear music of that type in church," Win says. "It's *just... so... mortifying*. Like the Rivercats trying to generate an offense yesterday."

That gets a laugh out of Feldy.

"These praise songs, they take you out of the Mass," Win says. "They jerk you back into the world. They interrupt the flow. They make you focus on the words, the people, instead of on the Sacrifice. Not to mention, the words are Protestant. They celebrate people, not the Sacrifice."

"That part about 'eat his body, drink his blood' goes to prove a Protestant wrote it," I say. "Because whoever wrote that, apparently doesn't know that the laity doesn't drink the wine."

"Every good Protestant knows it's whiskey we drink, while we're praying to idols," says Birdy.

Win, Feldy, and I all laugh; Duffy and Sander glance at us for a moment, like they wonder what's up.

"From what I understand," Win says, "it's licit for the laity to drink the wine, but hardly any parish does it. Because of accidents. I remember Monsignor Koudelka explained to me that it would be bound to get spilled sometimes, if the congregation drank it, and that would insult Our Lord."

That makes Feldy and Birdy look funny at Win, like maybe they think he's taking it all too seriously, but I find it interesting, what he's saying.

"That's what I'm talking about," Win says. "That's a song about us communing. It's directed to the congregation, not to God. It doesn't speak to the glory of God. It's inviting us to pat ourselves on the back. And 'They will know we are Christians by our love': same thing. That's us congratulating ourselves. It doesn't have any place in the Mass.

"And don't get me started on the Prayer of the Faithful. The Mass was always a beautiful thing to me, when I was a kid—it still is, but it *really* was, when it was in Latin. Even in English, you know, it still has some of the... I don't know what you might call it. Majesty, maybe. But less than it had, in Latin. And these other changes make it even worse. They deface the Mass. Like taking a magic marker and drawing tattoos on the *Pietà*."

"But what's wrong with the Prayer of the Faithful?" Birdy asks. "It seems to me that it makes people think about what Christian love consists of—in more concrete terms."

"There's a place for that," Win says. "But not in the Mass. Not to pray for things that are of the world, like the Rivercats, or for things people disagree about, like Vietnam."

"The Cats need whatever prayers they can get," Feldy says. "Clearly they're experiencing God's wrath, right now."

MAYBE I'M GOOD AT SOMETHING

We won the next game, though, the following Saturday. We were on the road, against the University of Washington, and they're a perennial power, so they were supposed to clobber us. They didn't. I was over at our house, listening to the game on the radio with Sander and Duffy. I can't explain it. We won all the way, 27-7. State City was hopeful again.

On the Tuesday evening following that game, Joe Barnett called me at my dorm.

He said, "You wouldn't believe the notes and phone calls we've been getting since Saturday. They were all saying the same thing, you know: 'Where's that sweet little Terri Feldy?'"

"I'm hardly sweet, or little," I said, but I noticed that I couldn't remember having ever felt quite so flattered.

"Evidently you sound sweet and little over the airwaves. Anyway, people seem to react well to you. It's too late to include you next week, when we're in Madison, but Sonny and I were thinking we'd like to have you in the booth for as many home games as you're up for, the rest of the season. Not just Homecoming. Would that suit you?"

I should have at least hinted that I ought to be paid, but frankly I don't have the nerve and I'm not sure I deserve any pay.

The Rivercats were 10-point favorites at Wisconsin, which is having a "rebuilding" year. We should have won. We were leading 13-7, late in the fourth quarter. We lost, 16-13, due to a series of foul-ups that I won't go into.

Last week, Homecoming, I was back in the broadcast booth. Nobody expected us to beat Purdue. We came close, but "moral victories" don't count. Boilermakers 17, Rivercats 14. Some fans have written the whole season off. Some are saying that Brosnan should be canned. But look: If it hadn't been for some awful bad luck, the Cats' record so far might be something like 3-0-1.

We've got Minnesota this afternoon, at home, and they're not a strong team. We should win this one. It's a miserable day. Pouring down rain, all afternoon. I'm not in any discomfort, up here in front of the mike, but nobody in the stands looks very happy.

The field is all mud, and neither team can move the ball. None of the runners or receivers can get a footing; the ball is almost uncatchable. In the first half, each team managed to cross midfield only once. Beebe completed just three short passes in that half, in ten attempts.

Early in the third quarter, we got the ball down to the Gophers' 32-yard line, and Abúi kicked the field goal. The score held up for the rest of the quarter. The Gophers have no offense whatever.

Joe said, over the air, "These two teams aren't playing in mud; it's more like oobleck!"

Now it's early in the fourth quarter, we're up 3-0, and we've taken over the ball at midfield. Our next two plays from scrimmage—both runs—net two yards. We have it third and eight on the Minnesota 48.

Ordinarily, this would be a passing situation, since we want to keep driving downfield and maybe get another score. But Beebe hasn't been passing well. It might make more sense to call another running play. If by some miracle it works, great. If it doesn't, Beebe can punt, and with luck, Minnesota will be inside their own five-yard line, where a fumble or an interception would set up another score for us.

"Bay and Miscowicz both split wide as the Rivercats come to the line of scrimmage," says Joe. "The fake is to Baumhauer. Beebe fading back, looking for Bay... and it's picked off! The ball was tipped, and the Minnesota linebacker, number 53, Bierman, picked it off right at the line of scrimmage, brought down immediately by a pack of Rivercats, but that's where the Gophers will take over: first and ten at their own 48-yard line!"

"I hear a little booing as the Rivercat offense comes off the field," I say. "I don't think that's called for, although you can understand the fans' frustration. Let's hold 'em here, Cats!"

"First and ten for the Minnesota Gophers, on their own 48," Sonny repeats. "They get up to the line... Hagen going back, looking to pass on first down. The throw is to Litten, going deep, he's got Vanderdender beat... and he has it! He's into the end zone! Touchdown, Minnesota!"

We hear more boos from the stands, and Minnesota makes the extra point.

Poor Vanderdender. He's a junior this year, a completely unremarkable defensive back. Not great, not terrible. There's not a defensive back in the world who hasn't been beaten on a long pass route at some point.

Trouble is, Vanderdender is also the off-back on the ensuing kickoff. Bay is our primary return man, but if the ball is kicked away from him, Vanderdender will catch it and return it.

The kick is well to Bay's left, and short, so Vanderdender steps up and catches it at about the 10. He runs with it a good 20 yards before a Minnesota tackler hits him—and strips the ball loose. Another Gopher falls on it.

The only merciful occurrence is that on the next play, when the Minnesota quarterback, Phil Hagen, drops back to pass yet again, he throws to the other side of the field to another receiver—so Vanderdender at least isn't entirely responsible for the second touchdown, which is what that play is.

With the extra point, the score is 14-3, Minnesota.

"This game has completely turned around in hardly more than 20 seconds," I say over the air. "But we've still got almost a full quarter to play."

The crowd is quiet, as this time Vanderdender holds onto the kickoff, and runs it back to about the 25. Baumhauer gains three yards up the middle. On second down Beebe calls for a screen pass. The blockers, and the intended receiver, Baumhauer, set up well, but Minnesota runs a zone blitz that takes Beebe by surprise. He's smeared for an 11-yard loss. Third and 18, now, on the Rivercat 17-yard line.

The fans are booing again. It's getting louder and louder. These aren't just a few boos, scattered through the stadium. This is tens of thousands of boos, a huge black cloud of boos, a torrent of boos.

"Maybe Beebe should have anticipated that blitz," I say, "but maybe he couldn't have. Once again, it was the kind of blown play that can happen; it wasn't because of any hideous mistake on Beebe's part, nor anyone else's. I don't know if the fans are booing Beebe, or the team, or the situation in general. The fact that everyone is soaking wet doesn't help."

Joe says, "This is probably the first time in the history of Rivercat football that a quarterback has had to wave his hands to ask the crowd to dial down the booing, so that the team can hear him calling the signals. They're lined up for a pass. Beebe is fading back… and now he goes for a quarterback draw, up the middle! The Gophers are completely fooled! But he's brought down at the 27. It's still fourth and eight, and the boos are picking up again as the punting unit comes on the field."

Minnesota has to punt, too, a few plays later, so the Cats have the ball back, but deep in their own territory. This time, Brosnan sends in the second-string quarterback, Ted Blaha. The booing picks up again.

"They can't be booing Blaha," Joe tells our listeners. "He hasn't played a down yet today. I can't understand this."

"It's like a stadium full of little children crying from frustration," I say. "Only it's booing, not crying. I'm appalled."

"Again, Blaha has to quiet the crowd before he bends over center," Joe remarks.

Blaha gives the ball to Miscowicz on an end-around, and the play only picks up a yard. Blaha throws an incomplete pass, intended for Mankiller, that's almost intercepted. Some of the fans begin chanting "We want Beebe! We want Beebe!"

On the next play, Blaha gives the ball to the halfback, Keenan, on an option—and Keenan throws incomplete to Bay. Again, the punting unit comes on.

At this point, the boos are almost crazed, almost feral.

Minnesota can't score on its next possession, either, but it's too late for us to score two touchdowns, even if we had it in us to do it. Fans are leaving the stadium: not straggling out, but streaming out, with still nearly four minutes left.

The final score is 14-3.

We go to a commercial. Off-air, Joe says, "That's all she wrote for this year. We're not going to win another game—or maybe one, by accident, if we're real lucky. That's the end of Brosnan."

"The booing made me sick," Sonny says. "I'm ashamed of the fans."

"It was bad," I say, "but it's hard to blame them. Sure, some of those mistakes just happen, in this kind of weather... but how can you laugh off something like that?"

It's a good night to go back to my dorm and study, so that's what I do. Both my roommates are back in their respective hometowns for the weekend. I have supper in the dorm cafeteria; practice my cello for an hour; read my biology text-book. I hate biology. My mood isn't helped by the knowledge that this is Saturday night and I'm in my room, working. I play the Glad Game, and remind myself to be glad of this opportunity to get the biology over with.

At ten o'clock, I go downstairs to the TV lounge to catch the news. A lot of it is about the Presidential campaign. The latest polls indicate that Humphrey might be catching up to Nixon, which makes me feel hopeful. The sports report comes on at about 10:15. The game wasn't telecast, but KCRG had a crew at the stadium to interview Coach Brosnan and the players. The sports report leads off with a description of what the sports an-chorman calls "an embarrassing game, and embarrassing behav-ior by some of the fans at Rivercat Stadium."

There's film of Baumhauer, the fullback—still in his uniform, covered with mud—telling a reporter, "I was shocked. I remem-ber last year when Beebe was our star and everyone was saying he was the greatest thing since indoor plumbing. Now he has a bad day and they turn on him like that."

Then, a clip of Coach Brosnan talking to reporters. He says, "I hope the booing was meant for me, and not for the players. You have to wonder about people sometimes; you have to won-der how they might feel if it were their own boy out there on the field, getting that treatment."

Finally, a clip of the Gophers' coach, Murray Warmath, telling reporters, "That was the most sickening sound I've ever heard in any stadium."

At Our Lady, this morning, Monsignor Koudelka has this to say in his homily:

"People have failings. The Church reconnizes that man is sin-ful, that man will sin. God forgiffs sin when there's genuine re-pentance, and genuine reparation whenever possible. God forgiffs failure much faster than sin. You must confess your sins, but failure, when you're trying your best, is no sin. The Church reconnizes that Jesus wass the only perfect man, and that while we might try to live up to the standards that Jesus set for us, we will fail. God unnerstands that we will fail, and He forgiffs.

"When we fail in life, God doesn't turn His back on us. He doesn't heckle us. He doesn't boo us. He may feel sorry when He sees us failing, but He doesn't try to make us feel worse about it than we already feel. God unnerstands that most of us are trying to do His will. He unnerstands that most of us are striving, that most of us have good intentions. When we fail, God feels as badly about it as we do. Maybe even worse. But instead of booing us, or shaming us, He roots for us to conquer our faults and do better next time."

In the *Examiner*, on Tuesday, it's reported that Coach Warmath, in a speech to the Minneapolis Quarterback Club the day before, had said, "The Minnesota fans who came to State City were embarrassed to be in that stadium. They were embarrassed that those Rivercat fans would treat their own boys that way. I don't know of a tougher place to play football than State City. The fans are enthusiastic, no question of that, but they're exceptionally critical and unforgiving. Thank goodness Minnesota is Minnesota and not State University!"

§

The awfulness continued through October, into November. Our next two games were Northwestern, in Evanston, then Indiana, in Bloomington. Against Northwestern, Beebe had another awful day. He completed only nine of 23 passes and threw two interceptions, but it wasn't all his fault, because he was getting no protection at all from the offensive line. Once again, our defense was great: better than anyone had expected it to be at the start of the season. Northwestern could only manage nine points: three field goals. But our offense couldn't even do that. The final score was Northwestern 9, State 3.

Feldy told me, when we were all having lunch at the Coffin Corner the next day, that he was going to advise Brosnan to try a Wing T formation for the Indiana game. He diagrammed it on his napkin for me.

He said, "I'm trying to help the poor guy keep his job. Maybe this'll work."

The Wing T did work that next Saturday, for the first two quarters. The Rivercats were leading 10-0 at the half and I was thinking that Feldy was the greatest genius ever.

But in the second half, Indiana seemed to figure out how to stop it—and the Cats' defense, which up to that point had been the big surprise of the season, ran out of gas all of a sudden. The final score was Indiana 24, State 17.

Baumhauer had a pretty successful day running the ball. He was the player who got the most ink the next day. The *Register* quoted him as saying, "I want all the people of Iowa, everybody who follows State University football, to know that the team is behind Coach Brosnan 100 percent. He introduced several new plays at practice this week and he did a perfect job of teaching them to us; we all agreed that his game plan was brilliant. We should have scored a couple more touchdowns, and we would have, if we could have executed better. Then we would have won, and Bob would have gotten the credit he deserved.

"I feel that we've been letting Bob down, all this year. I'm as much to blame as anyone. This season is not Bob's fault."

It was Feldy who deserved the credit for that game plan, but Baumhauer wouldn't have known that.

§

November 5, 1968: Election Night. I have never seen much difference between Humphrey and Nixon on the issues, but it's a given in the Feldevert family that Humphrey is our hero. Especially to Birdy. She thinks he's adorable.

I liked Humphrey the first time I saw him on TV, when he was running for the Democratic nomination in 1960. Of course, we had all been for Kennedy then, but we loved Humphrey anyway. I was struck by that almost comically sharp voice, coming from that tiny mouth that seems to peck at each word like a hen. He has that high bald forehead and red cheeks that make him look almost like a clown-doll. Birdy loves his emotion, even if he never says much of substance. I think he's kind of corny, but I can understand how Birdy feels.

I've been at our house since late afternoon, helping Birdy set up for the watch party. Guests started arriving at around seven o'clock: Jake and Silda Rosen; Dr. and Mrs. Ingram; some other couples that my folks do Democrat stuff with. Earlier in the evening, Nixon appeared to be getting the breaks in several states that had been expected to be close—but now, the results are closer than a lot of people had anticipated. George Wallace is running behind expectations—although he's carrying several states, so we could have a deadlock in the Electoral College.

We have, finally, about a dozen guests, and, gosh, it's tense. But fun-tense—for now—because most of us are feeling scared but hopeful. Just after ten o'clock, Humphrey pulls slightly ahead in the overall popular vote. Birdy whoops aloud when the numbers appear on the TV screen.

"By golly, we might do it!"

Birdy is, I won't call her drunk, but "she's a drop taken," as she herself might have put it, and I have never seen her in this condition before. Ever. She's drinking scotch and chain-smoking while the results come in. I hardly ever smoke, but I light one of her Kents, now, for solidarity.

Feldy sits in his usual chair, with a clipboard in his lap, noting the results on a chart he has designed, letting the socializing go on around him, not talking much. He has been working on the same glass of scotch and soda all evening, but most of the guests are making up the deficit for him. The party is getting a little raucous. I go over to Feldy's chair and crouch down next to him.

"How does it look?"

"See for yourself." Feldy hands me the clipboard. "Humphrey doesn't have any way to be elected, but if Nixon doesn't get a majority, it goes to the House, and they're sure to choose Humphrey—especially if he wins the popular vote. So, there's a chance. The way I see it, it depends on New Jersey, Illinois, Maryland, and Missouri." Feldy points with his pencil to the calculations he had made on paper, for each of those four states. "Humphrey's got to take Illinois plus at least two of the other three, to send it to the House—but if he can do that, he's in."

"How about California? They've just started counting the votes there."

"Hell, if Humphrey were to carry all those states plus California, he would actually be elected, outright. But I can't see Nixon losing California. It might be close, but if Hubert has to count on California, he can give up now."

"Anyway, Ray's winning," I say. "Get ready to run for Governor two years from now."

New Jersey totters for another three hours. At 1:00 in the morning, it goes for Nixon by a whisker. But Maryland looks like it's going to Humphrey. By this time, most of the guests have left. Birdy is sitting on the couch, looking half-anæsthetized.

"There's still hope for Illinois and Missouri," Feldy says. He gets to his feet and says to the company, "Stay as late as you like. They'll still be counting votes in the morning, though. I'm going to bed."

I go up to my old room. I brush my teeth but not my hair. I say my prayers—a shortened version, but still as always ending with "Please help me to be the person you mean me to be"— then I fall onto the bed.

I'm up at 7:00. Birdy and Feldy are drinking coffee at the kitchen table. Birdy looks somewhat the worse for wear. The TV, from the den, is reporting that returns from Illinois and Missouri are still inconclusive—but Nixon is ahead in both.

"We can still hope," Birdy says.

"Hope in one hand and poop in the other," Feldy says. "It doesn't look good."

"God doesn't want it," I say. I pour myself some coffee.

Birdy looks reproachful, like I ought to be more broken up.

"It's going to be okay," I tell her.

"But we gave his campaign $600! Oh, I know, that shouldn't be important, but I can't help thinking about it."

BROSNAN IS DONE

On the following Saturday, the Cats were back home—against Michigan State. The Spartans were 24-point favorites. That Friday morning—the day before—the *Register* ran a story by George Conroy stating that "Brosnan will resign at the end of this season rather than face the humiliation of having it announced that 'he'll be offered the opportunity to fulfill the fifth year of his contract in some other capacity.' Almost as inevitable is the statewide acclamation that will sweep Leo Feldevert back into the position of Head Coach. Whether the State University administration likes it or not, Feldy will command both posts—Head Coach and Athletic Director. It's what he deserves."

Feldy killed that rumor right away, or at least he tried to, by issuing a statement:

"I am not interested in coaching again—anywhere, ever—and I do not appreciate these rumors, which are only serving to undercut Coach Brosnan and the team, all of whom are doing their best. I can't help being flattered but I'm also upset that Mr. Conroy would publish such a story."

I knew the first part of Feldy's statement wasn't true, but what else could he have said? As for the second part, probably some people doubted his sincerity. But if they did, they were unfair.

Michigan State chewed us up and spat us out. Maybe it was because we hadn't played a team as strong as the Spartans so far this year, but our defense was unrecognizable. The only reason the final score was 35-0 was that the Spartans emptied their bench in the last quarter, and took care not to make it worse.

Our two quarterbacks, Beebe and Blaha, completed ten passes in 25 attempts (with two interceptions) for 59 yards. They were sacked seven times, for a total loss of 59 yards, which, when you subtract it from the miserable 75 yards we got on actual rushing attempts, makes our total offense just that: 75 yards.

The stadium looked only about two-thirds full at kickoff. By the fourth quarter, it was almost empty. Maybe two or three thousand fans stayed to the end. It was beyond eerie. It gave me the creeps, up there in the broadcast booth.

"Don't say anything about nobody's left in the stands," Joe said to me and Sonny, during a commercial break. "It's bad enough; no need to rub it in."

In Columbus, the next Saturday, against Ohio State, it was almost the same story. Buckeyes 38, Rivercats 0. State University's Big Ten season is over, with an 0-7 record. We still have one non-conference game: at home, against Mason Dixon University.

"That's it," Feldy said to us the next day, when we were driving away from church, to the Coffin. "I'm firing Brosnan."

Now, this is Feldy's version of the story. He told it to me over the phone on the next Tuesday night, when I called him from my dorm room for an update. Feldy told me that on Monday morning, he phoned down the hall of the Fieldhouse to Coach Brosnan's office, to cancel the private meeting that the two of them always have on the Monday after a game. He told him, "The Board in Control of Athletics will be holding a closed meeting tomorrow afternoon at three, as you've probably been notified. I'll see you there." Brosnan must have known what was up, if he and Feldy were both were ordered to attend the meeting.

"When we got to the meeting today," Feldy said to me, "Professor Mathers told Brosnan that the Board had voted unanimously to ask him to resign, and he would be allowed to coach the last game of the season if he chose to, but they wanted his resignation now, so that we could start the process of finding a new coach.

"The stubborn bastard says," (here, Feldy tried to do an impression of Brosnan), "'I still have a game to coach on Saturday; I've got another year left on my contract. You'll have to fire me.' Mathers looked over at me, as much as to say, 'You know what to do,' so I told Brosnan, 'Okay, then. The Board is authorized to ask you to resign, but they can't remove you. That's the Athletic Director's prerogative. I intend to issue a statement tonight that you and your staff will be relieved of your duties, effective at the end of the season, and that you'll be re-assigned for the last year of your contract.'

"I was the only guy in the room looking at Brosnan. The Board, all of them, were kind of sneak-looking at him, out of the corners of their eyes. Like they thought they had something to feel guilty about. I was ashamed of them."

Judas, Murphy, and Jethro. Feldy just made a huge mistake. This is going to make him look awful. Not a soul in Iowa expected Brosnan to stay on as Head Coach after this season. But next morning, Conroy of the *Register* editorialized:

> The reason why the Board in Control of Athletics at State University decided to fire Bob Brosnan as head football coach isn't any deep dark secret. The school had lost confidence in his ability to bring in a winning team. But he should have been allowed to finish the season without it being known that he's a lame duck. He should have been allowed to leave with more dignity. It's to the shame of State University that he wasn't.

In his column in the *Examiner* that afternoon, Brady was harder on Brosnan than the *Register* had been, but even he agreed that the situation was mishandled:

> We have to admit that it's time for Bob Brosnan to go. It would not be fair to call him a bad coach, but he is not the right coach for this program. His fate was sealed on the first day of the season, the moment that Winnemucca defensive back ran that interception over the goal line.
>
> But the Board in Control of Athletics should have withheld any decision on Brosnan's future for one more week. Brosnan should have been allowed to lead his team into the last game of the season without having been publicly humiliated in advance by the people he has loyally served for so many years.

The worst article came on Wednesday evening, in *The Cedar Rapids Gazette*. Their sports editor, Wayne Pulliam, is a complete horse's butt. He thinks he should be writing for *The New Yorker*, obviously. So fake-literary, so "the poet as sportswriter."

Grey and rainy is the mood at State University, and grey and rainy was this morning, when a beleaguered Bob Brosnan showed up at Rivercat Stadium to lead his team in one of the last practice sessions of the season—naturally to find the press waiting for him. He did not look much more cheerful than the weather. He waved to us—to us, the vultures assembled for the feast—and tried manfully to work up a smile.

"Nothing now," he called to us, as he walked into the locker room entrance. "After practice, after I've talked with the team."

I did not hear, at first hand, what happened next. Team meetings are closed to the press. This was told to me by one of the players. I talked to other players and coaches, too, and they all told me substantially the same story.

Brosnan called his players and assistant coaches together in the locker room, when they were suited up and ready to go onto the practice field. Some sat on benches next to their lockers; some stood; some squatted on the floor, all of them attentive. Afterward, to me, they all kept coming back to one word, when they recalled what Brosnan said to them: "class."

"Fellas, I want to start by saying that I'm proud of all of you. You've all of you given nothing but your best, all year long. That goes for the players, the coaches, trainers, equipment managers, everybody. We had one big win against a real good team. As for the games we lost, some of them, we got outplayed; some of them, we got outcoached; a couple of times we were just plain unlucky. But at no time did I feel that any of you let any of the rest of us down—and I hope you don't feel that I let you down."

"**** Feldy!" came a voice from the back of the room.

"Now, none of that," said Brosnan, but while he was saying it, a couple of other players started to chant, "****

Feldy! **** Feldy!" before some of the other players shushed them.

"None of that," Brosnan repeated. "Nobody was coaching this team except me. If you have to blame somebody—I don't think you should blame anybody, but if you have to blame someone, blame me and nobody else. Now, we've still got one game to play, so let's get out there now and have a good practice."

After no more than a second of silence—according to people who were there—a few players started clapping, and in another couple of seconds, everyone in the room was on his feet. Everyone but Brosnan was clapping, yelling, whistling. Fred Baumhauer, the hulking fullback, shouted, "We love ya, Bob!" Brosnan looked bashful—but appreciative.

"Thanks, fellas. Let's get on out there."

In not much more than an hour, the team was back indoors. Brosnan invited us—the vultures—into the locker room, where he more or less reiterated to us what he had told his players.

"I would have looked forward to rebuilding the team after what was obviously a disappointing year. The Board and the Athletic Director have decided to go in a different direction, and it's their decision to make. I want to thank President Esterhart and the rest of the administration, the State University faculty and staff, the students and alumni, my own staff, and above all, I want to thank my players.

"I want to emphasize that I hold no hard feelings toward anyone. I wish all the best for the State University football program, and if I can contribute to its future in any way, I will."

We didn't have many questions for Brosnan, and he had no future plans to reveal. He hadn't had time to think about whether he would stay at State for the optional fifth year he had been offered, he said.

"I'm more concerned about my assistants, but I'm not worried; I'm sure State University will treat them fairly."

And so, we will say goodbye to a fine man who simply was not cut out to cope with the pressures that are peculiar to coaching at State University, and that his successor will have to face—unless his successor is, himself, the primary source of those pressures.

What a bastard. Pulliam, not Brosnan.

Then on Thursday morning, people driving to work along Highway 6-218 got a bit of a jolt from what they saw hanging from the Blackhawk Avenue viaduct: a life-sized dummy, dangling from a traditional hangman's noose, dressed in regulation Rivercat sweat pants and shirt, with signs saying "Feldy" hung across its shoulders, front and back. The fire department sent a hook-and-ladder truck to take it down—but not before the *Examiner* got a photo of it, which ran on the front page that afternoon. With no comment, except to say where it had been found.

§

Win and I have gotten into the habit of meeting up once or twice a week in the Lower Lounge—which is a big dimly lit circular room in the basement of the State University Memorial Union, next to the snack shop—whenever we both have a few minutes, to update each other without the rest of the family around. We talk about our studies, mostly, but today, all we can talk about is this situation.

"It makes me sick," I tell Win. "Reading all this stuff. It's so unfair. To a lot of people but especially to Feldy. I'm thinking maybe I ought to drop my music major and focus on journalism. I don't know what kind of journalist I'll be—you know, newspapers, magazines, radio, whatever—but it makes me furious when reporters don't get the facts, when they poison people against other people. I feel like maybe it's my duty to be a journalist who *doesn't* give the profession a bad name. You know, if there are just a few journalists who are honest and trustworthy... I don't know; what do you think?"

"I can see that," Win says. "But music might be a way to distance yourself, you know. Remove yourself from too much involvement with that sort of thing."

"It's like every sportswriter in Iowa has got something against Feldy," I say. "It's their fault, if the whole rest of the state thinks Feldy's the bad guy. It's the administration's fault, too. Esterhart, and the rest of them. If they wanted to have a winning football team, why didn't they let Feldy keep coaching?"

"Everybody needs a scapegoat in situations like this," Win says. "It's complicated. Probably some people resented Feldy for not continuing as coach, when he must have known that nobody else was up to the job. Like, they've twisted the story around in their heads so they can think that Feldy let the team down, somehow. Plus, everybody likes Brosnan. He's a nice guy; people don't want to pile on him when he's down. The story that everybody wants to believe is that Brosnan had an impossible situation and did the best he could with it—with his biggest problem being that Feldy has been sabotaging him all along. Maybe it's easier to believe that, than to find out whether it's true."

That makes me smile.

"You mean Feldy is taking on the sins of the whole football program?"

Win laughs.

"I see where you're going with this. No, that's not a licit comparison, but there's nobody stronger than Feldy—nobody living today—and nobody who's more willing to take on a burden. If it helps the program for everyone to blame Feldy, temporarily, he can handle it. It's harder for us than for him."

§

Saturday is my last turn in the broadcast booth, at least for this fall. The Rivercats look fired up against the Mason-Dixon Surveyors. Like they want to prove something. Even way up in the press section, I can feel that they've got extra energy today.

Beebe throws for one touchdown; Keenan runs for another; Abúi adds a long field goal right before the gun to give the Rivercats a 17-7 lead at halftime.

In the second half, Mason-Dixon starts reading Beebe's passing habits better, and his receivers can't get clear. On a fourth down, Mason-Dixon's defenders break through the line and block a punt, inside our 15-yard-line—and two plays later, they've got another touchdown.

A few minutes after that, Beebe throws an interception, which gets run back for a touchdown. All of a sudden, it's Surveyors 21, Rivercats 17. In the fourth quarter, Mason-Dixon scores another one. On our next possession—which could be our last, with about three minutes to go—we bog down at the Mason-Dixon 35.

"Brosnan is sending out the field goal unit," Joe observes over the air. "I'd have thought Beebe would throw a Hail Mary, here on fourth down, since the Cats need 11 points and time is ticking away, but what do I know?"

I say, "Maybe Coach Brosnan is thinking: score three here, then try an onside and hope for one more series to score a touchdown. Then a two-pointer would tie it—but it's a slim chance, either way."

"There's the snap," says Joe. "Abúi's kick is up… and good! The Rivercats are still in it, if barely."

Inevitably, we do try an onside, which is always a low-percentage play, and sure enough it doesn't work. Mason-Dixon fields the ball, and that will end the scoring for both teams. The final will be Mason-Dixon 28, State 20.

As has become usual, only a few thousand spectators have stayed to the end.

"The final seconds are ticking off," Sonny says over the air, "and Mason-Dixon is not lining up for a play; they're going to let the clock run out…"

All of a sudden, Joe straightens up in his chair, and sounds way more animated.

"Sorry to cut in, Sonny, but the Rivercat players on the sideline have picked up Coach Brosnan; they've hoisted him onto their shoulders! There's the final gun, and the whole team, the whole Rivercat team, is forming a pack around their coach.

"The spectators who are still in the stands are standing and clapping—I can hear very little cheering, mostly clapping—as the Rivercat players end what must have been a heartbreaking season by carrying their coach off the field."

Joe's voice is catching; I glance over at him and see that he is literally weeping.

Oh, for the love of... I have to force myself not to roll my eyes. People feel what they feel.

§

Despite the hanging in effigy, despite the wailings from the press about the way Brosnan's firing was handled, Feldy is still a legend. He still has the majority of the fans behind him: I'm convinced of that. Jack Brady writes in the *Examiner*:

> It sounds like Feldy is willing to accept a draft. He didn't issue a "Sherman"; he didn't even issue a "Coolidge." He might be poor-mouthing his own abilities, but he hasn't said "never," and popular acclaim is on his side.
>
> Can we imagine anyone more qualified than Feldy to coach the Rivercats? He might find some other good coach to take the position, but wouldn't we, in that case, be settling for someone other than the obvious choice?
>
> Feldy might be worried about his legacy. After a disastrous season like this one, it's hard to imagine that we'll have a winning team next year, no matter who coaches. But with Feldy at the helm, we would be certain to pick our game up in two to three years. As for 1969, we'll probably be underdogs in every single game on our schedule. If the Rivercats under Feldy can pull off, say, three upsets, we'll be on our way, feeling confident about the future.

Two of Brosnan's assistants have found jobs as Head Coaches: one with the Mongols of Faber College, in Pennsylvania, and one with the Saskatchewan Rough Riders of the Canadian Football League. Conroy of the *Register* thought it might be the time to see whether either of them might be talkative. Mind you, he doesn't cite either of those coaches as sources, but anyone with even one brain cell to spare would have to be pretty sure where he got most of his material. I refuse to believe this information is entirely true, but the most effective lies are mixed with the truth.

Some observers have said Brosnan's failure can largely be blamed on recruiting. When Feldy was coach, NCAA recruiting rules were more lax; he was able to bring almost anyone he wanted onto the team. Many of Feldy's players, it must be admitted now that they're long gone, would not have been allowed onto a college campus today.

That doesn't tell a fair story, though, because all NCAA coaches have to deal with the same recruiting restrictions.

One person close to the scene reports, "When Feldy was coach, we would entertain the recruits and their parents at one or another of the great steakhouses in the area. We would travel to Chicago, Milwaukee, St. Louis, even to Philadelphia sometimes, to recruit. When Feldy became A.D., it was 'I don't want you going out of town every week.' We were told to take the recruits and their parents to meals at the Coffin Corner cafeteria. We were given a strict budget for long-distance phone calls. It was obvious, right from the start, that Feldy had an attitude toward Brosnan—and it was clear that Brosnan wasn't going to make it. The situation started out bad and got worse week by week, over the years."

I refuse to believe that Feldy "had an attitude" toward Brosnan. But that's the narrative, and enough people are promoting it to make most of the college football world believe it. So, imagine that you're Leo Feldevert, following a disastrous season where it was clear all along that the football coach would have to be let go—and then, right at the end of the season, an article like that one gets published, while you're looking for a new Head Coach.

On paper, State would look like a great opportunity. Say you're an ambitious coach who hasn't made a reputation yet. You could take over a team that could hardly get any worse than it had been the year before, where even a little improvement would get you all kinds of praise. You'll have a five-year contract—if you got the same terms that Feldy and Brosnan had—and unless you made as much of a shambles as Brosnan did, you'll have that full term, to build a team that's identifiably yours.

Coaches all over America would leap at a chance like that, wouldn't you think?

Think again.

Feldy isn't under any pressure to hire this coach or that one. He has his pick of whoever is available.

So Feldy picks up the phone and calls Coach Able.

"Hey, Able, Feldy here. You know, we're short a head football coach. Our freshman team was the only bright spot this year, so there'll be a lot of talent coming back next fall. Care to fly into State City and talk about it?"

Able says, "Gosh, thanks for thinking of me, Feldy, but I'm happy where I am." Even though Coach Able is at some second-tier college with a completely lame football program.

Feldy calls Coach Baker. Gives him the same pitch. Gets pretty much the same response. He calls Coach Charlie: same. He calls Coach Dog: same.

Then, maybe Coach Easy thinks about it. Maybe Coach Easy comes out to State City to visit with Feldy; he looks at the stadium; he talks with the administration—and maybe he thinks good and hard about taking the job. Feldy tells him that the job is his if he wants it; Coach Easy flies back home to consider—and late on a Friday afternoon he issues a statement declaring that "having changed my mind several times, I have decided, with great gratitude in my heart, to decline the offer."

I don't know: could Feldy have a blind spot? We all have them. Could it be that Feldy is thinking, and wondering, about why he can't find anyone to take this job, while the real reason is staring him in the face every morning when he shaves, and he just won't see it? Whether or not he deserves the reputation he has—and I don't believe he does—that's the reputation he has. It's not like the world of college football coaching is that big. These guys all know each other; they talk.

"Now Appears Feldy Will Coach," says the top headline of the *Register*'s sports section on Monday, December 20. The main article sums up the situation. Conroy's column, also on the front of the sports section, says in part:

It appears that Leo Feldevert, or at least his reputation, is what is keeping any other good coach from accepting the job in State City. Thus, he has two choices: dissociate himself with State University entirely, or take over the helm as Head Coach. In my opinion, the latter would be preferable. I say to the administration that allowing him to remain as Athletic Director would be a small price to pay. To keep Feldy out of the coaching job, at this point, strikes me as contrary to ordinary sense: perhaps an act of spite.

Instead, this same day, Feldy calls a press conference to announce that Tobias Timmerman, whose Mason-Dixon Surveyors beat us in that final game of 1968, will be coming to State University as the new head football coach. This afternoon's *Examiner* runs a photo of Timmerman, who flew in from Pennsylvania for a secret meeting this past weekend, standing next to Feldy.

Judging from the picture, Timmerman is really handsome— by my standards. He's 38, with wavy hair and a big dimply smile, but he looks more like a real estate agent than a football coach in his conservative suit and narrow tie.

Even I have never heard Feldy mention Timmerman's name. Mason Dixon's 1968 record was only 5-5: Timmerman's best in four years there. Mason Dixon looked lousy against the Rivercats; they only won that game because our mistakes practically handed it to them.

Maybe Timmerman didn't like his chances of improving on that 5-5 record at Mason Dixon. Maybe Mason Dixon didn't think highly enough of him to hold him to that last year of his contract. Maybe Timmerman thinks it will be a lot easier to go (say) 3-7 at a prestigious school like State, and be praised for it, than play out one more year at Mason Dixon with not much chance of improvement or appreciation.

Toby Timmerman tells the press, "I'm thrilled to be coaching in the Big Ten. And I'm sure Feldy will give me plenty of support with recruiting."

Brosnan has taken another job, too. Up in Green Bay, Head Coach Phil Bengtson has decided he needs an offensive backfield coach for the 1969 season.

VACATION AND VOCATION

Our family flew out to New York City for Christmas, to celebrate the holiday with Lou's in-laws-to-be, and see Lou get married. Had a great time. Grandma and Grandpa Duffy booked three suites of rooms at the Roosevelt Hotel, to accommodate everyone. We went to Mass at St. Pat's. Now we're flying home.

Before Timmerman was hired, I was half hoping and half dreading that Feldy would end up coaching again. Now I'm half relieved and half disappointed that he won't. Everything has been so crazy, though, what with the wedding and Christmas and all, that this is my first chance to get Feldy's thoughts.

I have the window seat, in the plane; Feldy is in the middle; Win is on the aisle. Sander, Duffy, and Birdy sit in a row behind us. Win is reading Aquinas' *Summary of Theology*, and making notes on a yellow pad. It's late afternoon; we're flying into the lowering sun. I'm dazzled by those icy clouds below us, against the bright blue sky, and the contrast with the almost-orange sun is one of the most beautiful works of God I have ever seen. Since we're flying west, the sunset will last and last.

"Isn't this beautiful, Feldy? Do you want to switch places with me so you can see it better?"

"That would be kind of awkward. Anyway, I can see it fine. Yeah, it's something."

"Are you happy with how it all turned out?"

"You bet. That's a real nice girl. If all you kids choose as well as Lou did, you're all going to be very happy."

"Oh, no. I'm sorry. How could you have known what I meant? No, I mean about football. This new coach, and all. Are you happy with how that turned out? Do you wish you were coaching again?"

"You never stop wondering, 'what if?' Sure, there's part of me that misses it. Realistically, though, all those rumors about how I was going to coach, there was never anything in them. No. Coaching again, at this point in my life, that would be a step back. Gotta move on."

"Have you thought any more about politics?"

"That's a pretty remote possibility. I'm sure there are Democratic politicians out there who want to be Governor or Senator more than I do. If you're going to win, you need to really *want* to win. You need to want it more than anybody you're competing against, because whoever wants it most... well, maybe they don't win every single time, but that's the way to bet."

Feldy thinks for a moment, then he says, "I might like to find a way to stay in academia. Public service doesn't interest me, to tell you the truth—at least, not running for office. I've got the wrong personality for it. But I do sometimes feel like I'm spinning my wheels in this job."

"Well, President Esterhart's retiring in the spring." I give Feldy a big grin to show that I don't completely mean it—even if I sort of do. "You could go after his job."

Feldy laughs. "I'm not a scholar. Sometimes a university will hire a lawyer or a businessman to be President, but not an ex-jock, no chance. People like me are not regarded as intelligent by the people who make those decisions."

"But if you're spinning your wheels here, what else would you be thinking about?"

"That's the problem." Feldy sighs. "Football is all I know. It's frustrating as hell, not coaching. But realistically, I've been out of it too long for the NFL to be interested in me... and coaching at some other university, well, that would be pretty anticlimactic, wouldn't it? Not to mention what it would do to my health. I could look for some kind of business opportunity—Grandpa Duffy would help me find something—but I don't want a gig that I got because my father-in-law pulled a string or two."

I'm stuck for anything to say.

"Enough about me," Feldy says. "Tell me about you. How's your year going?"

"It's already overwhelming me, and I'm hardly taking anything I want to take. It's almost all core courses this year, plus my cello lessons. It'll be more of the same this spring. Then my sophomore year is really going to get crazy, whether I choose Journalism or Communications for my other major."

I don't want Feldy to think I'm complaining, so I gave him a rundown of my current classes, and tell him about my roommates—leaving out the part about one of them sleeping with an instructor. I tell him about Mona Shapen, and what a great cello teacher she is—because she is.

"You still going to be a sportscaster?" Feldy asks. "Listen, you did real well this fall. You were the best thing about the team. I know that's not saying much, but I'd say it even if we had had a good year."

"I'm sure thinking about it. But for right now, I'm relieved that the season's over. I have no time for anything except my classes. I haven't seen a movie or play all semester. Haven't gone to a party except for the Greek events that pledges have to show up for. I do miss doing the games, though. I have no idea if I'll be invited back next fall."

"You have to make that happen. Call Barnett and Bell tomorrow. Tell 'em you're interested. Be insistent."

I don't have to do anything of the kind, because before I can make that call, the next day—in fact when I'm putting away the breakfast dishes—the phone rings, and it's Joe Barnett for me. I figure it has to be good news of some kind, and it is.

"We want you to maintain a presence on KSCR for the rest of the year. You made a heck of an impression. Ever since the season ended, we've been getting cards and letters and phone calls asking us where you are, and can't we get you back on the air?"

I am floored. I was practically walking on clouds, at the start of the football season, when fans called into the station to say they missed me on the Cats' first road game. Now, apparently, they still feel that way.

"I was thinking you might do a broadcast," Joe says, "maybe one morning a week, where you give an update on what's going on with the Cats, whatever sport happens to be going on at the time. Like, basketball, wrestling, swimming this winter, then in April you'll be able to report on the spring football practice, the baseball team, so on. Only you wouldn't just be reporting. You'd be editorializing, giving your opinions. It'd be good practice for you, plus you'd get a good general knowledge of all the sports programs, not that you don't have it already."

It's hard for me to believe that. People want to hear my voice. Joe is implying that my presence on-air will be good for the station—bring in more advertisers, maybe. I have to admit it to myself: I'm in people's minds. I'm popular.

"But that's a thing," I say. "I'll bet you anything that people are already talking about how I'm only working the football games because I'm Feldy's Girl. If I'm doing a broadcast every week where I'm talking about all our sports programs, when everyone knows who my father is, how much credibility do you think I'll have?"

Joe sees the sense in that, so we agree that I'll do these four-minute broadcasts at 7:25 every Monday morning, during "drive time," and that I'll editorialize on anything except the Rivercats. I'll stick to commenting on professional sports, maybe sometimes talking about other college teams if something of particular moment is happening—but only in the rarest of circumstances will I even acknowledge the existence of the Rivercats.

And again—I realize after I have hung up the phone—*again*, I have forgotten to talk about money. It's too late now; I'd feel like a complete idiot if I called Joe back to haggle.

So, starting in mid-January, every Monday, I get to get up even earlier than usual and walk from Radcliffe Hall to KSCR, and at 7:25 my listeners hear, "Good morning again, Eastern Iowa: this is Terri Feldevert, speaking of sports."

I explain to my listeners that the Jets' victory in the Super Bowl had not surprised me—and should not have been that much of a surprise to anyone who knows football.

"The smartest thing Joe Namath will probably ever say, in the whole of his career in football, was the statement he made a few days ago, when he said, 'We'll win; I guarantee it.' The Jets could have had the same attitude that we saw from the AFL in the first two years of the AFL-NFL Championship Game, in which the Chiefs, and then the Raiders, each played with the intention of not embarrassing themselves against the Packers: being able to walk off the field with their dignity intact. Namath was the first AFL quarterback to come into the Super Bowl with a winner's attitude. What's more, he knew he would never live it down if he guaranteed a win and then didn't produce it. He put pressure on himself to succeed, and it was exactly the right kind of pressure.

"It's hard to say whether a quarterback, or any athlete, can *acquire* an attitude like Namath's. It might be something you're born with, or it could just be confidence in your own abilities. Some people said Namath was being arrogant when he guaranteed a win, but he wasn't just talking about himself. He was talking about the team, letting people know that he was confident in the New York Jets.

"Confidence like that is infectious. It can pass from one player to the team, and it can turn into a sort of collective will to win. It can infect players who might not have felt so sure of themselves, and sure of the team, otherwise. I can't help thinking that the Jets' coach, Weeb Ewbank, had something to do with that too."

Maybe I'm not sounding professional, yet, but here I am still 18, still not used to editorializing on the radio, so I'd say I'm doing pretty good, even if it's me saying it. I go on to a brief analysis of what the Jets did right and what the Colts did wrong. At three minutes and fifty-eight seconds exactly, I say, "This is Terri Feldevert, reporting."

§

It's the second semester. I'm on the staff of State U's daily paper, *The University Statesman*, in a small way. It's a few hours each week—time I can't afford—culling items from the Associated Press and the United Press International that might be a good fit for the inside pages. It's a way of gradually learning the business and getting known by the senior staff. I'm also a "stringer." That is, I'm supposed to stay alert for newsworthy occurrences, and propose stories to the higher-ranking editors, who might or might not assign me to write them.

I'm still studying with Mona Shapen—only now, we usually meet at Mona and Mike's apartment. The Shapens live pretty near Radcliffe Hall, closer than the music building, which is important because winter in State City is brutal.

They live in a side-by-side duplex. When you come in the front or back door of the house, you encounter two more doors, left and right; the right-hand door, at the front of the house, leads to Mona and Mike's place.

It's a hippie couple's apartment. They've got a mandala tapestry on one wall of the living room; an old couch covered with an Indian blanket; a poster of *Yellow Submarine*. The living room smells of incense, patchouli, and cigarettes; the kitchen smells of curry. It's neat and clean, anyway. Lots of books, and I've heard of some of the authors: LeRoi Jones, William Kunstler, Eldridge Cleaver. Copies of *Ramparts* in the bathroom. Sometimes I wish I were a person who would live in a place like this, and sometimes I'm glad I'm not.

In the other half of the house lives a young lady about the Same age as Mona and Mike, named Vicki, and her husband, who's called Red. At least, I assume it's her husband. They don't wear rings. Vicki is in Mona and Mike's place pretty often: to socialize, and sometimes to use their bathtub, since her apartment only has a shower stall.

I can tell, from the way Mona's face lights up when Vicki is in the room, that Mona has a little crush on her—maybe because they're so different in their looks and personalities. Vicki is almost as tall as I am, built like an athlete—I can tell because Vicki usually wears jeans—and she's not conventionally good-looking but she's compelling nevertheless if that makes any sense. I won't say "beautiful" because that's such an over-used word and it's so debased that it doesn't mean anything—and Vicki *isn't* beautiful. She's not even that pretty. She just grabs you.

She's got dirty-blonde hair, and eyes that can be blue, green, or grey depending on the light. She's got a big wide mouth and big front teeth that stick out, and a chin that recedes a little. She has this loud, nasal, braying voice with a Long Island accent (which I know is a Long Island accent only because she mentioned that she's from there).

Mona looks all shiny-eyed at Vicki, as though she wishes she could be Vicki. Sometimes Vicki comes out of the bathroom, in a heavy terrycloth robe and her hair up in a towel, while Mona and I are in the middle of a lesson, and changes back into her regular clothes in front of us. Mona doesn't even pretend she's not looking. I don't blame her. I get feelings I know I shouldn't have, when I see Vicki naked.

Once—it was at night, and the snow was coming down hard—Vicki remarked that she would love to get on her horse and ride around in the dark, in that weather. That was when I found out she's from Long Island: she mentioned that she had horses, at her parents' estate there. Mona said she had only ever gotten to ride horses at summer camp, as a girl. Vicki promised to take Mona to one of the stables around here, when spring finally comes along, and I said, "I'd love that, too. I've only ever ridden a little, but I love it. Maybe we could all go together."

I'm spending more time at the Shapens, these days, visiting with Mona and Vicki, and sometimes Mike. Sometimes Red knocks on the door, but he doesn't visit much; he usually just wants Vicki to come home. We have tea or Mogen David wine—and we talk politics more than music. Sometimes other friends of Mona and Mike's are there. They look a year or two older: mostly men with long hair and beards, or angry-looking women.

They all smoke cigarettes, except for Mona and me. Once one of the male guests brought something out of his shirt pocket—I couldn't see what it was—and I heard Mike say, "Ah! Ah!" and saw him nod in my direction. The guest immediately put whatever it was, back in his pocket, so I assume it was a marijuana cigarette.

No, I wouldn't inform on anyone, if they smoked it in front of me. But I would feel uncomfortable, and I wouldn't be able to pretend I wasn't. So, I was relieved that Mike stopped that guy, but I was displeased with myself for being the killjoy.

The phrase "the movement" comes up a lot, in the Shapens' apartment, but I'm not quite sure what it means, other than upsetting the existing order.

Mona says Nixon is as bad as Johnson and it doesn't much matter who is President: it's the corporations that run America. She says the revolution will be against the corporations, against capitalism, more than against whoever is President.

"It starts here in academia," she says. "This university has research contracts with Dow, which makes napalm, and other corporations that deal with weapons, bombs, chemical warfare. If we can prevent all the major research universities from doing business with these corporations, maybe that will make it harder for them to do what they're doing—and maybe if we put enough pressure on companies like Dow, they won't want to do business with the Department of Defense. It all adds up."

This makes sense to me in a way, but it does occur to me that maybe that's an oversimplification, that maybe it wouldn't be possible to abolish wars by abolishing weapons, or abolish weapons by abolishing research. But I don't trust myself to argue with Mona about it, since I get a feeling that Mona—unlike some of the other people in the room—is... she's not *dumb*, obviously, but she's too idealistic to think things through. And she has told me about her parents—who voted for Henry Wallace, back when she was a baby, and sent her to socialist summer camp, and all that. Who knows? Maybe one of us has been indoctrinated wrong, and maybe it's me—but I very much doubt that.

SPRING MEANS DEMONSTRATIONS

On a Monday afternoon, I'm leaving the Liberal Arts building, walking across University Common, past Territorial—the building that was Iowa's Capitol building in the 1840s (before Iowa

103

became a State and Des Moines became the capital city) and now partly a museum and partly the University President's office. Territorial looks like a miniature model of the U.S. Capitol Building in Washington, with the gold dome and all.

I'm headed for the Music Building, which is a couple of blocks to the north and two more blocks to the east, but I stop for a minute in front of the grand staircase of Territorial, because for some reason this afternoon it's packed with students: demonstrators, probably between 100 and 200 people. It looks like they're trying to block the entrance. I can't see any police. This wasn't brewing earlier in the day, so the crowd must have assembled just during the past 50 minutes while I was in class.

Demonstrations materialize pretty often on University Common—the huge lawn that connects Territorial with State University's four other oldest buildings—and they usually end up on the front steps of Territorial, where one speaker or another holds forth with a bullhorn. The police hardly ever have to get involved; these meetings break up of their own accord after an hour or so. This is a bigger crowd than usual, though, and it looks angrier. I see a hand-lettered sign: "Dow Off Our Campus." Another says, "State University Takes Blood Money."

This looks like a garden-variety operation that won't amount to anything but shouting and sign-waving, so I keep walking to the Music Building, where I have my last class of the day; then I walk back to Radcliffe Hall—in a different direction from Territorial, so I don't see the resolution of the demonstration. It's wonderful sunny weather, so I sit on the grass outside the dorm, studying, till dinnertime. After dinner, I practice my cello in my room for a few minutes, to get warmed up before my lesson.

I get to the Shapens' apartment as usual, to find the house dark and nobody at home. I knock on Vicki's entrance, too, but, same story. I figure maybe Mona has plumb forgotten about the lesson, or maybe there has been some sort of emergency; in any case I can't think of anything better than to lug the cello back to my dorm room, explain the situation to Karen (who is lying on her bed studying) and ask if it would be okay if I practice there.

"Play something meditative," she says. "Help me concentrate."

Maybe 90 minutes later our phone rings, and it's Mona.

"Teresa, I'm sorry if you stopped by earlier," she says. "Mike and Vicki and I all got arrested, this afternoon. They just let us out of the police lockup, about an hour ago. It's a long story and I can tell you tomorrow, if you want to reschedule our lesson. Again, I'm sorry I wasn't able to get word to you."

§

"Yeah, what you saw on the steps of Territorial was the rear guard," Mona is telling me. It's Tuesday night. Nobody else is in Mona's half of the house; we haven't begun the lesson yet, although I've taken the cello out of its bag and I'm sitting ready to play. "Mike and Vicki and I were three of the 12 people who had agreed to go into the President's office and barricade it, so that no campus business would get done for as long as we could hold out, or till the University met our demands."

"Which were…"

"First, turn over its draft records to us, for destruction. Then, cancel its research contracts with Dow and a few other companies. We spread the word around, that this would happen, so we had a lot of people following behind.

"We went into Territorial a few minutes after noon, when we were pretty sure nobody would be in the President's office. There was just one secretary in the anteroom and we told her it might be better for her if she left. Then we locked the door from the inside and barricaded it with bookcases. We had enough food and so on to keep us supplied for four or five days, including toilet paper, and buckets, if it came to that, but it would have been quite a mess if we had stayed there for long."

"Doesn't the President's office have a private bathroom?"

"So it turned out. We guessed that there would be one, but we weren't sure. Then we called the *Statesman* and the *Examiner* to let them know what was going down, and what our demands were. A lot of the people who had followed us, were out there on the front steps of Territorial. Only, we heard about that later. We couldn't see them because the President's office's windows face out the other direction. They were blocking that entrance-way, but our original plan hadn't been to occupy the whole building. We didn't think we had enough people to secure all the entrances, and hold them, if the cops showed up.

"We hadn't been in there for more than a minute or two before some of the people who had pens and magic markers started writing slogans and various words that didn't have anything to do with what we were about, on the wall of the office."

Mona shakes her head and looks mournful.

"It's such a beautiful office, too, if you can call an office beautiful. This lovely dark wood paneling. If there was an office in Heaven, that's what it would look like. I wanted to stop them, but I realized I couldn't, and I didn't want to get Mike into a fight, which would have happened if he had tried to stop them.

"It was maybe half an hour later that President Esterhart showed up and knocked on the door and said who he was and asked to come in. Not shouting or anything; just speaking so that we could hear him through all the furniture we had piled up against the door.

"He said, 'There's nobody with me, no police. I'd like to talk. May I come in?'

"Mike and I said to Vicki that maybe we should talk to him, so we shoved the bookcases aside enough to open the door a crack, then Mike you might say made himself our spokesman by default, but Vicki and I were standing right next to him so that Esterhart could see the three of us. So that we would look like a team, and so that he couldn't see past us to see who else was in there. But he could hear them, for sure, because a lot of them were yelling things at him and calling him names that I would rather not repeat. I have to say it: in this movement, you have to deal with some pretty awful people. I was embarrassed, because, you know, he looks like quite a nice man, and he was being so quiet and humble."

Mona shakes her head.

"He's so distinguished-looking, with that wavy white hair. I'm sure you've seen him."

"Well, my parents know him, of course. He looks like a college president from a movie."

"I didn't think he should be treated that way," Mona says. "I called out to everyone to keep quiet but they wouldn't. Just kept shouting over him, chanting and so on. He asked us if we had any hostages, if we were holding any of his staff in there…"

"Would that have been part of your plan?" I ask. "Like, did you think about holding that secretary…?"

"No! Absolutely not. We told him we weren't violent, and we weren't there to hurt anybody, then Mike told him what our demands were. He asked who we were, so Mike gave him his name and mine, and Vicki's. Then he asked if he could come in or if some of us would come into the hall and talk. A bunch of the guys behind us—it was mostly guys; just me and Vicki and one other woman—they were chanting 'Bullshit! Bullshit!' and calling Mr. Esterhart anything you can think of.

"Finally, Vicki said, 'Cool it, all of you, let's listen to this guy,' and, you know, she's almost as big as you are, not that I'm sure that that was the reason, but she was able to make it stick. Anyway, they quieted down for a minute or two at least.

"Mr. Esterhart told us that he had had an idea of what our demands were going to be—after all, that's what a lot of the talk has been about, for months, now. He started explaining to Mike—he was calling him 'Mr. Shapen'—he said these research contracts were all tied together in a great big package of work that the university does for the government, and how if they canceled those contracts it would pretty much wreck the university in terms of what it could offer the students. He said that without those contracts, the university would have to be made way smaller, and it would hit the hospital and the medical school hardest of all. He also said that none of the university's contracts with Dow had to do with anything military as far as he knew. Mike said maybe they didn't, but whatever the university does for those corporations is going to free up more of their resources to go to weapons, right?

"Mr. Esterhart said he might be in favor of setting up some kind of review process that would include students, that could go over the contracts and decide which ones ought to be gotten rid of. When he said that, some of the guys behind us started shouting him down and insulting him again. I was so embarrassed, by this time, and I turned around and, forgive me, I said, 'Any of you assholes want to take my place?' Which shut them up for a second while they were trying to figure out what I meant. And they're not used to hearing me talk like that.

"Of course I was implying that they'd be afraid to step up and let themselves be identified, which might have been unfair, I don't know, but some of the men in the movement really are… not very manly, sometimes.

"Then Mr. Esterhart said that he couldn't agree to any of our demands as long as we were holding his office for ransom. He asked if there was anything he could do that would persuade us to leave, and Mike said he guessed not. Then Mike said he was sorry, you know, trying to be polite—so Mr. Esterhart said he was sympathetic to a lot of our demands, and he didn't want the cops to intervene, but he was afraid they were going to have to.

"Which was what we wanted. We wanted to force a confrontation; we knew perfectly well that Mr. Esterhart wasn't going to give in to all our demands right there in the hallway.

"But he was concerned about what would happen to his office; he said he had a lot of historic documents in there—I gather he was a history professor before he became President—and he asked Mike if he could count on him to make sure that none of it was damaged. Mike said he would be personally responsible…"

Mona looks down at the floor, shaking her head.

"Stuff got damaged after all, huh?" I say.

"It wasn't as bad as it could have been. Mr. Esterhart shook hands with Mike, through the door, and as soon as Mike had shut the door and we had started moving the bookcases back in front of it, one of the assholes starts yanking the drawers out of one of the file cabinets. He dumps all the papers out of one of the drawers, and a couple of them start skating around in the papers…"

"Oh, no."

"There are some people in the movement who are more into destruction than anything else," Mona says. "Their cause isn't the war, or what companies the university does business with. It's like they want to destroy for the sake of destruction. And what can you do? We can't drum them out of the movement."

("You could shoot them," I say to myself.)

108

"Anyway, that almost started a brawl. I shoved one of them away, and he pushed me back, then Mike slapped his face and he started punching Mike. Only, it was actually kind of funny, because that other guy hit like a girl—even I could see that—so it was all I could do to not start laughing at him, right there."

Mona actually starts laughing, at the memory of it, and it takes her a few seconds to compose herself. She has to grab a Kleenex and wipe her eyes.

"Oh, I'm sorry. But it was so funny, how he hit like a girl. Like a silly little ten-year-old girl! And he was practically crying. Mike said that was from the humiliation of being slapped instead of punched. God, men are so weird.

"But, anyway, Vicki and I got between them and things calmed down slightly. I picked up the papers as best I could and got them back into the filing cabinet, although I could see that some of them were torn up and had dirty shoe-prints on them. I'm sure they weren't in the right order. I feel so guilty about that.

"Then Mike and I stood in front of the cabinet, and after a couple of minutes, Vicki, she got us to all sit down and sing, but still we were not feeling as good about the situation as we had been when we went in there—all of us pretty much angry at each other, you know—so I was almost relieved a few minutes later when the cops showed up."

"You let them in?"

"Of course not; that was the point, but the cop in charge, I don't know what rank he was, he did the same thing—asked us to open up so we could talk—and we wouldn't do that because if it was a bunch of them, they could storm in, right? So Mike said they would just have to shout, and the cop said if we opened up and came out, we would be arrested for trespass—which was a simple misdemeanor—but he said they could bring a fire truck up to the window, then break the window and throw in some tear gas, and then… and then he said, 'then we'll arrest you the hard way.' He said in that case there would be felony charges for sure. He said he would give us five minutes to think about it."

"But you wanted there to be violence, didn't you?"

"No! That's not what we're about. Okay, maybe a couple of us would have liked it if the cops had over-reacted and gone crazy on us, like Chicago, but those were the same ones who were trying to wreck President Esterhart's office. Mike told everybody that we had made our point, that it was going to be in the papers and on TV for sure, so we might as well come out, especially since there would be more damage if we stayed, and he and Vicki and I finally pretty much won everybody over.

"It was pretty orderly after that. Mike called to the cops that we were coming out but we didn't want any rough stuff; the cop said there wouldn't be; and there wasn't. There were maybe 15 cops and Sheriff's deputies there; they had a couple of lady cops to frisk and handcuff me and Vicki and this other girl, then the cop in charge read us our rights from this card he had in his hand, and asked each of us if we understood. There was one guy who I thought was thinking about giving some kind of smart answer, but I guess he thought better of it, being handcuffed.

"Then we all got marched out of the building—I thought they were going to march us down the front steps, which would have been great, since there was a pretty big crowd of our supporters standing out there, and who knows what would have happened when we came out? But they took us down to the ground floor and out a side exit, then along that sidewalk that goes around to where the back of the Liberal Arts building faces Lincoln Avenue, where they had a bunch of cop cars and a fire truck.

"You know, it's hard to walk with handcuffs on. Especially going down steps. I never thought about that, till I had to do it. How much you use your hands and arms when you walk. Or maybe you don't even use them so much, but you know that they're there, to help you keep your balance. If you can't use your arms, you're always afraid you might fall. Anyway, us three girls got to ride in the back of a squad car, while the guys got put into a paddy wagon. They took us to the county jail—then they did the fingerprinting and photographing and all that."

"Didn't that freak you out?"

I've been sitting still, listening, and now I realize that I'm slack-jawed. I ask the question mainly to get my face working.

"Well, the process itself isn't much of anything, except you get your fingers all covered with ink, then they have a sink there where you can wash it off. Being photographed... when it was going on, I was thinking, 'Is this me? Having a mug shot taken?' I have to admit it was pretty embarrassing to think about how my family would react if they found out.

"We each had one phone call, so... maybe I should have called you, but I couldn't be sure you would be in, and Mike called Bill Pickens, who's a lawyer who's... one of us, you know, and I was hoping Mr. Pickens would get us out, so I asked if I could wait to make my call.

"Then they moved all the guys into the drunk tank, you know, this big cell that holds a lot of people. They took Vicki and Norma and me and put us each in a cell of our own..."

"Oh, my gosh, what was that like? Being locked in a cell?"

"Like what you're probably thinking. Just weird. First, it's like when they're taking your mug shot: you're thinking, 'Is this me? In a jail cell?' Then you're horrified when you realize, 'Oh, my God, I'm actually locked in a cage. I can't leave. I can't get out of this room!' It was a room, not a cage. With cinderblock walls and a toilet and sink and a cot that's maybe a foot across. You feel so powerless then. Like you have no control over your life at all, and for all you know you could be left in there to die."

"How long were you in there for?"

"Mmmm... See, that's another awful thing about being locked up! You lose track of time, and it really puts you on edge. It makes you feel even more helpless, and like maybe you're going crazy. It was at least four hours, maybe five or six, must have been. Long enough that they had to feed us.

"I got something that looked like scrambled eggs—only they might have been those reconstituted eggs that you hear about them using in the army—and Spam, and Wonder bread or something like it... and coleslaw, and that fruit cocktail from a can. Then some time after that, the lady deputy opened the door and told me to come on out, they were turning us loose. I didn't know what was going on. Then there was Mr. Pickens in the Sheriff's office to meet us and... and I could see by the clock on the wall that it was about 7:30... So then Mike and Vicki and I walked home, and Mike explained to us..."

"They let you out just like that?"

"The cops got hold of President Esterhart, and he said he didn't want to file a complaint, he didn't want anybody making a spectacle out of this. Then Mr. Pickens did some talking to somebody, I'm not sure who he would have talked to, maybe the County Attorney. Finally, we all had to sign these 'desk appearance tickets,' like you have to sign for a traffic ticket, only I don't know since I've never had a traffic ticket. The charge is 'disorderly conduct,' and we all have to go to court in the next few days to deal with that unless Mr. Pickens works something else out, but meanwhile we're here.

"And, oh, my God, Teresa, last night, Mike and I... it was so *intense*. Like those few hours in jail were an aphrodisiac, or something. Oh, I'm sorry. I'm making you uncomfortable."

Actually, she's not, but somehow I wish she were. Anyway, she immediately switches over to talking about my lesson.

§

I never thought it would happen, but I've been slacking off on my studies, since that incident, because I've started spending three or even four evenings a week at Mona and Mike's: sometimes to work with Mona on the cello, but more often to learn what I can about the political situation. I'm not sure I accept everything they're telling me, but it's interesting to hear the talk.

I have a feeling that some of the men who visit the apartment are uncomfortable with me because I'm so much younger, and I know I look old-fashioned, the way I dress and all. Sometimes I catch one or another of them giving me the hairy eyeball. Once a guy stopped himself in the middle of talking about organizing some kind of demonstration, then he glanced over at me, then said to the others, "I'll finish that thought later."

I'm not sure I like the atmosphere in that apartment, when some of those people are there, but I love Mona. She's almost the big sister I never had. Mike is okay—a little arrogant, but okay—and Vicki has a snarky sense of humor, at least, like I might have if I weren't such a goody-goody. Most of their friends strike me as angry at the world as though they *enjoy* being angry at the world. And deliberately rude. Almost as though they think it's a *virtue* to be nasty, or like it makes them more *real*, somehow. Plus, they clearly don't like me. Once when I asked Mike, "What is all this fighting about, anyway?" a couple of the men in the room snickered.

Mike gave them this little annoyed glance, then he turned back to me, looking terribly earnest.

"We're fighting to overthrow everything that is old, ugly, bigoted, and repressive," he said, oh-so-soft-and-dramatic. "All of that—all of it—must be pushed into the sea and never allowed back into our society. We used to be able to do that through peaceful demonstrations. Earlier in this century. But that model has become obsolete, now. The March on Washington... when was it, six years ago? That was probably the last time we'll ever see a demonstration like that, that accomplished anything.

"We hate violence, but we might be at the point where the need for violence has been imposed on us. We need to resort to violence because we're fighting for our own survival. We survived Chicago. If we survived Chicago, we can win."

He was so busy talking that his cigarette burned all the way to the end, and he had to light another.

"What exactly are you trying to overthrow, though?"

"We're trying to overthrow everything that prevents people from being free and equal. People are not free, and they're certainly not equal. For the past year or so, the movement has been exposing the repressive structures, the propaganda... When the Yippies tried to hold their own event, last year in Chicago, they were gassed, the way the Nazis beat and gassed and imprisoned people. It's the same treatment that black people get when they try to run their own communities, or that students get when they want to run the universities that they're paying for. The only freedom we have is the freedom to shut up and stay in our places, like good slaves.

"If people are sincerely opposed to being violently oppressed by capitalism, maybe they're starting to learn that to get rid of it, you have to fight. Maybe one day, we'll put an end to army and police as we know those terms."

"Wow," I said. "No army, and no police, at all?"

"If the United States was attacked, invaded, citizen armies might resist—unless they welcomed the invasion, in which case, no problem," Mike said. "I guess we would cross that bridge when we come to it, but let's be real: it's highly unlikely that any other country is going to invade us. In terms of the police, what we hope is that we can replace the state-run police force with volunteer community patrols, one in every neighborhood, that the people in that neighborhood would oversee, that would be in charge of making sure that no real crimes were committed— like murder and rape—instead of being enforcers for the State. As it is, the people who most need protection sure aren't getting it from the police."

I didn't know what to say.

§

Spring drills are happening for the football team, and Joe Barnett has invited me to a practice session, as a credentialed reporter. The team is drilling on one of the practice fields near the stadium. Spectators are wandering along the sidelines, which is tolerated as long as they don't get in the way.

This is my first chance to see the new coach in action. He cuts a good-looking figure on the sidelines, in his chinos and a Rivercat-brown polo shirt, but I'm off at a distance and can't hear anything he's saying to the players.

He's talking to this tall blond guy, who Joe tells me is Gary Schoyer: the quarterback for the freshman team last fall. Beebe is graduating, so Ted Blaha, who was the second-string quarterback in 1968 season, is likely to be the starter this coming fall. Schoyer will probably be his backup. Joe tells me that Schoyer looked good on the freshman team, which finished 6-4: way better than the varsity squad did.

The players aren't wearing helmets, so I can see Schoyer's head and face clearly. He has got to be the handsomest male I have ever seen.

His hair is grown over his ears and down his neck; he's got a big smile; I can't tell if his eyes are blue or grey from this distance but they're lively; they make him look almost a little crazy, even when he's smiling. He's broad-shouldered—they're not wearing pads, either, so I can tell—and probably about as tall as I am.

I'm watching the offensive drills—the running plays, the pass patterns—being run at half-speed with no contact. Schoyer is quicker than Blaha, and smoother in his handoffs. He carries himself with more confidence: I can't quite explain how I know that. Blaha has a loose, easy-going body language, while Schoyer looks tenser, more mercurial. Blaha will probably be the better quarterback this year, but Schoyer might be experienced enough to beat Blaha out for the starting job in 1970.

I've never met either of them, but I've been aware of Ted Blaha for several years, since he's local. He's the son of Frank and Ruth Blaha, who own several jewelry and gift shops in and around State City. My parents might be slightly acquainted with them. Ted was a star athlete at State City High—not Visitation, even though I'm pretty sure the Blahas are Catholic—and a year ahead of me.

Gary Schoyer is a graduate of Clinton St. Mary's high school, 60-odd miles to the east of State City, but he's virtually a State Citian, since his big brother, Paul, was the starting quarterback for the Rivercats in the 1962 and '63 seasons. After that, Paul had five seasons in the AFL, as a second-string quarterback for the Jets, the Patriots, and the Oilers—but he never quite made it. I know that Feldy hired Paul to be the Rivercat backfield coach even before he hired Timmerman.

I'm also noticing number 40, whose name I don't know yet: a tall black guy with a short "natural" hairstyle, plus a little moustache and an imperial; long legs, and even broader shoulders and a slimmer waist than Gary Schoyer. He's taking handoffs from the quarterbacks. Incredibly graceful, like an impala or an antelope.

Timmerman tells the players to go grab a shower, and Joe walks me over to Timmerman to be introduced.

"Oh, sure," says Timmerman. He has a strong handshake; his expression is friendly but neutral. "You're Feldy's Girl. They say you're real smart about football."

"Who is that number 40?" I ask.

"That young man is Charles Watkins," says Timmerman. He grins. "Not Charlie, not Chuck. Charles. He's very insistent on that. I'm not surprised you noticed him. He's got tremendous potential. He's so darn fast; he's agile—and he's got good football sense."

"He wasn't on the team last fall, though, was he?" I ask. "I don't remember him."

"He was on the freshman squad in '67," Joe explains. "Then Brosnan redshirted him last fall so that he could catch up academically. Plus, as I recall, he wasn't that big when he was a freshman. He has really filled out."

"Yes, he's very strong," Timmerman says. He begins walking toward the locker rooms; Joe and I keep stride. "I'm sure he's going to contribute. I won't say we'll win the Big Ten this fall, but we're going to be competitive, and you can say I said so."

"No reflection on my predecessor," he adds. "Bob Brosnan had such an unlucky year. He didn't have as much talent as he deserved to be able to work with, and he got a lot of terrible breaks. I'm lucky that I've got so much new blood coming in this year. If we execute, we'll have a winning team."

I report that conversation to Feldy, the next time I'm home. Feldy comments, "That was a nice hedge. Obviously, this guy knows how to be diplomatic. He can sound good without saying much. That's a useful talent. I never developed it."

I can't tell whether Feldy is praising Timmerman, or putting him down.

VICKI IS A MESS LATELY

It's been almost two weeks since Mona, Mike, and Vicki got out of jail, and I'm noticing that Vicki seems to have started drinking a lot. Maybe because she's lonely. Red has gotten into drug dealing, which she says involves a lot of time on the road. Also, she says Red is mad at her for having attracted attention to herself, getting arrested, because if the cops know where she lives, they know where he lives. Probably she meant Red was afraid the cops would be watching their apartment or something.

Vicki has started bringing a bottle of vodka into Mona and Mike's apartment, instead of sipping Mona's wine. She just sits there swigging out of the bottle. She's got no life in her eyes. She says she's depressed; she says she sometimes spends all day in bed, lately, because she's too sad to move.

Too sad to move. I can't even imagine that.

Vicki gets more talkative when she's schnockered. Sometimes she'll laugh suddenly at nothing, or tell a funny story about her childhood that has nothing to do with what's being discussed. She's pretty intense about politics, but when she's had a few, she'll say something about "the movement" that some people might take as sacrilegious, and she'll laugh, while the other people in the room mostly ignore her or roll their eyes.

Sometimes, Vicki will wink or cock her head at one or another of the men, and they'll leave for a few minutes. We can hear them going into Vicki's side of the house; then in maybe ten minutes they'll be back.

Tonight, though—Saturday—it's just me, Mona, and Vicki in the apartment, and Vicki is pretty well along. She takes a swallow from her bottle and declares, "I love how much more sociable vodka makes one feel. So much less inhibited. Especially about sex. You know, I never have been all that crazy about having a dick up inside me. Not even Red's. For one thing, it makes me feel like I'm not in control. I'm all about control. It's why I enjoy riding horses so much, maybe. I find that I can make it last as long as I want to, if I'm sucking a guy's dick, or get it done really fast if that's what I prefer. I can do anything I want. I'm the boss. Yeah, there's something way exciting about that."

I don't like hearing that kind of talk. Mona shifts a bit in her chair—obviously trying not to cringe. I don't know what to say.

I have heard my two roommates making remarks about sex, now and then; it stopped shocking me a long time ago. Karen is still a virgin, but she has a boyfriend, now, and she tells me she's thinking about altering her status. I make a point of not advising her one way or the other, because anything I would say would just push her in the wrong direction. I avoid saying anything in response, when either of my roommates brings up the subject.

What Vicki is saying, tonight, is the most graphic talk I have ever heard. Neither Mona nor I say anything in response, and after a couple minutes, Vicki says, "I think I'll mosey downtown and see if I find anybody who wants it done."

I guess I'm looking incredulous, dumbfounded, whatever, because when Vicki has left, Mona looks apologetic at me and says, "It's what she does. She goes into these blue-collar bars and picks guys up, and… gets her satisfaction that way. Some of the women in the movement say some pretty awful things about her… well, some of the men, too, because frankly, some of the men are not masculine enough to be her type, so they resent her for… for not bestowing her favors on them. It's her thing. It's not something I understand. Not the act, nothing against the act. But with strangers, like that… I don't get it."

"But she's married."

"I guess she and Red have an open arrangement," Mona says. "Anyway, they might not actually be married. I don't ask. That's another thing. Vicki tries not to show it, but she has a horrible fear of being abandoned, of being left by anyone she feels close to. And now Red seems to be growing away from her. Spending all that time on the road; criticizing her for spending time with people like us. That's really messing her up. Because she thinks it's all her fault."

"Why did she get involved with him in the first place?"

Mona shakes her head. "Don't ask me, except that lots of girls are attracted to that sort of guy. I think it happens when the girl doesn't have much self-esteem, although that's crazy, since… my gosh, if anyone should have a high opinion of herself, you would think it would be Vicki. She seems so confident, but sometimes I have to wonder if that's an act. Some of this stuff, you can't figure out. But what she's doing now, with these other guys… I wouldn't be surprised if she's looking for some kind of… I don't know. Assurance? Maybe she just… maybe this is her crazy way of proving to herself that she's somehow worth something, to guys. On some level. It's a mess."

I have heard rumors of people who behave that way, but so far as I know, I have never known anyone, aside from Vicki, who goes out and does stuff like that, with whomever. It's odd that I don't feel particularly scandalized by what Vicki is doing. Maybe I'm becoming *blasé* because I've already been corrupted by the evils of the world, ha-ha.

I'm walking back to my dorm now, and thinking more about what Mona said. I reflect. I'm drawing a distinction between Vicki's behavior, and Andrea Schedl sleeping with her art professor. Maybe I don't approve of what Andrea is doing, but I can understand it. At least Andrea isn't boasting of doing those favors for random men.

I'm thinking about Mona's speculations on why Vicki drinks and does that other stuff. Maybe Mona is right, that Vicki has some awful doubts about herself, about her worth: doubts that I can't even imagine.

I have to admit I don't like Vicki, not anymore. It's not that she's disagreeable, but she seems to stand for everything that I've always been taught was wrong, in terms of personal values and morality. Plus, I've always felt a vibe from her: nothing she has ever said to me. Just a feeling that she looks down on me for being so square.

I've already been including Andrea in my prayers every night, and I'm thinking I ought to pray to St. Victoria, for Vicki. But now I wonder whether that would be presumptuous on my part, or impertinent—because everyone needs prayers, and I can't intercede for every individual in the world. I also wonder whether I'm being proud, or like a Pharisee: singling out Andrea—and now Vicki—as though I'm somehow better than they are. It would probably be more acceptable to ask prayers for Mona, too, since she's almost family, and for Karen, to keep her on the right path, and then somehow it might be more okay to pray for Andrea and Vicki. I don't know, but that's what I'll do.

Andrea—if she knew what was in my prayers—might smirk and ask me why I'm not praying for a boyfriend. I would tell her it's frivolous to pray for something that isn't a spiritual need— but we're never going to have that conversation.

§

Okay, so here is what Mona tells me when we see each other in the Music Building on Monday: She tells me that Vicki didn't return home under her own power, Saturday night. The way Vicki told it to Mona, she didn't remember most of that night.

"She couldn't even remember that she had been visiting with us, earlier," Mona says. "She must have been way drunker than she looked, when she was with us, but I suppose she was already having a blackout.

"She says all that she can remember is lying on a blanket in the back of a panel truck with her jeans and panties down around her ankles, and from the light coming in the front windshield she can see this big, husky guy going through her purse and getting her wallet out of it. She also… she could tell that this guy had just… had his way with her, right? I mean, raped her. While she was out. Only she says he must have been looking for her address, because so far as she could tell, he didn't take anything out of her wallet. Then she was sort of hazy, and the next thing she knew she was being dragged out of the back of the truck and dropped on the front lawn in front of our house.

"She says she can't remember when she finally got on her feet; she says it could have been anywhere from five minutes to five hours later; then she just went inside and slept it off."

"Did she call the police?" I ask. "File a complaint?"

"Well, she can't remember who the guy was. Can't remember much about what he looked like, what he was wearing, anything. Plus, is she going to trust the police to listen to her? They'll ask her to prove she didn't give consent, and how is she going to do that? I bet there would be plenty of witnesses who saw her leave the bar with that guy, whoever he is. Probably some of them would have seen her getting into his truck."

I'm listening to this and asking myself, would a rapist have been considerate enough to go through the purse of the drunk girl he had just raped, without taking anything, looking for her address—then give her a ride home? A man who thought he had

120

just done it with someone who had been willing might do that, sure. But a rapist? I'm skeptical. I don't say this to Mona.

Now Mona is telling me that she and Mike and Vicki are going to be part of an operation on the following day, to block all the entrances to the Memorial Union. They have heard that the University has provided some temporary offices in the Union, to representatives of Dow Chemical—and Dow will be interviewing and recruiting chemical engineering students about to graduate. This group of protesters is going to trap the Dow people inside that building, and make sure that no students can get in there to be interviewed.

They have an informant, in the University administration offices, who has told them that a luncheon for the Dow people and some higher-up University officials has been planned in one of the Union's private dining rooms, and that the interviews are scheduled for that afternoon. The protestors are going to set up their blockade during that luncheon. They'll allow people to leave the building for the first few minutes, to give students and other "innocent parties" a chance to evacuate, but then nobody else will be allowed in or out till the Dow people agree to not only leave the building, but leave State City entirely.

I ask, "Don't they have a right to be here, the same as anybody, even if you don't agree with them?"

"They're murderers." Mona's eye muscles contract. Her voice is still soft and sweet, but she's *so* serious. "They kill people with poison chemicals, and they're here to persuade students to be criminals along with them. Technically they're not breaking the law, and even if they were, they wouldn't be arrested. So decent people have to stop them. We don't want to hurt them—unlike them, who do want to hurt people—but we just want to trap them like rats and get them out of this town."

I'm hoping that Mona won't ask me to join them, but it's like she's reading my mind, because she says, "If you don't feel right about joining us, maybe you could write about it for the *Statesman*. Maybe ask the editor if they need somebody to be there."

§

I've stopped by the Engineering Building, where the *Statesman*'s press rooms are, and left a note for the editor-in-chief, telling her that I'm on the story unless I hear otherwise from her, and at this point she has no way to get in touch with me. I've skipped my 12:30 class—Intro to Philosophy, and I've already read the material the lecture will cover—to show up outside the Memorial Union, where the demonstrators are assembling.

I've walked around the perimeter of the building, and I estimate maybe 20 demonstrators so far, at each of the entrances. And, yeah: they're telling people they can't go in. The people being turned away are just obeying, just accepting it, apparently, without any questions or dispute.

At the east entrance—the main one—Mona, Mike, and Vicki are sitting together, at the top of the steps leading into the building, overlooking maybe 40 other people occupying the steps. Facing them, on the street in front of the steps, are another 20 or so students, almost all male, all dressed in business clothes rather than class clothes. I suppose these are the engineers who are trying to enter the building.

Nearby, in front of the building, are about ten municipal cops, the county sheriff, and seven deputies. I look back the way I came, and I see President Esterhart himself, walking down the hill from his office in Territorial, toward the Union. Even at a distance, I see that his face is haggard; he's clearly upset. He doesn't look well. He's red in the face, or maybe he looks unusually red because of that white hair. He's almost trotting as he gets nearer the Union.

Mike calls to me, "C'mon up here!"

"I'm not here to demonstrate," I holler back. I smile at Mike, though, to pretend to be with him in spirit, or something. "But I'll come up there and get a quote from you."

I start to climb the steps; several young men try to block me, but Mike hollers, "Let her through! She's cool!" I manage, one step at a time, to wiggle my way past demonstrators who are trying to let me pass but are finding it hard to open a path for me.

"Thanks," I say to Mike, when I finally get to the top of the steps, although I'm not sure what I'm thanking him for. Mona and Vicki are laughing, like they're high on the fun of demonstrating. I look down at the crowd and I see President Esterhart talking to one of the cops, gesturing. I can't tell whether he's asking the cop something, or telling him something, or discussing strategy.

"How long are you planning to stay here?" I ask Mike. "And what's the next step?"

"The next step is, they'll have to arrest us," Mike says. "Unless the criminals we've got trapped here agree to get out of town."

"Do you have a right to say who gets to be in this town?"

"The city government throws people out of town all the time," Mike says. "Tramps and so on. People who haven't committed any crimes. These are actual criminals."

I keep writing in my notebook; I notice out of the corner of my eye that a couple of the engineering students have stepped forward and are trying to push their way up the steps, but the demonstrators in the front rank are locking elbows and swaying back, against the elbow-locked rank behind them. One of the engineers tries to crawl between the demonstrators' legs, but the bodies are so packed together that he soon gives it up. The crowd on the steps cheers.

"Stand by," Mike says. "There's something happening here." Then he realizes what he just said, and grins, and adds, "What it is ain't exactly clear."

And now I have that stupid song in my head: Pong… ping… pong… ping…

The police and sheriff's deputies have moved up in front of the demonstrators and are starting to make arrests, but each time they try to take someone away, he goes limp.

"Gonna be a long afternoon," Mike says.

Some of the demonstrators are singing Chopin's Funeral March, wordlessly—"Dum, dum, ta-dum; dum, ta-dum, ta-dum, ta-dum"—each in his own key, which sounds ridiculous. For a few seconds I'm mentally playing counterpoint on an imaginary cello to see if I can get them all on-key. I'm seeing colors again: first a bluish green; it's morphing into a red-orange but still with flashes of that bluish-green. Kind of stylized diarrhœa.

I'm jarred out of it when I hear one of the engineering students—one of the bigger men, athletic-looking—who's standing in front of his colleagues and hollering, really loud, "You know what, guys? Fuck this! We are not going to let these freaks tell us what we can't do and where we can't go. We are gonna break through that line. I am gonna lead you. Ready?"

Why don't they go to a side entrance, where there would be fewer people to charge through, and they wouldn't have to do it up a flight of stairs?

These guys form a wedge—one guy, then two, then three—each man grabbing the trouser waistband of a guy in front of him, with the two or three girls at the back, and the leader just bulls his way right smack into that line, head down. I don't think he's a football player, but he should be playing center or guard.

It looks like he's trying to find a seam to break through—like they're playing Red Rover, Red Rover—but one of the demonstrators puts himself in the way, so the leader of the wedge butts that guy in the pit of the stomach and takes him down—and since they're all elbow-locked, the demonstrators' front line collapses. The engineers are trampling them, and the second row of demonstrators is trying to fight them back.

It's hard to charge up-hill, let alone up a staircase, but these people are determined. All of a sudden, it's a *mêlée*. The cops and sheriff's deputies aren't trying to be gentle. They're charging in, with their batons. The engineers are still a few steps down from where we are—me, Mike, Mona, and Vicki—but I'm thinking we should open the door and escape into the Union building. Only, the doors open outward and we're being crushed against them.

Mike and Vicki are trying to get at the engineers, to help push them back, but their own people are in their way. Mona, next to me, is trying to sit on the top step and curl into a ball to protect herself. The next thing I know—I don't know how it happened—Mona has gotten shoved or jostled so that she's tumbling forward, and down a couple of steps.

It's the most horrifying sound I have ever heard. The sound a wild animal would make if an eagle got its claws into her, only louder. I can't believe I will ever hear anything so terrible, as long as I live. I know it's Mona's voice.

I can see that Mike has stopped fighting and is trying to get over to Mona—he's bleeding, from over his right eye—and shield her. He gets his arms round her and turns his back to the fighting, trying to help her up.

Mona is bleeding, too. She's holding up her left hand, looking at it. It's covered with blood.

By this time, enough people have been cleared off the steps so that I can move a little. Mona and Mike are too far away, now, for me to reach, and I can't see Vicki at all, but I can get the front door open. Mona and Mike are my friends, but this is not my fight. I'm a reporter, but I'm not going to get clubbed or thrown in jail for it. I can see a cop stepping up to Mona and Mike; I can't tell whether he's trying to help, or arrest them, or what.

I duck into the Union. Luckily, I know the layout. I know where the nearest ladies' room is. I run toward it, getting down the hall and out of sight before any cop can get in that door. The ladies' room is empty, so I sit there in a stall, writing in my notebook what has happened, trying to get as much of it down as I can, as accurately as I can.

As each minute goes by, I feel more thankful that I can't hear anyone coming into the restroom. I also feel guilty for having run out on my friends—and convinced that I'll never make a reporter if I'm such a coward as to run away from a story.

Then I play the Glad Game, and tell myself I'm glad I escaped. I could have been hurt or arrested, and I wasn't.

After maybe five or six minutes, I hear someone else coming in, so I stay dead-still in that stall. When I look under the door at the feet, I can see it's not a cop: just some other girl, needing to answer a call of nature, so I'm okay. But I stay there, very quiet, writing in my notebook, listening to her bodily noises. I stay for another 20 minutes, after she's long gone. Nobody else uses the john during that time.

I come out of the stall, wash my hands even though I've done nothing to get them dirty, then put my ear to the entrance door to try to hear whether there's anything out of the ordinary going on inside the Union. I emerge, trying to look innocent.

It looks like business as usual. A few students sitting in arm-chairs in the lounge area, reading. A few people walking through the building, like always.

I want to go back the way I came, to see if anything is still going on, on the front steps—but if there's still a fight or something, I don't want to get into it. If the fight is done, there might still be cops there. They might recognize me as someone who was on the steps before. I go down to the basement level, get a Coke at the snack shop, and sit in the Lower Lounge, nursing it, for another hour or so. At last, I leave by a side exit, and walk around the building. I'm walking on the other side of the street. I don't see any demonstrators, or any cops.

I walk over to the Engineering Building. There, in the news-room, I find an empty desk with a typewriter. I see only two other people in the room; they can't tell me whether anybody else is covering the story. I find a phone, at a neighboring desk, and call over to the County Jail to see if anyone had been arrested, but I'm told that people are still being processed; the Sheriff can't release any names yet.

As it turns out, the *Statesman* had assigned another reporter to the story. This reporter had much more complete information than I had, by press time, but she incorporated some of my material. "Teresa Feldevert contributed to this story" appeared at the bottom of the article the next morning.

ESTERHART CRITICAL: SUFFERS HEART ATTACK DURING STUDENT UPROAR

What I had not seen, because it happened a second or two after I bolted from the brawl on the Union steps, was President Es-terhart suddenly turning white and falling to the ground. The *Statesman*'s article calls it a "massive" heart attack. He's not dead, but he is going to have to spend several days in the hospital at least, and he's in critical condition.

The spin, in most newspapers across Iowa, was that he had fallen in the line of duty, trying to calm a situation created by campus radicals who had had nothing better to do than to prevent other people from going about their lawful business. That was not the point of view of the *Statesman*. Its article merely noted that Esterhart had been observing a student demonstration when he was (oh, purely coincidentally) stricken. A brief piece on the editorial page suggested that it was regrettable that the point of the demonstration had been overshadowed by that fact.

It looks like this has been a public relations fiasco for the Movement, and I'm not sure whether I'm glad of that or not. In the end, there weren't many arrests—partly because the cops didn't have the manpower to arrest everyone; partly because the engineering students had finally broken through the demonstrators in front of the steps, and entered the building. When word of this got around to the other demonstrators, who had been blocking the other entrances, those crowds must have all broken up and slunk off.

That explains why the situation stabilized in just the half-hour or so that I spent sitting in the ladies' room in the Union—during which time, I was assuming that Mike, Mona, and Vicki had all been arrested. It turned out that none of those three had been.

MONA'S HAND

"I refuse to feel guilty," Mona says to me. It's night, and I've come over to Mona and Mike's apartment, even though Mona called me earlier today to tell me I might need to find another cello teacher. I'm here especially because of that. Mona told me over the phone that she spent last night in the hospital for observation, and her hand is crushed. Lots of the bones and nerves in her hand and fingers are involved. She'll have to wear a cast for weeks. The doctors can't promise that she'll recover enough to play the cello much, ever again. The injury might not have been such a disaster if it had been her right hand—her bowing hand—but it's almost certain that her fingering abilities are going to be compromised at least. Destroyed, at worst.

I said, "Let me come over tonight anyway." I had been standing in my dorm room, by the door, facing the corner of the wall while I talked, and this news was making me feel almost literally nauseated. "Just to see how you are. It would make me feel better even if I can't do anything for you."

I'm sitting on a pillow on the Shapens' floor. Mike sits next to Mona on the sofa, with his arm round her. They both tell me a more complete version of what happened at the Union. Mona snuggles close to Mike, like for protection. Mike has a gauze bandage over one eye, with a folded red bandanna tied round his head to hold it in place. Vicki is sitting on the sofa too, not drinking. Usually, drunk or sober, she acts pretty cheerful, but now she looks grim.

"Will you be able to finish the semester?" I ask. "What else can you do? Do you have any alternatives, if you can't play?"

"I can still finish my academic classes. I only need one hand for those, and Professor Meregaglia agreed that since I already gave my recital for the year, I get an A. But I don't know the status of my scholarship. I'm not going to be getting a Masters in cello performance now, that's for sure. If I'm lucky, I might be able to switch to a degree in musical scholarship, or pedagogy. Or maybe even conducting. I don't know. I'll have to find out."

Mona half-smiles: bitter, and I've never seen her bitter, but I guess I would be too. "This is what I get for being on the right side of history. Anyway, the… I don't know, the implications? The full impact? Really hasn't sunk in yet. I'm surprised I feel pretty calm, but I have a feeling that's not going to last."

"And Mike, what happened to you?" I ask. (My assumption is that he got hit with a policeman's night-stick, but I'm not going to say that.)

"I don't know for sure what happened. I would like to say that a pig clubbed me, and maybe one of them did, but I can't know. I don't remember being hit. I just know I was on my knees, feeling like I was going to throw up. Then I heard Mona scream, so I got up and found her. Didn't even think about it."

Mike tells me the rest of the story. He was shielding Mona with his body as best he could, he says, and he had hustled her down the steps and out of the way of the violence, at about the same moment that President Esterhart had collapsed. Mike steered Mona over toward Esterhart, since that situation was distracting the cops' attention away from arresting people.

"Probably the fact that Esterhart was down, in the street, helped to stop the fighting," Mike says. "I figured that if Mona and I could get close to Esterhart, and keep quiet, there would be an ambulance coming any minute, and we could show Mona's hand to the medical people and ask if she could go along to the emergency room.

"We were real lucky that the cops right next to Esterhart were decent about it and didn't try to run us off—they could see we were both hurt—so when the ambulance showed up, I showed Mona's hand to one of the porkers and he asked the, I don't know what you call them, the medics, he asked the medics if they could bring her along. He didn't seem to notice that my head was bleeding, or maybe he did notice and decided I had it coming. Or maybe he took pity on Mona because, you know, good-looking girl in distress. Anyway, they took Mona along.

"They took her and Esterhart to University Hospital, but Mercy Hospital is closer to the Union—probably not even a mile—so I decided to walk over there and present myself at the emergency entrance, you know, all innocence, like maybe I'd tripped and hit my head on a curb. That was plausible, because I wasn't exactly clean and neat. Anyway, they stitched me up and didn't ask any questions."

"I feel bad about Esterhart," Mike says. "I have nothing against him personally; I don't think Mona does, either." Mona shakes her head. "Mona and I tried to see him, today, at the hospital. Just to let him know that this wasn't an outcome that we were happy with. But he wasn't allowed to have visitors."

"That's why I feel... maybe not guilty, but sad," Mona says. "I wanted to tell him how sorry we were that that happened to him."

"He maybe isn't a bad guy," Vicki says, "but he's a tool. And glad to be one. It's too bad, but I can't say I feel sorry for him.

People like him have to die before we might have peace and justice in the world."

"What do you mean by peace and justice?" I ask. "And why do people have to die for it?"

"Because they're the generation that's in control at the moment," Vicki says. "They're too old to learn any different, even if they wanted to learn. And too comfortable where they are, to be part of any revolutionary movement."

"Vicki's probably right," Mike says.

"You two are out of it for a while," Vicki says to Mona and Mike. "At least, you should be. I'm going to pick up the slack for you. Maybe I wasn't as into this business as I should have been, but I've got to be, now."

Vicki looks so stern that I almost laugh. Vainglorious. That's the word that comes to me. It's like she's preening.

"We'll get there," Vicki says. "In any revolution, you'll have maybe 20 percent of the people who are on board with it. Twenty percent are against it, and 60 percent in the middle don't give a shit. If we get that 20 percent, we've got it locked."

Mona smiles, faintly, from under Mike's arm.

"We've radicalized you," she says.

"It's something to do while Red's away. I'll tell you what I think did it. Getting raped. By that… that Iowa redneck."

I want to ask Vicki, "Did you really get raped? How do you know? If you were so drunk that you don't remember anything, how do you know you didn't give consent, if you were coherent enough to get yourself downtown, looking for action? Don't you think you probably propositioned him? And if he really did take you forcibly, didn't you put yourself in the way of it?" But it's not the time or place to say any of that.

"He was America personified," Vicki goes on. "What he did to me, we're doing to the rest of the world—and to black people in this country."

"It doesn't matter so much what struck the spark with you," Mona says. "As long as you're part of the movement."

"Teresa, you're so quiet," Vicki says.

"I'm listening. It's interesting." I'm not sure how interested I am, but I can't think of anything to say, and at least I'm learning about what they're thinking.

"Maybe if we had elected Gene McCarthy last year, things would have been different," Mona says. "But he and Bobby were the only good ones in that bunch, and they weren't going to be allowed to succeed. I can't know it, but I can't help wondering if Sirhan was hired by Johnson. Or by the CIA, or both."

I have to stop myself from rolling my eyes at that, so I say the first thing that comes into my head:

"I'll ask St. Teresa to pray for him."

Vicki gives me a "What are you talking about?" look.

"For... Esterhart. I never knew him, really. I met him once or twice, at events, because of who my father is, you know, but just to be introduced. Anyway, I'll pray for him."

"How does that work?" Mona asks. "Praying to a Saint. As opposed to praying to, you know, the Big Guy. I don't know anything about that."

"Well, when you pray to a Saint, you're not directly speaking to God; you're asking the Saint to speak to God on your behalf. We ask a Saint to keep us in their prayers, because we think their prayers might carry more weight with God than ours do. We pray directly to God, too, but the Church has so many prayers that have been prepared for us to recite to God, so we use those. If we improvise a prayer to Him, it'll be short and simple, and it won't include asking Him for anything specific. If you ask God for something specific, sometimes He says 'no.'"

Mike is looking uncomfortable. Vicki is smirking, kind of, but Mona looks serious.

"I hardly knew any Catholics, or hardly any Christians for that matter, till I came here to Iowa," Mona says. "Everybody here is *so* Christian. I shouldn't assume that people look at me like I'm from outer space, but I feel like it sometimes. Not so much here in State City, but in other towns. Like Cedar Rapids."

"Every town in the Midwest has a few Jewish families," I say. "But around here it's mostly heretics like Lutherans and Methodists, plus us Catholics. We won't eat you; that's just a story."

"But religion is so primitive here," Vicki says. "Where I grew up, some people went to church, but it was something one did to look respectable. Not because anybody actually believed that stuff. Here, it's like people mean it."

"Some of us do."

"But don't you think it does more harm than good, now?" Vicki asks. "If it ever did anybody any good, which I wonder."

I have no idea what to say to that.

"Cavemen made up stories to explain the universe," Vicki says. "People are naturally fearful, so we created demons to explain danger, sickness, whatever. But now we don't need those stories. Religion doesn't help us anymore, if it ever did. It actually works against humanity."

I want to ask how the Sam Hill she gets the idea that religion works against humanity, but Mike jumps in before I can.

"The first problem with religion is that it assumes the truth," he says. "If empirical fact contradicts the myth, then somehow you have to find a way to deny the fact, or twist it to suit your myth. If you're not inside that bubble, this will look insane to you, but if you're on the inside, and you can't hear anyone contradicting or questioning you, then it makes sense, or at least enough sense that you'll be comforted by it."

Now I'm getting annoyed.

"I don't see how anything I believe is insane," I say.

"For example," Mike says, "you might say that the stories of the ancient Egyptian gods are clearly bullshit—and you'd be right—but then you have no problem with the story of Eve talking to a snake. While here I am, saying, 'They're both folk tales.'"

"But we don't believe that there was a real talking snake. At least not all of us. Most Catholics accept that a lot of Genesis is myth. Or allegory. We're not Baptists."

"Okay, maybe not, but you do believe you'll be sent to Hell and burn for all eternity if you don't believe that Jesus was God, and that God created the universe, and so on. Would you love some human who would do that to you? Send you to Hell? Then why would you love a God who would do that to you, much less worship a God like that?"

"God doesn't do it to you. You do it to yourself. God offers you His mercy. You can choose whether to take it or not."

"Mercy for what, though?" Vicki asks.

Oh, boy. I have a very unkind response in mind, but I don't deliver it.

"If God is always telling you what to do, you're not thinking for yourself, are you?" Vicki asks. "So, if you always do what God tells you, how can you do anything wrong?"

"You can't," I say, "if you do exactly what God tell you to do, all the time. But nobody's that perfect. Sometimes we know what God is telling us, but we do bad things anyway. Sometimes we don't listen. Or sometimes we don't even hear."

"Only, it wasn't God who wrote the Bible, or the Koran, or whatever," Mike says. "It was people. People telling you how to act. That's why I say religion's purpose is to control you. See, it allows people with power to create a hierarchy—with themselves at the top, and a few privileged overseers under them to control the masses. Then you have those masses, who are too intimidated by religion to rise up against the people controlling them. Too intimidated even to ask questions."

"Catholics are supposed to ask questions," I say. "There's this idea that if you're religious you're not supposed to question, but Catholic scholars question everything. All the time. That's why there are so many books about Catholicism."

"Okay, but it's not just Catholicism; it's any religion," Vicki says. "You're proud to be part of whatever herd you belong to."

"Maybe we should stop defining ourselves by the different myths we believe in," Mona says. She sounds timid, like maybe she thinks she shouldn't be chiming in. "If we're going to have any religions at all—and maybe we don't need to have any, but if we have them—they need to be about working toward love and kindness to everybody, *from* everybody."

Poor Mona. She does mean well.

"Look at all our religious books," she goes on. "I mean from just about any religion in the West; maybe not so much in Hinduism or Buddhism or Taoism, but Western religions. They talk about kidnapping, rape, murder, enslavement, what have you, as though these things are all okay so long as you're doing them to someone outside your group. But then we're taught that 'God is love,' and religion is all about love and peace and nice stuff. Meanwhile men are being sent to Vietnam to kill the 'other.' This is a religious war almost as much as it's a racial war."

"And here's a biggie," Mike says. "Religion justifies inequality. Religions encourage men to treat women like property, and women are supposed to be glad to be property. Religion justifies treating different races differently; it justifies some people being richer than other people; it justifies the whole notion of social classes. It justifies hatred of your fellow human being. It does all of that—for the sake of keeping the powerful in power."

Mike lights another cigarette.

"They teach myth," he says. "Then they teach you that if you don't believe the myth, you go to Hell. Science can pretty much explain the world. And anything we can't explain now, science will explain it, pretty soon—but religion demands that we just believe. It's not God who wants us to be ignorant, because there isn't any God. It's the people in power, who want to hold onto their power and wealth. They want us to keep believing myth, because that makes it easier for them to dominate us."

Now I'm laughing and shaking my head, because frankly I would like to stuff a back-issue of *Ramparts* up Mike's poop-hole. I'm sorry, I hardly ever use that kind of language, but I would.

"But I always had plenty of science classes, in the Catholic high school I went to," I say. "Including evolution. We don't say there isn't science. We know there's science. But we believe God's behind it."

"It's not so much the science that bothers me," Mike says. "I know lots of religions don't deny science. The main thing I hate is the way some people in power use religion to justify... oh, any kind of crime you can think of. Like they do in Vietnam. God loves America, right? Everybody knows that we're on God's side, and God's on our side. So, we can burn whole villages, with women and children in them, and it's okay. It might not look nice, but it's okay. Because one way or another, you can use the Bible to justify it."

"That's not religion. That's politicians misusing religion."

134

Mike shrugs. "I hear that a lot," he says. "If you see Christians behaving badly—or Jews behaving badly too, for that matter—somebody's gonna say, 'Well, that's not really Christianity,' or, 'He's not a good Jew.' My point is that it really *is* Christianity."

If I hadn't been so tired, I might have said, "The same way you'll probably tell me that Russia under Stalin was 'not really Communism,'" but as it is, I let the conversation drift to another subject—and a few minutes later I can tell them it's way past my bedtime, and leave without looking like I had lost the argument.

§

I can read Feldy pretty well. I think the reason why I get along so well with Feldy—why Birdy and all my brothers get along with him, but maybe me especially—is that I've learned to read him. I know more or less what he's thinking, and I'm pretty good at reacting the right way, if I need to react. If I say so myself.

It's five days after that demonstration, Sunday night. Feldy and Birdy are having Coach Timmerman and his wife to our house for dinner. Win and I are there to help Birdy with the cooking and setting up, and to keep Sander and Duffy from monopolizing the conversation at the table.

The Timmermans have five children: a girl, 17, is the eldest. The kids haven't come to State City yet, but Timmerman is wrapping up the spring drills, and his wife is along for a few days to find a house big enough to hold all of them.

Sander and Duffy are under strict instructions not to ask Coach Timmerman too many questions, but that's forgotten as soon as we're all at the table. Timmerman doesn't seem to mind.

"I'm glad you two fellows can tell me so much about the team," he says. "I need all the information I can get."

Mrs. Timmerman is pretty the way her husband is handsome: so wholesome, so all-American. She's asking Duffy and Sander about their athletic interests, to get them talking so her husband can eat.

"You might enjoy meeting our older son, when he gets here," she tells them. "He's a pretty good athlete too; I can't think of a sport he doesn't play. And, Teresa, you might like to know our daughter Gail. She's about to graduate high school, and she'll probably be going here in the fall. You can show her around."

I tell Mrs. Timmerman I'd be glad to do whatever I can for their daughter, but from reading Feldy, I get the impression that we're not going to be socializing much with the Timmermans.

It's not actual dislike that I'm sensing. Suspicion? That's not quite it, either. Disdain? Not disdain. Timmerman is Head Coach of the football team and Feldy isn't: that's the best way I can describe whatever Feldy is giving off, here.

Inevitably, the Battle of the Union Steps comes up.

"This is a hell of a way for a guy to end his career," Feldy is saying to Timmerman. "I feel awful for Esterhart. He's a scholar. He has no idea how to deal with the situations we're seeing now. We're going to see worse—more of these demonstrations—and he would never have been equipped to handle it. You can understand why the students are frustrated, but they shouldn't have been allowed to get away with that. They've got a lot of outsiders stirring them up. Professional troublemakers.

"Toby, that's something you're going to have to watch for. There's a discipline problem with young people in general these days—except for our own kids, who are perfect." (Feldy gestures to all of us, and laughs.) "The mindset that's infecting these demonstrators has rubbed off on the kind of kids you wouldn't expect to see it from. That includes athletes. They seem to have this idea that the university belongs to them, that they should be allowed to decide how it should be run, that they're entitled to make the rules, even to the point of deciding who gets to come and go. I'd advise you to keep an eye on it. Be fair, but be firm from the start, if there's any unrest on the team."

I don't bring up the fact that I had been there on the Union steps. But now it's later; Win is driving me back to my dorm in his Rambler—and I confess it to him.

"I feel almost like I have some sort of responsibility for what happened," I tell him. "Obviously, I don't; that's crazy thinking. I'm still trying to figure out whether the demonstrators were right to do what they did. Maybe if he was that sick, Esterhart would have had the attack sooner or later, for some other reason. But the fact that I was there, it makes me feel almost dirty."

"Would you have felt dirty from being there, if Esterhart hadn't had the attack?"

"No."

"You were observing. As a reporter. Correct? So don't make yourself responsible for everything that goes on in the world. That's scrupulosity, in a way."

"You're right. If I'm being rational, you're right. I don't know where these feelings come from. But I have them."

It isn't till Monday morning that I see in the *Statesman* that Esterhart died the night before—probably at right about the same time that Win was driving me back to the dorm. The obituary says his retirement would have been effective in another three weeks, and that he had been looking forward to teaching and lecturing, at State University and elsewhere.

MY FIRST DATE, I GUESS

On the evening following the last day of classes—that is, the week before final exams—I had what I guess was the first real date of my life. What I did with Jim Wagner, back at Visitation High, wasn't really *dating*-dating. This is the first time ever, that someone asked me out because he was—I'm assuming—attracted to me. His name is Andrew Palinkas.

He sat near me in Intro to Philosophy all semester. He's nothing to look at. He's tall—taller than I am, for sure—and on the stout side, although not really fat. He's already going bald on top.

I knew who he was, in high school. He went to State City High; he was a good actor. Jim and I went to a few performances by the State City High Drama Club, because we were both into theatre then. Andy was two years ahead of me. So this is his junior year. He had never spoken to me before except for "Hi." The other morning, when we were getting up to leave at the end of the hour, he leaned over to me, and muttered—without looking at me—"I want to see that *Romeo and Juliet* movie, downtown. Want to see it with me, this weekend?"

I wanted to see the movie no matter whom I saw it with, so I said "Sure." He said he would be in the lobby of Radcliffe Hall on Friday evening, and he was.

We saw the movie, then we walked around the corner to Hamel's, which is a bar and restaurant where a lot of the Drama and Music majors hang out, to get a pizza. Andy told me he's majoring in Business Administration because he decided majoring in Drama would be too much work. He knows who Feldy is, because he's a football fan "even though I never could play it." He told me he got to hear me on the radio because the football games were broadcast into Rosen's Men's Store, where he works on weekends. But Andy didn't talk much. He mostly let me talk. I think he might have been tongue-tied. He seemed not at all sure of himself. Insecure.

At one point he kind of burst out, "I can't believe you're out with me. I was flabbergasted when you said yes, and I was afraid you were going to cancel at the last minute, or stand me up."

I didn't know what to say to that. I just looked at him, and asked him what other courses he was taking this semester. Andy went all red in the face.

"Me and my big mouth," he said. He tried to laugh. "Don't mind me. Anyway, what else I'm taking… I'm taking this Philosophy class because this is the first semester that I've had time to take courses that really interest me. I'll try to do more of that in my senior year."

"You sound like you're not quite focused, yet," I said.

"I like to think of myself as a Renaissance Man." Andy grinned. I don't know: that rationalization made me take him less seriously, although maybe that's not fair of me.

Andy walked me back to my dorm; I wasn't sure whether or not he would try to kiss me goodnight, but I didn't want him doing it—so at the front door of the building I held out my hand and said, "Thank you, Andy. This has been such a nice evening."

He asked me if I would like to get together and study, before the final, which is on Monday, but I told him, "Oh, I've got so much to do. I know I'll have to study at some point this weekend, but I don't know what my schedule will be like. I'll see you on Monday, though."

And thus ended my first date ever: evidently with both parties slightly disappointed.

Now it's Monday; I've just sat the exam. Andy asked me if I'd like to get coffee at Hamburgher's café afterwards and I didn't want to refuse, but when we were sitting in Hamburgher's I made a point of telling Andy that our family is traveling up to Wisconsin for most of the summer, not returning till August.

"But I'm sure I'll see you in the fall," I said—hoping I was coming across as polite, rather than either teasing him or dismissing him.

"Could I write to you?" Andy asked. I told him I didn't know the street address in Wisconsin, and gave him my address in State City. "It'll get forwarded to me." Now I'm wondering if I handled it right.

BOOK III

SOPHOMORE YEAR AT STATE

I took a Greyhound back to our house in State City ahead of the rest of the family, because I had volunteered to cover the River-cats' summer practice and write a report on their prospects, for the fall semester's first edition of the *Statesman*. I'll be working with Joe and Sonny again, too, during the football season, and resume my weekly morning sports report.

Coach Timmerman always waves hello to me, when he sees me on the sidelines, watching the team practice. He usually has time to take a question or two.

A few of the football players know that I'm Feldy's Girl, but I don't know any of them to speak to. That big Negro linebacker, Abiatha Turner, always waves to me. He might be one of the team's most talented defensive players. He sure looks strong, in the contact drills. Maybe the strongest guy I've ever seen on the football field. Charles Watkins still looks impressive in the offensive backfield. So fast for a big man.

Gary Schoyer is handling the ball as much as Ted Blaha, at quarterback, as far as I can tell. I approach Coach Timmerman on the sidelines, at a moment when he doesn't look too busy, and ask him, "Have you made up your mind about who's starting at quarterback?"

"Blaha's going to start. He's got the experience and the seniority. Schoyer is going to see some playing time. I want a definite number-one guy, but I need two quarterbacks I can depend on."

The more I watch them drill, the more convinced I am that Schoyer is more naturally skillful than Blaha. He's definitely faster and more graceful. Speed and reflexes can't be taught. Smoothness in handing the ball off, or passing it, can only be improved so much.

I try to tell myself it doesn't matter, but Schoyer is a lot better-looking, too. Blaha is tall and lanky; his hair is getting a little thin already, although not as bad as Andy Palinkas. Schoyer is big, too, but more compact, more muscular. He trots past me at one point with his helmet off and I see that his eyes are light blue, not grey; they seem to lock onto whomever he's talking to.

The word "fanatical" pops into my mind, when I notice how intently he looks at a coach or teammate when he's talking or listening to them. It's not a threatening or unfriendly look. But fanatical: that's all I can think to call it. Maybe because his eyes are so sky-blue. He doesn't look stern or angry. He smiles a lot, when he has his helmet off. But he's always tending to business, on the field.

I can't interfere with practice, to talk with Gary, but I can wait outside the exit of the locker room and waylay him later. I'm a reporter, working on a story. If he'll fall for that.

Here comes Ted Blaha, in his street clothes: blue jeans and a brown Rivercat t-shirt. I'll approach him and introduce myself as a reporter for the *Statesman*; I just have to run the risk that Gary will come out and walk past us. I step up to Blaha and introduce myself, and he says, "Sure, I know you, you're Feldy's Girl."

He and I are just the same height. He is not unattractive—regular features and all—but Ted Blaha is one of the most ordinary-looking guys I have ever seen. What's remarkable about his appearance is that there's nothing remarkable about it. His voice is the same as any other guy's.

I ask him, "What do you see as the biggest challenge for the Rivercat offense, this fall?"

He smiles, and he's saying "I'm not the guy who should be saying anything about that. That's for Coach Timmerman to talk about," when Gary comes out of the building and is about to walk past us.

"Hold it right there, Schoyer," I holler, but I'm smiling to show goodwill. "You're next, as soon as I'm done talking to Blaha, here." I have never spoken to either of them before; I'm surprised at myself. They both laugh, and Gary stops walking.

"She's from the *Statesman*," Blaha tells Gary. "Trying to get us to divulge our secret plays."

"You'll never get 'em out of us," says Gary. His eyes twinkle; he has such a breezy voice. So light, but baritone. Manly. And those dimples, when he smiles. Like, I would not imagine that he would have enough face to support dimples as deep as those.

Sure enough, I get nothing but generalities from either of them. The closest they come to saying anything at all committal is when I ask them if they're competing against each other.

Gary says, "Coach has made it clear that Ted's the starter. I'm fine with that. This is just my first year as a varsity player. I've got a lot to learn. It wouldn't work to have us fighting over the job during the season."

Gary has a slight accent. It's not a regional accent, but he has a peculiar way of pronouncing some words. His "L" is funny: apparently he does something with his lips and tongue so that you really notice it. Words like "clear" and "player" come out, almost, as "kel-*lear*" and "pel-*layer*." That grabs me. It's as though he's channeling his dimples and his blue eyes, with that one little trick of his speech.

I'm walking with both of them toward a parking lot near the practice field, one of them on either side of me. It turns out they're parked near each other. Ted has a green Oldsmobile 88, and Gary has a black Camaro—both convertibles, both late models. They both tell me, "See you later" before they get into their cars.

I'm impressed with myself. By engaging Ted Blaha first, I made it look less like I was trying to break the ice with Gary. I know, it was sheer luck, but I'll pretend I played it brilliantly.

§

Fall semester is starting, and I've moved into Iota Delta Theta house, across DeWitt Street and a few buildings north of Radcliffe Hall. At most of the sorority houses at State University, the number of girls living in the house depends on how many want to pay for a single room. The members who want a single room get priority. The singles are barely big enough to accommodate a bed, closet, desk, and chair, and they never sell out, so a few will be turned into doubles, with bunk beds. Three larger rooms are big enough for two bunk beds, so they sleep four people. The house has a telephone switchboard, and each bedroom has one phone, so if you're sharing a room, you share the phone. Each of the inhabitants of double and quadruple rooms has further closet space in a shared area, plus their own desks, in carrels, in common study rooms.

I have a double. My roommate is a skinny little girl with wavy black hair: Janet Fletcher. She's a dance major. We don't find much to talk about, but she likes to practice her dance positions while I practice my cello—although there's barely enough space in that room for both of us to practice at once.

Iota attracts a lot of music and art students. I got along great with Karen Whittlesey last year, and I hardly saw Andrea, but I'm happier now that I'm living with girls whose interests line up with my interests.

I have an "Iota name." My sisters call me Brenda, for Brenda Starr, since I'm a Journalism major. They kid me about being a grind, but what am I going to do: deny it?

Gail Timmerman, the coach's daughter, is a freshman. I looked her up, as soon as the Timmermans were moved into their new home, and encouraged her to visit Iota during the rushing season. When I told my Big Sister, Renée McAloon—we call her Lefty, because she's the most left-handed person in the world—that I'm hoping Gail Timmerman will commit to Iota Delta Theta, Lefty said, "She's a nice girl. Very smooth. But what is this, the football sorority?" Lefty wasn't seriously objecting, though, because Gail is one of our pledges now.

I phoned Mona and Mike Shapen the day before classes started. Mona told me the cast was off her hand, but she could barely move her fingers.

"The doctor gave me some exercises to help rehabilitate it, but he's not optimistic that I'll ever have full use of it, so I'm looking at other options," Mona said. "The University is continuing my scholarship for this year, but it's going to take me a third year to complete my degree, because I'll have to switch over to something else: conducting or pedagogy, probably; that remains to be seen. It depends on whether I can get into the conducting studio—but either way, I'll have to find a way to pay for that extra year. I would still love for you to come over here when you can, and play for me, so I can at least enjoy it vicariously."

Mona told me that now that it's sunk in, what's happened to her, she feels like crying almost constantly. She says it will probably get worse when classes start and she sees other instrumentalists going ahead with studying and planning their careers, while all of a sudden she's done with that.

I had to reject a boy for the first time in my life. Andy Palinkas called our house, and Birdy told him I was living in Iota. He phoned me here to ask me for a date, the first week of classes.

"Andy, thank you. Really. The thing is, I won't have time to date at all this year. I just have too many activities having to do with my sorority, not to mention my studies."

Andy didn't say anything, but I could feel his disappointment, through the phone, almost as though it were a physical sensation: a sort of lowering of my own spirits.

"We'll see each other around," I said. I felt like a first-class heel. "I'm sure we'll see each other around; maybe if we do, we can get coffee and catch up."

Andy kept quiet for a few seconds, then I heard a little sigh.

"I'm sorry. I blew it. I shouldn't have written you those letters."

"Aw, no you didn't blow it. You didn't blow anything. That one date was probably the only one I'll have till I graduate. You're very nice. I mean it. You take care."

I felt guilty about hanging up the phone, too. I had to tell myself: Andy hadn't blown it by sending me those letters—I mean, there were only two, and all they were was him telling me a little about what he was doing with himself, and saying he hoped I was having a nice summer and he looked forward to seeing me again when the fall semester started. Nothing effusive or even flirtatious. But if I had been on the fence about him, those letters *would* have blown it, because he would have made me wonder: if he's got nothing else going on, why should I be interested in someone who's so unpopular? And why is he so interested in me? I'm nothing much; I know I'm not especially pretty. What's he got wrong with him, that he's attracted to me?

Well, okay, there's plenty wrong with Andy: mainly he's balding, completely non-athletic, and apparently directionless as to his future. Like, I'd date that? I'm being cruel, and I'm kind of joking—but only kind of. I should have told Andy, "Next time you're interested in someone, act like you're not. Make it look like it's her idea." But that would have implied that I could have been interested in him in the first place.

§

It's the same evening. I've brought my cello over to the Shapens. Vicki is here too, sitting with Mona and Mike on the couch. She looks awfully glum; she gives me a tiny smile and sort of mumbles a hello. Mona has a gob of Silly Putty in her left hand. She keeps kneading and kneading it, stretching it, re-gathering.

"I'm trying to get my hand back. I still can't use it for fingering, but the doctor said maybe if I keep working it, it might come back. He wasn't optimistic that I'll regain full use, but he said there was a chance. Fortunately, you don't need much movement in your left hand to conduct—if I develop the knack for it."

I play the prelude to the First Bach Cello Suite. Mona nods, and she's about to comment, when Vicki stands up, headed for the bathroom, and I see she has a small baby bump.

I smile at Vicki and say, "Congratulations!" but Mona and Mike both wince enough for me to notice. Vicki smiles the least bit and said, "Thanks, I guess." I wonder for an instant whether I'm mistaken, if Vicki is just overweight, but no: I know what a pregnant belly looks like, and this one appears to be around the fifth month. Then I realize what happened five months ago, and I'm mortified, but I try not to show it; I certainly don't apologize.

"Your bowing is a lot smoother," says Mona. "You must have put in a lot of practice this summer."

But as soon as Vicki is in the bathroom, Mona says, very softly, "It might not be a good idea to talk about..."

"I know, I know. I'm sorry. I wasn't thinking."

"Red took off," Mona whispers, "since obviously it's not his."

"Why obviously not his?"

"Because she doesn't do that with Red. At least that's what she told me: that she hasn't done *that* with Red in a long time. Just other stuff. So it can't be his, and now she'll have to bring it up by herself. She's on the outs with her parents, now. She saw them, back in June. They wanted her to stay on Long Island and get an abortion. They were really putting pressure on her. She told them where they could stick it, and she came back here."

Vicki comes out of the bathroom, and Mona says, in normal voice, "It's great that you're working on Bach. I know he's not your favorite, but there's no other composer like him if you're a cellist. It's the fact that those suites are so difficult that keeps people playing them. They're so educational."

§

The first game of the 1969 football season didn't impress anybody. It was a 17-0 loss, at home, against Arizona State. The defense looked pretty good, but the offense was horrible. Charles Watkins made only 50 yards on 18 carries; Blaha had terrible trouble finding open receivers. He didn't pass badly; he just couldn't find anyone to throw to. He was sacked six times, and completed only 12 passes in 30 attempts. Gary took over for almost all the fourth quarter. He didn't do much better.

The following week was the first conference game of the season, against Purdue: also a home game. The Boilermakers have a strong team again this year.

Blaha went down with what looked like an ankle sprain in the second quarter, with the Rivercats behind, 14-0. Gary took over and drove the Rivercats downfield. Watkins ran the ball in from the 10-yard line for the first Rivercat score of the season—in the sixth quarter the team had played this year. Blaha was out for the

146

afternoon. Gary did well—he completed more than half his passes—but the final score was Purdue 28, State 14.

The third game of the season was on the road, against our in-state rival, the University of Des Moines—which has always had a weak athletic program. Its football team is part of the Big Eight conference—and it's a joke. U. Des Moines hasn't had a winning season in ten years.

I traveled along with Joe and Sonny to Des Moines, in Joe's Ford LTD. Now we're laughing and actually singing, on the way back to State City. It was a blow-out. Blaha's ankle was still recovering, so Gary started at quarterback. UDM could do nothing; Gary could do nothing wrong. He completed 18 of 25 passes, three for touchdowns. Watkins gained 113 yards rushing and scored another touchdown. State 38, UDM 0.

"All of a sudden, I've got a good feeling about this year," Joe says. "Hate to say it, but maybe Blaha getting hurt was the best thing that could have happened. Schoyer looks like a leader. You can see it from his posture. He's got such confidence."

"That confidence, it's infectious," Sonny says. "If it rubs off on the rest of the offense, you never know what could happen. And that Watkins! Oh, boy, when he's on, he's on."

"Has Schoyer asked you for a date yet?" Joe asks me. He's driving; I'm next to him in the passenger seat, with Sonny in back. Sonny guffaws. I can feel my face getting hot.

"You've gotten acquainted with him, a little, though, haven't you?" Joe asks. "You two would be a natural."

"Oh, please," I say. "He's got the whole campus to choose from. Plus, he'd have to be crazy to date the A.D.'s daughter, don't you think?"

"It would make sense," Sonny says. "But no young man would date you for political reasons." He laughs again.

§

I'm trying to be a good Sister, at Iota, so I almost burned myself out, the first week of October. Homecoming happens in the middle of the month. Meantime, Iota is involved in various Greek-led activities: the blood drive, the United Way foot-race, the co-ed flag football playoffs. I'm glad the Rivercats were on the road yesterday, against Michigan, and KSCR didn't want to buy me a plane ticket. I'd have gone, but it would have cost me a day I couldn't have afforded. I heard the game on the radio.

Blaha's ankle sprain is a bad one. He's off crutches now, but still couldn't play yesterday. Gary played the whole game, and he rattled off three touchdown passes in the first half before the Wolverines could get unstuck. We were ahead 21-14 at halftime. Early in the third quarter, Charles Watkins broke loose and ran 60 yards for another score. Michigan scored twice more to tie it up—but with a minute to go, Michigan fumbled on its own 25-yard line. Gary ran a couple of plays; then Abúi kicked a field goal at the final gun. Rivercats 31, Wolverines 28.

I know Gary lives in the athletic dorm—footballers have to, at least in their freshman and sophomore years—and I suppose he got back from Michigan last night. He probably slept late, so I'm going to phone over there in the afternoon to see if I can get him to do a tape-for-broadcast interview for my radio show tomorrow morning. That's against my usual rule—to avoid talking about the Rivercats—but it's an excuse. Maybe I can casually lead him into other subjects. Like, does he have a steady girl-friend?

"I'm at Iota Delta Theta, pretty near you, so it would be no trouble for me to come over," I tell him over the phone.

"You'd get better sound quality if we talked at the studio," he says. This surprises me: why would he be the one to think of that? "That would be silly, though, if it's for a four-minute show. Listen, I could drive over to Iota and pick you up; we could go for coffee someplace and talk for a while; then you'd have enough so that there's sure to be something you could use."

Now I'm astonished. I wasn't expecting that.

"Would now be okay? I could be there in ten minutes."

I want to run around the house telling all my sisters whom I'm about to spend part of the afternoon with, but I'm thinking it might be much more splendid to let them find out. I put on a sweater, grab my cassette recorder, and run downstairs to wait for Gary on Iota's front lawn. Someone is sure to see me getting into a black Camaro. Even if they don't know whose it is, they'll be sure to remark on it.

It's a grey day, cold for so early in October, so Gary doesn't have the top down. I let myself into the car, and before I say anything, Gary says, "Let's pop over to Hamburgher's. They've got the best pie and ice cream in town. But we can sit in the car before we go in, and do the taping there, so there won't be any background noise."

Hamburgher's Cafe is right nearby, downtown, on Iowa Boulevard. That's where we're parked. I start the machine.

"So, you'll be the starting quarterback, this coming Saturday. Have you and Coach Timmerman got your game plan ready?"

"You always go in with a pel-*lan*, but you forget it as soon as you get hit. Anyway, with any luck, Ted will be good to go on Saturday. I just borrowed his job for a couple of games. If he's ready to pel-*lay*, I'm sure he'll start, and I'll be rooting for him."

I tell myself, that's the quote I'm going to use tomorrow. That "L" is so sexy.

"Yeah, I had a good day," he says. "But I had such a good day because the whole team did—and because Coach Timmerman had us ready to go. He's a real good guy to work with."

Now we're in Hamburgher's, where we've had coffee and pie (Gary had peach; I had blueberry) with ice cream. We've been talking for nearly two hours, almost entirely about football. I've got studying to do, and my cello to practice, but too bad. I'm feeling so easy with Gary. So far, we've hardly talked about anything but football, but it's what we're both comfortable with. It's like we can't stop the conversation.

"Coach sends the plays in," Gary says. "He says he wants me and Ted to both get to where we can mostly call our own games, but that'll probably be next year."

"My father told me it takes a lot of experience for a QB to call his own games," I say. "There were only a couple of years, when he was coach, that he had someone he trusted to do it. Both times, we went to the Rose Bowl. One of them was your brother, in '63."

"We're not going to the Rose Bowl this year. But we're good. We're real good. Next year I think we could do it. Say, want to drive around for a few minutes? It's a great day for it."

The sky is gloomy; it's getting late in the afternoon—but the fall colors are just hitting their peak. Gary is driving west on Highway 6, and now we're starting to talk about other things. I'm telling Gary about my music, and how I'm writing a few articles for the *Statesman*, this year.

"I feel guilty," I tell Gary. "I've got too much going on. I don't have the time to give all my interests the attention they deserve—but I would feel just as guilty if I gave up one thing, to focus on another. I should be able to handle everything."

Gary has such a warm laugh: just a soft little chuckle. It's adorable.

"Athletes have it easy, in a way," he says. "We're not expected to do much in the classroom. If we do, it's unusual. If we do the minimum, if we just show up most of the time, and pass, we're okay. Gosh, come to think of it, I don't think I've ever heard any teammate talk about classes. It doesn't come up."

We're traveling along a flat stretch of Highway 6 where there are fewer trees: mainly pasture, and silos. Those silos always comfort me for some reason, whenever I'm driving or riding along a country road. They make me feel safe and secure—maybe because they have food in them, so they suggest prosperity—but they also make me feel wistful, somehow.

"No, wait," Gary says, and I snap out of my little reverie. "I do remember a story. You know Tragakis? The DT? He signed up this fall for an art class, clay modeling. The instructor told him he wouldn't even have to do any work. His job would be to stand at the classroom door, and hand out clay to the students as they went in. He wouldn't even have to go into the classroom."

"Really? I mean, sure, I've heard rumors that that sort of thing goes on, but you mean he didn't even have to attend the class?"

"Well, but it gets better. The way Tragakis tells it, there's this really pretty girl who comes in last, with nothing but a bathrobe on. She won't take any clay. So, the second time she does this,

Tragakis decides to go into the classroom and see what's going on—and what does he see but this young lady up at the front of the classroom, wearing not a darn thing, with the rest of the class making clay models of her. You can bet Tragakis was right there, working with the clay, every day after that."

"I'm sure."

"He's crazy. He's actually one of the brighter guys on the team, but he's crazy. Loves a party. Which, no problem as long as he does his job. I'm probably telling you too much."

I can't make myself laugh, but I smile a little.

"Don't worry, I'm not going to report back to my father. And I'm not going to ask what the partying consists of."

"Nah, he's okay. I mean, he doesn't go overboard. Say, I don't know if you'll believe this, but I've got studying to do. I know you must have some. We better head on back."

We're quiet for a few seconds, then Gary asks me, "What's your plan for Homecoming Week? What's your house up to?"

Judas, Murphy, and Jethro, is he going to invite me to do something? I tell him all the activities that Iota is involved in, and then there's the Homecoming parade and bonfire on Friday night, the game on Saturday afternoon, and the dance that night, and I'm thinking, hoping, that he might be up for the dance…

"You know, it's ironic," Gary says, "but the football team doesn't get to do any of that Homecoming stuff. We all have to get to bed early on Friday night; then we're usually too sore after the game to do anything except recuperate for the next 24 hours. You're lucky: I won't get to have a real Homecoming till I'm one of the alumni coming home."

Well, that kills that.

HOMECOMING

Ted Blaha started today, against Northwestern, but he didn't look sure of himself. Gary took over in the second quarter. He passed for a touchdown; we were tied, 7-7, at halftime.

It's the second half; Ted and Gary are taking turns at quarterback on each possession. There's no question which of them looks better. Gary passes for a touchdown; Northwestern kicks a field goal; State is ahead, 14-10, at the end of the third quarter.

"Schoyer seems to be faster and more agile," I say, over the air. "Blaha still seems to be favoring his ankle. So far, both quarterbacks are passing accurately, but Schoyer has been gaining more yardage from his passes."

"Teresa, if you were the coach, which quarterback would you go with in this final quarter?" Joe asks. He smiles sidelong at me, and winks, the so-and-so.

"If Coach Timmerman keeps on rotating the two of them, I'm sure he knows what he's doing," I say. "It might depend on the situation. Blaha has experience, and he's steady. Schoyer might be more likely to deliver the big play."

Gary plays most of the final quarter, and passes for another touchdown. Northwestern can only manage another field goal. The final score is State 21, Northwestern 13. The Rivercats are 3-2, halfway through the season: the first time they've been over .500, at this point, since Feldy was coach.

"The stands are still full; nobody has left," I say into the mike, with the clock ticking down. "It's been a long time since we've heard cheering like this."

"Not since your dad was coach, I'll bet," says Joe. "There seems to be a real sense of optimism, both in the stands and on the sidelines, as Schoyer falls on the ball. That'll be the last play of the game; the gun sounds; the two coaches are meeting at midfield to congratulate each other..."

It's about 1:00 in the morning, and I'm walking back to Iota house from the Homecoming Dance at the Memorial Union, with my roommate, Janet, and two other sisters: Lefty McAloon and Tina Ferguson. All my sisters were at the dance; it was expected of us. The other attendees were almost all Greeks, too. I gather that the Homecoming Dance used to be a fairly high-toned event, with the men wearing suits or sport jackets and the ladies in party dresses, but the formality has pretty much disappeared. Almost half the guys were wearing jeans. This kind of party is considered hopelessly square, now—or it would be, if the term "square" weren't so square.

I danced a lot. I didn't see any football players in the crowd. I didn't know any of the guys I danced with. I just seemed to attract them—almost non-stop for about four hours—which astonished the daylights out of me. I sat out all the slow numbers, talking with whichever guy I had been dancing with. Several of these guys already knew my name. Two of them said they enjoyed hearing me on the radio. Any one of them would have been someone I wouldn't have minded getting to know.

The walk back to Iota means a long climb up a steep hill in high heels. I'm guessing that each of my sisters would rather take her shoes off and ruin a good pair of nylons—I know I would—but nobody wants to be the first.

"Well, Brenda, you sure were busy," Lefty says. "You were the belle of the ball!"

Janet and Tina both laugh, then they start whistling that waltz by Leroy Anderson, "Doo-doot, da-doo-doot, da-doo-doo-doo-doo-doo-doo." I can feel myself blushing, but I start whistling a tune in counterpoint till we all get the giggles and stop.

"It was just a fluke. It must have been. Maybe I stood out because I'm tall, and they had to ask someone to dance."

"Yeah, sure," Lefty says. "Julie Newmar. That's what we're going to have to call you now, instead of Brenda Starr."

"Yeah, that's who you look like," Tina says. "With those mile-long legs of yours. All you need is a Catwoman costume."

§

According to rumor, while I was at that dance, Gary was recuperating from the game a little too publicly. In a bar, where people saw him. The drinking age in Iowa is 21, but the State City area has plenty of bars that aren't particular about whom they serve, so long as they behave. I gather that he didn't end up in any kind of a sticky situation, but you know how it goes.

Someone sees you in a bar, they report that you're drinking too much. If they actually see you ingesting alcohol, the story will go that you were getting blotto. If you're seen acting exuberant, forget it: you were passed out, puking, exposing yourself, and grabbing waitresses—all at the same time—and half the town saw it.

The story of Gary having been seen drinking in a bar (which was true) and getting completely out of control (almost certainly not true) didn't get into the papers. It got around, though. I heard about it on Monday, in the newsroom of the *Statesman*. A reporter from the *Examiner* asked Coach Timmerman about it at his press conference that day, and Timmerman said, "It's not surprising that those rumors will start, but I've got a lot more important things to do than to chase down gossip. Gary looked good on Saturday; he did everything I asked of him; I'm going to trust him to behave himself off the field. I believe that's what he's doing."

He also revealed that Gary will start on Saturday, when the Rivercats go up to East Lansing to play Michigan State.

"He's earned it. Ted looked good on Saturday too, but his ankle is still doubtful, and I want to be sure he's completely healed before I start him again."

I want so badly to call Gary to say hello and get his side of the story—I'm pretty sure he wasn't doing anything too terrible except maybe drinking illegally, or maybe he wasn't drinking at all—but I know better than to contact him before he contacts me. I don't even know if he's involved with anyone, and I have to assume he is. How could he not be? I'm on the phone with Feldy now, to get his opinion of how the team is shaping up— just because I want an excuse to talk football, then bring the conversation around to Gary, and maybe get Feldy's opinion of him. I'm so cagey and clever. I can't let Feldy know I have any ulterior motive, though. I could, but he'd tease me half to death and I'd never hear the last of it.

Feldy and I talk about the game; I tell him how much fun the dance was; at last we get around to Gary. Unfortunately, when Feldy brings him up, it's to talk about those rumors.

"If Timmerman is smart, he'll nip this in the bud," Feldy is telling me. "You don't have to do any serious detective work to find out if it's true he was drinking in a bar. People saw it. It doesn't matter whether or not he was drunk. He was breaking the law and making the team look bad. Was me, I'd crack down on him good and hard. Suspend him for a week, make it plain that he's in the dog house for the rest of the year, tell him he's still got two years to pull himself together and make something of himself—and tell him to chalk this year up to experience."

"Maybe you're right, theoretically," I say, "but we haven't got a third quarterback. Nobody Timmerman could trust to play for any length of time, if Blaha gets racked up again—and Blaha, you saw him on Saturday. He's not a winning quarterback, not this year. Gary could be, eventually."

I hear a chuckle on Feldy's end—and I realize that I said "Gary," not "Schoyer." But Feldy doesn't say anything about it before we hang up.

§

Okay, so the Rivercats did not play well at Michigan State. The Spartans were favored, but most of us figured that the Cats would at least make a fight of it. The final score was 35-10.

I heard it on the radio. Gary didn't utterly disgrace himself, but his overall performance stank. On our first possession, he fumbled a handoff deep in our own territory, which set up a Michigan State touchdown. He completed fewer than half his passes—not entirely his fault, since (according to Sonny Bell, on the air) the Spartans' coverage was brilliant. And, in the third quarter he threw an interception that set up another touchdown, which made the score 28-3 and put the game out of reach. Blaha took over for most of the fourth quarter, and drove the team downfield for a "courtesy touchdown" in the closing minutes, playing against the Spartan bench.

I know, *know*, that a girl should not phone a guy, not *ever*. I did it the other day, but that was for business. If Gary is interested, he'll call. But I forced myself away from the phone on Sunday, Monday, and most of today, till evening, and I could hardly touch my dinner for thinking of Gary—so I'm weak.

"I just called to see how you're doing. I wanted to tell you not to get discouraged. It was just one game. They had the better team. Are you feeling okay?"

He sounds happy to hear from me. We go over the game for a few minutes.

"You're not recording this, are you? I would hear a beep if you were. At least that's what the phone company tells people."

"No, I'm not calling as a reporter," I tell him. "Just as a friend. Wanted to make sure you were okay. I know you'll get 'em on Saturday."

Stupid, stupid. Why am I so stupid?

I thought about calling Gary again, later in the week, to see if he needed cheering up, when Coach Timmerman told the press that Blaha's ankle was good to go and that he would start against Indiana. I wanted to call. But I prayed to St. Teresa to grant me the strength not to. She came through for me.

I was in the broadcast booth as usual, on Saturday, but there wasn't much excitement to report. It was a rainy, mucky day. Blaha played almost the whole game. Neither team had much luck moving the ball. The Rivercats led, most of the way, but it was low-scoring. With five minutes left, the Rivercats were up 14-10, but they had to punt one last time—and our defense couldn't hold. I could see they were tired. Indiana started at its own 35, and slowly drove the ball downfield. I felt this awful sense of inevitability, all the time they were doing it. With less than 30 seconds on the clock, their left guard and tackle opened a huge hole. Their tailback ran it in from the eight-yard line; the final score was Indiana 17, State 14.

The headline in the sports section in Monday's *Register*:

RIVERCATS INVOLVED IN POST-GAME CAR CRASH

Davis Briefly Held; He, Schoyer Unhurt

Daniel Davis, a tight end for the State University Rivercats, was taken into custody by State City Police at approximately 2:00 on Sunday morning, following a two-car accident on U.S. Highway 6. No injuries were reported, but Davis, who was driving one of the vehicles, was briefly held at the State City police station. He was later released without charge. Gary Schoyer, the Rivercats' second-string quarterback, was a passenger in the vehicle...

Similar headlines and stories appeared in the *Statesman*, that morning, and in the *Gazette* and the *Examiner*, in the afternoon.

I can read between the lines as well as anyone. I inferred that Davis was hammered, but got a break because he's an athlete, so the cops let him go once he'd sobered up. I stopped by the *Statesman*'s newsroom that morning, where I was told that it was lucky that nobody had been killed. It was only a two-car crash, but it barely missed being a multi-vehicle pileup involving several other football players, who had been in cars following the one Gary and Dan Davis had been in. Everyone had been drinking, although that was never proven.

I decided it was time for me to take a hand in this nonsense. I walked over to the athletic dorm this afternoon—with a note, in case Gary wasn't in. He wasn't, so I left the note with another footballer—who said, "Hey, you're Feldy's Girl!" which made me pretty certain that he would make sure Gary got it. It also made me say to myself, "You're darn right I'm Feldy's Girl."

> Dear Gary,
> Please call me when you get this. Let's go for a walk this evening if you have time. I have an idea or two that I'd like to bounce off you, just to see whether I know what I'm talking about.
> Teresa.

Gary phoned me back, later in the afternoon, and said he would stop by Iota Delta Theta at around 7:00.

It's a nice night, not too cold. Gary is wearing a black leather jacket and blue jeans, and he seems pretty upbeat, like he doesn't have a worry of any kind. Like he doesn't know of any car crash.

We're walking away from Sorority Row, away from the campus, toward a residential area: near where the Shapens live.

This is State City's north side. The houses are old wood-frames, from the turn of the century or older, and big: some have families living in them, and some are broken up into student apartments. Not many other people are on the streets; we almost have the neighborhood to ourselves. I'm telling Gary about Mona and Mike and some of the people I've met through them. I tell him that Mona injured her hand (but I don't tell him how) so that she might never play the cello again.

"You've got all kinds of friends, haven't you?" Gary says. "Yeah, athletes all live in fear of that day when we'll get the injury that'll finish us. A knee, or something. But if it happens, at least we knew it could. Must be harder for your friend. I guess playing an instrument isn't usually dangerous."

"But let's talk about you," I say. "Too bad you didn't get to play more on Saturday. It was an unlucky day all around. We should have won; it looked like we just ran out of steam before they did."

"I'd have won that game."

Gary sounds bitter, all of a sudden.

"What would you have done differently?"

"I'd have passed more, and I'd have run the quarterback option if Coach had let me. Watkins is a good runner, but with field conditions the way they were, Ted wasn't executing his handoffs fast enough, and Watkins wasn't able to take advantage whenever a hole opened up. I'd have thrown a lot of quick, short passes, play-action passes.

"Look, I'm not knocking Ted. He wasn't calling the pel-lays. But if I'd been in there, I'd have talked with Coach about changing things up a little. See, Ted's not bad, he's not dumb, but he's not assertive enough."

"It must be frustrating," I say. "You're just going to have to bear down in practice and hope Timmerman notices how hard you're working."

"I feel like I'm not in charge of my own destiny. I understand Coach feels like he ought to play Ted, because he's earned it, and what am I supposed to do? Go to Coach and say, 'Listen, I'm better; can't you see that?'"

"No, you can't say that. I'm betting you'll have more playing time on Saturday, though. You need to work extra hard this week, so that when you do get the call, you're ready."

I hesitate; I work up my courage.

"That means not putting yourself in situations where people can spread rumors about you," I say.

Finally, I get to it. I wasn't meaning to bring it up quite like that, but it's out of my mouth now. I can't see the expression on Gary's face—I don't have the nerve to look him right in the eye—but I sense it.

"Oh, God, it's all over town, isn't it? I was *not* drunk. I had two beers."

I'm not sure I believe that.

"I was half asleep, in the back seat."

Okay, now I don't believe "two beers" at all. He hardly played, in that game, and two beers don't put you to sleep.

"I didn't even know what was going on, till all of a sudden I get this jolt like I'm being gang-tackled. For a second I actually did imagine that I was on the football field; then I woke up enough to realize what the situation was, and I told myself, 'Get out of the car before it explodes,' so I opened the rear door and kind of half-crawled and half-rolled onto the asphalt, then the next thing I know I'm up on my feet and I run over to the median, you know, that grassy area in the middle of Highway 6. Thank God, nothing did blow up.

"I'm guessing what happened is that Dan tried to change lanes and just plain didn't see the car in the lane next to him. He had to crawl out of the passenger side of the front seat, because the driver's side was wedged up against that other car."

"Was he drunk?"

Why am I asking that? I know what Gary will say.

"No. Unless he was drinking way more than I saw him drink, and that was hardly any. So the cops showed up and they took Dan off in the patrol car. Then a paddy wagon came to take me and the people in that other car back to town. Then they let Dan go later when they found out he wasn't drunk."

"The papers said you were 'unavailable for comment.' Did they try to talk to you?"

"A couple of reporters left messages at the dorm. I didn't call them back."

"What did the coach say about it?"

"Dan and I told him at the team meeting this morning, that we hadn't been drinking. And we hadn't. Not enough to amount to *drinking*-drinking. And he said he believed us but then he gave us this business about, 'From now on, you've got to be above suspicion. Don't even put yourself in any situations where there can be any question about your conduct.' Which I thought was unfair since we hadn't done anything but have an accident. But I knew better than to open my trap."

We keep walking without saying anything, for a few seconds, while I work up a little extra nerve.

"I believe you too, but it doesn't matter," I say. "You're not even supposed to have one. Not even half a one. Not where anyone can see you, and certainly not during the season."

Another little silence, and I wonder if Gary is mad at me.

"Do you want to play in the NFL after you graduate?"

I'm asking because I'm curious, not because I'm throwing out some kind of challenge.

"Doesn't everybody?"

"You know, when my father was coach here, he used to tell the players that their first commitment in life, always, was to God. He said as long as they weren't married with families, their next most important commitment was to their studies, to getting their education. And the only thing that should matter for them, after that, was the Rivercats. I wondered sometimes whether he believed they should come in that order. But he was right. God, your studies, and football. Nothing else, right now."

I can see that Gary is smiling, a tiny bit.

"Then what am I doing walking with you, right now?"

"This is about football. I'm here walking with you because of football. I want the Cats to win, and a lot of that is going to have to do with you, for this year and two more years. And at least for the rest of this season, I'm going to keep my eye on you. I'm going to make sure you help the team as much as you can."

"Whoa. What is that going to consist of?"

"Just remember that I'm on your shoulder. I'm your good angel—and now that I've told you I am, you're going to remember it. You've got lots of bad angels around you. Maybe they're not bad guys, but they're not thinking about whether they're doing you any good. If you spend your time with them, you're ignoring those three things you've got to be committed to. If you get your name in the papers for anything other than football, that's a distraction. Even a rumor is a distraction."

"Yes, ma'am."

I'm afraid I've shot my bolt: run out of things to say without having thought of the *right* thing. Gary clears his throat.

"I've got a girl I see, you know. A steady girl."

"I figured you did."

I'm trying to be nonchalant, but let's face it: I'm pretty chalant. It's true that I figured he had one, but I've been hoping he *didn't*—even though there's no possibility of that, none. He'll have at least one girlfriend, if not a whole harem. So, I'm telling myself that this isn't about trying to get something going with Gary. It's about helping the team.

Then I realize that that is such ridiculous B.S. I almost laugh out loud at myself for even pretending to kid myself that way. Then I play the Glad Game. I tell myself I'm glad that I'm not Gary's girlfriend because I can speak more frankly to him, and give him better advice than I could if I were concerned about keeping him happy.

"So, tell me about her." I don't want to know, but I have to ask, to pretend I'm not fazed.

"Well, we've gone together since high school. You might know her. She's a Tri-Delt. Robin Hunsaker."

"I might know her if I saw her. Are you two serious?"

"It's tough. You know, there's this emotional thing between us, because we've been a couple for so long. We were able to spend plenty of time together last year because freshman football wasn't that big of a deal and we were taking a lot of the same classes, but this year—gosh, varsity football is a whole different story. It takes up so much of your time and energy; plus, I'm actually trying to do well in my classes. We don't have as much time for each other as we used to, and… and maybe we both think we're still too young to tie each other down; I don't know."

"Things might change when the season's over, you think?"

"Anything's possible. You must have guys all over you."

"I'm way too busy to date."

That's true, but I say it because I don't want to say anything disparaging of myself—such as admitting that I hardly ever get asked—and then I remind myself that I did seem to impress a lot of guys at that Homecoming dance.

"I'm spending more time…" I'm about to say, "with you, right now, than I can afford," but instead I say, "on my class work and my music than I ever thought I would have to. It cuts my fun time down to nothing at all. And I had better get back; it's pretty late."

"Thanks for calling me," says Gary. We've gone nearly a mile from the sorority house; now we turn right, walk a block, turn right again, and head west. "It was nice of you to try to cheer me up. I guess you're right. I just need to work harder, and hope Coach notices."

"And don't get noticed for anything else."

I can sense that Gary is finally getting tired of being badgered.

"You're really dancing on my nose tonight," he says.

"I'm just giving you a hard time," I say. "I know you haven't done anything wrong, not really."

I don't know it, not really. I suspect the worst. I bet Gary has been partying too much. I don't know that it's interfering with his performance in practices and games, but it might be. Anyway, mission accomplished: Gary knows I have my eye on him—and he might even keep that in mind.

At the front door of Iota, I say, "Thanks for the walk, Gary," and I give him a soft punch on the biceps. "Get 'em Saturday."

§

He did, sort of. The Cats were in Champaign, Saturday, against Illinois, and we figured to win, since Illinois is having a miserable season. Blaha started, but when it became clear that it would be a blowout—which happened before the first quarter was over—

Timmerman sent Gary in. The two quarterbacks saw pretty equal playing time, and we won, 45-7. Blaha did well. He completed seven out of 13 passes and threw for a touchdown. But Gary completed nine of 12 attempts, two for touchdowns.

I had planned not to contact Gary at all, for the next week. I've planted the "good angel" idea in his head, and now I don't want to be pushy. But on Sunday, when Mass had ended and we were walking out, there was Gary in one of the back pews. He saw me; he smiled and winked. Then he called, that afternoon.

"Want to meet up for coffee tomorrow? We can talk about the game, and, y'know, whatever."

It's Monday; we're sitting in the cafeteria in the basement of Radcliffe Hall. This is a public cafeteria, like at the Coffin Corner, but not heavily populated in mid-afternoon, so we have privacy and I don't think anybody is noticing us. Gary gives me a run-down of the Illinois game.

"So, two more to play," he says. "We've got no more than a fighting chance against Minnesota, and I'd like to pretend we have any chance at all to beat Ohio State, but we have no business on the same field with those guys. Nothing against Ted, I like him personally, but I think I know how to beat Minnesota and I'm not sure he can do it. Only, I can't just come out and tell Coach that. It's frustrating."

"I'm sure your performance got noticed. You're not going to be warming the bench."

"I know I shouldn't, but I'm already thinking about next year. It's gonna be me and Ted again, and he'll be a senior; it won't look right if I'm the regular QB and he plays behind me. But he's never gonna play in the NFL. He doesn't have it. I'm starting to wonder if maybe I should transfer to another school next year."

I give Gary a "pffft."

"You're getting more playing time than any other sophomore QB in the country. If you work hard and keep playing well, they won't be able to keep you off the field. You're not the one who needs to worry about how much you'll play. Just earn it."

WHAT A GAME

Judas, Murphy, and Jethro, what a game.

Minnesota was the last home game of the season, and my last game in the broadcast booth till 1970. The Gophers have a good team this year, for a change: just not quite good enough to beat out Ohio State for the Big Ten championship. They came into State City with a 6-2 record, compared to our 4-4; Las Vegas made the Gophers 15-point favorites. Timmerman started out by alternating Gary and Blaha on each possession, but toward the end of the first quarter Blaha got totaled by two Minnesota tacklers, just as he released a pass. The ball got intercepted and run back for a touchdown; Blaha got helped off the field.

Gary played the rest of the half. He drove the Cats downfield for a touchdown; Minnesota added another; we got close enough in the final seconds of the half for Abúi to kick a field goal. At halftime, we were down 14-10—but still in contention, and our offense had seemed to gel in that second quarter. Gary looked confident and he seemed to be on top of things.

The second half was nuts. State's defense held for most of the third quarter, while Gary passed for two touchdowns—and just like that, we were up by ten. The Gophers put together a drive and scored a touchdown at the end of the quarter, but still the score was State 24, Minnesota 21, with only 15:00 to play.

Gary had been hitting his receivers, but he threw two incompletions on State's next possession. The Rivercats had to punt. Minnesota scored another touchdown, six plays later.

Looking down at the sidelines from the broadcast booth, I could see Blaha talking with Coach Timmerman. I couldn't begin to know what the conversation was, but I fantasized that Blaha was pleading his case to get back onto the field. Gary had just gotten done looking bad, in that previous possession.

I was tempted to speculate on this, over the air, but I decided that wouldn't be smart. I was surprised at how apprehensive I felt about the possibility of Blaha being sent back in. I wanted Gary to stay in there and show that he knew how to win, as he had boasted to me a few days before—plus, I knew in my gut that we wouldn't get the lead back, if Blaha were under center.

I felt relief like I can't describe, seeing Gary run onto the field after Minnesota's kickoff. He started at the 20, and slowly led the team into Gopher territory, mostly with play-action passes and a couple of key running plays by Watkins. With first and ten on the Minnesota 40, he sent his wide receivers long, then flipped a sideline pass to the tight end, Dan Davis, who ran it clear down to the Minnesota 12. Then Watkins ran a sweep for six yards.

The next play, I believe—with 20-20 hindsight—might have been the key play of the afternoon, and it showed how smart Gary is, if what I think happened, happened. Timmerman had sent a substitute guard into the huddle—presumably with a play to pass along to Gary. They came out of the huddle and lined up with three receivers on the strong side. Obviously, they were all going to head for the end zone, and Gary would throw to whichever of them was open. But I'm pretty sure that when Gary got to the line of scrimmage, he saw that the Gophers were lined up in anticipation of that kind of play. They would have been sure to stop it.

An "audible" is when the quarterback changes the play at the line of scrimmage, as he shouts the signals, by rattling off a series of numbers that are code for a play other than the one that had been called in the huddle. In this case, the numbers that Gary shouted amounted to, "I'm changing the play. We're running Watkins on a student body left. You linemen, your blocking assignments have changed. You two guards, you've got to pull, and clear a path for him."

What I am pretty certain Gary did *not* shout, among those coded signals, was that he didn't intend to hand the ball off to

Watkins. Instead, Gary planned to fake the handoff to Watkins—then keep the ball and run it on the other side of the field.

An audible is always risky. The quarterback has to hope that every man on the team hears and understands what he's saying to them when he shouts, for instance, "Three! Brown! Forty-Seven!" This play—in which I am 99.99 percent sure Gary was fooling not just the other team, but his own teammates—is a "fake them out of their jockstraps" play that can't work against a slow defense that isn't on its toes. It can only work against a quick, intelligent, well-coached defense like Minnesota's. They'll see the guards pulling and sweeping left (to the defenders' right), and they'll realize that the play isn't a pass after all. They'll see Watkins following his blockers, so they'll key on him—and miss the actual ballcarrier: Gary, clear over on the other side of the field, all by himself.

If they're too slow to react to our guards pulling, though—if they don't take the fake—Gary gets creamed.

The play worked perfectly. Watkins decoyed—and again, I'm dead sure that he had no idea that he was just a decoy, till he didn't get the ball in his belly. No, I can't be absolutely sure. I couldn't see the looks on the players' faces. I've just seen a lot of football; I can read situations. The whole Gopher defense went in Watkins' direction; Gary trotted into the end zone with not a brass knuckle laid on him. Abúi kicked the point-after; the Rivercats led again, 31-28, with 6:30 left on the clock.

Sonny said, over the air, "Certainly the most gripping game the Rivercats have been involved in this year. Teresa, your friend Schoyer is tearing the place up!"

"That drive showed how far the whole team has come this year," I said into my mike. I barely registered the "your friend," and thank God, there was too much going on for me to react to it. "The last three plays, especially—the sideline pass to Davis, the run by Watkins, and the scoring play—that showed a level of execution that we haven't seen all year."

"That scoring play was a brilliant call," said Joe. "It caught the Gophers completely unaware. Exceptionally smart move by Coach Timmerman."

Whoever made that call—and I'm convinced it was Gary—it didn't lock up the win. Minnesota had plenty of time to score, and they were trying to eat up the clock while they did it. Our defense looked pretty well exhausted.

Minnesota started deep in its own territory and took almost three minutes off the clock getting to midfield. Two plays later, on third and ten, they tried a pass that was calculated to get them a first down and no more—but our defense, and particularly the man covering that receiver, were so tired that when their receiver caught that pass, he had a clear field in front of him.

On the one hand, it was good for Minnesota that they scored the go-ahead touchdown. On the other hand, it was bad, for them, to have done it on a 50-yard pass play, leaving us just enough time to score again—if we had it in us to do it.

To make it worse for Minnesota, on the point-after attempt, Abiatha Turner broke through the line and blocked the kick. It was Minnesota 34, State 31. We could tie it up with a field goal.

Watkins took the kickoff and ran it up to the Rivercat 35, with not quite 3:00 left to play. It goes without saying that the stadium was as full as it had been at the opening kickoff. Most of the crowd was screaming, but some of them weren't daring to look; some of them were staring at the action with their mouths shut; some of them, probably, were praying. You're not supposed to pray for that sort of thing, but people are weak.

This was almost certainly going to be State's last possession. Our offense must have been nearly done for, but they were pumped; the Gophers' defense must have been not only tired, but frustrated by their inability to hold us.

Gary mostly threw short passes, toward the sidelines. That way, the receiver could step out of bounds and stop the clock, if that seemed like the thing to do. In four plays, the Cats were in Gopher territory. Three more plays, and we were inside the 30, but with only half a minute to play. That's within Abúi's range, but on such a windy day, a field goal attempt could have gone anywhere. In any case, what would we want with a tie?

On first and ten from the 28, the Cats lined up for a pass, but Gary gave the ball to the fullback, Tucker, on a draw play. Tucker is a substitute who doesn't get much time on the field; nobody was looking for him to carry the ball. He made it down to the 11-yard line before being shoved out of bounds.

On the next play, Gary sent three receivers into the end zone, then dumped off a safety-valve pass to Tucker, who once again hadn't been attracting anyone's attention.

"… and he's gonna score!" Joe hollered to the radio audience.

I had not heard a football crowd roar like that since Feldy was coaching. Not since 1963, our last Rose Bowl year.

"Tucker trots across the goal line almost before anyone noticed that he had the ball!" Joe shouted. "State 37, Minnesota 34; only nine seconds left on the clock here at Rivercat Stadium!"

Abúi kicked the point-after. The Gophers only had time for one play—an incomplete pass—before the clock ran out. State 38, Minnesota 34: the first time the Cats have won five games in a season since Feldy, with one game left on the schedule.

There was some confusion at the final gun, because some of the Rivercats seemed to want to carry Tucker off the field and some made for Gary, but they both shook their heads and pointed to Coach Timmerman, who was at midfield shaking hands with Murray Warmath. Timmerman got the carry-off. From the sound of the fans, it was a popular choice.

§

I wanted to call Gary, to congratulate him. I forced myself not to, on Sunday, and I didn't see him at Mass. I forced myself not to, again, on Monday, and on Monday night he called me.

He called me. No kidding. I was more relieved than thrilled, although I was both. Relieved, because I did not have to make myself obnoxious by phoning him up and reminding him that his good angel was watching him. He said he thought I might want to talk over the game since he knew I liked to be kept informed. I suspected that he wanted the chance to brag about his accomplishments to someone who knew about football. I'm trying, still, not to get my hopes up beyond that.

Anyway, we agreed to meet in the Radcliffe Hall cafeteria again, on Tuesday afternoon. I asked Gary if I would be causing trouble for him by spending time with him in public, but he said, "Robin's not interested in football. We talk about other stuff."

It was in the cafeteria where Gary confirmed to me that that fake sweep had been an audible, and that Watkins had thought he was going to get the ball. Gary said it had been his idea to dump the ball off to Tucker for the winning touchdown, too.

"Two of those receivers in the end zone were decoys," he said. "I wasn't watching them at all. Coach likes me to focus on one receiver, not look around to see who's open. So, on that play, I was only ever going to throw to Didrikson—except the coverage was all over him. I didn't have time to look for another receiver, but I knew exactly where Tucker would be, waiting for me to drop it off to him if I had to, so he could step out of bounds. Only he had a clear field in front of him, so he ran it in for the score, instead."

"You can use that against Ohio State," I said. Gary laughed.

"We'll need a lot more than that. I'm sure we'll do our best, but it might look like Christians versus Lions."

"Stay positive." I was a little stern.

"Anything can happen, but we have to be realistic. Ohio State hasn't come close to losing a game this year. They're number one in the nation; they're so much bigger than we are. Especially their down four. It's hard to imagine that Watkins is going to make any yardage at all."

Gary considered.

"But that's a thing," he said. "Watkins and I both have two years ahead of us, and he's still growing. He's gonna be a fantastic runner next year. Between me and him, we'll have a real good shot at the Rose Bowl."

"That's fine, but stay focused on Saturday," I said. "You can win it. Never say 'can't.' A lot of it is attitude, but you know that."

I knew as well as Gary did that we would have no chance at all—the line is the Buckeyes and 24 points, and we'll be playing in the Shoe—but, never say "can't."

§

I listened to Joe and Sonny reporting the Ohio State game on the radio with a few of my Iota sisters, who of course asked me if I'd seen more of Gary, lately, and I pretended I hadn't.

Gary started at quarterback, did his best, but got nowhere. The entire offense got nowhere. Our defense could not have been better, though: really strong, which was a big surprise considering how they performed against Minnesota.

The Buckeyes played a super-conservative, ball-controlling, clock-eating offense—they threw only eight passes in the first half, and scored one touchdown—and it was a dull, dull game. The third quarter was downright soporific. The Buckeyes added another field goal, to make it 10-0. Joe Barnett remarked that Gary didn't seem to be throwing with confidence.

"It seems like every time he puts the ball in the air, his objective is to avoid an interception, rather than to hit his receiver," Joe said.

Watkins, as Gary had predicted, wasn't picking up big yardage. He was quick, but his blockers couldn't create holes for him.

Blaha took over as quarterback in the fourth quarter, when it appeared that the game was out of reach. It might not have been anything to do with him—it didn't sound like he was playing above his usual level—but maybe the Buckeyes' defense was tiring. With about 6:00 to play, the Rivercats started moving the ball. On second and goal from the one-yard line, Blaha threw a rollout pass to the wide receiver, Didrikson. Seven seconds were left on the clock.

The Rivercats had to attempt an onside kick—then, if they recovered it, either throw a Hail Mary pass for the win, or kick a field goal for the tie. An onside kick rarely works, but in this case, Abúi laid it down perfectly, and the Rivercats recovered, on the Buckeye 48.

It would be a 65-yard field goal attempt, in all, for Abúi—a ridiculous distance, but the wind was at his back, and neither Gary nor Blaha would have any chance to complete a desperation pass when all eleven of Ohio State's defenders would be waiting for it. State lined up to try the field goal.

"A tremendous kick!" Joe shouted. "It might have the distance… it's almost straight… no. No, the wind pulled it just slightly wide to the left and it's not quite long enough, either. The gun has sounded; the final score: Buckeyes 10, Rivercats 7. But we have to believe that this game was Ohio State's toughest test of the year. Coach Timmerman looks smiling and happy, down there on the field, shaking hands with Woody Hayes. As for the players, it's clear from their body language that the Rivercats as a team are about as happy as it's possible to be following a loss."

I wasn't there, but when the team's charter flight touched down at Cedar Rapids Airport, 25 miles north of State City, late that night, a crowd of more than 100 fans was there to greet them. A record of 5-5 was way more than anyone had expected, considering what happened last year.

§

It's the Monday of Thanksgiving week, so I've got classes today and tomorrow; Wednesday is officially a day of classes but almost everybody cuts them. Gary and I are having lunch in the Radcliffe Hall cafeteria.

"I wasn't feeling as positive as everybody else," Gary says. "I had a sh… a crummy day. No getting around it. Ted was responsible for our one touchdown. Not the best way to end the season."

"You mustn't think that way," I tell him. "The whole offense couldn't do anything at all till that last possession, and Ohio State didn't care if we scored as long as we ran the clock down while we were doing it. If they had had to hold us, like if they'd been ahead 3-0 instead of 10-0, they could have. You had a great season. The whole team had a great season, considering, but especially you. Look, you're a sophomore and, yeah, you were officially the second-string QB, but you threw more passes all year than Ted, and I'm estimating you played about 60 percent of the time when we had the ball."

Gary looks startled.

"Yeah, I've been paying attention to the stats," I say. "You learn to do that if you grow up in a family like mine. You have nothing to complain about. Nothing to criticize yourself for, not really. This year was 'next year,' for you."

We're walking up the steps from the basement cafeteria to the street level, and Gary takes my hand. Nothing awkward about it, nothing tentative. I don't resist.

"Thanks," he says. "For the pep talk. And for being my good angel, the last few weeks. Maybe it really did help."

"Anything for the team."

I keep holding Gary's hand. I don't drop it till we're at the top of the stairs and ready to head out the main door.

"We don't want to be doing that, where people can see."

"I wouldn't have minded," Gary says.

Gary opens the door for me, and we pass outside.

§

Gary had told me, at some point during the season, that he had never had any conversation with Feldy, aside from shaking hands with him at team functions, which I thought was too bad, since if he wanted to make the most of his time here, it couldn't hurt to know the A.D. I knew Feldy would be glad to know Gary, too, since Gary could give him information on how the team was operating that he wouldn't get anywhere else—so over Thanksgiving break, I asked Feldy and Birdy if we could arrange to have him over for a meal. Birdy suggested that she could put a roast in the oven before Mass, a week from Sunday, and we could do that instead of our usual lunch at the Coffin Corner.

Sander and Duffy were even more excited by the prospect of meeting the quarterback than they had been for Coach Timmerman. So was Birdy. The plan was to find Gary some room in our Suburban, pick him up at the athletic dorm, take him to Mass, then back to our house.

I've been looking forward for more than a week to letting Gary see our house, and now he's here, sitting next to me at the dinner table, with Sander and Duffy on the other side of him, Win, Birdy, and Feldy at the other end of the table, and Birdy's roast beef and Yorkshire pudding in front of us. So far, ever since we walked out of Our Lady, we've been talking about nothing but the season, and Gary's role in it. Feldy seems especially interested in the offensive play-calling process. Gary tells him what I already know: Coach Timmerman sends in the plays, and Gary sometimes calls audibles at the line of scrimmage.

"Coach doesn't always call the right play," Gary says. "Usually he's okay, but every now and then he'll call a play and I wonder what he's thinking. If I come to the line and realize his play can't work, I'll try to call a time-out if I can, or I'll have to use an audible to call my own play. Like against Minnesota."

That gets Gary and Feldy going on that one play—that fake to Watkins in the Minnesota game—and Gary's touchdown.

"When I was coaching," Feldy says, "when your brother Paul was in his senior year, I wouldn't have to send in more than ten plays in a game. He was a smart young man. I wouldn't be surprised if you're calling your own game next year."

"I shouldn't count on starting next year. Ted's gonna be back, too. Plus, Coach gets upset with me calling those audibles. It's not like I do it a lot, but he thinks I'm second-guessing him, or questioning his authority somehow. Not that he minded when I did it against Minnesota. At least, he pretended it didn't bother him. But he thinks I'm trying to show him up. I'm not. He's got his good qualities as a coach; we get along; I just question his play-calling sometimes. I think he likes Ted because Ted does what he's told. Nothing against Ted. He's a good guy; we're friends. But he's an executioner. He follows orders. He doesn't think for himself on the field, doesn't make any waves."

"He seems competent, though, Blaha," said Feldy. "He had a lot of bad luck this year, all those injuries. Remains to be seen if he can come back from them—and whether he shows any improvement. He might look really good next year. But from what I've seen of the two of you, you seem to have more potential for improvement. Blaha may have reached his level."

Feldy pauses—maybe to let Gary think about that.

"So keep in shape over the winter. Then show up for spring practice as sharp as you know how to be. That young Watkins sure impressed me, too, this year. He'll be bigger and stronger—and he'll be both a running and a receiving threat, so the other teams won't be able to give your other receivers the coverage. It might be the same situation the Browns had a few years ago, when Jim Brown was still playing. The other teams had to concentrate on containing him—which made the Browns' passing game stronger."

"Watkins is terrific," Gary says. "So talented."

"What's he like off the field?" Feldy asks.

"He seems okay. If you've seen him around, you know how he dresses. That black suit, the narrow black tie, the stingy-brim. Like a cross between Jim Brown and a Black Muslim. Maybe he's cocky, but if I could run like that, I'd be cocky too. I don't know him all that well. The black guys and the white guys pretty much keep separate. Not because anybody's keeping us apart or anything; just that the black guys would rather stick together."

"I suppose that's natural," Feldy says, "but you have to wish it weren't. No false modesty here: I brought a lot more colored kids onto this campus than anybody ever did before, and I'm not only talking about the football players, either. When I started recruiting colored boys for the football team, other athletes followed—and when I became A.D., I made it clear to all the coaches that I expected them to go where the talent was, no matter what color or background.

"When other colored high school students—I mean other than athletes—started getting the word that State University was a good place for them, that they would be treated right, here, then they started coming in. We're getting more students from Chicago, St. Louis, even some of the southern cities, because of how our athletic department has gone after them. At least I have to think we had something to do with it. And I'm thinking there's less racial tension here, than on a lot of college campuses. I'm glad that maybe I can take a little of the credit."

Gary is nodding, looking serious.

"I realize there's only so much you can do," Feldy says, "but it might be a good idea, as a general thing, for the white athletes to reach out to the black guys more, make it clear to them that you're all teammates. I don't know, maybe you feel that you're already doing that."

"Yeah, that's a good idea. I get along fine with all the black guys, and I've never seen any racial stuff go on. But it can't hurt to be aware of it. Look for ways to reach out, like you said."

Now Gary is telling everyone about how I've been giving him little pep-talks between games, which is making me pretty embarrassed, but it would be worse if I tried to stop him.

"Teresa's real smart about football," Gary says. "She probably knows more than I do. Anyway, we'll have to find something else to talk about for the next couple months."

He winks at me, right there in front of everybody, and they all laugh. I'm sure my ears are bright red.

After we'd had dessert and sat around for a while, Feldy said he had some work to catch up on, then he handed me his car keys.

"Gary, you're welcome to stay as long as you like, but Terri can run you home whenever you're ready." Then Feldy gave me a wink, too, before he went off to his study.

Now I'm pulling Feldy's car up in front of the athletic dorm. Gary leans over and gives me a peck on the cheek. He wets his lips before he does it, so it's a real kiss, but just barely. I can't help giggling, which I know is childish, but I can't stop myself. Gary says, "See you," and gets out of the car.

I've officially been kissed by a guy. For the first time, at 19. I'd almost rather say it doesn't count. I'm pathetic. I'm also feeling all oogly inside, the way I've heard about girls feeling, at least I assume that what I'm feeling is what they're talking about, but it's so strange to me that I don't know what to think about it. It's almost like I'm searching in my mind for something that I ought to be feeling about it, but I have no idea what that could be.

I drive back home and hang out there for the rest of the afternoon; we watch a couple of NFL games and have some cold supper. (I'm strange. Roast beef is my very favorite dish but I prefer it when it's cold, especially if it's nice and rare.) Now it's dark, and Feldy is driving me back to Iota.

"Gary seems like a bright young man. Level-headed. It's too early to tell how good he's going to be, but he seems to have the mental makeup. If he stays healthy, he might end up playing on Sundays. Are you seeing much of him?"

"I don't have time to. We've gotten to be sort of friends—and I told him during the season that I was going to keep an eye on him. So, you know, we meet up and talk every few days."

"Sounds harmless."

We're at a stop light; Feldy looks over at me and smiles kind of grimly. "But be careful of athletes, especially football players."

He doesn't say anything more till we pull up to the curb in front of Iota.

"The thing is, nowadays, kids aren't waiting for marriage like they used to," he says. "Okay, times change; I'm not going to give you the big lecture about that. But girls are handing it out, now, like candy. I know *you're* not. But a lot of girls are, and athletes get a lot of those handouts. I've been in this business a long time. I've seen it. Especially in the last few years, now that they've got the pill and all.

"The athletes expect it. You know, a lot of athletes are just animals. I have to admit it. Some of them act almost like they think girls owe it to them, because they're athletes. So be careful. This boy's probably fine. But keep in mind what I'm telling you. Some athletes—well, and especially the football players—have that sense of entitlement... There have been times, here at State U, when a girl has gotten herself into bad trouble on account of getting involved with athletes."

"Pregnant, you mean?"

"That, and...well, getting hurt. Usually the girl is willing enough when these things happen, so they've got nobody to blame but themselves—and no regrets, probably—but there have been cases... well, some of these guys, when they get some booze in them, they lose control of themselves."

"Like, *rape*?"

"It happens. Rarely. Sometimes it's a matter of the girl putting herself in a situation that ends up going farther than she had expected it to... but there have been instances where a young lady really did get taken advantage of."

"It never gets into the papers," I say. "Don't these guys get arrested, if they, you know, beat a girl up or worse?"

Feldy inclines his head, and gives me a pained little smirk.

"The girls don't report it. Nobody would believe them, if they did, and they don't want to be known as someone who had it happen to them. That's another complicated subject. I'm not trying to be alarmist. This boy seems fine. I'm talking about athletes in general. But, who knows? Maybe music students are just as bad. Anyway, good night. Have a great week."

I hardly ever kiss Feldy goodbye, but I feel like doing it this time, so I do.

WHAT TO THINK OF ALL THIS?

I didn't hear from Gary for two days. That dismayed me—once again, to be honest, I was having trouble eating—and I felt more relieved than I wanted to admit when I did hear from him.

Birdy called me on Monday to tell me that a dozen white roses had arrived, addressed to her, with a note in which Gary asked her to pass thanks along to the rest of the family, "so that's why I'm calling you." I didn't tell Birdy that I was all wound up because Gary hadn't called *me*. Then on Tuesday he did call, to ask if I would like to see *Putney Swope*, before he goes home to Clinton for Christmas.

This is the second date of my life and so far, it's turning out to be almost a carbon copy of my first one, with Andy Palinkas. Gary showed up at Iota to take me downtown, and I could tell that the three sisters who saw him arrive were pretty impressed.

He said, "Hope you don't mind walking. It's not that cold, and you know what it's like to try and find a parking place at night." Which reassured me, because I figure it indicated that Gary didn't have any intentions that I might not want to go along with. At least, for tonight, he doesn't.

The movie, then to Hamel's for a pizza—and now in the restaurant Gary wants to talk about the racial issues in the movie.

"That's something I don't like about Watkins," he says. "He's one of those guys who seems to be always looking for racism, even when it's not there at all. Like, any time Coach criticized him, all through the season, he got that look in his eye, and he'd do that inhale thing…"

Gary looks exasperated, and inhales through his teeth as though he's trying to keep himself from showing his temper.

"Like that. And a couple times, I'd hear him talking: talking to the other black players about how Coach doesn't understand them, how he's extra hard on them, like he's hoping they'll mess up so he'll have a reason not to play them. Stuff like that. But I don't know where he gets that idea. I've never seen Coach doing anything like that. No, he doesn't go out of his way for the black guys, but he shouldn't. He's fair to everybody. He isn't any less fair to the black guys than to the white guys.

"A couple months ago—must have been right after Homecoming—Coach did give us a talk about how we had an image to uphold, how he wanted us all to look respectable off the field. He said 'conservative.' I remember now. He said something like, 'Some of you guys are looking a little too casual in your everyday appearance, and some of you are looking too flamboyant. Just keep in mind that you're representing the team, and try to look neat and conservative at all times.'"

"And that was wrong, why?"

"Well, because, the only guys you could say dress flamboyantly are some of the black guys," said Gary. "You know, some of them wear the natural hair, and the bright colors, like Jimi Hendrix. And berets, some of them, like they were Black Panthers or something. It looks silly, if you want my opinion. Nothing wrong with looking silly; we all do it somehow. Well, and Watkins, he's different, you know, with the suit and tie all the time. You could almost say he's so conservative that it's a way of being flamboyant. Coach didn't mention Watkins, didn't even look at him when he was saying that, so I'm sure he didn't have Watkins in mind, but I could see Watkins was steaming."

Gary shrugs.

"Anyway," he says, "he'll be even better next year, plus he'll have better blocking, so maybe Coach ought to just be glad he's on the team. But what do I know?"

We're talking about the basketball and wrestling teams. Gary mentions that he'll be playing lacrosse in the spring. I tell him about my cello lessons, and about a chamber concert I'll be performing in right before Christmas break.

We walk back to Iota. We're at the front door, and just like that, Gary leans in and kisses me, on the lips this time. He doesn't have to bend down at all, because with heels I'm taller than he is (if we were both barefoot, I figure I might still be just a shade taller), and it's too quick for me to resist but I don't want to. I try to kiss him back although I'm not sure I'm doing it right: I've never kissed on the mouth before. It feels sort of the way I might have expected it to feel. He's not trying to stick his tongue in my mouth, which is what I'm told most guys try to do. It's not even a second later and he moves his face back and smiles; I notice that I'm smiling too; then I give him that little hand-on-the arm thing (how do I know to do that? it's like instinct) to be friendly while stopping him from doing anything more.

I say, "Thank you so much for the evening. Good night, and have a wonderful Christmas." Which I know sounds cold, and I want to say something else, but I can't think of anything more to say that wouldn't sound insincere—so I smile and wave to him, and go inside.

Lefty and Tina have been watching from the window: not being furtive about it. I gasp when I see them and they laugh.

Tina sings, "Brenda's got a boyfriend."

"Ooo, and *such* a boyfriend," Lefty says.

I'm trying to be a good sport. I just roll my eyes and go upstairs to my room.

§

I was at home—Iota being closed for the vacation—on the following Saturday when the 6:00 evening newscast reported that Toby Timmerman had been named Coach of the Year by the Associated Press. For the whole nation.

Feldy said, "Oh, my God," in a stage-whisper. Birdy was in the kitchen; my brothers were wherever; I was sitting where I usually sat, in the den; Feldy lurched forward in his chair, looking like he was part furious and part dumbfounded. "They have got to be kidding," he said. Then in a few seconds he started chuckling, almost like he was forcing himself.

"So, now you get Coach of the Year for exceeding expectations." he said. "That's the damndest thing I've ever heard."

I got one phone call from Gary, who was 60-some miles away in Clinton, between Christmas and New Year's. It was on an afternoon; it lasted between five and ten minutes; he sounded cheerful. He said he had just wanted to say hi, since it had been a few days. We talked about how our Christmases had gone, then I asked him flat-out, "So. Coach of the Year. Did he deserve it?"

"He's a good coach, all in all. Not perfect, I don't agree with him on everything. But he did a good job. As a team we did way better than I thought we would, going into the season. So, yeah, I can see why they gave it to him. Not that he did anything great, just that he surprised everybody."

First day of classes, post-break. Gary and I are having lunch in the Radcliffe Hall cafeteria. Gary is saying, "I'm kind of upset right now. Robin and I had a couple of pretty intense talks, when we were back in Clinton. It looks like we're not together anymore."

I raise an eyebrow. Not trying to look cool: it's a reflex.

"Well, she said I wasn't paying her enough attention, and she's right that we haven't had that much time for each other, because she's as busy as I am with this and that, but she wants to see other guys, only she put it on me. Made it look like I was the one breaking up with her. In her mind."

"Did you tell her you wanted to stay with her?"

"I… maybe… maybe I didn't, y'know, I didn't beg her to change her mind. If that's how she feels, that's how she feels. I told her I was sorry but if she wanted to see other guys there wasn't anything I could do to stop her."

"You could have said you didn't want her seeing other guys. That's all it would have taken. If it mattered to you. If you still wanted to be a couple."

"Except… maybe I do want her seeing other guys. I don't want her thinking that I'm all that. Because I'm not. I don't want her to feel like she has to stick with me because we've been together since high school. Maybe it would be better for her to get to know other guys. So that whenever she does get married, she'll have a better idea of what she wants for the long run."

"My, you're terribly adult."

"What, you think I don't mean it?"

"Oh, I think you mean it. I don't think it's all about what she wants, though. Maybe partly it is. But maybe partly you want to not be attached, either. Maybe what you said about her is what you're thinking about you."

§

It amazes me how little most college girls know about sex. I don't have the benefit of experience, but I know more than a lot of the girls at Iota.

At Visitation High we only heard rumors about sex. My female friends would giggle and speculate about it—and every year, one or two girls would have to leave school on account of pregnancy—but I observed, pretty early on, that I was far better informed of the actual facts than any of the girls I hung out with.

Now I'm noticing that most of my sorority sisters will make catty remarks, in private, about girls they suspect are less than pure—while, of course, they're all pretending to be guarding their own virginities. Maybe some of them are. By their own accounts, some of them are doing "everything but," and others are claiming that they don't allow anything more than a kiss.

My hunch? I'm pretty sure that not many of them reach my own standards of behavior. I'm not saying that to suggest that I'm better than they are in any way; just stating what I suspect.

When they're talking that kind of talk, if I'm obliged to be in its presence, I stay pretty quiet. Usually, when the conversation turns that way, I'll leave the room as discreetly as I can. I'm careful not to make a big thing of it. I don't dramatically flounce out because the subject matter offends my virgin ears, none of that, but I'm sure my sisters notice that I have to go study, or practice my cello, when certain matters come up for discussion.

Some of them don't know that you can't get pregnant just from getting "it" on you or near you. I've heard it said that you can get pregnant, or get V.D., from a swimming pool or a toilet seat. Right. No kidding, I've heard people say that.

Some girls insist that you can't get pregnant when you're on your period; others say that that's exactly the riskiest time of the month—although they always add that they themselves don't "do it," so it's academic as far as they're concerned.

"Hand jobs" don't count. "That" might not count—if a girl were the kind of girl who would do "that," which they certainly are not. They say.

I might be the least experienced girl in Iota—maybe in the whole Greek community here—but if I want to know something, I bother to go to a book and look it up.

I'm also worried that most of my sisters will go to Hell. Nobody (or virtually nobody) goes directly to Heaven, according to Roman Catholic teachings. You go to Purgatory, which is almost as bad as Hell except that in Purgatory you have hope. Then, once you've purged yourself of your sins, you experience the Beatific Vision. But if your soul is utterly lost—if you die in a state of mortal sin—you go to Hell. There is no hope for you. People on Earth are not supposed to pray for souls in Hell, for they are utterly lost.

That's why you don't commit mortal sins. Because you could die at any moment.

I don't pray for my Iota sisters, though. I figure it's their lookout. I'm getting mean in my old age. But I started praying for Vicki again, this winter, as she got more and more pregnant. Then I started praying for the child, when it was born on January 31, 1970—Jack and Jerry's 24th birthday.

"It's so sad," Mona told me. It was that afternoon. Mona and I were working in a practice room of the Music Building. "Mike and I took her to the hospital at about four this morning. She came into our apartment and woke us up, said the pains were coming fast. Then when we got to the hospital, she was hardly in labor at all; the baby was out in way less than an hour. We got to see her and the baby right after, and… oh, God, Teresa, she's calling it 'Little Red.' She's calling him Richard, Jr., officially, but Little Red is what she was calling him this morning, even though he's got a full head of black hair and doesn't look like Red even a little."

"Is Red in the picture at all?"

"Long gone. Vicki used to hear from him sometimes. He's in California. He would call her every couple of months to see how she was doing, but he hasn't done that since maybe October. She knows he's not coming back."

"What's she going to do?"

"Raise the baby herself. Here. Which means Mike and I will be stuck with some baby-sitting. She says her parents are helping her financially, whether she likes it or not, but she's not moving back with them."

"Is she taking classes?"

"Well, she didn't register for this semester, since she knew she'd be too busy. I don't know how prepared she is to bring up a baby. She told me she isn't going to breastfeed, which didn't sound right to me. She said she didn't want to ruin her body any more than she could help."

"Vanity."

"Poor Vicki," says Mona. "I think she resents the baby. For interrupting her life. And she was constantly complaining that she couldn't drink as much while she was pregnant. She is so messed up. Mike and I are going to do what we can. As much for the baby's sake as for Vicki's."

I still have hardly any time to spend with Gary. We don't have any classes together; we don't even have subjects in common. Now that I'm a sophomore, I'm expected to participate more in musical performances. Gary and I have to fight for the time to get together once a week; twice in one week is unusual.

Still, we seem to have fallen into a pattern in which I can't deny that Gary is my boyfriend and I'm his girlfriend. We hold hands when we walk together. I usually initiate it. Sometimes, I'll take his arm. The kisses are getting longer and more complicated, but so far, Gary hasn't tried to take it any farther.

It does occur to me that maybe Gary has other girls for that sort of thing. But unless I know for sure otherwise, I'll assume that he's as chaste as I am, and as principled.

One evening, over dinner, Lefty gave me this little sidelong smile, and said to me in front of everyone, "It's like a novel, or a comic book, isn't it, Brenda? The football hero dating the Athletic Director's daughter. You two could play yourselves, when they make the movie."

For the rest of the meal and well into the evening, the sisters were devising plot lines, subplots, all kinds of ridiculous scenarios, around the romance of me and Gary. They threw in various speculations about other romances involving football players, with girls from other sororities. It didn't take long for the conversation to become pretty crude—although they left me and Gary out of it when they went in that direction, so I sat through it, feigning amusement.

§

On Tuesday, March 31, 1970, Isaiah Monroe, President of the Afro-American Student Association of the State of Iowa, issued a press release including a list of demands that would supposedly end what he called "an intolerable situation" for black athletes at State University. The list ran in the *Statesman* the next morning.

Monroe claimed that an agreement reached the previous spring between the athletic department and the AASASI—one that had promised "increased social opportunities," "an end to persecution," and "greater team participation" for black athletes—had not been complied with. The release added, "If the agreement is not immediately honored, discussions are in process as to strikes by Afro-American athletes at State University."

The press contacted both Feldy and Coach Timmerman, that day. Timmerman claimed he had not heard of any agreement; much less had he heard of any of its particulars.

"I was busy organizing spring drills at that time last year, as I am now," Timmerman said. "I didn't hear a word about this, or about any grievances from any group."

Feldy was quoted as saying that the association had sent him a letter, "which I don't remember the specifics of, off-hand. I'll have to look for it and read it again." He recalled that the letter had listed certain grievances and requests.

"I did, in fact, address some of those grievances, but no formal agreement was ever reached," he said. "I never met with the people who sent me the letter. I acknowledged in my response that some of their complaints were legitimate, and I passed them along to President Esterhart. He promised to look into the matter—but then of course he died. I have no idea whether President Nash has had a chance to address this."

What the press didn't know at the time—but they found out fast enough—was that Isaiah Monroe may have been reacting to a team meeting that had taken place on the day before he issued that release, in which Timmerman had spoken to his players about what he perceived as sloppy conduct off the field.

"That wasn't a regular meeting," Gary is telling me. We're sitting in the Union's Lower Lounge. We're supposed to be studying together, but first I show him that article in the *Statesman*, so we have to discuss that first.

"We weren't supposed to meet till Friday," Gary says. "Then, you know, spring drills start on Saturday. But Coach let us know over the weekend that he was calling a meeting for yesterday. Had to have made a lot of long-distance calls, with most of us out of town for Easter. Anyway, we all showed up at the Fieldhouse, last night, and Coach was talking about several issues, but the main one was about some of us getting in trouble various ways—you know, our grades mostly, or too much partying—and how this was affecting the team, and the program. He singled out these two black guys: Shawn Eddings and Booley Norton. He said right there in front of everybody, 'Yeah, I'm talking about you, Eddings, and you, Norton. It's people like you who are hurting the team and hurting the program.'"

"Oh, no. In front of everybody? That's not smart."

"No kidding. As soon as that meeting broke up, some of the black players were talking about getting an apology. Watkins told me that this guy from the Afro-American Association had been trying to get the black players involved with the Black Power movement, and he was also—this Monroe guy—he was trying get money out of the administration for the Afro-American Association to have their own meeting house, on or near campus.

"Watkins allowed as how he was going to call Monroe right away, about how they could use this incident to put pressure on the athletic department to come up with the money for that. He said something to me, like, 'They're using us as black gladiators. They owe us.'"

"Oh, come on."

"Seriously," Gary says. "I was thinking, 'What does the athletic department owe you that they don't owe the white guys?' I didn't say it, but I thought it. Watkins must have seen that that's what I was thinking, because he said, 'Educate yourself, man.' Which made me want to say, 'Oh, f…' I mean, it made me want to tell him to take a hike, but I, you know, I let it go."

"Still, you can see how the black guys would have felt they were being singled out," I say.

"Oh, for sure. Plus, what you have to realize about Watkins is that he's one of these guys who might or might not be intelligent, but he thinks he's the brightest bulb in the circuit, you know? Well, he's articulate. Not that I understood what he has to complain about. He has a full-ride scholarship just for playing football."

§

On Friday, Coach Timmerman issued a statement announcing that two members of the Rivercat squad—both starters the previous season, both black—would not be allowed to participate in spring drills. They were the two he had singled out at that meeting: Roger "Booley" Norton, defensive back from West Memphis, Arkansas; Shawn Eddings, defensive tackle from Toledo, Ohio.

"Both of these young men are dealing with some personal challenges," the release said. "It is in their best interests to not be distracted by spring drills. It would also not benefit the team, if we included them in spring drills and built up our expectations of having them on the team in the fall, although we hope to have them back with us when August drills start. For the sake of the squad, and to ensure that they have the best chance of making the squad this fall, they will not be with us during spring drills."

The release didn't specify what the problems were, but I knew. Norton wasn't much of a student, and Eddings had been arrested, the week before, for passing a bad cheque.

Aside from those articles about the pre-season practice that I wrote at the start of the year, I'm not covering sports for the *Statesman*—I'm back to being nothing but a stringer, not officially on staff—but I'd love to ask Timmerman, "Is that going to have a significant impact on the team's performance this year?"

That's the kind of question that's tough to answer without looking bad. If you say, "They're going to be hard to replace," or "they'll be a big loss," then you're suggesting that the team isn't going to do well on account of missing those two key players—thus making it look like you're blaming them for getting into trouble, and at the same time implying that other players on the squad aren't good enough to replace them. If you say, "I don't think their absence will significantly hurt the team," you're implying that those two guys are nonentities. In that case, what were they doing in the starting lineup the year before? Besides, Eddings is too big an asset to pretend that his absence won't damage us badly.

Obviously, Timmerman put out that statement on a Friday, hoping that it wouldn't get much notice, but when two black football players get suspended from the team—one of them a star—people are going to talk. If it had been two white boys, people would have assumed that they weren't any good, and were being suspended as a way of getting rid of them.

Feldy wasn't at the first practice session, the next day, but I was. Feldy, Birdy, Win, Sander, Duffy, and I are having Sunday lunch at the Coffin Corner as usual, and I'm giving them the full report.

"Pretty routine. No contact drills, no incidents that I could see. But everybody seemed really tense. It was nothing I could put my finger on; just something I felt. An ugly vibe. Like everybody was on guard, maybe angry, too. Losing those two guys is bound to make them feel less optimistic."

"How does your boyfriend look?" Feldy asks.

"He looks sharp. So does Blaha. I got to talk to both of them for a minute afterwards, and they both said they're optimistic.

And the freshmen look good; they'll be a big help in the fall now that we lost Norton and Eddings."

"Shouldn't count on anybody filling their shoes, though," Feldy says. "I don't understand Timmerman's reasoning. First, with regard to Norton, did he take any initiative to prevent Norton from getting into trouble academically? Did he pay any attention to the courses Norton was taking? Did he contact Norton's instructors to see how he was doing? I mean at a point in the year when it might have made a difference."

Feldy shakes his head and pauses for effect before going on:

"This sends out the wrong signal to the rest of the team. It makes them think that their coach isn't looking out for them, not sticking by them. They'll think he won't have their backs if they get into any kind of trouble. Especially when he announces it like that. Why didn't he just *do it* and hope the press wouldn't notice? Don't volunteer it, for crying out loud."

I say, "Gary told me Norton's failing everything."

"Okay, so maybe he is. We're going to see what we can do about keeping him eligible, but Timmerman has undermined the squad's confidence in the whole Athletic Department. The colored kids are gonna be especially suspicious. And did he ever talk to Eddings, to get an idea of what he did off the field?"

Birdy says, "Well, Feldy, is Eddings going to tell anyone he's kiting cheques?"

Feldy sighs. "No, I suppose not. I appreciate that it would have looked bad if Timmerman had let him participate. But there's such a thing as being too transparent. Those are two important players. We want them on the team this fall. That's the bottom line."

VICKI, GONE

"I'm glad we were able to find you," Mona says. "I guess you were at church and with your family all morning, and the only place we could leave a message was at your sorority house. No-body was home when we called your parents."

It's Sunday afternoon. Grey and drizzly outside. Mona and Mike are sitting together on their couch; I'm sitting on a pillow facing them, and we're all still trying to process. They're both white in the face, and drawn. Little Red is asleep in a bassinette in their bedroom. Mona is holding her left hand in this strange, rigid way, her fingers all stiff. It looks completely paralyzed.

The way Mona and Mike are telling it to me, they had been taking care of Little Red overnight, since Vicki was out partying, "and I'm damn glad we were," Mike says. "He's still not sleeping through the night, so it's a pain in the ass, but better than leaving him alone in Vicki's apartment. If she was going out for the night, sometimes she would drop him off with us and collect him in the morning, but I have to think there were a few times when she just left him there."

"We both sleep like logs, whenever he'll let us," Mike says. "It would take an earthquake to wake us up—except when it's him. He makes any kind of noise, and we're awake. Anyway, it must have been about five this morning when he's starting to make noise—and what woke me up even faster is that I could see the flashing red lights, you know, reflecting on our windows and walls, so I know it's a pigmobile or an ambulance outside, or both, and right by our house too.

"Of course, the first thing that pops into my mind is, 'Vicki's in trouble,' because, what can I tell you? She's always been a tick-ing time bomb. I'm asking myself, 'Did she fall and hurt herself, or is she getting arrested for something, or what?' I come out here, and look out the front window, and sure enough it's two cop cars and an ambulance in front of the house, so I go back into the bedroom and get my pants and a pair of slippers, and I go out there just in time to see her body being carried out on a stretcher and put in the ambulance. I mean, I know it's her. It's covered up.

"There's pigs all over the place, and I ask one of them what's going on, and he says, 'There's been an accident.' Looking at me all stony-faced, like they do, you know. I ask him, 'Is she dead?' although it's obvious she's dead, and he says, 'It looks very bad.'

Like, I don't know, maybe they're not allowed to say any more than that.

"Then he asks me, did I hear anything during the night, but no; Mona and I went to bed around 11:00 or so and I was out cold, till Little Red woke me up. I ask him are there other people hurt, and he says no, just the one, and he says it again, 'It's very bad. Lieutenant Stamp is inside; he might want to ask you if you know anything that could help.'"

I'm still just sitting there, listening to Mike; I can't think of anything to say.

"Then I see this guy in a trench coat coming out of the door of Vicki's apartment; I assume that's Stamp. He's got 'cop' written all over him. Then two more people come out—civilians, as far as I can tell. A black guy—he looked older than you but younger than me or Mona—and a white woman quite a bit older, maybe 40, and a uniformed cop behind them. I'm watching them put these two people into the back of one of the squad cars, only they're not handcuffed: it doesn't look like they're in custody.

"Then the guy in plain clothes, he comes back to where I am, and, yeah, he tells me his name is Lieutenant Stamp, and he takes my name and asks me is this where they can find me if they need to; then he gets into that patrol car and they drive off—him and one of the uniforms, and the two civilians. The one in the uniform that I was talking with is still there, and I'm feeling like I'm going to puke or pass out or something, so I say 'Excuse me, sir,' which I'm aware is ridiculous, but I say it, then I run back in here before I really do pass out."

"His face was *green*," Mona says. "I was up, I was getting dressed enough to go out there when Mike came in. He sort of collapsed on the couch, and told me to stay in here, and that Vicki was dead."

"I didn't want Mona going out there because if she got to talking with anybody—I know you wouldn't have meant to do it, Mona—but if you had somehow let it slip that we had Vicki's baby in here, then the pigs would have come in here and taken him away, for sure. And then who knows what would have happened to him?"

"They did come knocking on our door pretty soon after that," Mona says. "A detective—not Stamp, a different one—and a guy in uniform, but by that time we had Little Red stashed away behind a closed door, and they just wanted to know our names and if we had seen anything. Then they asked us if we paid any attention to who came and went in her apartment, but you can imagine, Mike and I don't want to put innocent people in trouble."

Mike lights another cigarette.

"I was hoping that maybe—well, God knows, it's bad enough that she's dead," Mike says, "but I was hoping that if she had to die, maybe she went off in her sleep. Like maybe she finally drank herself to death. Or an overdose, although so far as I know, she wasn't using anything she could O.D. on. But the detective made it clear that someone killed her, although he wouldn't give us any of the details yet.

"I thought maybe those two people coming out of her house… I thought maybe they'd been partying with her, and maybe she collapsed, and they called an ambulance. But the detective said they had come into her apartment and found her body there… again, he wouldn't tell us how it happened, but evidently there was foul play of some kind. I asked him if it was the two people we saw, but he just said they're being questioned. I didn't recognize either of them."

"I wonder…" Mona is looking like she doesn't want to go on, but she does. "She's been seeing this black guy, lately. She told me about him. I saw them once, going into her apartment together: he's kind of a big guy… and I guess she was trying to break up with him, because he was scaring her. She told me his name, but I don't remember it."

Mona isn't looking at us, and this is no more than my intuition, but somehow, I can feel it: She's not telling us what she knows. She's holding something back.

"Who is maybe the guy I saw this morning," Mike says. "I've never seen a black guy with Vicki, but I'm not observant like Mona; I don't pay as much attention."

"From the way you describe him, it sounds like that's the one," Mona says. "She's been bringing guys home, and she never used to do that."

"Yeah, it seemed like it got worse, after the baby was born," Mike says. "The almost compulsive sleeping around. Well, not *sleeping*, but... It was... I don't know why, but maybe it was like she had to prove to herself that she still had it."

"It's because she felt so alone," Mona says. "Without Red. She told me she's been... well, actually *doing the deed* with guys, so to speak. Instead of just doing what she prefers to do with them. Because she was telling me she was desperate to be with someone, you know, have someone in her life, and she felt that she couldn't keep a guy unless she did... that thing that she didn't like to do."

(The best way to keep a guy is to not do that thing, if he's not your husband, I say to myself, but what do I know?)

"She told me she was learning to like doing it, with this guy, but then he..." Mona is obviously about to reveal something, but she stops herself. "Oh, God, how awful it would be if the police try to pin it on one of them. I mean, sorry, that sounds so awful: 'one of them.' I didn't mean that the way it sounded. I mean if a black man did it, if they can prove he did it, then we have to live with that. But I hope that now they don't just choose someone who looks like he's the most convenient scapegoat."

"We have to make sure they don't," Mike says. "We'll have to get people out on the street, to let them know that we won't tolerate any legal lynching. That's gone on for way too long in this country and we have to acknowledge that it's still going on."

"I wish I could have done more... no, I wish I *had* done more; I could maybe have kept this from happening," Mona says. "Maybe I was too busy trying to show myself how broad-minded I am; maybe that's why I never suggested to Vicki that she shouldn't be living the way she was. It wasn't my place to say it, and it would have made me sound like some kind of Republican. But maybe if I had..."

"She wouldn't have been advised by you, Squeeze," Mike says. "Or by me, or anybody. She was gonna do what she was gonna do. Getting raped made her crazy. Not that she didn't have her problems before, but that—that and having the baby—multiplied those problems geometrically. She was so depressed, almost all the time, and... doing that sort of thing, that was the only thing that would make her feel better. You can't talk someone out of that attitude, or talk them out of doing whatever they do to deal with it."

"We told the cops—I'm not proud of this—but we told them we didn't know off-hand who her next-of-kin were," Mona tells me. "We're trying to find some way to get word to her parents before the police do. Because otherwise they'll be sure to tell the police that she has that baby, and then they'll come here and cart him off to an orphanage or something."

"Well, Vicki's parents would claim him," I say.

"That would be almost worse," says Mike. "From what Vicki has told us about them. They're exactly the rich country-club trash that children ought to be kept away from."

"I had better call the *Statesman* and see if they have anybody on this story," I say.

I know, I'm awful. Mona looks shocked, but Mike says, "Good for you. Get on it. Phone's in the kitchen."

Since it's Sunday afternoon, the editor-in-chief is there, working on Monday morning's edition. She tells me she's already got someone on the story, but I persuade her to let me contribute an interview with Vicki's neighbors. She also tells me as much as she knows about what happened—almost all of which I know already: Vicki died violently; the police have not made any arrests, but they're questioning the two people who found the body; no report on what the violence might have consisted of.

"The cops haven't released any names," she tells me, "but we have our sources. People who happen to see things. Their names are Cindy Phillips and Charles Watkins."

Oh, Judas...

I pass that information along to Mona and Mike as soon as I'm off their phone—they have no idea who Charles Watkins is, that's how little they care about sports—and I explain that I need to call my father right away, in case he hasn't heard.

I get Birdy on the phone and tell her as briefly as I can about what has happened, and ask her to put Feldy on. I tell him a slightly more detailed version, including that Watkins is being questioned, and I tell him I'm going to stay on it, because I've got an assignment from the *Statesman.*

Feldy's not saying anything for a few seconds, then he says, "If Watkins turns out to be a suspect, we are going to be in a world of trouble. What in hell was he doing in that house, at that hour of the morning? I wonder if Timmerman knows about it yet. I need to call him now. Thanks for telling me this, Terri; keep me posted if you hear anything else. And don't write anything more in the *Statesman* than you know. Just the facts. But you know that."

The University Statesman, Monday, April 27, 1970
RIVERCAT GRID STAR
QUESTIONED IN DEATH

State City police are investigating the death of Victoria Ann DeGroot, 23, a former student at State University, whose fully clothed body was discovered in her apartment at 419 Kirk Street early Sunday morning. According to police and other sources, uniformed patrol responded to a call from the apartment at 4:01 Sunday morning. Charles Watkins, 21, a State University student and a member of the State University football team, told police that he discovered the body when he paid a late-night visit to Miss DeGroot along with his friend Cynthia Phillips, 33, of State City.

Mr. Watkins has been questioned and released, according to police, while Miss Phillips is being held in State County Jail on an outstanding bench warrant for failure to appear to respond to a previous charge of solicitation. Lt. Vernon Stamp, of the State City Police Department's detective division, says a patrol car arrived at the victim's apartment approximately five minutes after the police station received the call, and Watkins and Phillips greeted them outside the front door of the building. Inside, police found Miss DeGroot's body. Stamp would not release the cause of her death, but said she had "obviously suffered severe trauma."

"The body is still being examined," Stamp said. "We don't know, yet, what was the direct cause of her death. At this point, neither Watkins nor Miss Phillips are suspects, although unfortunately Miss Phillips has been detained on outstanding charges. They are both cooperating with the investigation. Based on the information they have given us, it's likely that we will be interviewing several other people. We are not naming any suspect or suspects."

I don't have time for it, but I skip lunch and stop by City Hall to see if the police can tell me anything more. I ask for Lieutenant Stamp; I give the desk Sergeant my name; in a couple of minutes this youngish-looking guy in plain clothes—a well-built guy, medium size, with glasses—comes out of his office and gives me a big smile.

"You're Feldy's Girl, aren't you? And you're doing a piece for the *Statesman*? Come on back." So, I'm sitting in Lieutenant Stamp's office, across the desk from him. I know darn well he would not have been so forthcoming except that I'm Feldy's Girl. I tell Stamp that I knew Vicki, so I was especially concerned about the case. Stamp repeats that no arrests have been made, and the autopsy report won't be completed for weeks—and when it is, it won't be available to the public.

"It's pretty bad," he says. "I would not want to let you see it."

"Do you have a suspect?"

"We have several people we're talking to, but we haven't charged anybody. You said you knew her. Is there anything you can tell us?"

Here's a dilemma. Do I tell Stamp that Vicki was notorious for picking up strangers? Or, since I don't know the names of any of the people Vicki claimed to have serviced—aside from possibly Watkins—would that be relevant? In that case, should I not speak ill of someone who has just been murdered?

"She told me... that she had a lot of boyfriends, nothing special. And a husband, who I gather she wasn't faithful to, and I understand he left town when he found out she was pregnant."

And there, damn it, I let it slip that she had a baby, and now is Stamp going to ask me about it, and then are the cops going to beat down the Shapens' door to get the kid?

"Yes, we heard about the husband and the baby," Stamp says, and boy do I feel relieved that he didn't get it from me.

"We tracked down her parents, and they told us about him, and said that if we hadn't found him in her apartment, her neighbors would know where he was. So, we visited Mr. and Mrs. Shapen, and… well, it's irregular, and we could theoretically get in trouble for it, but they pleaded with us, they even asked us to call Vicki's parents back again, from their phone, to see if they would let them keep the baby there at least till the parents arrived in town. That's where we left it, and the parents will probably collect the kid today or tomorrow."

Back at Iota, late that afternoon, I find a note that Gary had called. I have no idea how much he knows, and I don't feel like talking to him right now. I figure I have to, though. He deserves to know what I know, if I can tell him anything new.

"Listen, do me a favor," he says, when I call him. "Try not to say too much about Watkins, when you're reporting. I'm sure it wasn't him, and we need him on the team in the fall."

"He's not a suspect, so far as I know," I say, "and I'm not going to keep mentioning that he found the body."

"He's not a suspect?" I can hear the relief in Gary's voice. "Thank God. He's got enough trouble already. Oh, man, Coach might kick him off the team just for having been someplace where he could have found a body at four AM of the morning."

"He's not a suspect; that doesn't mean he's been cleared. The detective told me they haven't ruled anybody out, so they might still be looking at him."

"Shit." I can tell Gary is upset, since he almost always watches his language around me.

"Watkins pretty much keeps to himself," Gary says. "I've always been friendly with him, but I don't know that much about him, or what he does off the field."

"Don't worry," I say. "I'm going to mention him as little as I can. So, listen, this week is crazy. Start thinking about a movie or something we can do Saturday night. I'll need it, I'm pretty sure. Take care, Honey."

That's the first time I've ever called anyone "Honey," and I did it without thinking to do it. Why did I, right then, after a conversation like that?

§

It's amazing, how fast a story travels. Everyone in Iota Delta Theta would have known the outline of it this morning, but now they all seem to know more about it than I do—or at least they're pretending to. At the dinner table—we're having chicken à la King, over rice, and it's really good, only I can't fully enjoy it— I'm hearing that everybody knew that that girl who got killed was the slut of the campus, especially when it came to black guys. I am pretty certain that none of the sisters ever knew Vicki at all, unless one or two of them knew her by sight. And if they had known about her reputation, they certainly didn't get it from me.

I don't think any of them know that I knew her. If I were to bet, I would bet that whatever the girls at this table know about her has only just been invented for the sake of this conversation. It's amazing how that happens. You wish it wouldn't, but it does. People can be really vicious. Especially girls.

Christine Smith starts to sing:

Negroes in the night, exchanging white girls
Taking their delight, but you can't see them
Not unless they smile, and then they glow for miles…

"Oh, Chris, that's awful," Lefty says, but Chris keeps going:

Dooby-dooby-doo, da-da-da-dee-da…

§

Mona and Mike have been busy dealing with Vicki's parents, who are in town to make arrangements about Vicky's body, and the baby, too, I imagine. I'm wondering why God would allow Vicki to die like that: obviously not in a State of Grace, in a way that probably means she's in Hell now. I'm thinking it might be my fault, at least to some extent. I didn't bring Vicki to repentance; I never even came close to trying to.

I remind myself of what Mike said to Mona—"She wouldn't have been advised by you"—and I tell myself that Mike was right. Plus, if Vicki would not have listened to Mona, there's no way she would have listened to me. But I should have tried. I'll confess that, on Saturday, and pray on it before that.

WHAT MONA IS TELLING ME

This was not a random break, enter, and kill. Whoever killed Vicki, knew her. I'm at Mona's apartment ostensibly to play my cello for her, so she can critique me, but really, I've come over to commiserate. Mike is at an opera rehearsal; Little Red is sleeping in his bassinette. Mona sits on the sofa; I'm ready to play, but I'm still listening to Mona's latest.

"We have no idea what our legal status is, with regard to the little guy. Vicki's parents are letting us foster him, for the time being; they've agreed to help us, financially, so we hope they'll let us adopt. We don't know what the legal procedures are. We're not going to talk about it with her parents yet, because, you can imagine, they're broken up about what happened, and we're all still trying to come to terms with it. I guess it'll be decided before too long."

Mona simpers.

"Mike and I hadn't planned to start a family so soon. But it would be nice if we could bring up Vicki's baby for her. I still feel guilty—like we could have done more for her when she was alive. So maybe this all wouldn't have happened."

"I feel the same way," I tell Mona. "Not that she and I were ever that close, and... and what could I have said? I can't even vote, yet, and I'm supposed to tell her not to drink so much, or not to... you know?"

"I know. She liked you, but she would never have listened to you. She thought it was funny that you were so old-fashioned..."

"Old-fashioned girls don't get into situations like that."

I know that's mean of me to say, but sometimes I don't care if it's mean. I can see from a tiny twitch of her face muscles that Mona doesn't like hearing that, and I don't want to get into a discussion of the implications of what I just said. I want to get to the point.

"Charles Watkins. Did she mention a Charles?"

Mona looks away from me.

"Charles was the name. I remembered it, not when you told us, but next day, when I saw it in the paper. I don't know what Charles Watkins looks like—I don't follow football at all—but this guy was big enough to be a football player, for sure. I don't know what to do, now."

"Is there anything more that you know, that the cops don't?"

Mona still can't look at me.

"For God's sake, he killed her," she whispers. "The guy I saw her with. I'll bet you anything. I don't know for a fact he did it, but... but I know he did it."

I've been holding onto the faint hope that no matter how bad it looks for him, maybe Watkins had nothing to do with Vicki getting killed—but Mona obviously believes what she's saying.

"We have to look at that possibility," I say. "What makes you so sure, though?"

Mona is looking at the floor, shaking her head.

"I can't talk about it."

"You don't have to. You don't have to tell me. But if you know something, if you have real evidence, maybe you should take it to the police."

"It's not evidence. Just stuff Vicki told me. About this guy."

"What? Did he beat her up, or threaten her, or something?"

"Not exactly, but pretty close. She told me…. well, that… he likes to do certain things that she doesn't allow. Specifically, the back door. Sorry. I'm shocking you. Sorry."

"No, it's nothing I haven't heard before."

Actually, up to right this minute, I have only heard that that act exists; I do not want to believe that anyone does it, although I have to admit to myself that homosexuals probably do.

"Well, she told me he tricked her into doing that. And she didn't want anything more to do with him after that."

I squinch my face up.

"How can someone *trick* you into doing that?" I genuinely want to know the answer. "I believe she told you that, but how is it possible? That's such a small hole. I can see how a really strong man might hold you down, and force himself on you, but how would he *trick* you? If you don't mind telling me."

Mona looks horribly embarrassed. I don't blame her.

"Well… the way she told it, she was crosswise on the bed, see. He was standing up, and she had her legs up over his shoulders—which is a really fun way to do it, for your information, but when you're in that position, you can't move. You're at the mercy of the guy you're with. So according to her, all of a sudden, he… pulled out, and then… he put it someplace else."

I scrunch myself into a ball, bringing my knees almost to my face: it's a reflex.

"Yeah," Mona says. "I've never… had it *there*, so I don't know, but she said it was like having her guts torn out. Like being shot, she said. She was bleeding, and all."

"Oh, no…"

"Yeah, and she said she, you know, *staggered* to the bathroom and was trying to, I guess, repair herself, and he's saying, 'I'm sorry, baby, it was an accident. You know it was an accident.'"

Mona makes the same kind of face I suppose I'm making, then she goes on.

"Vicki was scared to death, besides being in so much pain. I mean, what if something was broken in there?"

"That's horrible."

"Then, she said, he kept on apologizing, saying it was an accident, saying 'I love you,' and she just waited for him to leave, because what else could she do?"

"If it was Watkins, she couldn't have thrown him out. I don't know, do I need to tell my father about this?"

(And what if I do tell him? Could I tell Feldy those details?)

"She told me that after that, she wouldn't talk to him on the phone, when he called, and she wouldn't let him in, the next time he came by the house. She said this was when Mike and I weren't home. She told me he scared the hell out of her. She said he was pounding on the door, first, then he yelled... oh, I can't remember exactly what she told me he called her. 'A dime-a-dozen hole,' or something like that. She told me she was looking for Red's gun, but he must have taken it to California with him.

"Then a couple days after that, she told me he had come by again, acting all sweet and nice and just wanting to talk, and this time she let him in to talk but he started getting really mad when she wouldn't do anything with him. She said she bolted out of the apartment—left him there, you know, with the door open— and hollered that she was going to find a phone booth and call the cops if he didn't get out of there and get clear away. So he did. But not for long."

"Okay, but what was that other woman doing with him? Did they kill her together, do you think?"

"No," Mona says. "I'm thinking that if he wanted help killing her, he wouldn't have brought a woman. The paper said they'd gone there to get his hat. But that's so strange. Why would he go back for his hat? How would anyone know it was his hat?"

"Ah, see, if you followed football, you'd know that Watkins is notorious around campus for that hat. For the way he dresses, in general. Maybe he knew that *you* knew he had been in Vicki's place before—or that *someone* knew. Maybe someone saw him harassing her. He knew that he would be a suspect—so he had to pretend to find Vicki, so as to throw suspicion off himself."

Mona looks all, "Aha!"

"So," Mona says, "he brings his friend along so that she can say they just happened to be visiting..."

"Bingo."

"At four in the morning?"

"Yeah, that's a tough one," I say. "But the longer he lets Vicki lie there, the more likely someone else will find her, and his hat. His fingerprints are probably all over the apartment, too."

Mona leans forward, on the sofa, and grips her left hand with her right, like she's trying to flex it. It's not completely paralyzed like it was a few days ago.

"I could have encouraged her to go to the police," Mona says. "But I figured she knew what she was doing, she was a big girl— and I expected it would blow over, he would find some other girl to bother. It's like I killed her, now."

"For one thing," I say, "you don't know for sure *he* did it. And if he did, it's not like you made her... do what she was doing."

"I can't help thinking that whatever happened to her was another 'accident' except that it got way out of hand," Mona says. "Or maybe he wanted to have another accident with her, and she tried to fight him off and... and that happened."

Mona's face is going red and I can see her eyes welling up, so I get up out of my chair real fast and sit down next to her. I put my arm round her shoulders and give her a hug, which is not like me.

Mona hugs me back with both arms and puts her face into my shoulder. Now she's sobbing, really heaving, and crying out loud, although my blouse is muffling it. This is something I've never dealt with before, not even with one of my younger brothers—well, when they were little boys, they were too tough to have needed any comforting from me.

What I most want to say is, "Look, you need to go to the cops and tell them everything you know. Because this story's pretty important, don't you think?" But I don't say it; I let her cry.

"I can't remember her face," Mona says. She's still sobbing her heart out. "Isn't that awful? I can't remember her face. I've forgotten what she looked like."

"You'll remember it," I say. "It's just right now it's not coming to you. It's how you're coping. You'll remember her while that little guy grows up, and it'll be sad, but you'll remember Vicki, too. There'll be something nice in that."

"She might have had fun with him." Mona is calmer: sniffling, now. "I know she wasn't perfect, but she had... such a flair for life. She was hell on wheels, wasn't she?" Mona half-laughs and half-sobs into my blouse.

"Little Red will never know her. Which is another thing. We can't call him Little Red. Richard Henry DeGroot, Jr. We can't call him Richard or Dick, because of Nixon. Hank, maybe."

Mona reaches over to a side table for a tissue and wipes her nose; then she wriggles her left hand out from between us and holds it up in front of my face.

"Could you work my fingers for me? They're seizing up."

I try massaging her hand with both of mine.

"I've been bowing," Mona says. "I've been playing the open notes. At least I'm improving my bowing technique. It makes me sick when I try to finger. Sick from frustration, and literally almost nauseated from the pain, sometimes, if I move certain joints too fast. Sometimes it'll get completely paralyzed. Usually when something upsets me emotionally. Well, like when I heard about Vicki. I couldn't move my fingers at all, till yesterday. But I still hope I can work through it."

She takes her hand back from me, gets another tissue, blows her nose, and tries to grip the tissue with her left hand.

I have an idea.

"Come for a walk," I say. "It's such a nice night, and you need to get out of the house. We can take Little… Hank with us: you've got a baby carriage, don't you? I bet he could use some air, too."

What Mona doesn't know is that I'm going to walk her in the direction of City Hall.

"That's a thought," Mona says. "Yeah, thank goodness the carriage was in the back entranceway. I don't suppose the detectives would have let us into Vicki's apartment to get it. Not that I could ever have gone in there. Anyway, yeah, we could go for a walk. Mike won't be home for at least another hour."

I'm intending to keep Mona out longer than that.

I say, "Leave him a note, just in case. That we've gone out. I'll leave my cello here, so he can be sure we'll be back." I go into my purse and grab a note-pad and a pen; Mona writes fast.

Mona says, "Would you walk with me over to City Hall? Like now, before Mike gets home and talks me out of it? Maybe nobody will see us. Nobody who knows us, I mean."

Telepathy?

I keep it light, on the way over there. The thing is to keep Mona moving, keep her spirits up, keep her as energized as I can, so she doesn't get cold feet and turn around. It's only about a 15-minute walk to City Hall. Lieutenant Stamp won't be on duty, I'm sure, but I suppose any detective will do.

Mona and I and Little Red in the carriage all approach the front desk, and I tell the desk officer, "We believe we have some information about a murder you're investigating, and we'd like to talk to a detective." The officer says he ought to call Lieutenant Stamp and bring him into the station.

"He probably hasn't gone to bed yet. He's the guy you should talk to. He'll know what questions to ask." He picks up the phone on his desk. "Why don't you two have a seat over there?"

"Tell him it's Teresa Feldevert, and a friend. That way he'll know it's not just a crank."

The officer looks startled. "You're Feldy's Girl?"

I nod. For some reason that question annoys me, this once.

"How about that? I'll be darned," he says, while he's dialing.

Mona and I sit there for about 20 minutes. The desk officer offers us coffee, "or something from the pop machine?" We each have a Sprite, and I keep Mona talking, mainly about music. Then Lieutenant Stamp arrives through the same public entrance that Mona and I used. He's wearing a brown suit without a tie.

"Evening, ladies," he says. "Good to see you again, Teresa. Mrs. Shapen. I hope you can tell me something good."

"Mona's the one you want to talk with," I say. "I'll watch the little guy for you out here, Mona."

I sit there, scolding myself for having left my purse and my note pad in Mona's apartment, and wishing that I could write a to-do list for the next few days. Or a list of what I might write for the *Statesman*—if there's anything for me to write. Or do something, instead of just sitting here with a baby, losing time. I play the Glad Game: I'm glad that Little Red is being so quiet.

It's nearly ten o'clock, and Stamp is bringing Mona out from his office. She has obviously been crying some more—her face is horribly red and puffy—but she seems relaxed; she's even smiling at something Stamp just said to her, that I didn't catch.

"Again, thanks so much for coming in, Mona," Stamp says. At least they're comfortable enough that she's "Mona," now. "This was real helpful information. And, Teresa, thank you for standing by your friend."

"Is there anything you can tell me?" I hope I'm not sounding over-eager.

"Not at the moment. If I were a reporter, though, I would be on the lookout for something to happen in the next day or two. We've been finding some other clues. Aside from what Mona has told us. Just saying."

Stamp turns to the desk officer. "Dave, I'm going to be here a while. Let's see if we can give these ladies a lift to wherever they're stopping."

"No, wait," I say. "We don't want anybody to know we were here. Not for now. We'd better walk; it's not that far."

While we're walking, I want to say, "Mona, you did the right thing. I'm so proud of you." But that would be wrong, and patronizing: me saying that to someone who's four-five-six years older than I am. I feel almost ashamed to have thought of saying it. I also don't want to remind Mona that she might have to testify in court, too, one of these days. That really makes me feel guilty. I let Mona tell me what she told the detective, which is pretty much what I already know. I'm surprised that she's retelling the whole story to me, on the way back to her place, but I guess she's blowing off steam by talking.

Back at Mona's place, I start to play my cello while she puts the baby down, but Mike comes home about five minutes later. Mona doesn't tell him where we were. Maybe she will when I'm gone.

§

The police made the pinch at Watkins' rooming house on South Marquette St. early the next morning. Watkins was marched out, in handcuffs, and booked into State County Jail on an open charge of murder. The *Examiner*, that afternoon, ran a photo of him being led into the Sheriff's office. I saw it, when I got back to Iota after classes. I also found a message to call Birdy, so I did.

"Do you think Gary would like to come over for supper on Sunday night? Feldy wants to pick his brain about the situation with the team. But don't tell him that, when you're inviting him."

I called Gary, and he accepted the invitation, but he told me, "You can't be wearing your reporter hat. I need your absolute word that you won't quote me on anything I might say about the team, or Watkins, or mention me, or use anything I say to you."

"I don't know what to think," Gary is saying to Feldy. "I don't know enough to have an opinion. It could have been Watkins. But I don't know anything, except that it's gonna hurt us for sure if Watkins can't play this fall."

This is an informal supper. Birdy has the makings for tacos all set out, and we're concocting our own mixtures and chowing down. Gary has been entertaining Sander and Duffy with funny stories about the spring drills, but now Feldy has brought the conversation around to Watkins.

I can't say anything about what happened with Mona, the other night, although they all know that my friend/teacher lives next door to that apartment. I feel bad that I can't tell them all I know, but it's thrilling that I share some critical information with only a couple of other people, at this point.

"I don't know for sure," I say, "but I've been told that a witness has come forward who definitely implicates Watkins."

"Just what we need," Gary says. "The militants, that guy Monroe, they're gonna make a big stink out of this. They'll say he's being framed. They could do anything. At least spring drills are over after next week. Maybe things will be different in August, but who knows? I'm sure Watkins was... you know, partying with this girl. Let's face it: a lot of that goes on. Girls making themselves available to athletes..." Gary looks around. "Sorry. I shouldn't be talking that way in mixed company."

"The ladies and the youngsters in this house are pretty hard-boiled," Feldy says. "There's always going to be some of that sort of goings-on. It's inevitable, when you've got athletes and pretty girls, and the environment we've created in this country. But I've never heard of it coming to this. Incidents happen, but I don't believe any State University athlete has ever been involved in a crime like this—ever."

"I never would have thought any of us could have done something like that," Gary says. "I'm sure hoping Watkins didn't do it. But how can I know what he might be capable of? Plus, in a case like this, you're guilty no matter how innocent you are. And it makes us all look guilty, because the talk is gonna be, 'Oh, those football players, they're all a bunch of animals.'"

"Exactly," Feldy says. "These kids have gotten too big, or something. There was a time when they weren't this crazy. You could count on the athletes to discipline themselves."

"I almost want to say something about it on my show tomorrow morning," I say. "I know, I keep trying to not talk about our teams, but sometimes I have to do it. Just to point out that the athletes are the face of the school, whether they like it or not."

"That might not be a bad idea," Birdy says. "It might sound different coming from you. You know, someone who's well known, who has a stake in the situation."

"Oh, Birdy, that's funny! Okay, I guess I am well known, but it's funny whenever I'm forced to stop and think about it."

"We've got at least three famous people at this table," Feldy says. "And a few more who will be. Except Win, here, who's going to go really far—but always in the background."

Gary is driving me back to Iota, and I ask him, "You think Watkins did it, don't you?"

Silence for several seconds. Gary stares out at the road, where there isn't much traffic, and bites his lip.

"Obviously he could have. But I can't imagine it. I have to think it's got to be some stranger. Or maybe I'm hoping it is."

For some reason, neither of us feel like exchanging more than a quick smooch when we say goodnight.

The next morning, on the radio, I spoke mostly about the start of the Major League Baseball season. But I used the last 90 seconds or so to make a short speech.

"I'm the daughter of State University's Athletic Director, and for that reason, I avoid mentioning any news about any of the Rivercat sports teams. But I have to speak out on this issue. With the recent arrest of running back Charles Watkins—who I pray will turn out to be innocent of the charge against him—it's become clear to many of us that State University's athletes have got an image problem. It's an unfair problem for them to have, because I know a lot of these young men, and they're good guys. They don't get into trouble; they certainly don't cause trouble.

"With regard to Charles Watkins, let's not rush to judgment. I, personally, believe he's innocent. But athletes at State University need to understand that whether they like it or not, they represent the university to the rest of the community. To the rest of the world if it comes to that. They need to be above suspicion at all times, and remember that they are teammates always. Not only on the field: always. They are a band of brothers, and as good brothers do, they need to police each other.

"Maybe it's time for each one of our athletes to take a good look at themselves and ask, 'Am I doing what I should, to look after my teammates?' This is Terri Feldevert, reporting."

I lied. I don't believe he's innocent.

STRIKE

That was Monday, May 4, 1970. On that day, before the news of the shootings at Kent State had gotten out, the Afro-American Student Association of the State of Iowa (pronounced, "ah-SAH-zee") issued a press release, stating that they had forwarded a demand to the new President of State University, David Nash, and to Feldy: that the University stand bail for Charles Watkins, and provide him with full legal services.

Nash sent the AASASI a polite, conciliatory letter—which the *Statesman* published the next day—inviting them to a conference at his office at 11:00 Tuesday morning.

I was there: I volunteered to cover it and got the assignment. University Common, in front of the Territorial building, was already thick with demonstrators, because of what had happened at Kent State, but they were orderly. The Watkins case maybe distracted a lot of the black students from the peace movement.

Quite a sight, though: off to the side of the main demonstration were 20 or so black guys—no females—almost all of them dressed up like Black Panthers in what looked like military fatigues; all of them wore sunglasses; most of them had goatees and naturals. They had to get through this throng of anti-war demonstrators, to get to the President's office, and they were being led through the crowd by a flying wedge of cops (whom they would have called "pigs," ordinarily, as in "off the pig"). I was right behind them.

It must have gotten back to Nash that this visiting committee would be too big to fit in his office. Since he wanted other members of the faculty and administration present as well, he got the idea to move the meeting to the old Territorial Senate Chamber, which has been preserved just as it was in the 1840s, very elegant, with nice carpeting, wall sconces (that now hold electric lights in the shape of the candles they used to hold), and wooden chairs from that period. When we all entered that room, Nash and his secretary were arranging those chairs in a big circle so that he would be on an equal level with the visitors.

President Nash is in his early 40s, on the short side, with Robert Kennedy-style hair and a rumpled blue suit. If Lawrence Esterhart looked like Central Casting's idea of a university president, David O. Nash looks like that same organization's idea of a crusading professor. He started the meeting with a speech to the effect that the Territorial Senate Chamber is the seat of Iowa's oldest deliberative body—and therefore worthy of the wise people assembled in it on this day. I thought that was more than slightly butt-kissing, but what do I know?

"Only, how can you call it Iowa's oldest deliberative body?" Isaiah Monroe demanded. Monroe is this tall guy who was wearing a red bandanna over his natural. By the way, they were all still wearing their sunglasses, even in the Senate Chamber. "Our brothers, the First Americans, were deliberating here for thousands of years before the white man started killing them off."

My face about broke from eye-rolling.

"That might be a discussion for another time," Nash said, "but I want to address your current grievances, as quickly and efficiently as I can. What can we do for you, right now?"

"Why isn't the University standing bail for brother Watkins?" Monroe asked, in a loud voice. "There's parietal rule here, right? You are acting *in loco parentis*. Wouldn't a parent bail his son out of jail? Or is it just the white students who are your children? Mr. Watkins is just a field hand, and now that he's gotten uppity, you're happy enough to see him disciplined—at the government's expense. He was white, he'd be out on bail now—if he'd even have been arrested in the first place."

"That's simply not true," said Nash. "The University has never stood bail for any student who was arrested. That would be completely improper, and unworkable. I don't like to say so, Mr. Monroe, but quite a few University students get arrested during any school year. For drunk driving, bad cheques, petty theft, drugs—and I'm sorry to say, sometimes for violent offenses. If we bailed one of them, we would have to make it University policy to bail them all. We're sorry if Mr. Watkins can't make bail, but the University is not going to involve itself."

"We also want a formal apology from Timmerman," Monroe said. "For demeaning black athletes. For making it clear that black athletes don't matter to him or to the University except as gladiators in the Forum. For deliberately humiliating two fine young athletes and not standing by them, as though they didn't matter to him unless they're winning football games for him."

Yes, Monroe said "gladiators in the Forum." Displaying his scholarship and general knowledge.

Finally, on behalf of the Association, Monroe handed President Nash a list of other demands, having to do with how black athletes were being treated generally. Nash looked at them without comment, and promised to discuss them with the Athletic Director, and act "as quickly as is prudent."

"We can only be so patient," Monroe warned. "We'll expect a response by the end of the day tomorrow." He stood, and the rest of the delegation did too, and walked out.

That must have been agreed on, like, "At a point, we're going to get up and leave like he's not worth listening to."

Word came down to Timmerman—either from President Nash or more likely from Feldy—that he would have to eat dirt for the sake of the University. He made a speech of apology at a meeting of the full squad that afternoon. Gary repeated it to me, as best as he could remember.

"It was not prudent of me to have announced the names of the suspended athletes," was Gary's version. "If I had been asked directly about their absence, I would have had to provide an explanation, but in retrospect it was a mistake for me to have brought the subject up myself, and I apologize.

"It was also unwise of me to have singled the two players out in front of the whole team. I can only explain that I was frustrated with the situation, and I acted without thinking my actions through. I apologize for that, also."

"Some of the black players were grumbling about that," Gary told me, "then one of them—Leroy Marshall—he gets up and says something like, 'This apology only goes so far and we doubt that you're being sincere. Our association has presented a list of demands to President Nash, and we are fully prepared to walk off of spring practice if the Association's demands aren't met.'

"That got Timmerman good and mad, I could tell, although he was doing a real good job of keeping cool under the circumstances. He said, 'You all know my policy regarding unexcused absences from practice. You probably remember that I dismissed one of our starters, last August, for missing a practice. That will happen this time, too.'"

§

We were hearing, all last week, about campuses all over the country going insane because of what happened at Kent State, and at

Jackson State, too, but the commotion never got much above a dull roar here at State University—hardly any violence, and not much property damage—because there were two competing protest movements going on. The anti-war demonstrators, and the various black-led groups, were split and didn't organize any kind of unified incidents.

On Wednesday afternoon, 16 black players—including seven freshmen who would have been on the varsity squad in the fall—didn't show up for practice. Timmerman told the rest of the team—and the press, following the practice session—that they were dismissed from the squad. Four black players—all four of them starters, and highly regarded—did continue to show up for practice, so they're still on the team.

When reporters asked Timmerman if those 16 might be able to rejoin the squad later, Timmerman said, "They're off the team. Period. They will not be playing as Rivercats this fall. This is going to hurt the team, and it's going to hurt the young men who have left the team. We have one set of rules here. Those rules have to apply to everyone equally, on an integrated team in an integrated university. I feel terrible about what these young men have done to their futures, but it was their decision. I'm sure they're all adult enough that they'll be able to live with it.

"The men who have remained with our program have decided that they want to win football games. They're the type of students I consider deserving of State University's resources."

On Thursday, a new organization—calling itself the Black Athletes Union—released a statement that it called "an open letter to the public," and sent it to several newspapers and radio and TV stations in Iowa. It said, in part:

> We wish it known that we do not have now, and never had, any intentions of not partaking of the intercollegiate athletic programs at State University. Our primary concern is to demonstrate through our protest that an intolerable situation exists at State University for all Afro-American people, not just athletes.

We want assurance that the machinery has been set in motion to alleviate the situation as it exists. Complete satisfaction and not pacification is our goal.

It has been stated that State University has an integrated football team and an integrated community. We maintain that this is false.

Athletes and athletics obviously play a major part in the lives of Afro-American people. Outstanding Afro-American athletes are often hero symbols to Afro-American children. However, if Jesse Owens sets a world sprinting record and is subsequently only allowed to race against horses, if Muhammad Ali wins the World Heavyweight Championship and is subsequently sentenced to prison for being an uppity nigger, if Jim Brown sets rushing records and still has to quit professional football because he isn't being paid enough to make him want to keep playing, that does not represent progress.

Such is the case of the Afro-American athlete at State U. There are problems unique to the Afro-American athlete and those of a more general nature to the Blackman. The resolution to both is imperative.

Brought into focus here is the slave-master relationship. The Afro-American athlete, for example, is the gladiator who performs in the arena for the pleasure of the white masses. He is brought from the Afro-American plantation, typically called high school, which is predominately Afro-American and is in the business of providing athletic fodder. By any human standard, predominately Afro-American high schools are unequal to that which exists for the white community in the grand plantation that is America: noted for their out-of-date textbooks, inadequate supplies, and poorly prepared teachers.

The Afro-American gladiator brought into this oppressive campus environment, representing approximately one percent of the population, is trained to razor athletic sharpness and used to thrill the white spectators. Incidental to this razor sharpness is the problem of eligibility. Eligibility has two faces: one is the image; the other is academic.

The image is supposed to conform to middle-class standards, so the ideal Afro-American athlete must remain quiet and unobtrusive. The academic face represents the greatest paradox.

The requirements of athletic eligibility do not meet those of graduation. Why? Simply because it was never intended for the Afro-American athlete to graduate. At the end of four years, the Afro-American gladiator may be tossed back onto the Plantation, or sent to die in Vietnam, exhausted from his toil and exploitation in white man's America, and now expelled from it.

It is intended that he be broken, exhausted, in body, mind, and spirit, because otherwise, healthy and able-bodied, he potentially represents the greatest threat to this society, politically and revolutionary.

We hereby resolve to resist the white pig-masters. The Afro-American athlete will not accept the treatment of old.

It sure looks to me like this organization is working against the black athletes they claim they're trying to help—whether they realize it or not.

By Sunday, May 10, that statement had appeared in several newspapers, including the *Register*. On Tuesday, May 12, the *Statesman* reported that the seven freshmen who had left the team had disassociated themselves from the BAU and were asking to be reinstated. The *Statesman* quoted a spokesman for that group of freshmen as saying they believed State University and the

214

athletic department "are doing the best they can to fix the problems" that led to the boycott and dismissals.

Professor Mathers, chairman of the Board in Control of Athletics, issued a communiqué that same day, to the effect that "steps are being taken" to offer improved counseling and guidance services to State University athletes of all races, and the Board is "exploring ways" to extend financial assistance to athletes beyond the terms of their eligibility, without giving them preferential treatment on account of their being athletes, or on account of race, etc. But, the statement went on, "the Board reaffirms its policy that matters of team morale and discipline must be dealt with by the coaches and squad members concerned."

In other words, the Board will not reinstate the striking players.

That afternoon, I was at a press conference where five spokesmen for the BAU listed their group's demands. They added that the Board's statement was generally in accord with those demands. It was pretty clear to me that they were trying to walk back the walk-out, so to speak. The demands are:

1. Better and more specialized academic counseling
2. Financial aid provided up to graduation, even if it takes more than four years.
3. A five-year scholarship for athletes who need an extra year for graduation.
4. Relaxed rules about athletes' personal conduct, including political expression.
5. An allowance of $20 per month for athletes.

Mathers was quoted in the next morning's papers: "For nearly a year, the Board has been reviewing the program of counseling services for athletes, as well as rules concerning grants-in-aid, both regarding the monthly allowance, and aid to athletes who need a fifth year.

"The Board has reaffirmed its position in favor of the increased aid in the fifth year, and has advised our faculty representative to the Big Ten to support or initiate these charges.

"We have appointed a committee, chaired by the University Counseling Service, to coordinate implementation.

"All of this was reported to the black athletes on Monday, May 4, and preceded the boycott of practice by 16 athletes on May 6, which has led to their current status."

So, if Mathers were telling the truth, the higher-ups had been in the process of granting some if not all of the striking students' requests a couple of days before, but the students struck anyway.

Meanwhile, the AASASI, and several other individuals and organizations, have been trying to raise ten percent of Watkins' $100,000 bail in cash, and find someone who can put up real estate as surety, to get Watkins out of jail.

I have heard that they approached the one truly wealthy negro family in State City: Sonny Bell's parents, Nelson, Sr. and Geraldine Bell. The elder Nelson Bell came here from St. Louis, long ago, and founded a shoeshine parlor in downtown State City in the early 1920s. He hired men who were just passing through town: hobos who would work for a day or two, or maybe a week or two, then move on. Everyone in town supposed Mr. Bell did pretty well, since nearly every man in State City came into his store for a shine, or to get his shoes re-soled. Mrs. Bell got a good reputation as a seamstress. But nobody ever saw Mr. Bell or his wife spending any more of their money than they had to.

What the Bells were doing, all those years, was investing in land: in real estate that nobody else wanted. It wasn't arable land; it was mostly scrub and woodland outside of State City, that they could buy for almost nothing. They knew, obviously, that State City was sure to grow, and that one day, developers would be interested in that land.

The Bells probably never foresaw the building of the Interstate Highway, in the 1950s and 60s. That was when they hit the jackpot. The Federal government paid them top dollar for huge chunks of land. Today, the Bells may be the richest family in State City, but you would never know it from the look of them.

Mr. Bell, Sr. is a stringy, grim-looking old man. His wife looks like a female version of him. I've never been introduced to her, but I've known Mr. Bell ever since we moved to State City.

When I was little, Feldy would take me into Bell's Shoe Repair sometimes, and we would both get a shine. Mr. Bell isn't much of a smiler, but he was always so friendly and polite to me, like it was a special treat for him whenever I came in. He would always call me "Miss Feldevert."

He and Mrs. Bell still live in a little house in a neighborhood that used to be the "colored section," back when State City was segregated. But Mr. Bell has sold his shine parlor, and he and his wife spend a lot of time traveling.

Nowadays, whenever I see Mr. Bell on the street, he always has time to talk. He'll tell me about how he and Mrs. Bell just got back from Italy—where they visited the Vatican and saw the Sistine Chapel, and attended the opera at La Scala—or from Japan.

"Tokyo surely is exciting, Miss Feldevert, but my wife and I fell in love with Kyoto. It might be the most beautiful city in the world." Like that.

I've been told that when the Charles Watkins Bail Committee approached him, Mr. Bell said something to the effect of, "That boy's guilty as hell. Why am I gonna trust him to show up for his trial? You show me someone else in this town who's fool enough to put up a chunk of their real estate, maybe half of that figure, then maybe we can talk."

The committee appealed to Mrs. Barfield Temple, one of my parents' friends. She's white, a widow; her husband was a banker and one of the big wheels in the Democratic party. Mrs. Temple said she "would be honored to join forces with Mr. Bell to help right this wrong," i.e., chip in a piece of her own real estate.

So, Charles Watkins has been indicted for first-degree murder, and released on bail. His trial has been set for August, although it will probably be postponed for several months beyond that. He's not going to be playing football this fall.

BACK TO WISCONSIN

My sophomore year is almost over. It's finals week. Our family is scheduled to drive up to Door County, to stay for at least two months. I can't wait. I am exhausted. Some days, I feel like a zombie, forcing myself along. It seems like I can't think of anything besides how much I would love to sleep.

But I can't believe how much I got done this year: my reporting; my Monday morning broadcasts; practicing my cello as I can; the orchestra concerts; the chamber music performances; participating in various activities at Iota, such as Greek Week—and very, very occasionally spending time with Gary.

Gary and I are lounging on the grass, on the banks of the State River, outside the Memorial Union. We're not really studying, not really having a discussion, not really making out, but a little of each. We've been talking about Watkins, and about girls who get involved with that type of guy—and how athletes seem to have such an advantage, just from being athletes, which is not hard to explain.

"There are girls all over town who just love to do it with athletes," Gary says. "I don't mean to shock you, but it's true. Some of them prefer the black ones."

"How would you know?"

I'm only half joking. I don't want to hear the true answer. I've known all along what Gary has just told me. And I know, from the talk at Iota, that young men need "relief." I suppose there's a good chance that Gary relieves himself in the way most athletes are able to do, but I don't want to think about it. I can't help torturing myself with the idea that he's using some other girl, or more than one.

"Guys talk. They ask me about you, too." Gary grins at me. "I tell 'em you're Miss Kel-*lean*."

That is what I have been. We got up to French kissing, a couple weeks ago. I wasn't too crazy about it at first because neither of us seemed to know how to do it very well, but now that we have the hang of it, it's not bad. Obviously, Gary's previous girlfriend never bothered to teach him to do it better, or maybe she didn't know any better either.

The couple of times when Gary has tried to touch my breasts—over my clothes—I have gently taken his hand away, while still kissing him, to show that I'm not offended even if I don't want him going there. Considering the stories I hear from other girls, about other guys, I have nothing to complain about. Gary has been more than respectful.

"You're really gonna wait till you're married?" Gary is asking me now. He's grinning, but he wants a discussion. I'm not going to give him one.

"Thou shalt not commit adultery," I say. "That's as clear as it gets. Nothing more to be said."

"What's the farthest you're allowed to go that isn't adultery?"

"I don't think about how far I'm allowed to go. It's how far I allow myself to go. Which is this far, right now. Sorry, Dear."

I squeeze Gary's hand; I want to console him somehow.

"But you're the only guy I've ever gone this far with, if that means anything."

Gary can't think of a clever response.

§

We got up to Wisconsin in time to catch the last day of spring turkey season. I got one. Birdy, Feldy, and us four younger kids are here for the whole summer; Lou, Jack, and Jerry have each visited for a weekend with their wives. Those who enjoy fishing (not me) have been going after perch and musky. We all play golf, every day when it isn't raining, at the country club nearby or at one or another of the resort courses in the area. Usually we break into two threesomes, each with a girl and two boys. If we're in a hurry, we play a sixsome scramble.

Win might not be much of an athlete in general, but he's on the State University golf team. On championship-level courses, his game is about 75, from the tips. Win is unflappable on the course. Even after a horrible shot, I never hear him say anything stronger than "darn," or "rats." Feldy shoots somewhere around 80; Duffy and I generally score in the mid 80s (I hit from the ladies' tees, so it's not the same); Birdy shoots around 90, and so does Sander, but he'll do better when he's full-grown.

I love and hate golf. It refreshes me, because it takes my mind off of everything but the next shot. If I have any worries, I can pretty well forget them for as long as I'm on the course. But golf drives me crazy, because it's all about consistency. A golfer's goal is to play well all the time, to never hit a truly bad shot. But we all hit a bad shot sometimes, and when I do, it enrages me—internally. I have never, even as a child, had a tantrum on the course. If my performance is off, I'll just steam, quietly. Then at the end of the round I'll head over to the practice green or the driving range to work on whatever part of my game is failing me.

Playing golf with Feldy can be frustrating. I've never seen Feldy be anything less than a gentleman, anywhere else—but not on the golf course. He's a fast player—to him, it's almost like a round of golf is a race—and the group that's playing ahead of him never goes as fast as he wants them to.

Feldy can't always control his urge to hit into them. When he hits into a group, he'll call, "Sorry," then at the next tee, he'll ask if they mind if we play through—if they're so dense that they haven't already offered to let us.

In State City, at all three of the public courses, everyone knows that it's best to always let Feldy's group play through. This embarrasses the heck out of me. It's like Feldy is taking advantage of being Feldy. It lowers the stature of everyone else in his group, when he does that.

On this day, at the Sturgeon Bay Country Club, Feldy, Win, and I are walking off the 18th green, and Win has just shot a 72—even par, on a difficult course. I ask him, "Are you going to join the tour after you graduate? You ought to. You should be able to shave another couple of strokes off your score."

Win laughs.

"That would be great, but even if I consistently shot under par on a course like this, that's nothing like the level a touring pro has to play at."

"Yeah," Feldy says, "It's different if you're doing it with your career on the line. That's a hell of a way to try to make a living. Golf is the hardest game in the world to play really well, consistently. There's a world of difference between a first-class amateur and a touring professional."

"No, I've got an idea of what I'm going to do," Win says, more to Feldy than to me. "When I graduate. I'd like go on to seminary. I'm pretty sure that's where I belong. I've thought about it, and prayed on it. I'm not absolutely sure that I've been called, but I'm leaning in that direction."

The three of us stop at a vantage point above the 18th green to watch Birdy, Sander, and Duffy hit up. I feel suddenly and terribly disappointed at what Win has said.

"But you'd make such a wonderful father," I tell him. "Father of children, not capital F father. You'd have such a great family. Are you sure you want to give that up?"

"Like I say, I'm not definite, but I have the feeling I might serve God better in the priesthood."

It's horrible of me; I should be ashamed for even thinking it, but I wonder if this is Win's way of beating the draft. Maybe he's still holding back on a final decision—and then if the draft is still going on, when he graduates in 1971, he can claim the religious exemption, or forget the whole thing if the draft has ended.

I know, I *know* that's not what's in his mind—but *I* think it, because there's a part of me that's bad enough to think it.

"You know, Win, I'm not surprised," Feldy says. "We all knew you were considering it, at least Terri and I and Birdy did. You used to mention it even when you were little, and what else can you do with a degree in philosophy? If you've got a Catholic family with lots of boys, the one who can't catch the football is the one who's gonna go into the priesthood."

"Hey, I was never *that* bad."

We watch Birdy, about 20 yards away, hitting out of a sand trap. Duffy and Sander are already waiting on the green. Birdy can't hit for much distance, being small and thin, but she strikes the ball so precisely. That's her secret.

"No, you weren't, but you were never the athlete of the family," Feldy says. "You're our best golfer, though. That's a big, big advantage if you're a priest."

Win and I both laugh, then we're all quiet, watching the rest of the family putt out, below us. When they're done, Feldy calls down to them, "Hey, Win just shot a 72. He's going places."

It's nighttime; Win and I are sitting in the screen porch at the back of the house, him with his guitar and me with my cello. We're trying to harmonize with the cicadas outside.

Win says, "I'm embarrassed. You've taken yourself so much farther than I have. I can't play at your level."

"Well, I'm a music major. It makes a difference."

"Too bad you're not a guy. You'd have torn it up, as a priest. You've got the right personality for it."

"Me?"

"You're sincere; you work hard; you actually think about what Catholicism means. You certainly couldn't go into a convent. But I don't see you as a concert cellist. Or a music teacher."

"Oh, come on. I'm going to combine cello and journalism. Whenever I'm on tour, I'll dig up the hot stories, every town I go do, research them, file the story, give my concert, then on to the next town. And show up at one NFL stadium or another to do the broadcast on Sunday. What could be easier?"

"Oh, sure," Win says. "I hadn't thought of that. Easiest thing in the world."

I bow a few notes. "I'm keeping all my options open." I play a few more notes; Win puts in a chord. "I have no idea what I'm going to do. Still have two years to figure it out. The idea of doing the sportscaster thing full-time, though. That speaks to me."

"Go after it," Win says.

Feldy and Birdy come in from the dining room. They listen to us playing, for a few minutes, then Feldy asks Win whether he has made a list, yet, of seminaries he would want to apply to. Win mentions a few.

"How about you, Terri?" Feldy asks. "Missing your boyfriend yet?"

"I wouldn't say he's my boyfriend. But, yeah. Anything can happen over the summer. We might both meet new people."

"Why not invite them up here for a week? Him and his brother. I wouldn't mind seeing them again too, maybe talk shop. We've got plenty of room."

§

Duffy and Sander are twice as excited as I am, about having Paul and Gary Schoyer here for a week. After all, I'm only excited to see Gary. They get to hang out with a quarterback *and* an assistant coach who used to play on Sundays. Duffy is going to be off to his freshman year in the fall, at Devaney College, in Minnesota, where he plans to major in music but he'll play football too. Sander is saying it's a cinch he'll be a starter this fall at Our Lady—although he's a lineman, not a back. They figure they'll spend this week getting their heads crammed with information from Gary and Paul.

It's the first night of their visit. We're at the dinner table, and Gary is telling us that it looks like he might be a running back, this fall. Instead of quarterback. "Paul just heard about it a couple days ago," he says.

"Yeah, Coach Timmerman told me he was going to try Gary as a running back, when we start the drills next month," Paul says. Paul Schoyer looks like Gary will look, a few years from now. A little heavier. "Coach isn't going to let Watkins back onto the team while he's under indictment—and then we lost all those other players. We don't have *anyone* in the backfield. So Blaha will start at QB, and it looks like Gary's going to be our tailback. Gary has mixed feelings about that. Don't you, Gar?"

Gary snorts. "You might say that. I ought to be starting under center this year. Ted's a nice guy and all, but he's not that good."

"Maybe he'll learn, this year," Feldy says. "Timmerman dug himself into a hell of a situation. What you might consider, Paul, since you've got Timmerman's ear, why not suggest to him that Gary could be an all-around type of back, not just a runner? One of those guys who runs, passes, and catches passes, the way Gifford operated for the Giants, or Hornung for the Packers.

"Gary, this might be a blessing in disguise, as far as your future's concerned. You'll be a good tailback, if you can get the blocking. You know how the season's going to go—if we do lose all those colored players, if Timmerman won't take them back. But you could be the one star on a bad team."

"Don't be so gloomy, Dear," Birdy says.

"It's the plain truth," Feldy says. "Timmerman didn't have any alternative to kicking those guys off the team after that damn strike, but he's been clumsy all along. He hasn't been handling himself well. Yeah, he won five games last year, great. But he won't have the personnel, this fall. And I wonder how good he is at coaching off the field. I have my doubts about him."

"We've got to get those guys back," Gary says. "Somehow. Sure, some of them were expendable. But without some of those guys, we won't have a team."

"That's it," Paul says. "Whatever you think of Timmerman— and he really is not too bad of a coach. He's not you…" (he points at Feldy across the table) "but I won't say he's hopeless. Yet. Gary, look at it this way: If we… if we go all to shit this year, if Ted's QB, at least he'll get the blame, not you. Not that it'll be his fault, either, necessarily, but he's the guy everybody's gonna take it out on. Him, and Timmerman."

Paul might be a little tiddly. He took seconds on cocktails before dinner. I know he got divorced recently, but I haven't heard any of the details of that. Maybe he's sad.

Birdy and I are in the kitchen, cleaning up, when Birdy asks, "Are you going to look after Gary again this year? I have a feeling he's going to have his problems if he doesn't start thinking more positively." Birdy gives me a big smile. "You'll need to keep him feeling good about himself, whatever happens, because the team's not going to have much, besides him."

"It's looking that way. I'll control the damage if I can, but I don't know there's much I can do."

It's still light, so Gary, Win, Duffy, and Sander are outside, running pass patterns. Birdy and I join Feldy and Paul on the screen porch. They're sipping brandy from snifters; Birdy and I each pour ourselves just enough to wet the bottoms of our glasses.

"Bengston can't last," Feldy is saying. "The Packers will have another so-so season, at best. Then they cut him loose. I'm putting out feelers. Discreetly. I've got connections; I'll be on the short list, anyway. Which will be tricky, you know, if Brosnan is still an assistant there. I wonder if he's shaped up. Frankly, I'm hearing positive reports of him. He was always a good assistant for me. He wouldn't be able to continue with the Packers, if I were Head Coach, but if he's come around, I could find him something with some other team, or maybe help him get back into college coaching.

"No promises, Paul, but if I get that job, I'll need a new backfield coach. I'll keep my eye on you, this fall."

Paul looks intrigued.

Feldy glances over at Birdy and me, now that we're sitting down too. "I'm telling Paul about the situation at Green Bay," he tells us.

"Bengston was a first-rate assistant coach for Lombardi. Low-key guy, knew what Lombardi wanted him to do, executed Lombardi's plan, let Lombardi be the guy everybody hated. Now he's Head Coach and he doesn't know his ass from his elbow.

"Okay, I'll grant you, he doesn't have the playing talent that Lombardi had, but think about it: Lombardi didn't have great talent to work with, either. Hornung was really good for maybe three years. Jimmy Taylor, okay, he was consistent. Starr, he never had great tools, but he's got composure. He's just the quarterback you want, if you've got a smart coach behind him.

"The difference that Lombardi made was, he knew how to win, and he knew how to procure players who knew how to win, who were used to winning. The Head Coach's job is to win. The assistant coach's job is to make the men under his charge as good as they can be—as good, technically, and as good as possible at executing the Head Coach's plan, whatever that is. An assistant coach might be good at what he does—but then he's made Head Coach, and he's lost at sea. Take Brosnan. He was a terrific assistant, but he had the wrong personality for Head Coach. I knew that, but I had to give him his chance."

Feldy is considering for a moment; it seems clear to all of us that he's just pausing, so nobody else says anything.

"There might have been more going on between Lombardi and Bengston than met the eye," Feldy says. "I believe Lombardi set Bengston up to fail, so that Lombardi would remain the legendary coach, so that Bengston wouldn't supplant him. I can't prove it, but I'm guessing that Lombardi wouldn't have cared if Bengston hadn't won a single game for the Packers. Now Lombardi will probably take the Redskins to the Super Bowl this year. It'll take the Packers years to rebuild."

"They say Lombardi's sick," Paul says. "Maybe cancer."

"That's the rumor," Feldy says. "I'm having a hard time believing it. I'm praying it's not true. But my point is that you're going to rise, not to your level of competence, but to your level of *in*competence. As long as you're doing your job well, you keep getting promoted, till finally you're out of your depth, in a job that's too much for you, or that you're not fit for. Even if you could learn to do that job eventually, it'll take you too long to become competent.

"Paul, this season will be a great opportunity for you to grow, because Timmerman is going to have to rely on his assistants to work with the talent they've got. It'll be up to him to devise a system; it'll be up to you to make sure your boys execute it. Then it's up to the players—and how much they want to win.

"Plus, it's going to be up to you to help Gary adjust to the new situation, whatever it turns out to be. I'll be interested to see how he performs."

§

I'm spending a lot of time with Gary. Birdy warned me not to play golf with him, "… unless you're sure he's good enough that you can't possibly beat him. He won't like it if you do, and you won't like it if you have to let him win." So we don't play golf. We're spending most days on Green Bay (the bay of Lake Michigan, not the city), swimming, and lying around on the beach. We also use the smaller of our family sailboats, to explore the bay.

I don't like to admit it to myself, but I'm feeling a lot more, what? tingly? amorous? in these situations where we're both wearing less. It makes sense: Gary is amazingly well built. Tall and muscular with long limbs and no fat that I can see. I don't like to describe what it is that I feel around him sometimes, but it feels more physical than mental and I'm not going to talk about the physical part. I don't know; I have nothing to compare it with. I've never felt any romantic longing for anyone, at least not for any real person. But, oh, gosh: Gary in nothing but his trunks, with his hair longer than he wears it during the football season, and blonder, from the sun? This is a whole different deal.

I know I've gotten better-looking as I've gotten older: I can't help but notice that. I hardly ever exercise for the sake of exercise, but probably being so busy all the time keeps me fit. I reproached myself a little, at the beginning of the summer, about this bikini I bought. I guess you'd call the color "shocking pink." It's not modest. It's not the kind of thing I ever thought I would wear. I'm not going to let Sister Timothy know about it. But I have to let loose and be a little naughty sometimes. I won't have the figure for it forever.

Gary seems to appreciate it. I'm getting to where I really like kissing Gary. I love the way he smells, and gradually he has learned how to kiss in a romantic way that makes me feel all like I can't describe exactly. It's not sloppy at all. I must be improving my technique, too.

Yesterday afternoon, Gary and I were making out, on the floor of that sailboat in the middle of the bay, and I'll just say that Gary's physical reaction to my charms became obvious, which amused and horrified me, both. I knew I wasn't supposed to be looking, but it's not easy to tear your eyes away.

I told him, "We'd better stop."

He said, "We'd better keep going."

"Uh, not in public."

"Not in public, but maybe in private" was not what I meant to imply, but I had to come up with a diplomatic way to cease operations. Not that I wasn't interested, which is another reason why I wanted to stop. There were other boats within 100 yards or so of us. But I could tell that Gary was frustrated, even though he kept smiling. We turned the boat around and headed for shore, a few minutes later.

Gary said, oh-so-casually, "I'm not going to be living at the athletic dorm this fall. One of my buddies and I are getting our own place. You'll have to come see it, when we're back in town."

I immediately knew what Gary was hinting at, but I said nothing except, "That makes sense."

Then, late this morning, the two of us packed a picnic lunch and tramped into the woods near our house, where we wandered for a good hour before we came to a grove of ash trees, and no people nearby, so far as we could tell. We found a clearing that looked nice to settle on. I had known perfectly well, before we set out, that the main purpose of this little outing was to find a spot like this.

It didn't take us long, once we'd done eating, to start making out again. I'm wearing jeans and a blouse, and this time, almost before I know it, I'm allowing Gary's hands to go under the blouse. Oh, come on: I did know I was going to allow it, and now I'm allowing it, and his fingers have started trying to creep under my bra.

I would not have believed I would ever do such a thing, but it's like I'm telling myself, "Time to do it and have it done."

I whisper, "Hold on, that's not going to be comfortable." I sit up, shuck my blouse off over her head without unbuttoning it, toss it aside, and unhook my bra from the back.

Gary looks like he can't believe what he's seeing. My bra is still on—for the moment. I smile sidelong at Gary and let it drop off. I lie back down.

"Have at it. But that's as far as we go."

Several of my sisters at Iota have agreed that guys always say exactly the same thing when they see your boobs for the first time: "God, they're beautiful." And they say it in this awed whisper, as though they're looking at some priceless work of art.

I've been told that no matter what your boobs really do look like, that's how a guy will react to them. I don't know men's criteria for judging boobs, so I have no idea, but that is what Gary said, in just the tone of voice that the Iota girls demonstrated.

He doesn't know much about stimulating them. Doesn't know about nipple power, which I've known about since I grew breasts. I'm not feeling anything special, physically, but that's not the point. What I am feeling is that this is the appropriate time to make a territorial concession. Another thing I'm feeling, more than anything else, is that I want to laugh at how Gary is acting like he's found the pot of gold at the end of the rainbow.

I'm also flattered. I've been assuming that Gary is much more experienced than I am. And maybe he is, but he sure doesn't seem to know much. I can teach him, if I care to.

This is on my mind for a couple of minutes before I take Gary's face in my hands and say, "Okay, sport, that's it for today."

Gary looks surprised, then he chuckles, maybe because he appreciates my turn of phrase. I take the opportunity to slide out from under him, sit up, and slip my bra back on. I'm smiling at Gary, who is still half-lying, propped up on his elbow, but I can think of nothing else clever to say. Neither can Gary. A few minutes later, we're wandering back in the general direction we came from. We're holding hands, not talking.

Gary doesn't say anything till we're getting to the edge of the woods and not too far from our house. Then, as though we had been talking about it—and we hadn't, for a couple of days—he says, "It makes sense to let Ted take all the heat."

I have to say, "What?" reflexively, even though I did hear him, because it takes me a second to register what he said. Then I say, "Never mind, I heard you."

"If we do have to go ahead without all those guys Timmerman got rid of, we'll have no blocking whatever. In passing situations, he's gonna have to get rid of the ball so fast, the receivers won't have time to get open, and if he hands off to me, if I'm playing tailback, there won't be anyplace for me to run to—except backwards. But he'll get more of the blame than I will."

After dinner, the whole bunch of us are sitting around talking in the front room. In a sort of circle. Not enough seating for all of us, so Gary, Win, and I are on the floor. Gary is talking about the players who walked off of spring drills.

"Paul and I are going to go to bat for them if we can," he says. "I mean, we'll talk to Coach about it. We've got to have them; I don't want to be a tackling dummy, 20 or 25 times per game. If I'm gonna get killed on the football field, at least it's gotta be on a Sunday. Even if I don't get banged up, if I average minus five yards per carry this year, I'm never gonna play on Sunday at all."

"Maybe you're right," says Feldy, "but I've always believed that talent is nowhere near as important as desire. If you've got guys blocking for you who maybe aren't great athletes, but who can execute, can do what they're supposed to do on each play, who can play as mean as they need to play—then you should make some yardage this fall."

"But we do have to have them back," says Paul. "No way we can win a single game, without at least some of those guys."

"It's not going to look good for anybody, if they're not reinstated," Birdy says. "It'll make the team look bad; Timmerman will lose whatever goodwill he earned last year; the program will look bad." She looks over at Feldy. "So will you, indirectly."

"Maybe," Feldy says. "But I'd have been even tougher on those kids than Timmerman. I've been told that he's going to let them re-apply, and let the team vote on them one by one. I wouldn't have done that. I'd have made examples of them even if we lost each game 900 to nothing. I bet in the long run, that would be the way to attract more young men who really want to play football, who want the discipline.

"But that's me; you know how I can get. Probably we'll have to reinstate some of them, anyway. But I would advise Timmerman to look at them individually. Figure out who the real troublemakers are, make sure they don't get invited back. There'll be a few who are good kids, who just got led on. If they can play, those are the ones you want to give a break to."

The next morning: Sunday. I was not able to get to confession on Saturday. We go to Mass and I feel completely unworthy to accept the Sacrament, because of what Gary and I were up to. But what am I going to do? Sit in the pew, not go to the rail, and figure out how I'm going to explain to Feldy and Birdy why I'm not taking Holy Communion? So, I'm up here at the rail, feeling as dirty as I have ever felt. I can barely get my tongue out to receive the Host. I rationalize. I can confess next week. I feel the Holy Spirit telling me, "You will be forgiven," but a black screen is clouding my sight.

After mass, the Schoyers get into Paul's Chevrolet Biscayne to drive back to Iowa. I dare to give Gary a kiss on the cheek and a quick hug in front of everyone. Feldy is grinning at me. Now the family is headed for the golf course.

"They're good boys," Feldy says to me. He and I and Sander are walking from the first green to the second tee. The threesome that Feldy is in, always goes first—so that if he gets mad at anyone for being too slow, it won't be any of us. "I can see why you like Gary. I hope he can get through the year and not look too bad. It looks to me like you've gotten pretty serious about him now, huh?"

"Not that serious. I'm not in any hurry. Not going to do anything that would interfere with my career with *The NFL Today*. And as the next Jacqueline du Pré."

The second hole is a long, flat par five. Feldy, as he always does, tees up at the tips without any ceremony, and takes one waggle. He drills the ball straight down the fairway, about 275 yards. He stares after the ball, nodding, as though he's telling it, "Good job."

"Way to hit 'em, Feldy," Sander says. He sets up at the tips, too. His drive isn't his best: a duck hook that goes into the rough, about 220 yards along. "Shit." He's about to slam his clubhead onto the ground, but stops himself because Feldy would have shamed him.

"You're not bad there," says Feldy. "You've got a clean shot. You'll get a birdie yet."

We walk forward to the ladies' tee. I hit my drive about 200 yards, on the same line as Feldy's, so that I lie not too far behind him. We walk off the tee together, while Sander peels off to the left to find his ball.

"They're good boys, both of them," Feldy says again. "The older boy, he was a good quarterback for me, a few years back, but he does have a way of letting Mr. Emotion take over for him. And he was drinking a little, did you notice? You might want to watch Gary. That sort of thing can run in families."

BOOK IV

JUNIOR YEAR AT STATE

Dear Mrs. Feldevert, and Coach Feldevert:

Thank you so much for your hospitality. Paul is sending you a letter of his own. I wanted to let you know what a great time I had with you and your family last week, and I enjoyed our discussions, especially about the team.

I'm sure you've heard by now that the team voted to let seven guys back on the squad, but I'm a little disappointed. A lot disappointed, to be honest. Five of them are sophomores. Only two upperclassmen were voted back on. The five guys we didn't vote back onto the squad were the biggest troublemakers but two of them were guys we really needed: Osgood and Greene, you know, both offensive linemen. Possibly we'll have an adequate O-line after all but it's hard to see how. D-line isn't much better.

That means we're going to start the season <u>without</u> 14 players we expected to be on the team this fall. The four who didn't apply for reinstatement. The five we voted not to allow back. Watkins. The two that Coach Timmerman kicked off the team last spring, which got the whole thing started. And then Ciganowicz, the wide receiver, got racked up in a motorcycle accident last month and can't play. Tragakis has decided to quit football and be a pro wrestler, just for variety. We were counting on Tragakis this year.

Sincerely,

Gary Schoyer

Dear Terri,

You can read the letter I wrote to your folks, and I'll tell you more when you get back to State City. I had a great time with you. I'm looking forward to the season and mostly to seeing you again. You really are my good angel. Sorry I can't think of anything more poetic.

Miss you.

Gary

Dear Feldy and Birdy,

Thanks so much for hosting Gary and I. We had a real good time, both of us, and we're both so grateful for your generosity in sharing your home with us for a week. Above all, thanks to you, Feldy, for your advice. I did what you said. I requested a private meeting with Toby, as soon as we got back to State City. We met the next day, and I advised Toby to forget the vote, and just let the players back onto the team. I made the point that if he didn't want to give them much playing time, I could understand that, but we've got to have a bench. I also suggested he talk with Gary, to get a sense of what the team was feeling, and he did meet with Gary. Gary confirmed what I said, and I gather he told Toby which guys he thought would be key for us to reinstate. It was the O-line that Gary was most concerned about. Without them, we have no blocking.

Anyway, Toby did hold the vote after all, and we got seven guys back, which is better than nothing.

Once again, I can't tell you how Gary and I enjoyed our visit, and how much we appreciated your advice. I hope we can put our heads together during the season, too.

All the best,

Paul S.

Feldy, a day or two after receiving this letter, called Timmerman again, ostensibly to congratulate him for putting the strike behind him at last. They also discussed Timmerman's decision to put Gary at tailback. I know all this because I begged Feldy to let me listen in on the extension. Feldy went into the kitchen and got a dish towel, handed it to me, and said, "Put this over the mouthpiece. If you sneeze, you're dead to me."

"I appreciate that you've got nobody else," Feldy said to Timmerman. "But however you use him, you're going to find that Schoyer is the backbone of your offense. Blaha is willing enough, but he just hasn't got it."

"Blaha has grown," Timmerman said. "He's showing me more than he showed last year. As long as he stays healthy, he'll do okay. We don't have a fast man in the backfield, except Schoyer. And he's not a power runner. At this point I'm starting to think about converting one of our linebackers to a blocking back."

"Jesus. Well, it's done now, but we've got to discuss how we can prevent this ever happening again. Once was bad enough. Now, about how you use Schoyer, you're the man, it's your call, but he's not a power runner. What he might be, though, is a one-man backfield. Like Gifford, or Hornung…"

I have a beat, this fall, on the *Statesman*. I'm the "campus politics" reporter. It's a boring beat, because how many different articles can you write about Vietnam War protests? Mona and Mike feed me information about what they and their friends are up to, and they've taken me to a few of their meetings, but it still doesn't amount to much. Some of the campus politics revolves around the football team, this fall, on account of the strike, but that's more the sports desk's province.

All the black players on the Rivercat football team, and some of the white ones, are wearing black armbands over their uniform shirts to show solidarity with Watkins, who is attending classes, but has not been allowed to rejoin the team. His trial has been rescheduled for January, right after the holidays.

The football season was down the drain before it started. This is a team that I was thinking, last spring, might go 6-4, or even 7-3. I figured we would contend for the Big Ten championship.

That's not going to happen. Ted Blaha is not doing too badly at quarterback, considering how the offensive line was devastated by the boycott—and considering that his receivers are not talented. They try, but that's not enough.

Gary, at tailback, has been proven pretty nearly correct in his prediction that he would have nowhere to run but backwards. He usually doesn't get the blocking he needs to make a big gain, if he gets the ball on a conventional handoff. But Coach Timmerman has developed an option play, where Blaha pitches the ball out to Gary, who runs to the outside if he sees daylight, or drops back to pass if he sees an open man. Or, if neither option looks feasible, Gary will lateral back to Blaha—who, because the defenders have momentarily lost interest in him, might then be able to complete a pass, or run for a few yards.

There's no doubt in my mind that Gary and Blaha resent each other—quietly—because of their rivalry for the starting quarterback's job, but they're teammates first. They're friends, they like each other, and Gary doesn't ever say anything to me about any personal problems between them—not that we have any more time to talk, now, than we did before. Still, I have to imagine there must be tensions. They work together great on the field, no matter what might be in their heads. They seem to think alike, on almost every play. Their cooperation is the only consistently effective weapon the Rivercat offense has, this year.

Our defense is a lot stronger than I had expected it to be, but you can tell they're demoralized when they play their hearts out to hold the other team to 20 points or so, and our offense just can't score. We've got this wide receiver, a tall black kid named Rudolph Valentino Binks, who's surprising everybody—his agility is improving with every game—but Blaha can't throw to him on every down. Besides, if the interior line can't block worth a darn on running plays, they *really* can't pass-block. On most plays, the pocket gets broken, scattered all over the field. If we make a big gain on any play, it's almost always by accident. Our second-string QB is Michael Flick, a sophomore who seems to have no clue. Maybe he'll learn the position before he graduates, but he's no help this year.

I'm watching the home games from the press box at Rivercat Stadium, still doing color commentary for KSCR. People stop me on the street to tell me they prefer to listen to the games on radio than go to the stadium—because of me. I can't believe that, but yeah, I do know football—as well as Joe and Sonny do—and I guess I have a natural talent for communicating what I know.

This puts me in a delicate position, since the team is doing so badly. It didn't matter so much in 1968, when it was clear that Coach Brosnan was finished. In 1969, I didn't have to be diplomatic because we were fairly good. But this year, we're not producing, and I can't help pointing out when a play is blown, when Blaha throws a bad pass, when Gary fails to see a hole, when a lineman misses a blocking assignment.

I especially hate to make any negative remarks about Gary. I let Joe or Sonny do that—worrying, all the while, that one of them might remark something like, "Gee, Terri, your boyfriend flubbed that one." But they never do; they never refer at all, on-air, to my relationship with Gary. Which suits me, because I'm not sure about the nature of the relationship myself. I'm too busy to date anyone else, but I'm far from certain that Gary is Mr. Right. I probably haven't met my husband yet.

The fans and the press are blaming Coach Timmerman for this lousy season to some extent, but they generally don't consider him the main problem. The consensus is that the black players' strike, and the Watkins deal, were not Timmerman's fault; that Timmerman has done all that any coach could have done; that he's in an impossible situation at least for this year.

From what I hear—at the *Statesman*, and around town—Feldy is coming in for more criticism than Timmerman. It hurts my feelings when I hear this, but I can't say I'm surprised. Sometimes I wish Feldy would keep his big mouth shut. He does say stuff, in private to the family, and I can't doubt that he says a lot of the same stuff to other people.

During the 1969 season, Feldy kept pretty quiet. He didn't talk much to the press; he avoided exposure. That was smart, too, because he was expecting Timmerman to have an awful year, and he didn't want to publicly criticize a coach he had hired. But then Timmerman surprised everyone by over-performing.

Some people have said—and this is absolutely unfair, but they're saying it anyway—that Feldy could have done more to keep the black boycott from happening. There seems to be a sense—with nothing but intuition, no real evidence, to back it up—that Feldy isn't supporting Timmerman, doesn't want him to succeed. I know this hurts Feldy and Birdy; it sure hurts me. But at least Feldy has a thick hide. Way thicker than mine.

Ted Blaha is getting some of the blame. People are making allowances for the fact that he doesn't have any blocking, but they're saying that if Gary were under center, he might complete a few more passes than Blaha, and maybe we would be 4-4, with two games left in the season, instead of 1-7, which we are.

Most people feel sorry for Blaha, though. He has never been a standout. I can't imagine that any NFL team would draft him, unless maybe as a late-round afterthought.

Gary seems to be a special scapegoat of the fans and the press—even more than Feldy is. It isn't unanimous: a lot of people think he's the only bright spot on the team. But everybody knew, at the start of the season, that he was not happy about being moved over to tailback. So now, when he has a bad game, we hear vague grumblings about his "attitude," and accusations that he "isn't hustling."

I don't believe that. He has just as many problems as Blaha has, with that ridiculous offensive line. Sometimes, if a play gets blown, he can't do anything more than protect himself. Sure, he has pulled off a few impressive runs this year, but his overall statistics are not much. In eight games, so far, he's averaging 3.2 yards per carry; he has completed only ten of 22 passes; he has also caught 22 passes, mostly for short gains. The fact that he is doing all those things—running, passing, and catching passes—is great, but there's a limit to how well he can perform when he doesn't have a team to back him up.

It was a couple weeks ago, the day after the Homecoming game—on one of those rare afternoons when the two of us have had some alone-time—when Gary let it all hang out, so to speak.

We were out walking along the riverbank, holding hands, when Gary told me, "I understand Coach feels he has to use me at tailback. Ted sure couldn't be a running back. But he seems to expect me and Ted to just figure out how to get it done. He doesn't have much of a clue, himself. I don't know if it would do any good, but Coach needs to tell our offensive line that they're playing like a bunch of Liberaces. He needs to tear into them, tell them they're supposed to at least *try*. These guys have given up. It's like they don't care at all. Or maybe they cared at the beginning of the year, till they discovered how bad they were."

"Do you think maybe it's Timmerman who doesn't care?"

"Oh, he cares. It's his career he's got to be worried about. But after everything that happened with the boycott, he's… It's like he got the hell beat out of him before the season got started. He's still trying to recover from that. I think we're all just looking ahead to next year. Ted's going to be gone; there's no question that I'll be under center, but I'm disgusted by the attitudes I'm having to deal with."

So, it goes both ways. If some people think Gary isn't giving his best, he obviously thinks the same thing about some other people. I'm also afraid that sometimes, Gary's tongue gets loose and he says stuff he shouldn't be saying. I can't be his Good Angel all the time: nowhere near as often as I ought to be.

I didn't know Gary when he was on the freshman team in 1968. But I have been told that the freshman coach had a few discipline problems with him. Not always giving his best in practice, partying too much: that kind of thing. Then, during his sophomore year, came those one or two little incidents. That was why I made it my mission to be Gary's Good Angel, last year, whether or not I was thinking of him as boyfriend material: to keep him away from temptation as much as possible. I don't know whether I deserve any credit for it, but he behaved—last year, and so far this year.

But I'm pretty sure Gary's partying was never as bad as all that. He has this reputation that he doesn't deserve, so if he parties at all, it gets blown way out of proportion. Timmerman himself once complained to a reporter, "Gary Schoyer can stop into Topsy's at lunch hour to play the pinball machine for a few minutes, and within hours the story will be all over town that Gary was drunk on his ass at Topsy's."

The day after that Homecoming game—while Gary was with me, I suppose—Timmerman had gotten a call from Jack Brady at the *Examiner* to ask for a comment on the report that Schoyer had been picked up for drunkenness by the State City police at 2:00 in the morning. Timmerman tried to find the source of the story—and he told Feldy about his efforts, at their next weekly meeting. Which is why I found out about it, a few days later, at Sunday lunch at the Coffin Corner. Feldy then told us:

"Timmerman said to me that he's given up trying to run down the rumors on Schoyer. He said he asked Brady where he'd heard the story. Brady said he couldn't prove it, but that his brother-in-law had told him the story. Timmerman called this brother-in-law, and *he* said the story had come from the girl who baby-sits his kids. So, Timmerman called the baby-sitter! This high school girl. She said her mom heard the story at a party. Timmerman says he asked to talk with the girl's mother; *she* couldn't remember who told her, but she thought it might have been the lady two houses up the street. Timmerman asked her for that lady's name and this girl's mother said she was pretty sure that family was vacationing in Europe and couldn't be reached—and of course you have to wonder: if she was in Europe, how did she see Schoyer drunk the night before? People are going to believe what they want to believe."

Then, just over a week after I heard that story from Feldy—on a Monday morning following our hideous loss to Illinois—this was the headline in the sports section of the *Register*:

SCHOYER BLASTS TEAMMATES, TIMMERMAN FOR 'GIVING UP'
Others Call Running Back 'Party Boy'

The article consists mostly of unattributed quotes from other players, from acquaintances of Gary's—plus a couple of attributed remarks that Gary has made at one time or another during the season. It's the kind of stuff that Gary has said to me, and he should have known it would make him look terrible if it got into print. But some of it, I can't believe Gary said. I have to believe it's a distortion of what he might have actually said.

When that *Register* article came out, yesterday, with Gary's first- and second-hand quotes, the press asked Timmerman about it. This morning, Timmerman was quoted as saying, "I have no idea how accurate these quotes are. There's no question we're having a disappointing season, but on the whole, I'm pleased with how hard these young men have been trying, against teams that tend to be bigger and stronger."

With regard to Gary's off-the-field behavior, Timmerman said, "We had some minor problems with Gary, in regard to training rules and such, last year, but this year Gary has been behaving himself 100 percent. He assured us prior to the season that he wouldn't be in any bars, and as far as I know, his conduct has been exemplary, on and off the field. I'm proud of Gary, because he's been taking a lot of abuse from the public during this season—abuse that he doesn't deserve—and he's been dealing with it like a gentleman."

That was for public consumption. Before Monday afternoon's practice, Timmerman called Gary into his office to discuss the article—and their conversation upset Gary enough that he called me, tonight, to tell me.

"It was like being a kid in the principal's office. He didn't holler at me or anything; he was all Mister Calm and Collected, you know: giving me this look like he's Moses laying down the law or something. Telling me that he didn't appreciate my 'popping off to the press,' was the way he put it. Then he said, 'If you want to play next year, you better adjust your attitude.' As though I was the one with the attitude problem. I've been playing my heart out for that guy."

"But you did say most of the stuff that the papers said you said. I've heard you say some of it."

"Yeah, some of it I did say, and it's the damn truth. Listen, do you think I don't beat myself up too, sometimes, for the way I'm playing? I can't point to any one thing that I don't do right, on the field. Every game we've played, this year, I thought I played my best, considering the overall quality of the offense I had to work with. But I never feel like I'm playing *well*.

"Maybe I'd play better if I felt more positive. You know, if I didn't have to think about how we're almost certain to blow the next play, because we always *do* blow the next play. Or how I would have seen that open receiver that Blaha didn't see, on the previous play. Stuff like that."

I've got as good a vantage point, up in the broadcast booth, as anyone has in that stadium. As far as I can see, Gary *has* been trying as hard as anyone, and harder than most of the team, all season. But it does occur to me that one thing I'm not hearing, in this conversation, is Gary taking responsibility for much of anything—aside from losing patience with his teammates.

"I'd love to get your dad's advice," Gary says. "But that wouldn't be quite right, if I went and told him about what was going on. It would look like I was snitching to him, you know?"

"Yeah, that wouldn't be too smart. But you'll see him. You're coming to dinner on Sunday night, aren't you? You can tell him some of what's going on, at least, without, you know, denigrating anybody. Maybe bring Paul along, so Feldy can hear it from both of you. I'm sure he'll have some advice."

Gary and I have been kissing a lot, on those hardly-ever occasions where we're not only alone, but unobserved. A few times, this fall, we've parked at night in neighborhoods that aren't heavily populated, where nobody is likely to spot us. The first time, Gary tried for second base again, and I gently rebuffed him. He didn't say anything, but I could tell he was hurt and maybe a tiny bit mad, so I decided during the next parking session that I had better allow it once again, or he might decide that only seeing me with my blouse on is not worth the trouble. But I have been absolutely adamant against going any farther than that.

During one session, in the dark, in his car, Gary took my right hand in his left, then placed it on his area (his trousers were still up, zipped, so my hand was definitely over the cloth), and encouraged me with his hand to take a grip, and maybe rub a bit. I allowed this for a few seconds; then I took my hand away.

"Gary, I'm not going to do it to you once so that I can repent of it, and never do it again. Better not to do it even once. I'm sorry to frustrate you. Really." I kissed him again, this time with my hands on his face to show that I still liked him. But I did feel guilty about not accommodating him.

I know: masturbation is a sin, but I also know the Church takes a lenient attitude toward it. If I were to do that for him, maybe it wouldn't be adultery, strictly speaking. But if it isn't, it's close enough that I prefer not to do it.

Gary hasn't tried again. But I worry that he's losing patience.

TWO AND EIGHT

By some miracle, the Cats won the following Saturday, at home, against Wisconsin. Gary had his first really good game of the year. He rushed for 116 yards. Then the season ended on the Saturday before Thanksgiving, with a 17-7 loss on the road, at Minnesota. Gary completed a pass, on that option play that he and Ted worked out, for our only touchdown.

I'm living in a single room at Iota Delta Theta this year. Gail Timmerman is now a sophomore, so she's living in the house, too. I'm wondering whether I made a mistake, last year, encouraging Gail to join this sorority.

We got along fine during Gail's pledge year. She thanked me several times in the course of that year for having been so welcoming and helpful to her: getting her into Iota and showing her the ropes. But this fall, with the two of us living in the same house, sitting together at meals, working together on events, Gail is keeping a distance. She'll act pleasant enough if I speak to her, but she hardly ever initiates conversation with me.

I suppose this is because she assumes I'm spying for Feldy: maybe trying to get inside information on her father from her. Which would be a natural enough assumption. I don't blame her for thinking it.

To be honest, I might very well pass secrets along to Feldy, if Gail were to tell me any. I'm giving her all the space she wants, although I'm trying to make it clear that I would be happy to be better friends if Gail wants it to happen.

I got especially uncomfortable about having much to do with Gail during the football season, since I was pretty sure that if I tried to commiserate with her after a loss, it would be taken the wrong way. Only after our two wins, was I able to say something congratulatory to her about her father's coaching—but at least I made a point of doing it when I could.

Feldy might be less interested in inside information about the football team, now, than he would have been a few months ago. Governor Ray was re-elected to another two-year term, at the beginning of this month, but the election was surprisingly close, against an opponent who hadn't been expected to give him much of a contest.

Grandma and Grandpa Duffy came down from Madison for Thanksgiving Day, and when we were passing around the pumpkin pie, Birdy mentioned to them that a few days after the election, she and Feldy had gone out to dinner at the University Club with several big wheels from the Iowa Democratic party.

"Some Democrats are thinking that Ray might be vulnerable if he runs again in 1972," Birdy says. "If he doesn't, we'll have even a better shot at the governorship. But we don't have a strong bench. No Democrat who's really popular and well-known—except Feldy."

"We met with them because you don't refuse an invitation like that," Feldy says. "But I told them up-front that I'm reluctant to go into politics. Unless Ray's next term is a complete disaster, he'll be unbeatable in '72. Nixon's going to run again, and he'll have long coattails. I'd rather not get into it if I can't win."

"You took one of the worst football teams in the country," says Grandpa Duffy, "and got three Rose Bowls out of them. You're the next Governor of Iowa."

"Yeah, I'll think about it," Feldy says. "I gave them permission to set up an exploratory committee, to see how much support there might be for me—but I warned them to keep it quiet."

§

Right after Thanksgiving, I wrote a feature for the *Statesman* on Abiatha Turner, one of the black players who had *not* walked off the team. Turner is a sociology major, a senior. He's going to start law school, next fall. My headline was, "I Didn't Go Along."

One of the men who refused to join the black football players' boycott last spring (and consequently remained on the squad all year long) describes himself as "probably a lot more radical than you would think." Abiatha Turner, 21, recently played his last game as linebacker for the State University Rivercats. He says, "It would be nice if the NFL drafts me this winter, but I'm not counting on it. Whether or not I play professionally, I plan to earn my law degree, here at State U. I feel that's the best I can do to help Afro-American people and other disadvantaged people."

Why did Turner choose not to join the boycott? He says his decision was about "helping and being helpful."

"I knew that if the Afro-American players boycotted, it would leave some bad scars on both sides," he says. "The brothers who joined the boycott, it's not going to do them any good if they want to have careers at the college level and maybe go on to play professionally. Clearly, it hurt the team, after we had had an encouraging season the year before, and 1970 was supposed to be the year when we were going to turn the corner.

"I thought, frankly, that the boycott was a fool's errand. I said so from the start. I was aware of the Afro-American union's demands. I can never be certain about this, but I felt at the time—I still do—that we could have gotten everything we were asking for, or at least most of it, without a boycott. Many of those points had already been implemented in some Big Ten schools. Some were about to be announced here at State University, prior to those demands being issued. State has always pushed its athletes to graduate. After all, we do publish our graduation rates. I always got academic counseling when I needed it, and I understand that five-year scholarships are going to be offered, from this year on."

Turner says he didn't make up his mind to stay out of the boycott till the day it was announced, when—almost at the last minute—he decided to show up for practice.

"I agreed that most of the Afro-American players' grievances were legitimate," he says. "I went back and forth in my mind for several days. It was, in part, the other black players who helped me decide. They were not being subtle about what might happen to me, socially, if I didn't go along, and I did get kind of blacklisted—pardon the pun. I didn't get invited to many parties the rest of that spring and summer.

"When I made my decision, it was based on how I would best be able to help my people. I thought that by setting a good example on the football field, then getting my degree, I would help them in the immediate term, and be in a better position to help them later, in the long term. I don't know, maybe that's a rationalization. It did cause a lot of ill feeling."

Turner says his relationship with Coach Timmerman has been positive, although now that the season is over, he feels less constrained about criticizing him.

"A lot of the fellows said Coach was insensitive. That's not the word I would have used. He was trying to be understanding of the situation, trying to maintain morale, but it was like Coach was almost completely unaware of what has been happening racially in this country. He maybe didn't have to face those issues when he was coaching at Mason Dixon—which is an expensive private school, after all. He knew whatever he knew, based on what he read, what he heard, what he got from interacting with the players in a football context. But realistically dealing with the issues that were affecting us? He had no experience with that. He wasn't ready for it.

"Plus, Timmerman never stood in our shoes. I don't care how good your intentions are, how much black history you've read, or books by black authors or plays by black playwrights. You won't get it. Not till you've lived as a black person, which is impossible if you weren't born that way."

Turner calls several white footballers, including quarterback Ted Blaha and tailback Gary Schoyer, "allies." He says that Blaha, Schoyer, and others stood up for the black players during discussions about whether they should be reinstated on the team in August.

"They advised Coach Timmerman and the rest of the guys to let bygones be bygones," he says. "That's how the team felt, most of us, but there were a few of the players who boycotted, who had said some pretty hard things, and left some bad feelings behind them. I think the white players were willing to patch things up, were thinking about the good of the team, but they were reluctant to let the worst malcontents back inside the teepee."

Turner says he no longer attends meetings of the AA-SASI, although he remains a member. He says he admires the group's former chairman, Isaiah Monroe, a State University graduate student who organized the boycott—but he questions Monroe's approach to the black players. Turner suggests that the issues should have been addressed earlier, and less militantly—at least at first.

"Monroe took an aggressive approach to the athletic system—which, in a way, was a good thing because it brought attention the exploitation of some of the players," he says. "From the standpoint of academics and counseling, the black boycott did some good. You have to admire Monroe's ruthlessness, his willingness to take casualties. On the other hand, I have to disrespect him in some ways because he didn't put himself at any risk, and he really hurt some people. He and his organization don't seem to care about that."

The editor-in-chief of the *Statesman* was so pleased with that article that she told me to get an interview with Charles Watkins, so that we can publish it before Christmas break. It looks like I'm going to do it. I got his phone number from Gary; I called his apartment. I could hear Watkins sigh briefly on the other end, when I finished telling him who I was and what I wanted.

"All right, let's be businesslike and professional about this so we don't waste each other's time," he said. I suspected he was trying to intimidate me, but that could have been my over-suspicious imagination. "I will talk to you provided you agree to ask me nothing about this case upcoming. We can talk about the racial situation on campus, the boycott, any of that. I'm going to contact Isaiah Monroe or one of his representatives and tell them to be present at the interview. I'll have either my landlady or my pastor here, too, to make sure that anything that gets written is exactly what I said. I also expect to have approval of the article before it's published."

I explained that I would be glad to interview Watkins with other people present, but prior approval of the article would be hard for me to promise.

"No newspaper ever does that," I said. Maybe Watkins knew that; maybe he was asking for more than he thought he could get. Or maybe he doesn't know how these things work.

I feel apprehensive about meeting Watkins in his apartment, naturally. I can't help thinking he might be trying to trick me by promising to have other people present, then he'll meet me alone and God knows what he might try. But realistically, I don't believe that will happen.

It's as cold as I've ever known it to be, in mid-December. We had the first snow yesterday, and then the big drop in temperature today. Here I am with a notebook and cassette recorder, in front of Watkins' building, which is an old brick house near the railway station, in what used to be State City's "colored section" and still is, to some extent. It's just a couple of blocks from where the senior Bells live.

A door to the right of the building's main entrance—a few steps down from street level—lets directly into Watkins' living room, which is very dimly lit, and low-ceilinged. Watkins answers the door, just says, "Hi," and without shaking hands he lets me in. The room is not only dim, but foggy with mentholated cigarette smoke, which doesn't have anywhere to go because of the low ceiling and it being too cold to open a window. The two living room windows are level with the sidewalk outside.

As best I can see, the apartment is tidy—which is surprising to me, since I've grown up with boys. I see several Day-Glo posters on the wall, and a large one of Jimi Hendrix. I don't know Isaiah Monroe, but I recognize him, sitting in a far corner of the room, smoking. He still has his sunglasses on. Watkins motions for me to sit on the couch; he sinks grandly into a stuffed orange Naugahyde armchair and lights a Kool.

"Brother Isaiah is here to listen," he says. Watkins avoids eye contact with me, so far. He's wearing his usual black slacks and white shirt, but no jacket or tie. "So, Miss Feldevert, what can I do for you?"

I start by reiterating that I won't talk about the trial, "But so far, we haven't heard you talk about how you're dealing with having missed the football season, your views on the boycott, and lots of other subjects."

That's all Watkins needs to get going. He's fluent. Clearly, he has organized his thoughts in advance. I'm not putting in a single word. The more he talks, the more he seems to relax. I'm writing in my reporter's notebook, but I'm looking up as often as I can. Watkins has started meeting my eye, now. He's looking at me pretty intently. I'm drawn to his hands, which are large and move about when he talks. He's making frequent open-handed gestures toward me, like he's trying to involve me, or to invite me to empathize with what he's saying.

When he talks about the boycott, he's mostly parroting the slogans I've been reading or hearing for months. But if I were an acting instructor, I would say he has "great understated energy."

Naturally, he's bitter about having missed the football season.

"I can't prove it, but someone didn't want me playing football this fall. One way or another, efforts were going to be made to get me off the team. Why? Because I'm visible. I never make trouble, but I'm considered a troublemaker. There's plenty of people in this town who are happy enough to see black athletes on our teams, so long as they know their place. I have my own ideas about what my place is."

He still hopes to play in the NFL.

"Missing this season was a big disappointment, but once my legal difficulties are cleared up, I'll still have two more seasons of eligibility. I might not have to use them. I'm sure plenty of teams in the NFL will be glad to consider me as a free agent."

I don't want to let Watkins drift too far from the present.

"Do you have any regrets?"

"Yeah, I regret having been in that house at the wrong time. Look, they found it convenient to prosecute me. I won't say there was some grand conspiracy to set me up, but when the opportunity arose to nail me, they took full advantage. A winning football team was secondary. More important was to find a black player they could make an example of, to ensure that the rest of the black players would be docile. Yes, I was in that house. So were a lot of guys. I don't like to speak ill of the dead, but there was all kinds of traffic in and out of that lady's apartment."

He catches his *double entendre*, and chuckles, grimly.

"A lot of in and out, right? They had enough to prove I had been in that room. That was all they needed. So instead of a career in the NFL, I might end up with life in the pen because someone had to make a point."

"Do you blame anybody specific for the situation you're in?"

"I partly blame Coach Timmerman for not sticking up for me, because he doesn't like black players. I think, frankly, that your father could have done more to make sure that I was provided with effective counsel in a timely manner, and maybe could have helped with investigations that could have cleared me. I'm not saying your father had anything to do with what happened to me; he seems like a decent guy. But there was a big target on my back, from the day I set foot on this campus. A big threatening virile black man: I had to be eliminated. Sure, I blame myself for getting involved in that situation. I had a lot of girls to choose from. I could have stayed away from that."

Monroe has not said a word, nor hardly stirred except to smoke, since I came in, but now he shifts in his chair and says, "Charles, careful."

"That's probably all I should say," Watkins says. "Did I give you enough?"

He shakes my hand when he lets me out. Monroe doesn't get up. I walk straight to the *Statesman*'s offices. I type out the story, as a straight interview, in about two hours. Almost 95 percent of the article is direct quotes from Watkins; it's practically a transcript. I've kept myself out of it, aside from the by-line.

He is so guilty, I'm afraid.

CHRISTMAS BREAK

The whole Feldevert family was home for Christmas: all seven kids, and three wives, now—and the first grandson. Grandma and Grandpa Duffy came down from Wisconsin again. They had to sleep in a motel.

Lou is six months into his job as an Army lawyer—he's wearing his Captain's uniform—and his wife has been hired as an associate at some New York City law firm. Mudge Rose, or some such name. They have no children yet. Jack and Jerry are still assistant football coaches. Jack's wife is a schoolteacher; Jerry's wife has put off a career because she's staying at home with the little guy and she's already pregnant with a second.

We didn't hear much talk about Feldy running for Governor, this time—because two days before Christmas, up in Green Bay, Phil Bengtson resigned as coach of the Packers, having gone 6-8 in the season that just ended. Feldy had been expecting this, and he put the word out, to the Packers' front office, that he would be interested in taking over as Head Coach and General Manager. He's waiting to hear from them on that.

It was a happy time for us, with everyone home and getting along, but I couldn't help feeling tension, since Feldy is getting his hopes up. He said so, to Lou, at the Christmas dinner table, and I overheard.

"I'm telling you, Lou, you can't imagine how I want to get out of this situation. Lord knows I've had experience in turning teams around. It wouldn't be easy, because the Packers don't have the personnel right now, but I could make them a winner in two years. You bet I could. The situation here is toxic. That boycott took away whatever credibility Timmerman earned in his first year. He's going to be another Brosnan. I don't want to be around to see it."

"Well, Pop, the Rams might need you too," Lou said. "Or the Eagles: they're in horrible shape."

"I've got the word out. But Green Bay is my dream."

I'm my father's daughter, all right. I have my dreams, too, but I've got too many of them to focus on just one. I'm at State University on a music scholarship, so that has to be my major, but I'm starting to think that I don't have a true vocation to music. Teaching doesn't interest me. The more I study and play, the less I see myself with a career as a great soloist. I enjoy playing in the orchestra. I might be happy with that kind of career. But I doubt I can ever get good enough to make a living that way.

Being a sportscaster is more compelling. It occurs to me, a couple days after Christmas, that Sister Timothy might get a kick out of it if I told her. I haven't seen her in more than two years, and I'm feeling guilty about that. So, we're meeting for lunch at Hamburgher's, which is an easy walk from the convent.

It occurs to me that I have never before seen a nun in a habit eating a tenderloin sandwich and fries. Sister Timothy apparently regards French fries as a delivery system for ketchup. She seems happy to hear what I've been up to for the past two and a half years. She says she hears me on the radio, but everything else in my career is news to her.

"And you're dating the team's only star player." She's smiling more broadly than I ever saw her smile when I was her student. "How about if you marry him and he makes it in the NFL? That would be quite an interesting combination."

I laugh too. "I like Gary, I'm attracted to him… well, I like him a lot, actually, but I don't… I don't know what being in love feels like, and I don't know if that's what I feel for Gary. Oh, I can't even sound like I'm making sense, can I?"

"You're still young to be thinking about that. Although you have to think about it a little. People change, they develop. You'll marry somebody. You're much too glamourous not to."

It never fails, still, to take me aback when someone talks about me being pretty, or glamourous. Brenda Starr. Julie Newmar. I know that I have grown out of my awkwardness. I know I don't look too bad, now. But "glamourous" is another level.

We talk about the murder. I tell Sister Timothy that Vicki was a friend of a friend, and I tell her about my tiny role in the investigation, and then about Mona and Mike and all the political stuff that they're up to. Sister Timothy looks more than faintly disgusted when I tell her about poor Vicki. I don't tell her the gory details, of course: just an outline.

"It's a turning away from God," Sister Timothy says. "People forget that their souls are immortal, or they believe in reincarnation, so that whatever they do in this life doesn't matter because they'll be something better in the next life. Oh, I understand the temptation. We've all experienced it. It's not the temptation to commit adultery or take drugs or whatever, so much. It's simply the temptation to sin for the sake of sin. The temptation to be naughty. People do learn through experience, sometimes—but you can never count on it. If a person decides, one day, that she wants God to take care of her... well, then God will. Ask and ye shall receive."

"Too late for Vicki, though," I say.

I want to say, "According to the teachings of the Church, Vicki is probably in Hell," but I decide not to.

"I like to think that because God is merciful, Hell is empty," says Sister Timothy—as though she were reading my mind. "But I'm not going to put money on it."

That thought stays with me after we say goodbye, all the while I'm walking home: that Vicki almost certainly is in Hell, according to my knowledge of doctrine. And I am expected to believe that that's how it should be: that Vicki, having turned away from God, did not die in a State of Grace.

It's maybe 20 degrees out, and a foot or more of snow on the ground. I should have suggested meeting somewhere that was nearer a bus line. But walking home in this: I'll offer it up, as my paltry penance for doubting.

Maybe Vicki was made insane by her alcoholism. If Vicki was out of her mind, that would make her less guilty—unless she had had the inclination to sin, and had willfully sinned, then drank to blot out her guilt. It's a chicken-egg question.

Another point. Did Vicki turn away from God? Could it be that God somehow never revealed Himself to her? Is God to blame for having turned away from Vicki? Jesus Himself asked why God had forsaken Him. But God forsakes nobody.

I stop walking for a moment—as I'm about to turn onto Hilltop Street—and I put my fingertips to my temples as though to physically banish those thoughts. I try to play the Glad Game, to give myself reason to be glad of this visit with Sister Timothy.

I'm glad that Sister Timothy was so tickled to hear me talk about my sportscasting, and about how I'm dating Gary. I conjure up a mental picture of Gary, which immediately makes me smile and feel happier. The Glad Game really does work, almost all the time. And now I'm thinking—just a random thought, but it hit me—that I have never had a substantial conversation with Birdy, about Gary.

Till Gary and Paul visited us in Wisconsin, Birdy might have thought the relationship between me and Gary was just casual. She said to me, then, "Gary seems very nice," but she has never said much more than that in my hearing—except maybe to remark on Gary's performance in one game or another.

If Birdy is home, I'll grab the first opportunity to find out what she's thinking about Gary, if she's thinking anything at all.

Birdy is sitting at the kitchen table, writing a grocery list; I sit down beside her without bothering to take off my coat, to tell her that Sister Timothy says Happy New Year.

"She asked about all of us. She said congratulations on the new grandson. She thought it was funny that I was dating the football star. Wanted to know if I was serious about him."

Birdy looks arch.

"And what did you tell her? You haven't even told us, yet."

"I told her I wasn't thinking about Gary that way. Which is true. I know what love means, in terms of loving your family or loving God, or your family loving you or God loving you. But that kind of love, you know, with a guy... how did *you* know it, when it happened to you?"

Birdy thinks about this for a few seconds.

"This might sound corny, but it was when I was watching Feldy play football for the first time. He was so impressive, running all over the field, knocking people over. Asserting himself. I didn't know then that he was the boy I was going to marry, but that was when I felt a real thrill, just seeing him. Do you feel that way about Gary?"

"I feel excited when he's on the field. I watch what he's doing. When I'm in the broadcast booth I have to keep my eye on everything, but... yeah, maybe a *tiny* thrill. I know I have these feelings about him. When I'm with him, and when I think about him. Feelings I can't describe except that I want to take care of him, like maybe he needs me. I don't know: is that love?"

"It might be," Birdy says. "Love is different for everyone. You might love him, but he still might not be the boy you marry. I hope you're taking precautions."

I stare at Birdy; I'm aware that my jaw is hanging wide open.

"I... there's no need to. You mean you thought... ?"

"Well, Honey, I didn't know. I just know everybody does it now. I was hoping for the best in your case, but how could I know? I wasn't going to ask, but... but if you're not, I'm glad to hear it."

It barely lasts a second—the least flash of bright red light—but this is the first time I can remember being angry at Birdy, aside from the occasional little conflicts we had when I was very young. It passes in a blink—but I don't think I'm ever going to forget that red light in my head. Probably Birdy never guessed that I was having any reaction. I let a few more seconds go by, to get my voice under control.

"You raised me better than that." I think I'm speaking softly. I hope I am. "If I were committing adultery in the first place it wouldn't matter to God if I was using birth control. But I'm not. Gosh. You thought I was."

Birdy looks flustered, now.

"No, Dear, I didn't think you were, but I didn't know."

"You thought you knew."

"I'm sorry. Maybe I wasn't fair to you, but we all sin."

"Did you?"

This question has never seriously occurred to me before—that is, I had never really entertained the possibility. Maybe I didn't care to think about it. But now I'm curious.

"No. We waited till we were married. Everybody did, then."

"Well, this one's still going to wait." I force myself to smile.

I think for a few more seconds, then I say, "Maybe if you hadn't waited, you would have finished law school. What I mean is, if you and Feldy had started... sleeping together... without being married... maybe then you would have put marriage off for a few years, till you had both gotten your post-grad degrees." I laugh, even though I don't feel at all like laughing.

"Yes, and maybe none of you would have been born. It's always a trade-off." Birdy stands up. "I need to get to the Hy-Vee. Come along if you want to talk more."

"Well, but are you happy with how things turned out?" My coat's still on and I'm ready to go. "I'm not criticizing, just curious: are you sorry you didn't become a lawyer? I'm not saying you're sorry you had us, but if you could have done both, somehow. Maybe you could have."

"I hardly think about it. In the final analysis, everybody does what they want. I wanted one thing more than I wanted another thing. No, I have no regrets now. Considering the family I have. You might find that that's all that's important, at the end."

I wonder if Birdy is fooling herself. Or maybe she's not fooling herself at all: only justifying bad decisions. Or maybe she doesn't consider her decisions bad. I keep quiet.

"The wash still needs done; meals still need cooked," Birdy says. She's getting her coat out of the front closet, and putting it on. "We still need to bring up decent children, or there won't be any but bad ones. Both parents have to have something to do with that, but one of them has to be in charge of that department. That's been my job, and I can't imagine that I would have enjoyed being a lawyer any more than the life I've got."

§

The weekend before classes resume—after New Year's Day of 1971—is also the last weekend of pheasant season. Feldy, Win, Sander, Duffy, and I all got up before dawn this morning, and picked up the two Schoyer boys. I'm hoping the talk won't turn to football—I'm sick of the endless rehashing of last season—but I know that's a negligible possibility.

It's not till the end of the hunt, when we've got the kill packed into the cargo area in the back of the Suburban, and we're heading home, when Gary remarks that he has had much better luck with pheasants, lately, than with football.

"But it's done now. It wasn't the greatest season of my life, but I've still got a year left to make an impression."

Feldy is driving; I'm sitting next to him; Gary is on my right (holding my hand, discreetly); the rest of the crew is in back.

"You made a better impression than you might think," Feldy says. "The important point is, you were noticed. You were doing a lot. You were in on almost every play. Maybe I would have used you differently. But I'm not the coach."

"If you had been, we wouldn't have gone two and eight," Gary says. "I don't like to complain about Timmerman. He did have horrible luck. But I have trouble trusting his judgment. Maybe he knows more than I think he does, but I doubt it. He's just not bright."

Gary has been reticent about criticizing Timmerman to Feldy—especially when his brother is around. But now, we're driving along and he's citing specific incidents, in specific games, where he believed Timmerman made some bad decision or other. Each time, he's turning his head back to his brother and asking, "Isn't that right, Pablo?"

"I get the impression that you think you would play better if you had better coaching," Feldy says. "Not just the team, but you in particular."

"I don't know. Maybe."

"Well, do your best, next fall. You can always talk to me. Look, with Timmerman as Head Coach, I don't see the Cats doing all that well. Maybe next year isn't going to be the disaster that 1970 was, but we've had a setback. I would be real surprised if you fellas have a winning record next fall. At least, not if Timmerman is coaching the team. That's going to impact your future no matter how well you perform as an individual."

I'm listening, hard.

"You're going to be under center again," Feldy goes on, "so you're inevitably going to get some of the blame if the team doesn't win. Then some NFL team is going to draft you—I can't imagine a scenario where no team drafts you—but unless you really burn up the Big Ten in the fall, you might not be a high pick. Which means they won't have much money to offer you, and they might not have the incentive to keep you on the team. I'm just being realistic."

My heart is dropping into my stomach. I know darn well that Feldy is right. I don't even have to think about it. This is terrible news for me. Terrible news for Gary. I glance over at Gary and I see how glum he looks. Now I'm holding his hand with both of mine. Nobody says anything more for almost a minute.

"I don't mean to discourage you, Gary," Feldy says at last. "You're resourceful. You'll find a way to make the best of the situation. Just give it all you've got. I'm here to help if I can."

On the morning of January 14, I see—and Feldy must be seeing at the same time—an article in the *Register* reporting that the Packers had interviewed Joe Paterno, the Head Coach at Penn State University, the day before. According to the newspaper, when reporters caught him on his way out of a meeting with the Packers' front office, Paterno said, "We had a nice talk. We discussed the job. They told me what they were looking for. That was it. Any other comment has to come from the Packers."

When I call Feldy at his office, in the afternoon, to see if he needs to commiserate, he sounds like he's holding up okay—but he tells me that not even five minutes ago he got a phone call from George Conroy at the *Register* to get his reaction to "what just happened in Green Bay."

"Did they hire Paterno?" I ask.

"No. Conroy says they went with Dan Devine. Who's a good college coach, but somehow I don't think he's got the personality or the know-how to coach in the NFL. Especially not if he's going to be General Manager, too."

"Oh. Oh, Feldy, I'm so sorry."

"Yeah, but it gets better. That's when Conroy tells me that Devine has announced that Bob Brosnan is going to be his offensive coordinator."

"Oh, no. Oh, he didn't."

"That's not a bad decision," Feldy says. "Brosnan's a good guy. He's not head coach material, but he's the ultimate assistant. I'm sure he'll do well. I'm not so sure about Devine."

"Oh, Feldy. I'm so sorry." I'm not just sorry; I'm also sounding like a broken record.

"One of those things. I'll get over it. I'm getting tired of all this, to tell you the truth."

"Feldy, you really want to coach."

"I have to admit it. I used to say I didn't want to grow old in coaching, but sometimes I think I would rather do that, than grow old *not* coaching. I remember what it did to my health, years ago, but a lot of that was to do with my not having the authority to do what I needed to do—plus all that trouble I had with Enslowe. I'm disappointed; I won't pretend I'm not."

"Maybe you'll be Governor after all. Anything new on that?"

"Not yet. It's still just talk, at this point. Probably they'll wait for spring, when the weather's less crazy and they see how the legislative session is shaping up. Then the party leadership will start making plans and seeing who wants to run.

"Or maybe—and keep this to yourself—maybe I'll still be A.D. but back to coaching the Cats, too, by then. Timmerman might decide to take a job that's more his speed. You never know."

LOOKING FORWARD TO VALENTINE'S DAY

I still have almost no social life. Now that classes have started up again, not only do I have schoolwork, but rehearsals, and practice sessions, and the newspaper—and everyone told me being a junior was going to be way easier than being a freshman or sophomore. They lied. They all lied. I have to fight for time to see Mona once a week, and it's almost as bad with Gary. I see him on most Saturdays and Sundays, but hardly at all during the week. Phone calls here and there.

I'm getting to where I wish I could let myself do more with him than just kissing and fooling. I'm not sure, at all, that Gary is they guy I'm going to end up with, but I can't help wishing I could pretend to be my old friend Andrea Schedl, now and then—and then go back to being me, as though I never was anything else. Crazy fantasies I have. I might be in love with Gary. I don't know. Maybe I'm not, but how can I tell?

Valentine's Day is Sunday, this year, so Gary arranged for us to drive up to Cedar Rapids tonight, Saturday, to have dinner at the Flame Room, and then we're going to drive back to State City to see the University Theatre's production of *An Ideal Husband*, and it has occurred to me to wonder if he's going to do something crazy, like propose.

I don't think that's likely: just a silly thought I had. But Gary did have a bouquet of red roses delivered to Iota yesterday afternoon, along with a "Quality Assortment" box of chocolates from Horner's Candy Shoppe downtown, so it looks like he's not indifferent to me, either. The card that came with the candy says, "Share these with your sisters. To my Good Angel. Love, Gary." Gary is not much into saying sweet nothings—never has been—but this is as close to soul-baring as he has ever gotten with me.

This morning, I walked downtown to The Shadow Box—which specializes in Catholic gifts—and I got Gary a sterling silver St. Christopher medal. I wrote on the card, "May St. Christopher bear you through any waters. Love, Teresa."

I'm enjoying this play—although I hate to say it but I'm noticing some pretty serious weaknesses in the script, and, I know: how dare I criticize Oscar Wilde? But I'm losing concentration sometimes because I'm thinking about how I gave Gary the medal over our dinner at the Flame Room, right before dessert was served, how surprised he looked when I passed the little box across the table to him, and how he looked really and truly touched when he read my card and saw what was in the box.

"Thank you, Teresa," he said; he was almost whispering. "This is way nice." He put the chain round his neck and dropped the medal inside his shirt. No, he hadn't brought an engagement ring for me, and I'm more relieved than anything. I never thought he would. But I'm patting myself on the back for that medal. It's exactly the right present.

Now I'm going to disappoint him. I know he'll invite me to his place after the play. He has been so good about not doing that, so far this year. Well, in the fall, with football and everything, it wasn't going to happen, and so far this semester he has only hinted at it, but his roommate is usually there. But I have a feeling that his roommate is going to be gone tonight, and it's way too cold to park, so Gary will suggest it, and I'll have to tell him that I still have work to do tonight before I can go to bed at all—which is the truth, but still—so he'd better take me back to Iota. And I know he'll be very nice about it, and he'll do it, but I know he'll be frustrated, and I'm sorry. Truly.

Then tomorrow's Sunday; he'll come by Iota in the evening, so we can drive over to supper with Feldy and Birdy and the crew. It'll be the same thing. He'll be all nice as pie; he'll talk shop with Feldy; he'll be such a gentleman to Birdy; he'll drive me back to the house afterward; we'll be having a great time; there'll also be that same tension that we're both getting so tired of.

§

Gary shows the medal to Birdy and Feldy almost as soon as he walks into our house. Like he's really excited that I had given it to him and wants my parents to know how much he appreciates it. So, I have to tell them how beautiful his roses are, and how those chocolates from Horner's are about the best I'd ever had, and how much I enjoyed the play last night. Birdy and Feldy are acting all tickled, and giving each other little smiles, all through the meal, which is making me feel like my situation with Gary is nothing problematic, nothing unusual.

Now I'm feeling warm and happy on the drive back to Iota, as cold as it still is outside.

"Thank you again, for the medal," Gary says. "It means a lot."

He's driving, so I don't want to distract him, but I do give his sleeve a touch.

"So, where are we going?" he asks.

I'm about to say, "Back to Iota. I've been hardly getting any sleep." But then I don't say it because I realize that that isn't what Gary means.

"You and me," he says. "Where do you see us going?"

It takes me a few seconds to come up with the right words.

"Well, Gary, I'm having wonderful times with you...and I treasure whatever it is that we have. I do have feelings for you, you know that. I don't know whether I love you in the sense of wanting to marry you, but I can't rule that out. I'm not thinking that far ahead, though, at this point. It'll be years before I'll want to get married."

We're pulled up in front of Iota. Gary nods, and sits back in the driver's seat.

"I can see that. But in that case, are you going to... well, I mean, I love you too, but do you expect me to just keep on with you in the relationship we have now... for, like, indefinitely, in... well, in Limbo you might say?"

"This is what we have now," I say. "I know you want to take it further, but you know where I stand on that. As for spending more time together, that's just a problem we have to put up with, for now. We'll have the summer, and a lot more time then."

Gary sighs. "It's like I'm staying in this relationship the way I'm staying in football. I'm hoping it'll pay off down the line.

Only, you don't want to get married for a long time, and it seems like neither of us is convinced that we want to marry each other. Since that's the situation… Well, I'm human."

"You want to see other girls? Go ahead. We've never had any agreement. We can stay friends. I'll always be your friend."

"I love you," Gary says. "Really and truly. But this is… you know, 20 years ago this might have been a normal relationship. But it's just not. Not now."

"In other words, it's not normal unless we're doing it?"

"Well yeah. In a word, yeah."

"Gary, if that's how you feel, go find a normal relationship. If that's what's most important to you. I wish you well."

"Now, wait, hold on. I'm not breaking up with you, I'm not saying I want to stop seeing you. I'm just telling you how I feel, you know? I'm… giving you something to think about."

I smirk, kind of. I look at Gary out of the corners of my eyes.

"Then I'll think about it, as much as it needs to be thought about." I sit up straighter in my seat and lean over to Gary. "Good night." I kiss Gary on the mouth, but just lightly. "Thank you again for the candy and the flowers. I'm not sharing the candy any more than I can help." I let myself out of the car.

"Thanks again for the medal," Gary calls after me. "I'll keep wearing it."

I wave, then walk into Iota without looking back. Now, I'm starting to feel this awful ache in my insides and I can tell it's not from indigestion, or menstrual cramps, or anything else physical. I know what the feeling is; I know what it's about; I know what's causing it—but I have never felt anything like it before. Everything around me is glowing yellow. I see my sisters sitting in the front room and there's a yellow haze in front of them so that their faces are obscure; so are the words they're saying to me. Whatever they're saying, I'm responding without knowing what I'm saying. I get upstairs to my room as fast as I can.

I know Gary and I haven't officially broken up. But I know better than to think this is not the end, or at least the beginning of the end. Gary has his position, I have mine—and mine is not horizontal. That was an ultimatum he gave me, and I know it. I know I don't have to be angry at Gary—and I'm truly not. I understand. I just feel sick. As sick as I have ever felt in my life.

I have a broadcast to prepare, for next morning.

I figure I'll give my listeners an analysis of the Ali-Frazier fight—I am pretty sure Ali can win, but Frazier hits so hard—so I start writing my script in longhand. I can't focus, though.

I turn to a blank page in my notebook and start: "Rivercat tailback Gary Schoyer last night revealed himself as a boor and a slob. While this might or might not affect his performance on the football field this fall, where he's expected to return to the quarterback position, I hope his balls rot off."

I never talk that way in conversation, ever. It's the first time I've used that kind of language in writing. At any rate, after I have written a couple more lines, I realize that I'm not being clever. I rip the sheet out of the notebook, crumple it, throw it in the wastebasket, and go back to Ali vs. Frazier.

Now—way late—I've done my evening duties, said my prayers, and gotten into bed. When I reach over to switch off the bedside light, I catch a glimpse of the flowers on my dresser, and I'm thinking of how happy Gary looked when he got the St. Christopher medal, and about how happy we've both been for a year and a half now. Any normal girl would be crying, and I wonder if there's something wrong with me that I'm not. I'm lying here in the dark, trying to play the effing Glad Game, instead of bawling my head off.

Okay. I'm glad: glad that now I can dismiss, once and for all, any idea that Gary Schoyer is Mr. Right. But that doesn't make me feel even a tiny bit better. And "1900 Yesterday," of all songs, is in my head and won't go away.

A GIRL CALLED BRENDA

Breakups between boyfriends and girlfriends of college age aren't all alike, but they do run to one of several patterns. One predictable pattern is that the breakup will occur with not much dialogue, and even less drama. Just a tacit agreement between the two parties that the breakup has happened, with both realizing it at the same moment or nearly so. And you might be surprised at how many of these breakups occur on Valentine's Day, or right after. Unless it has happened to you, at one point or another, in which case you might not be surprised at all.

Any member of Alpha Beta Gamma who was living in the sorority house and paying any attention at all would have been able to figure out that Brenda had broken up with her boyfriend Mitch, without her having to disclose the fact or even insinuate it. Feminine intuition is no myth. If Brenda were a little bit low-energy for a few days, right after Valentine's Day, it was easy for her sisters to figure out why.

Brenda felt more than slightly self-conscious about this, at first, because she did not like people knowing her business, let alone what was going on in her head, but once she had thought about it, she was just as glad that everyone at Alpha Beta Gamma seemed to know what was up, because the main fact was out, and if anyone asked for an explanation, she could reply that it hurt too much to talk about it. Behind her back, there's no doubt that at least most of her sisters made the obvious guess: Brenda and Mitch had *broken* up because Brenda wouldn't *give it* up, and Mitch had lost patience.

For three weeks, Brenda kept hoping—despite her previous protestations to herself that she was glad that at least she had made a clean break—that Mitch might call. He never did. Brenda would have considered it unthinkable to call him.

She couldn't discuss the situation with her cello coach, Shona Mapen. Brenda suspected that Shona secretly looked down on her: for dating a football player, for being a Greek, for being so straight and uptight.

Eeren McOolan, her "Big Sister" at Alpha Beta Gamma, would give Brenda a sympathetic look or a pat now and then. Eeren clearly understood what was going on. She noticed that Brenda wasn't eating much at meals, was losing weight and looking haggard. After dinner one night in early March, Eeren suggested that Brenda join her and a few other girls (from other sororities) for a drive down to Boca Cerrada, in Florida, for Spring Break.

"Nothing takes your mind off a guy like another guy," Eeren told her. Eeren was almost as tall as Brenda, but more voluptuous, with thick, flowing black hair: one of the more alluring girls at Alpha Beta Gamma. She kept her love life a mystery, but the other sisters assumed that she was sophisticated in that department.

"Eeren knows how to handle guys," was the consensus, but none of them quite knew what they meant by that.

"There's plenty to do down there," Eeren told Brenda. "And what happens in Boca Cerrada stays there. You don't have to do anything you don't want to do. It'll just be fun to get out of town and meet some new people. Nobody will even know how to get in touch with you after."

Brenda was tempted, but: "It's Lent," she told Eeren.

"So, ask for it back," Eeren replied. Brenda had to laugh.

"Just because it's Lent doesn't mean you can't dip your hiney in the ocean," Eeren added. "Nothing in the Bible about that."

On Friday afternoon, March 19, 1971, there were six of them in the car, from three different sororities. They had originally planned to drive clear to Boca, but one of them had found a special "no frills" airfare that would get them from Chicago to Miami and back for only $100 each, if they flew at night. That was perfect. They piled into Eeren's Buick Electra late on Friday afternoon, after they had all conscientiously attended their classes (which not many students did, on the Friday before spring break); drove to O'Hare Airport in plenty of time to catch a 9:00 flight; arrived in Miami around midnight.

Two young men, friends of friends, were there at the airport to take them to Boca Cerrada, to a beach house that belonged to someone's parents. Those six girls and two boys, plus two other boys, drank beer and listened to records (The Who, Led Zeppelin, Sandy Denny, and others) till about six in the morning, when Brenda found a mattress on a bedroom floor and sacked out on it, clothes and all.

One of the girls, sometime that afternoon, shook her awake.

"Brenda? You're going to miss the sun. Come on out with us!"

Brenda felt slightly hung over, but she obeyed. She didn't bother to wash up: just brushed her teeth, got into her swimsuit, and went out a side door of the house, which gave directly onto the beach. There, quite a party seemed to have gotten underway. Her five girlfriends were there, plus maybe ten other girls she didn't know. The young men she had partied with in the small hours of that morning were there, and quite a few more. A big grill was smoking; people were filling plastic cups with beer from a keg. Brenda figured a little hair of the dog might help, so she walked to the keg and helped herself to a cup.

It didn't hurt that the person currently pouring for himself was a slender, athletically built young man, with curly brown hair, wearing only swim trunks. He looked Brenda's age or a bit older. She thought he looked like he could be in one of those beach-blanket movies about a spring vacation in Florida.

The young man gave her a big smile and said, "Hi, I'm Ron."

"I'm Brenda."

"No, you're not," Ron replied, and grinned all the more. Brenda felt a shock, as though this guy had pierced a disguise.

"You're Julie Newmar," Ron added. "Totally Julie Newmar."

Brenda laughed.

"I get Julie Newmar a lot," she replied.

She also got a lot of Ron, that evening. She found out he was local: in law school at the University of Miami. ("But, gosh, let's not talk about that!" he added.) Brenda told Ron that she attended the University of Wisconsin, and was majoring in voice.

That night, she and some of the others, including Ron, changed into regular clothes and drove to a disco. Brenda rode in Ron's Thunderbird convertible. Maybe she was having too much fun to think straight, but it was not till they were on the way back to the house—Brenda was very tired and fairly drunk—that it dawned on Brenda that she was in a strange man's car, just the two of them, at about three in the morning.

For a moment, then, she experienced a wave of panic. Why should she trust this man to drive her straight back to that house? He did, though. Brenda was duly impressed: enough to lean over and kiss him goodnight.

It wasn't till she was in bed—alone—that she remembered it was Sunday. She also remembered that this would be the second night in a row that she had gone to bed without saying her prayers—but she fell asleep before she could persuade herself to stay awake to say them.

It was nearly noon when she woke. She decided that missing Mass on just one Sunday was the kind of sin she could atone for, easily enough.

Ron didn't show up that day, nor the next. Brenda started thinking of Mitch again, wondering what he was up to—and why she hadn't been able to hold onto him. Other girls, she knew, could keep a guy on a string forever, without going to bed with him, although she knew that that happened less and less often, these days.

She reminded herself that Mitch had probably not been the man she would want to marry. If he had been willing to wait, she might have considered him husband material—but he had not been willing to wait, and she was glad she had found that out, so that she could stop tempting herself into not waiting.

As for Ron, if he had not been interested enough to show up after that first day, Brenda was glad to know, early on, that he was not worth thinking about.

The beach cookout on Monday night got pretty rowdy. Brenda's memories of it were hazy, but she did remember having ended up in a kissing session, on some guy's blanket, then deciding that she had better stop, and move herself to a more crowded area of the party, before anything else happened. Later, when she was somewhat drunker, she found herself lying on another blanket beside another young man, also about her own age, who she had to admit later was a lot more attractive than the other guy she had been kissing—but at that point she decided that she had had enough of kissing strange men.

She tried to get up from the blanket; the young man tried to hold her there. She began to struggle. She whispered, "Let me up."

"Five minutes of hot sex and you can get up," he grunted. He was fumbling at Brenda's bikini bottoms.

Brenda slammed the heel of her hand into his nose, good and hard. Not making a sound, the man rolled off of her, rolled over on his back, away from her. Then he rolled over on his belly, his hands to his face. Brenda scrambled to her feet. She waited only long enough to see that blood was dripping from behind his hands and onto the blanket. He was still making no noise, not even whimpering. Brenda suddenly felt dizzy and nauseated. She walked away—as steadily and quickly as she could, which was not very—past the rest of the revelers, and back to the house.

She had had enough. She was furious: mostly at herself, but partly at her friends, for having gotten her involved with this sort of person. She wasn't mad at the young man whose nose she had damaged. Guys were guys. She was mad at herself for being drunk. She actually muttered to herself, "This is not the kind of person I want to be."

She found a bathroom, found a tooth-glass by the sink, drank two glassfuls of water, then sat on the toilet, peeing and drinking more water, simultaneously, till the room had stopped spinning and she was certain she was not going to throw up.

This time, when she had washed herself and gotten into her robe, she did kneel down by her mattress and pray. She was alone in the house, so far as she knew, but she would have done it even if observed. She prayed drunkenly, but she prayed.

She was starting to dread the next several days. She was liking the ocean, but she was not used to drinking this much, nor to dealing with aggressive guys. She resolved to keep to herself as much as possible for the rest of the week—then she fell asleep, still pretty disappointed in herself and in the situation.

Ron stopped by on Tuesday morning, to invite Brenda for a drive in his Thunderbird. Brenda forgot that she had been so disappointed the day before. They drove to Miami Beach, where they visited the lobby of the Fontainebleau Hotel. Brenda got to feeling less dismayed about the prospect of the rest of the week.

It occurred to Brenda, in the course of that outing, that she did not yet know Ron's surname. Let alone his religion, or anything else about his background—aside from him telling her that he was a law student. Brenda thought it odd, that she allowed herself to know so little, but she decided there was no point in asking for more information, since she would never see him after this week, and it might involve telling him too much about herself.

The fewer lies she had to remember, the better.

Ron was beautiful to look at, Brenda thought. Not big enough to be a football player, but an athlete of some kind: he had the confident way that athletes have. They ended up making a day and an evening of it: driving around Miami Beach while Ron pointed out the landmarks; stopping for dinner at a mid-priced seafood restaurant; arriving back at the beach house at Boca Cerrada at about ten that night. They walked out to a secluded strip of beach and sat there in the dark—listening to the water for a while at first, then kissing—for another half-hour or so.

Ron was the best kisser Brenda had met, so far. Better than Mitch; better than the boys she had met at that party on Monday night. He wasn't the "rush into it, leading with the tongue" type of kisser. He took his time. Someone had taught him. He smelled good: of soap, and of sweat. He was kissing her neck and her ears, too, and Brenda started to worry that she was enjoying herself too much. She put her hands on Ron's shoulders and pushed gently, and told him exactly that. Ron chuckled, and disengaged.

"It's your call," he said. Brenda snuggled against him, but in such a way that he couldn't kiss her easily.

"I could marry a girl like you," Ron said. He was still grinning.

"But not me." Brenda smiled back.

"Well, aside from living in Wisconsin, you're intimidating," said Ron. "I'm not going to move way up there, and maybe you're too ambitious for me. You're going to be an actress and an opera singer; how am I going to keep up with that? Maybe I should have said, I want to marry a girl who's *almost* like you."

Brenda knew perfectly well that she had no future with Ron, but she wondered, then, how many other guys might think the same about her. She laughed.

"Yeah. I'll have to marry a man who thinks as big as I do." She squeezed Ron's hand. "You better walk me back to the house, now," she said. "I've had a wonderful day. Let's see each other again before I go back up to…" (she caught herself at the last possible nanosecond) "Wisconsin."

"Sure," Ron said. He scrambled to his feet and gave Brenda a hand up. She was astonished by his not objecting to her ending the evening; even more astonished that he wasn't trying anything.

They were together for most of the next day and evening, too. They took a guided boat excursion through part of the Everglades. When they got back to the house, another beach party was going full blast. They joined in, but not before Ron told Brenda, "There's a beach that hardly anybody knows about, not too far from here. Really secluded. It's on an inlet, so the water's quiet and pretty warm. I can't get away tomorrow, but I'll take you to it on Friday."

Ron only stayed at the party for a few minutes before chastely kissing Brenda goodnight, and she went to bed that night thinking that she had just had two practically perfect days in a row, which she did not think she deserved. She mentioned as much, while thanking God in her prayers.

Most likely, if Ron and Brenda had stayed longer at that secluded beach, on Friday, not much would have happened. But the beach was a disappointment: not as empty of people as perhaps Ron had hoped it would be, and not as pretty as Brenda had envisioned. By noon, they were ready to leave it. There would be some sort of fun going on back at the house.

Sure enough, the grill was fired up—only, because it was Friday, Brenda would not eat meat, and the non-meat items weren't sufficient to absorb the cocktail someone handed her, which had all kinds of interesting fruit flavors in it—pineapple, cherry, raspberry, others that she couldn't identify—so she kept sipping at the tall glass and hardly eating anything.

The combined smell of the grilling meat and the suntan lotion, which she had been smelling all week, was starting to cloy. The other people there at the party, aside from Ron, were not interesting to Brenda. The bits of sand in her bikini, acquired earlier that day at that not-so-secluded beach, were irritating.

She and Ron wandered away from the house, Brenda's right hand holding her large drink; her left holding Ron's right hand.

About a half-mile along, where the beach became rocky and scrubby (and thus less inviting to strollers and sunbathers), they came to a sloping stand of palm trees of some kind, bordering the beach on the side opposite the water. Some sort of tall grass grew there, too, and ferns. Ron led Brenda toward this area. Brenda felt unsteady from the alcohol. On the spot where they ended up sitting, they seemed well shielded from any prying eyes: they were behind trees and ferns on all sides. Brenda couldn't see the beach, so long as she was sitting on the ground, nor could she see any houses. They began to kiss.

Probably Ron got Brenda's bikini bottoms off because he hadn't made any move toward taking her top off. If he had, Brenda might have allowed that, or she might not have, but in either case she would have known that within the next few minutes he would go after the bottoms—and she would have been prepared to resist.

It has been said that a girl gives sexual consent in the split-second that it takes for her to raise her hiney that fraction of an inch, enough for the guy to slide the panties (or in this case, the bikini bottoms) off of her.

That must have happened. Brenda must have done that. Maybe she could not remember having done it, but she must have done it. Which means that on some level, she wanted this to happen—even if, on another level, she did not. Okay, she was tipsy. Her inhibitions were inhibited, so to say. But if her inhibitions were, her nerve endings were not. She could feel Ron's fingers running through the hair down there, caressing her mound; she could not describe how wonderful it felt. She heard him whisper, "It's so beautiful. Like a flower." She remembered that Mitch had been similarly impressed with other parts of her.

Then in another second or two, Brenda felt Ron's face nuzzling at her labia and his fingers gently tugging at the hair. This combined action felt even better, and was making her nipples harden and stand up under her bikini top.

Then she felt his tongue playing with her labia, pushing them apart and searching till it found her button; she cried "Oo!" softly in surprise. She had known, for years, how it felt to touch herself there, but she had never felt anything remotely like another person's tongue on it.

She felt the sun hotter and brighter than ever on her face; she closed her eyes and saw dark blue, then bright yellow. She felt a tickling in her behind that made her wish (to her amazement and shock) that Ron would stick a finger up that other hole, but she didn't know how to ask him to do that and in any case she wasn't sure she could get any words out, or whether she wanted to. She started dragging her wrists over the lower part of her bikini top, pushing her nipples upwards.

Then the tingling crept up her body and down her legs so she was all pins and needles while her thighs squeezed Ron's head as tightly as they could; her arms flailed up and down at the elbow, beating the ground; she whimpered and gasped; she could feel her body twitching, twitching, twitching; she cried out; she heaved and squirmed; then that little button got too sensitive all of a sudden, so, still breathless, she whispered, "Oh, Ron, stop, please stop!"

Ron did, and in another instant he was on his knees, between hers, looming over her; his swim trunks were at his ankles.

Brenda, having grown up in a houseful of boys, had seen penises before, but they had been pre-pubescent, and about as threatening as those little canned Vienna sausages, even on the rare occasions when she had seen them erect. Her brothers had become much more modest as they grew up, so she had never seen an adult penis up close, let alone one that was ready for action. Ron's looked bigger than she had thought it might be, the times when she had imagined what it would be like to see one for the first time.

In that instant, she wanted Ron inside her—then in the next instant she knew that she *must not* have Ron inside her, that she must do whatever she had to do so that Ron would *not* be inside her. She grabbed hold of his penis (gently, she hoped), scooched up to a sitting position, and put her other hand on Ron's chest, pushing slightly. "My turn now," she said.

It didn't taste like anything in particular. Brenda had had other people's body parts in her mouth before, like during childish roughhousing when someone's finger accidentally had gotten in there, or when she and Mitch (and, in the past week, other guys) were kissing heavily. She could smell Ron's sweat, different

272

from the sweat on other parts of a man's body. She knew (how she knew, she could never have said) that she had to give him both suction and friction. Instinctively, she knew to gently but firmly fondle his balls to increase the sensation, till they seemed to contract into his body cavity and she could no longer get a grip, but only stroke the sack.

She didn't know which part of his penis required more stimulation—the shaft or the head—but as she went along, she sensed that it felt best to him when she had as much of him in her mouth as she could accommodate, and was providing maximum lip action to the bottom of the shaft.

She figured out how to breathe, easily enough. She had had a few lessons on a clarinet, when she had been much younger, so she knew how to breathe while playing a wind instrument, and this was not terribly different. She had to be careful not to let her teeth dig into her own lips and cheeks, but that only took her a few seconds to learn.

Brenda didn't have much sense of how long the whole process took. It could have been a minute; it could have been three; it could not have been much more than that, before Ron was breathing much harder all of a sudden. This heartened Brenda because she knew that the sooner he finished, the sooner she could stop worrying, for the immediate term, about her virginity. (She would reflect later that she had caused Ron to sin, by spilling seed, but she figured that that was his lookout, and if he cared to repent of it, fine.)

Then Ron moaned, cried out *"UNH!"* and about two seconds later Brenda felt hot gooey juice bursting into her mouth. The consistency was rather like shampoo, but it didn't taste like anything Brenda could have described: mildly caustic; not especially pleasant or unpleasant.

She supposed the most efficient way to get it out of her mouth would be to swallow it, so she did. Besides, she knew intuitively that spitting it out would have been insulting behavior.

The process of making this happen to Ron (she had to admit this to herself, even if she might have preferred not to admit it) had been delightful, thrilling. In its way, it had been even more fun than having Ron make it happen to her. Swallowing the results felt, to her, like a final flourish, or the concluding chord of a symphony.

Brenda started to sit up, and before she could stop herself, she belched—spectacularly. It might have been the loudest noise either of them had made during the encounter. They both lay back on the ground, laughing and laughing: Brenda still wearing only her bikini top; Ron with his swimming trunks still hooked onto one ankle.

Brenda knew she should put her bikini bottom back on immediately, but for some reason she didn't want to, yet, and she was enjoying the sight of Ron's penis even though it was now deflating. She allowed herself maybe 60 seconds of this mutual exposure before adjusting her uniform. Ron, without a word, did the same. After another minute or two of simply sitting, maybe contemplating what they had just done, they got to their feet and headed back toward where the party was still going on. Ron put an arm round Brenda's shoulders as they walked.

Brenda felt steadier than she had felt a few minutes before. She thought she felt herself glowing. Maybe she literally was. She felt happy, relaxed, ready to laugh at anything. Relieved, too. She had escaped from a tricky situation while having sinned only minimally, compared to what might have happened.

She also felt tremendous affection for Ron—but at the same time, all of a sudden, she wanted to be away from him. They were about 300 yards from the beach house. Brenda took the hand that was on her shoulder and gave it a brief squeeze before getting out of his grasp.

"You know, I need a nap," she said. "I'm going to go back to the house and lie down for a while—and maybe sober up. I'll see you again before you take off." Ron looked surprised, hurt, so she added, "Or maybe tomorrow. C'mere, give me a kiss," before she split off from him and headed for the house.

Brenda's head was starting to ache. Her stomach felt fine, though, and she was sure the alcohol was not going to make her sick, so she knew it would be safe to lie down. She entered the house and found it, again, evidently empty. She wandered to her mattress and flopped onto it, still in her swimming costume.

The next thing she knew, she was waking up in a room that was dark except for whatever light the night sky was admitting through the window. She needed to pee, something fierce. She got up and felt her way to the door, opened it, and stepped into the hallway, where she could see better because light was coming from the kitchen, down the hall. The nearest bathroom was directly across the hall from the kitchen, so she couldn't help glancing into the kitchen when she heard human activity there.

Brenda saw a man's naked behind. His back. The back of his head. The man was on his knees, on the linoleum floor of the kitchen, thrusting away, like a dog, at a naked girl who was on her elbows and knees, whose face Brenda couldn't see.

However, Brenda could see that the woman's face was half-buried in the crotch of another naked girl—Brenda identified Eeren McOolan—who was breathing hard, with her legs spread wide, head thrown back, eyes closed. The three of them were gradually scooting along the smooth floor as they ground against each other, but they finally found stability when Eeren fetched up against the refrigerator, and braced her back against it.

Brenda darted into the bathroom, shutting the door fast. She figured that Eeren must have opened her eyes, even if only for a fraction of a second, when she came into contact with the fridge—and must have seen that Brenda had seen her.

Brenda leaned against the bathroom door, laughing silently. She was revolted, in a way, but the laughter would come: nothing she could do to stop it. She was in total darkness once again, and didn't dare open the door to admit some illumination, so she had to feel around for several seconds to find a light switch. She then took longer about peeing than she needed to, to give the people in the kitchen plenty of time to finish up and clear out of her line of sight.

By the time she emerged, the man and one of the girls (one of those she had flown down with, but from another sorority), still both as they were born, were sitting in molded plastic chairs at the formica-topped kitchen table. Eeren, similarly attired, with her back to Brenda, was looking into the open refrigerator, seeking a restorative snack after all that activity. Brenda went back to bed as inconspicuously as possible.

Brenda sat up again on her mattress before dawn, having slept for more than 12 hours in all, not counting the bathroom break. She prayed, then, to make up for having missed her prayers again the night before. She also remembered that she needed to go to Mass on that day, Saturday, because they would all be flying back to Chicago in the wee hours of Sunday morning, then driving back to State City. Brenda was certain that any church in the area would offer a Saturday afternoon "cop-out" Mass. But, it occurred to her then, she would have to find a way to make confession before Mass. At least, she reflected, with a rueful smile to herself, she had *almost* fasted through Friday.

She dressed herself in the nicest clothes she had brought: a plain black dress with a skirt that went to mid-knee, and black high heels. She had brought this outfit along, in fact, with church in mind. It would be a matter of finding a telephone book, in that house; looking in the Yellow Pages for the listings of Catholic churches in the Boca Cerrada area; phoning around to a few of them to see if they had Saturday afternoon Masses and what the hours of confession were.

The difficulty was that most Catholic churches had confessions later in the evening, which was no good for Brenda if she wanted to receive the Eucharist on that day.

On her fourth try, a woman at the other end of the line asked Brenda to hold on for a minute. Then, "Father Ramirez will be glad to hear your confession if you can show up half an hour before 5:00 Mass. If you can promise to be there at 4:30, he'll be waiting for you in the confessional." The woman gave Brenda directions to the church, which Brenda hoped she wrote down accurately. Brenda audibly sighed with relief when she had hung up. When the first three calls had ended in failure, she had begun to feel more and more desperate, more and more convinced that her sin had been even worse than it was—that she had, *had,* to put herself back in a State of Grace immediately.

When Ron stopped by, late that morning—as she knew he would—Brenda took her lace veil out of her suitcase and came outside to get into the passenger side of the Thunderbird.

"Whoa!" cried Ron. "Going to a funeral later?"

"No, a celebration," Brenda replied, with a big smile that she hoped Ron wouldn't identify as fake. "Ron, I need a big favor." She kept part of the smile on her face, but conveyed *gravitas* with her eyes. "Only I think you'll enjoy it too."

"I bet you've never been to a Catholic mass before, have you?" Brenda sounded like she was offering Ron an extra special treat. "It won't be the full show, the high Mass with the candles and all. But it'll give you an idea."

Brenda told herself, as the words were coming out, that she didn't know why she was assuming that Ron wasn't Catholic. There's no such thing as "looking Catholic." But somehow she knew he wasn't, or almost knew.

"See, the thing is," (Brenda took Ron's right hand in her left, and slid closer to him on the car seat, still smiling) "what we did yesterday? I'm not going to pretend I didn't enjoy it, but it's… it's something I shouldn't have done, and I need to put myself right with God about it. Which means making a good confession, and doing penance, before I receive the Eucharist again."

She looked serious, then.

"If you don't want to, or if you don't have time, I'm sure I've got enough cash to take a taxi. But I really want to spend the day with you if that's what you've come for… if you don't mind doing that favor for me. I'd never forget it."

Ron had not looked overwhelmed with enthusiasm, when he understood what Brenda was asking of him, but at "I'd never forget it," his expression changed entirely. He looked like Brenda had vanquished him, in a way that left him her abject slave. He said, "Sure, I guess," but his tone was far more enthusiastic than his words, and he was grinning. "Sure I will."

"Lunch is on me," Brenda said. "Let's get it now so that I can fast for a few hours." She showed Ron the directions she had written down, and he allowed that he knew just where the church would be.

They drove for only about five minutes, saying hardly anything, till they found a nice-looking diner. Once they were seated in a booth, Brenda told Ron, "Okay, I'm going to give you my little speech now."

"Believe it or not," Brenda said, very softly, "I've never come close to doing what we did yesterday. And I'm not going to go any farther. That's nothing against you. That was… it was wonderful. And so are you. Really. But I have my standards and I let myself fall away from them, yesterday. That's all."

The waitress arrived to take their orders, then, which would have given Ron time to absorb this. Brenda went on as soon as the waitress had walked away.

"Ron, you're a wonderful guy," Brenda resumed. "I want you to know that. I think you're very nice and I'm glad we met each other. But we're too good for each other, like you said. I'm going home late tonight. Maybe we can keep in touch and maybe not; we'll see."

Ron thought for a few seconds. It looked to Brenda like he was concluding that he faced an immovable position. He shrugged.

"I've enjoyed knowing you, too," he said. "What's this confession, though? How does that work? Always wondered about that."

Brenda described the ritual.

"You mean you actually tell the priest… what we were doing?"

"Not in so many words. You can be somewhat vague. You can say, like, 'I went farther with a boy than I should have, but not all the way,' and the priest will know what you're getting at. If he's a gentleman, he won't ask you to elaborate."

"Then he forgives you and you're good to go?"

"For the time being. He absolves you, in God's name. You have to promise to shape up and not do it again. You know, 'Go, and sin no more.' And you have to make a sincere effort to do that. You can't just confess, knowing that you're going to do it again. Because God isn't that dumb. The thing is, we all sin; only one man ever lived who didn't sin—but you're supposed to be mindful and not get carried away, like I did yesterday."

Ron grinned, maybe bitterly.

"So, no more of what we were doing, before we say goodbye?"

"It doesn't mean I don't still like you," Brenda replied. "I do appreciate everything you did for me this week. Including Mass. You'll probably enjoy it."

"Well," Ron said. He looked glum. His eyes could barely meet Brenda's, suddenly. "Here's my address and phone." He dug into the breast pocket of his shirt and brought out a carefully folded slip of note-paper. "If you want to use it. Can I have yours?"

Brenda had anticipated this, but hadn't decided how she would handle it. She glanced at the paper Ron had given her, and learned his surname: Coffman, which she supposed was anglicized German, possibly Jewish, possibly not. She got a ball-point pen and a memo pad from her purse, and wrote, "Brenda Sheehan, 588 Glenn Drive, Madison, Wisc. 59683. Tel. 414-708-5039." She knew she would have to confess this lie, too, late that afternoon, to the mysterious Father Ramirez.

St. Dennis was a nice-looking church. Not fancy, not very old, but the appointments in the sanctuary were pretty traditional. Brenda approved. Ron sat in a back pew, waiting while Brenda made her confession. He saw her emerge from the confessional and kneel in another back pew next to it, praying. Then she got up, and came over to him, but didn't sit down.

"Thank you so much," she whispered. "We've got some time. We could sit here if you want, or would you like me to explain the church to you?" She was smiling, looking excited, like she was about to lead Ron on an adventure. "The inside of a Catholic church is fascinating, especially if you've never been in one."

She gave Ron another smile, which meant "get up."

"I'll show you why Protestants think we're idol-worshipers," she said. "Or, wait, do you know about the Stations of the Cross?" Ron looked puzzled. "That's where to start." She pointed to their left, to the front of the nave. They walked over to the wall, in front of and to the left of the sanctuary, under a small fresco titled, "Jesus Is Condemned To Death."

"This is all pretty self-explanatory," Brenda whispered, "but Protestants don't make as big a deal of Christ's sacrifice as we do." She walked Ron over to "Jesus Is Made To Bear His Cross," then, "Jesus Falls The First Time."

Teresa paused a little longer at the sixth station, "Veronica Wipes The Face Of Jesus."

"Veronica is my confirmation name," Brenda whispered, and she really did have tears in her eyes. "Because she showed mercy, the cloth she used to wipe Jesus' face bore his image forever after. Such a sad story, but so wonderful. Sometimes I go into church when there isn't any Mass at all, just to visit each Station of the Cross, and remind myself."

Ron said nothing, but he appeared to look impressed, or interested, or maybe he was being polite. The pews were filling up, and Brenda's watch showed five o'clock sharp.

"We'd better sit," she said. She genuflected to the tabernacle, there in the aisle, then took Ron's hand and led him into the nearest pew. She knelt; Ron followed her lead.

"Any questions?" Brenda asked, when they were walking down the front steps of the church after Mass.

"It was a lot to absorb," Ron replied. "But I'm not sorry I had the experience."

Brenda took his arm, and squeezed up against him. "Thank you so much," she said. "I know I asked a lot from you."

"Oh..." Ron looked embarrassed. They hadn't much else to say to each other, for a few minutes after that.

"It was nice," Ron finally said, in the car, when they were about halfway back to the house. "I dunno, moving, somehow. Not that I understood all of what was going on."

Brenda silently thanked God that there had been no guitars.

Another party was getting started when they arrived back at the house. The two of them stayed in the thick of the activity, not going anywhere private, till it was time for Brenda to hurriedly pack her stuff. She and her friends had already arranged rides to the airport, so Brenda said goodnight to Ron there on the beach. She gave him a real kiss, with small tongue action. She said, "I'll write to you."

She did, that night when the plane was airborne. She got stationery and an envelope from a stewardess.

Dear Ron,

First of all, thank you again from the bottom of my heart for the wonderful time you showed me this past week. You were so kind, generous, and fun, and it was an experience I'll always treasure.

Now I have to make another confession, in addition to the one I made to the priest today. I don't live in Wisconsin. I wanted to cut loose and have fun without any responsibility—and I was irresponsible. I could give you my real address now, and I'm tempted to, but it would be a waste of our time and our mental energy. I like you very much and I always will, but we are not right for each other in that way—Holy Matrimony—and we both know it. I wish you only good things, all your life long.
Affectionately,
Brenda

Brenda put no return address on the envelope. She mailed it from O'Hare. She never asked whether Eeren had noticed Brenda observing her, the night before. When they got back to Alpha Beta Gamma at about 5:00 in the morning, before they went to bed, Brenda whispered thanks to Eeren, for having invited her. After that, neither of them mentioned the trip to the other, ever.

Brenda was not proud of what she had done on her spring vacation. But she had done it.

TARZAN TAKES OFF

I've never been a big basketball person. Even as a kid, I didn't much like to play it, even though I'm tall. I'm not fast or agile enough to be good at it. As for watching it, it's only the last two or three minutes that matter at all—and if the game isn't close, at that point, you've wasted two hours. So, even though we had our greatest basketball season ever, in 1970-71—we won the Big Ten Championship with a 14-0 in-conference record, and an overall record of 22-3—I haven't been paying much attention. I've been only vaguely aware that our basketball team was seeded third, going into the NCAA tournament, and ranked third in the nation by the Associated Press.

We lost a heartbreaker, to the University of Florida, in the second game of that tournament—by one point in overtime. That was a disappointment, after such a buildup—but still, close to 200 people showed up at the Cedar Rapids airport in the wee hours to welcome the team and coach Gustafson.

I was out of town when "Tarzan" Gustafson resigned a few days later. Nobody saw it coming. He has been at State University for five years. I've been told he's strict, but the players and fans like him because he's loud and volatile on the sidelines (which is why they call him Tarzan), and a brilliant strategist according to his players. He smokes those long Benson & Hedges cigarettes constantly, on and off the court. What he's famous for—at least, he's been famous for this for the past couple of years—is that with him coaching them, the basketball team will fall behind, then stage a crazy rally at the end, and win in the last few seconds.

Pulliam of the *Gazette* once wrote, "The Rivercats will be down by four or five points with a minute to play, then Gustafson will call a time out, gather the team around him, and say, 'Okay, fellas, we've got 'em right where we want 'em.'"

That might be the only time Pulliam actually wrote something clever, and he almost wasn't kidding. Watching the final minute of a Rivercat basketball game can be a real heart attack.

Rumors had been going around that the University of Maryland had contacted Gustafson, about becoming Head Coach of the Terrapins. Nobody believed he would jump. Maryland was courting him, so what? They have a pretty weak athletic program. What would he have wanted with them? But then, over spring break—thinking to make as little noise as possible with the announcement, I suppose—Gustafson's office issued a statement thanking the players, the fans, the University, Feldy, and President Nash, and bidding us all "a fond farewell."

Gustafson said his wife couldn't take another Iowa winter (granted, the last two winters have been hellish, even by Iowa standards), but a lot of people in State City don't believe that was his real reason.

The basketball team's small forward, Ben Aldridge (the "small forward" is usually not at all small—Aldridge is six-six—but he's known as the small forward in basketball terminology), told the *Examiner*, "I felt it coming, all season long. The team was great. We all love Tarzan and we had a blast working with him. But we were always aware of the infighting in the athletic department, and the football players' strike and all, and we could tell that Tarzan was under a lot of stress."

So the narrative is that State University lost one of the finest coaches in collegiate basketball—this guy who turned our basketball program from a joke to a powerhouse—because of troubles within the athletic department as a whole. The "blame Feldy for everything" brigade is having a field day.

I don't get it. I don't get why people think everything bad that happens to any Rivercat team is Feldy's fault—but if something good happens, it's someone else who gets the credit. It's crazy. It's like people envy Feldy for being a legend, so they're bound and determined to make him look bad, any way they can do it.

Gustafson's resignation was the talk of the campus, that first day of classes after Spring Break. Which is mostly why I called Gary. Way against my better judgment. Sure, I'm telling myself I'm doing it because, as a journalist, I have to keep current with the situation in the Athletic Department, but that's nonsense. The Rivercats aren't my beat, and I could have just called Feldy.

Now here's Gary on the other end of the phone oh-so-jocularly asking me whether I met anyone over Spring Break.

"Several," I say (instead of "What the hell do you care?"). "Nobody I want to have much more to do with, though."

"Sowed your wild oats, huh?" Now Gary sounds all bitter. I don't say anything.

"I'm sorry," Gary says. "I didn't mean it the way it sounded. I'm being a jerk. I'm sorry things happened the way they happened, between you and me, and maybe it was my fault. And I really just ought to have a better filter in my head. Sorry. I have other stuff on my mind right now. Some decisions I have to make about football."

I raise an eyebrow, but of course he can't see that. I wait.

"The situation here is so tense you wouldn't believe it," Gary says. "Nobody's getting along with anybody. Basically, the guys

I've been talking with are divided into the pro-Timmerman and anti-Timmerman parties. The assistant coaches are split. Paul and Timmerman are at daggers drawn, anymore, like Shakespeare might have said. Paul has decided that Timmerman doesn't know his butt from a little white rock. And I agree. We had some confidence in him, going into last fall, but now…"

"Have you talked to Feldy about this? I mean in private. Maybe Paul should, too."

"Paul has talked to Feldy. And excuse my language, but Paul told me that he told Feldy that the shit is gonna hit the fan, big-time, unless Timmerman makes a few changes. I'm not sure what'll come of that, if anything. But if you think Feldy wouldn't mind seeing me, too, yeah, I ought to talk with him."

§

Four days later—three weeks before spring drills were to begin—the Big Ten's Athletic Commission announced a 90-day off-campus recruiting ban on the State University football team, for previous rules violations. The *Examiner* reported that afternoon, and the *Register* and the *Statesman* a day later, that the punishment had to do with a photograph that the Commission had received by mail a few days before.

The photograph had been clipped from an old edition of the *Register*. In other words, it had been published months before, but nobody had thought anything of it at that time—unless they were sitting on it, which is conceivable. It was an Associated Press wirephoto, snapped in Memorial Stadium, in Champaign, Illinois, during the Cats' game against the Fighting Illini last October. It showed the Rivercat bench, with quite a few of the players and coaches watching the game. Standing next to Coach Timmerman was a high school football star from Gary, Indiana, named Buster Johnson. Buster is his given name. He signed a letter of commitment to State, this spring.

That might seem like no big deal, but it was a major infraction in the eyes of the Big Ten commissioners. Big Ten coaches are not permitted to visit, or entertain, prospective athletes away from campus, except in the prospect's home town. Johnson did not live in Champaign.

The caption under the photo, in that old newspaper, did not identify Johnson. Nobody did identify him till the photo was passed along to the Big Ten—presumably with a note inviting them to be scandalized by Buster Johnson's presence in it.

Who would have sent that picture to the Big Ten Athletic Commission, months after the fact? Who would have known that it would hurt our team?

This may have been the—excuse me—the "shit" that Gary was referring to, when he told me that Paul had told him that it was going to hit the fan. It seems that Gary is not the only person in State City to whom Paul Schoyer made that announcement. The story I heard—and this may just be scuttlebutt, but Feldy himself told me this—was that Paul was saying that very thing at a party where several well-known Rivercat boosters had been present, and where he appeared to be talking a little recklessly.

The rumors began to spread. The inference is clear as day, at least to some people, that Paul Schoyer snitched on Timmerman—or he knows who snitched. Plenty of Rivercat fans think it's weird that this suspension would come down just a few days before spring drills. This makes it impossible for Timmerman to recruit off-campus till *July*. Who would have saved that photo till a time when it would do the most damage?

I can't think why Paul would rat Timmerman out. He can't hate him that much. I know he doesn't hate the team. Or, Judas, could it be Gary himself? Could Gary—I believe he's coming to detest Timmerman—have passed the photo along, whether or not Paul suspected in advance what might happen?

It's also possible that neither of the Schoyers has anything to do with this. It could be that when Paul predicted that the poop was going to hit the fan, he was talking about some other poop.

§

Yesterday afternoon, Wednesday, April 7—not in time to make that evening's *Examiner*, so the first word of it came out on the 6:00 Iowa news, on the local CBS, NBC, and ABC TV affiliates—Coach Timmerman's office announced that assistant coach Paul Schoyer had been fired.

"In conversation with me this morning," said the statement released by Coach Timmerman, "I asked Paul whom he regarded as the man he worked for, here at State University. He said that as far as he was concerned, he reported to Leo Feldevert. I told him that I required that his first loyalty be to me, the Head Coach of the football team, and not the State University Athletic Director. And on that basis, I have relieved him of his duties."

Huh? Loyalty? Who is the Head Coach? Does he rank up there with the Holy Roman Emperor? Or the Akhund of Swat? You might fire an assistant for doing a bad job, or for not doing the job at all, or for committing adultery with your fourth wife. But because he isn't "loyal"? What does that even mean?

I've been calling Gary's apartment every hour or so, all day, but no response. Nobody there. I phone over to our house to see what Feldy knows.

"Timmerman has the idea that Paul has been acting as my informant," Feldy is telling me. "Timmerman figures that he and I are enemies, and everybody else is on his side or mine. He knows that you've been dating Gary, and he found out that Gary and Paul were up in Wisconsin with us, so with one thing and another, that's what's happened. I've been looking around, trying to find Paul a good job with some other school; otherwise we'll have to reassign him here, and that'll be pretty awkward."

"It's going to be awkward for Gary, too, you think?"

"I wouldn't be surprised. This is a hell of a situation, isn't it? I have no idea how it'll play out, but it's a mess. Timmerman lost control of that team a year ago. He might actually be unhinged. Thinking there's some kind of conspiracy against him. It makes me sick to see this happening."

"What can you do about it? Anything?"

"Not much I can do. Legally, Timmerman had a right to fire him. And Timmerman hasn't done anything that I could fire him for. This is one of the most frustrating situations I've ever seen. Have you talked with Gary about it?"

I kept trying Gary on Thursday night. No answer. Evidently his roommate was gone too. Friday morning's *Register*, on the front page of the Big Peach, reported that the State University Board in Control of Athletics had called a meeting for that morning—to which several members of the football squad were invited, to "give testimony." I assumed the purpose of the meeting would be to discuss whether Paul Schoyer should have been fired, and what his employment status should be. Right below that bulletin was an opinion piece, by George Conroy:

> A matter not officially on the agenda, Toby Timmerman's reported dismissal of Paul Schoyer from his football staff, could lead to any number of showdowns. At the moment, the principal adversaries could be Coach Timmerman and former assistant Schoyer, or Timmerman vs. Athletic Director Feldevert (who is known to be friendly with Schoyer). The team could fall on any side or could split up into factions. For all we know, the meeting could end in a free-for-all with multiple injuries and arrests.
>
> It appears that the immediate central issue at hand is Schoyer's ouster, but the catalyst is probably the ongoing conflict between Timmerman and Feldevert, in which Schoyer might only be a pawn.
>
> The Board needs to concern itself with the larger picture: the future of State University football, with the Athletic Director and the Head Coach fighting a cold war that's getting hotter. Can that situation be resolved without one of them leaving?
>
> Whether or not it can be, all parties must take care not to get the student athletes involved. They will feel that they're caught between Scylla and Charybdis, and most of them are too young, too inexperienced, and too unassuming to handle the situation adroitly.
>
> As for the immediate matter at hand—if what I hear is accurate—Paul Schoyer has, in effect, been what Timmerman accused him of being: disloyal.

After that closed-door meeting, which lasted into the afternoon, the Chairman of the Board in Control of Athletics issued a prepared statement. It upheld Timmerman's decision to dismiss Schoyer, on the grounds that "assistant coaches of football shall serve at the pleasure of Head Coaches of football." But since Schoyer was under contract to State University, he will be retained through 1971 "with titles and duties to be assigned by the Athletic Director."

It occurred to me that Gary might have gone home to Clinton for the weekend, so on Saturday morning I called his parents' home. Mrs. Schoyer told me, "He's supposed to be here later today; I'll give him your message."

"I was so sorry to hear about Paul," I said. "My father is too. He feels terrible that it might have happened because Paul is friends with him."

"We'll have to wait and see," Mrs. Schoyer said. She sounded like she didn't want to talk with me, so I thanked her and hung up. Gary hasn't returned my message.

The next day, Sunday, an open letter appeared in all of Iowa's major newspapers, from Paul Schoyer, announcing that the Houston Oilers had hired him as a scout, and bidding farewell to State University. I guess this gets Feldy off the hook.

Before I leave State University for my new position with the Houston Oilers, I owe it to myself to address the lies that have been told about me, and to explain the true reasons for my departure. For these reasons I was fired:

1. I placed my loyalty to State University—not my loyalty to Leo Feldevert, as Coach Timmerman alleged—higher than my personal loyalty to Coach Timmerman.

2. Timmerman charged that I had socialized with Leo Feldevert, that I had spent days as a guest of Feldy at his summer home in Wisconsin—which is true—and that I was poorly prepared for the opening of August training camp because of that vacation, which is not true.

3. That I criticized Timmerman to anonymous sources, which is not true.

4. That I did not invite the Timmermans to a Christmas party held at my home. (I live in a small apartment.)

5. That my parents enjoy socializing with the Feldeverts but not with the Timmermans. (To my knowledge, my parents only met Leo and Mrs. Feldevert a very few times, years ago, when I was a member of the football team.)

6. That I had encouraged my brother and other players to transfer to another university, which is not true.

7. That I had informed on Timmerman to the NCAA about the recruiting violation that resulted in his 90-day recruiting suspension, which is not true.

I also point to an article in *The Fort Dodge Messenger* that quotes Timmerman as saying I had telephoned "some parents of kids we're trying to recruit, and told them not to send their boys to State." I deny that completely.

Just a few days before my dismissal, Timmerman was talking about my possibly taking over as the Rivercat offensive coordinator, if the current offensive coordinator, Red Stultz, got the coaching job he was being considered for at another university. I had no idea that Timmerman was unhappy with my performance. If he had been, and if he had not been intent on using me to worsen the conflict between him and Feldy, he would have told me so at the end of last season so that I could resign or reform. It upsets me that my reputation as a person and a football coach has been put in jeopardy for the benefit of others.

This is to say nothing of the ordeal of having to keep quiet and go along, as though I approved of Timmerman's methods. Time and again I worried that Timmerman had lost the confidence of his players and assistants.

Unfortunately, the Rivercats' performance last year proved my fears justified. It's hard to imagine that the Rivercats will win many games with Timmerman at the helm this coming fall, or ever.

I only hope that I have contributed a small amount to State University in return for the rewards it has given me as a student, football player, and alumnus.

On Sunday morning, I read that letter, met the family for Mass, had lunch with them at the Coffin Corner. Feldy confirmed that he had put in a good word for Paul with the Oilers' front office—of course, they already knew Paul, since he had played for the Oilers for three seasons—and he wondered, again, how Gary and Timmerman could possibly work together now.

"Looking at Paul's grievances," I say, "it makes Timmerman sound incredibly petty. Almost like a bratty little girl."

"Well, Timmerman *is* a bratty little girl," Feldy says.

"I haven't heard from Gary in a few days," I told Feldy. "I hope he's not doing anything crazy. Do you think it's true, what Paul said in that letter? Well, obviously Paul said it wasn't true, but do you think maybe he did inform to the Big Ten? Or that he did call people's families and tell them not to send their kids here?"

"No, that's crazy talk," Feldy said. "That's Timmerman's paranoia. I can't imagine Paul doing anything like that; can you?"

"Well, he is emotional," Birdy said to Feldy. "You know that. Maybe if he was in a bad mood, maybe if he'd been stewing about it and letting himself get all het up... possibly?"

"That's the only way it could have happened, but I still think it's pretty far-fetched."

SO DOES GARY, APPARENTLY

This morning, Tuesday, April 13, Gary and his friend Max Gruber, who's a guard, issued a joint statement to the press that they're quitting the Rivercat football team—mind you, this is less than a week before spring drills are going to start—and transferring to the University of Texas.

Gary still hasn't gotten back to me, so I didn't hear about this till just now, when I got back to Iota from classes and practice in time to sit down to dinner at 6:30, and naturally the sisters want to know my reaction to the news—which I didn't know till they showed me the article in this evening's *Examiner*.

290

"There is no way that either of us will stay at State University to play even one more down for Coach Timmerman," said the statement. "The University of Texas has agreed to welcome us as transfers, and we're grateful for the opportunity."

I don't have much of an appetite, but I'm forcing myself to keep calm and eat the lasagna. I have no idea whether this means that Gary has already left State City, or if he's going to finish the spring semester and then transfer. But he is not going to play any more football at State University. I make myself keep eating, and I start getting furious. It's like a betrayal, especially since he didn't discuss it with me. Intellectually, I can understand it, since Coach Timmerman just fired Gary's brother. But, still.

I've got to call Feldy. As soon as I'm done eating. Before I talk to Gary. I have an awful feeling. I'm scared to. But I'm going to.

"Feldy, I'm sorry to ask this, but I have to ask it. Please tell me the truth. Did you encourage Gary to do that?"

There's a second or two of silence before Feldy answers me.

"Of course not."

"Because I remember, after that pheasant hunt, you told him he wasn't going to help himself if he played here this fall…"

"Honey, I did not encourage him to do that. I did talk with him about it. But you don't have to worry about him transferring now, I don't think. You might want to worry about whether he'll be playing *anywhere*, this fall. The one I feel sorry for is this Gruber kid. He's just a stooge, and Gary dragged him along."

Now I'm confused.

"I was getting phone calls all this morning," Feldy says, "from the Board and from President Nash, all of them asking what the hell happened, so I might as well tell you."

There's a pause; I suppose Feldy is organizing his story.

"The other day," (Feldy is talking slowly, like he wants to be sure he's telling it right) "your boyfriend and Gruber came to my office and told me how unhappy they were, playing for Timmerman. They told me that they had been in touch with the Texas program and Texas had told them that they needed State University's permission to talk with them. That is, Texas needed our permission.

"So, I gave it to them. I called Darrell Royal, down in Austin, and I told him that as far as I was concerned, he was free to talk with them. Because for one thing, it's a free country and anybody has a right to talk with anybody, and for another, I'm not so sure but what it would be better for our program if those two young men were no longer associated with it. It's pretty clear that they're not happy here. We don't want malcontents on the team. One of them can make all kinds of trouble, and two are deadly."

I'm not saying anything, and Feldy doesn't say anything, either, for a few seconds.

"That damn Nash, though. Royal calls *him*, after he's done talking to me, and then Nash calls me to tell me that those two won't be able to play for Texas this fall. See, according to NCAA rules, a transferring player can only compete immediately if he has not been recruited by his original school, and never got an athletics scholarship. Well, Schoyer and Gruber were both heavily recruited—nobody's going to deny that—and they both have full scholarships. That means they'll have to sit out a year, at Texas, before they become eligible. Now, I knew that rule was in place, but there are work-arounds, and I was assuming that these young men had already explored them, and talked it over with the right people. It looks like they didn't do that."

I'm listening. Feldy pauses again.

"Let me see if I can reconstruct word-for-word what Nash said." Feldy talks in a higher pitch, and slower than he usually talks, trying to imitate Nash. "He says, 'They can play this year, if they receive a transfer-release agreement from us. They're not going to get one. Not while I'm in charge here.'

"Then Nash says he doesn't know if Texas explained to them that they're going to have to sit out for a year. He says we better find out whether that was done. He says 'We need to contact both the Athletic Director at Texas, and the football coach'— Nash doesn't even know those guys' names, I'm pretty sure— and he says, 'We have to let the NCAA know about this, too.'"

Feldy clears his throat, and I can hear him do that little inhale, like he's exasperated.

"It wasn't my job to do the due diligence for these boys," he goes on. "They should have known the rules, and Texas should have told them if they didn't know. Wasn't anybody on the ball down there?"

"What happens now?" I ask.

"God knows. I can't imagine that Timmerman will take them back. I'm not sure I would want him to. I know how you feel about Gary, but he's got an attitude. He's got a lot of growing up to do."

"Well, I know that."

That's all I can think of to say. I'm not going to complicate the matter by telling Feldy about Gary's and my little spat. I'm just sick about this. How could Gary be that stupid? And why didn't Feldy ask him whether he had considered that rule? I don't want to hear the answer. I thank Feldy, and hang up as soon as I can.

The following day, the University of Texas' Athletic Department issues a statement to the effect that the details of the two State University players' transfer are "still being finalized." Gary is quoted in the afternoon's *Examiner*: "This is a big shock to Max and I. We're still trying to work something out. One way or another, we're going to be playing for a major program this fall."

It's all I can do not to call Gary and scream at him (for saying "to Max and I," among other reasons—that's something I always have to remind myself of), and then maybe listen to his side of the story. I'm too upset, though. If he wants to tell me anything, he knows how to get hold of me.

I hope he doesn't. My plan for the next few days is to go into hiding as much as I can. I'll hole up in my room and study and practice. I'll go to classes, then come right back here. I've got a lesson with Professor Meregaglia on Friday. I've got my broadcast on Monday, only what can I talk about, other than this mess? I'll have to think of something. I also owe the *Statesman* a couple of articles, about the preparations for Charles Watkins' trial, which looks like it will *finally* happen in two weeks, and how do I keep football out of that?

I want to curl up and sleep for a month, and I can't. How do I play the Glad Game about this? How?

§

Okay, now here is what happens on Monday, April 19. That morning, Gary Schoyer's roommate—Matt Sayre, who is a senior about to graduate, a Comp Lit major, and not an athlete—hand-delivers a letter to the Chairman of the Board in Control of Athletics. He releases copies of it to the press, as well, and the *Examiner* runs it in the afternoon:

> Dear Sirs:
>
> In all good conscience I feel compelled to write this as a State University student (soon to be an alumnus), who feels grateful to the university and desirous of protecting it. The State University football program is under attack from within, and it is my duty to report it in hopes that you will act on my information.
>
> As you know, former Assistant Coach Paul Schoyer was recently fired by Head Coach Timmerman on the grounds of "disloyalty." While this charge has struck some people as ludicrous, I can testify to my certain knowledge that Paul Schoyer and his brother Gary were attempting, in various ways, to undermine the football team and coaching staff, and were indeed disloyal to Coach Timmerman.
>
> A few days after Paul Schoyer's dismissal, my friend and roommate Gary Schoyer announced, along with his teammate Max Gruber, that he refused to play another down for Coach Timmerman. The two of them subsequently were accepted as transfers by the University of Texas, but that arrangement has fallen through, and the two men are currently without a football team.
>
> In my many conversations with Gary on this subject, over the course of the school year, he mentioned to me more than once that Athletic Director Feldevert had told him that it would be impossible to have a good football program as long as Toby Timmerman was Head Coach. Feldy, according to Gary, believed that Timmerman had lost control of the team and his coaching staff. Feldy said

Timmerman should be made to resign, and in that case, Feldy would once again be head football coach as well as Athletic Director.

As a result of these conversations, Gary told me, he tried to organize a mutiny by the football team that would have forced Coach Timmerman out. However, in Gary's words, hardly any of his teammates "had the cashews" to go along with the plan.

I'm convinced that Gary would have stayed with the team and done his best to get along with Coach Timmerman during spring drills and in the upcoming season. However, when Timmerman fired his brother, Gary felt he had no choice but to leave the team, with Gruber going along with him as a gesture of solidarity.

I will go farther, and reveal that on the day when Paul Schoyer was fired, Gary received a phone call from Feldy. As soon as he had hung up the phone, Gary told me that Feldy had said, "It's time to make the move."

Little did Gary know that State University would block this attempt, making it impossible for him to catch on with another team.

I'm not saying whether I think Gary did the right thing, by trying to rebel against Coach Timmerman. I only know football from a fan's perspective, and I only ever heard Gary's side of the story. But I do feel that Gary was used as a pawn by Feldy and was regarded as expendable, as pawns often are. In all fairness, this situation needs to be exposed.

I have no reason to lie. I take full responsibility for this statement, but I am not the only one who knows the story behind what has happened. Others know more than I know, or they know it from different points of view, and will talk if they're not intimidated into keeping quiet.

I do not want to cause trouble for anybody: not for Timmerman, not for Feldy, and certainly not for the Schoyers, who are friends of mine. But you, the Board in Control of Athletics, need to be made aware of this mess that is killing State University's entire athletic program.

Ninety-five football players are immediately involved, but we have also, recently and suddenly, lost a popular and accomplished basketball coach who had just given State University its best season ever. Who knows how many other sports, and how many other student athletes, will be affected if this problem is not addressed? I cannot understand why grown men would allow all of this to happen because of their own selfish interests.

Professor Mathers, on reading this letter, called an emergency meeting of the Board for the following day, Tuesday, April 20. The *Register*'s headline that morning:

STUDENT RIPS FELDY: CLAIMS CONSPIRACY

… Sayre told the *Register* that a Board member had called him to let him know that the Board was taking his letter seriously, and to thank him for making the statement available. "He said it was real helpful to the Board," said Sayre. "He told me that the discussion they would have would just be the beginning, and I could expect a lot more to happen."

Coach Timmerman, when informed by the *Register* of the existence of this letter, would not acknowledge that he had been aware of it, saying, "I have positively, absolutely no comment to make in any way, shape, or form."

Athletic Director Feldevert could only say, "I never had any part in Gary Schoyer's decision to leave State University. I certainly deny trying to influence his opinion of Coach Timmerman, or their relationship."

Gary Schoyer, contacted by the *Register*, said, "I never talked to anyone at the University of Texas till the day I announced my decision, and in that one and only conversation I was told that I wouldn't be allowed to play for Texas in 1971."

Who's going to believe that? Unless Gary is technically telling the truth. It's possible that Gary never directly spoke to Darrell Royal or anyone else from Texas—because someone else, maybe Paul, was doing the talking for him up till the day when Gary went public with it. But in that case, Gary would still have known everything that was going on.

I'm still not believing that Feldy was in on this. I just can't see Feldy… okay, I can see where Gary might have gotten the idea that Feldy was at least *implying* that Gary ought to consider transferring, but I'm not going to believe more than that.

I tried to get Gary on the phone, last night, and I try tonight, too, before and after dinner, but all I get is that busy signal: "*bought… bought… bought…*"

I am not having this. I know Gary lives across the river in this big but fairly crummy three-story apartment building that's been renting to students since before my family moved here. I sent him a card on his last birthday, and one at Christmas, so I know his room number.

I walk down Jefferson Avenue hill—or gulch, more accurately—past the Memorial Union, then across the river on the footbridge, up another Godforsaken hill, past the art museum. Finally, I walk in the front door of the apartment building—having not enjoyed the walk one bit, but I'm playing the Glad Game and telling myself that this way, I'm getting a workout and I'll take Gary by surprise.

The building is blocky grey concrete on the outside—like East Germany or something—and the inside, at least on the street level, is nothing but hall and doors, like a hotel. I find room 112. I knock, and just when Gary opens the door—he's got the phone in his hand, and he's putting his other hand over the receiver presumably in preparation to say something to me—here comes Paul, down the hall, coming toward us from another entrance, at the other end of the building. Gary sees him and doesn't say anything to either of us: just says into the receiver, "Sorry, I gotta go," walks the receiver into the kitchenette, and hangs up.

Paul is going to walk into the apartment no matter what, and I'm standing in his way, so I figure the most efficient way to solve that problem is to enter in front of him.

It's the first time I have ever been in Gary's place. He is a slob. Towels and dirty socks all over the living room. The apartment smells like dirty socks. And very subtly, of what a guy's personal fluids smell like. I know: I have six brothers.

This other guy is standing there in the living room—he had been sitting on the sofa, reading, but he got up when Paul and I came in—and I'm saying to myself, "Is this the roommate? What is he doing, still living with Gary?" He's kind of a tall, thin, blond guy who looks like an owl with the big round glasses—he looks like anything but an athlete—and Paul starts talking to him. I can tell Paul is mad, but he's not yelling. He's telling this guy—obviously it is Sayre—that everything Timmerman had accused him of had been a damn lie, and that Sayre was making a bad situation worse with that letter of his.

"I'm going to keep denying everything," Paul says to Sayre. "It'll be Gary's and my word against yours."

"What would I invent that story for?" Sayre asks. "I haven't had any conversations with Timmerman; I've never even met him."

"We never had any conspiracy with Feldy," Paul says. "That's a bunch of shit."

"I was talking about conversations I had with Gary, and with other people, and we didn't talk about whether you were involved in a conspiracy, so I'm not saying you were. Maybe you were acting on your own; I don't know."

"Pablo, it's done now," Gary says. He looks like he's trying to get between Sayre and his brother. He doesn't even look at me. "I've got enough to worry about."

"You didn't tell this guy" (Paul jerks his thumb at Sayre) "to send that letter, did you?"

"I was trying to do Gary a solid," says Sayre. "Maybe it'll work."

Paul doesn't know what to say to that. He turns around and walks out the door—and presumably out of the building. I'm still standing there. Gary hasn't had time to say anything to me.

Finally, I say to Gary, "I just came here to ask you the same question Paul asked. Did you two cook up that letter together?"

"No," they both say. "It isn't 'cooked up,'" says Sayre, at the same moment Gary is saying, "Of course not."

I am not going to waste my time asking again, if they're going to deny it. But I don't believe them.

"That's your story." I say it as more of a statement than a question. "Gary, you're saying this guy here is telling the truth?"

Gary looks me right in the eye, but I know that's something most people can do, whether they're lying or not.

"Yeah. He could have gone into more detail, but it would have been a book, then, not a letter. He told the truth."

We stare at each other for a few seconds.

"And this is nothing against you," he says, "but I have to blame your dad for this. Why did he tell me it was okay to go ahead and do it when he must have known this would happen? It's what Matt says. Your dad was using me to stir up more trouble with the football program. Knowing I'd be a casualty."

I'm doing my very best to keep an even tone.

"It might be that you and Feldy misunderstood each other," I say. "But I don't appreciate what you're suggesting. Plus, that you would just up and leave without talking to me about it."

"Well, I'm not leaving till after the semester. And I thought we were broken up."

"You said we weren't. But of course, we are. I'm sorry I came disturbing you."

I turn and walk out the door, and Gary doesn't come after me.

Wednesday's *Register* quotes Feldy as calling Sayre's letter "a fabrication. A ridiculous, fantastic story. He's a confused young man who has maybe read too much literature and decided to get creative. I've told the Board that the statement is unreliable, and I'm pretty sure they'll take my word and put the matter behind them." On Thursday, Conroy comments in the *Register*:

Who's to say who's telling the truth, or whether anyone is telling the whole truth? It's time for President Nash to take charge of the situation. As I see it, he has three options: fire Timmerman, fire Feldy, or fire them both and start fresh.

I'm in the TV room of Iota, watching the 6:00 Iowa Report on WMT. Usually the sports starts at 6:15 or 6:20, but this time they start with sports. They're showing footage taken on the steps of the Iowa State Capitol Building in Des Moines, this afternoon. State Senator Lew McGrath, of Cedar Rapids—he's a Republican, a former State University fullback, and a first-team All-American in 1951—is letting loose on Feldy, to a clump of reporters:

"I have been a devoted Rivercat for 40-plus years. I grew up in the State City area. I have lived and died with Rivercat sports since I gained awareness. I have kept my counsel for as long as I could stand it. I've stood all I can stands, and I can't stands nummore.

"I take the unequivocal position that Leo Feldevert has worked consistently to undermine his two successors, Bob Brosnan and now Toby Timmerman. His actions have caused conflict and chaos at State University. I don't know whether his actions are the result of malice or stupidity—I suspect the former, because Feldy is not a stupid man—but one way or the other, he has probably cost State University more than one million dollars in football receipts.

"I insist that the Board of Regents meet with the appropriate parties without any further delay, and report back to the people of the State of Iowa about what the hell is going on in State City."

I sit there, not saying anything. The other sisters are pretending that this is not happening. Gail Timmerman is sitting right across the room, not reacting at all, although I'm sure she's laughing up her sleeve.

Can there be any truth to this? A grain. A grain isn't inconceivable. I mean, it's possible that people could think that maybe Feldy is behind all these troubles, because who doesn't know that Feldy wanted to be Head Coach and Athletic Director, both? But that was years ago, and I don't believe he wants it anymore. Not here. So why would he be behind any of this?

300

I want Feldy to do what makes him happy, whether that's coaching or something else. Only, I don't want us to move out of our house. I don't want Feldy and Birdy in some other part of the world. But I worry that the longer Feldy stays here at State, at this point, the worse it'll be for his career. People are so ungrateful. Other people have messed up the program that he built, and now he's getting the blame.

Plus, Birdy tells me the crank phone calls have started up again. Like they did during the 1968 season, when we were losing and everyone was blaming Feldy for it. Sometimes it's just people calling and hanging up. Sometimes they say awful things, sexual things, about my parents. There have been a couple of calls to Iota Delta Theta: guys leaving messages for me. Once I came to the phone and someone said something I'd rather not repeat.

On the following Monday, April 26, the Iowa Board of Regents drove to State City and met behind closed doors for 75 minutes with President Nash, Feldy, Coach Timmerman, and I guess a few other people. The Chairman of the Board of Regents announced after the meeting, "The situation with the Rivercat football team was the only topic we discussed, and no vote was taken. There are no plans to remove any member of the Department of Athletics."

Nash told reporters, "The Regents and the State University administration agree that athletics are, and have to be, a part of the university. That being the case, we see no reason why athletics should be exempted from University control and evaluation, any more than the English department or the College of Law."

That could mean anything, and it probably means nothing.

Spring drills are underway. Several players who were injured last year are back on the roster, and they look healthy. The four black players who were kept off the squad last year, after the boycott, are back on the team.

"All four of those young men have met me more than halfway," Timmerman is quoted in the *Statesman*. "They're all going to contribute this fall and I'm happy to have them on the squad."

Gary and Gruber, on the other hand, are not participating in the drills. I don't know where they are or where they're going next year.

I haven't spoken to Gary in a couple of weeks and I don't much want to.

WATKINS ON TRIAL

The trial of Charles Watkins also began on Monday, with jury selection. At lunch at the Coffin Corner the day before, Feldy told me, "I don't know how well the charge will stand up in court, but I would have to suspect he did it. Watkins is a type. I still remember quite a bit, from all my psychology classes.

"People like him lack empathy. That sort of young man will have very poor impulse control. He'll feel entitled to whatever he wants at the moment, and entitled to retaliate against anyone he feels has treated him with disrespect. Anybody who doesn't give him what he wants, when he wants it, that person deserves anything he can do to him. Or her, in this case. Unfortunately, you see that type quite a bit, among athletes."

Since my beat on the *Statesman* is campus politics, and since I campaigned my butt off to be allowed to cover the trial, I'm covering it. I'm going to have to miss a few classes from Tuesday on; I've already made arrangements with my instructors to make up the work, so that I won't have to take any incompletes.

Tuesday morning, and the prosecutor, Esther Solymossy, is making her opening statement. I don't recognize any of the jurors. Six men and six women, all white, but we just don't have very many Negroes in State City. The Judge is Nathan Oliver, whom I also don't know. He's a skinny old man; he's got a pencil-line moustache and black hair slicked flat to his head.

Mrs. Solymossy tells the jury that she will establish that the defendant, Charles Watkins, had been at the crime scene not only to discover the body, but before and during the time that the crime had taken place; had hit Victoria DeGroot on the face and head with a heavy glass bottle, then strangled her, using his hands; had absent-mindedly left his hat on the premises—and the bottle, which bore his fingerprints—and thus felt that he had to return to the apartment to create an impression of innocence.

The prosecution will show that another fingerprint of the defendant's—a bloody one—was found on the bathroom sink.

The prosecution will produce testimony that the defendant frequented that house. They will have a witness who will testify that he had insisted on taking her back to that house on the night of the murder, presumably so that he would have a witness to testify that they had just happened upon a crime scene.

That witness, who originally told the police one story about the defendant's whereabouts and behavior on that night, has since changed her story and will testify that the defendant had not been with her at the time of the crime. This witness will further testify that the defendant insisted that she come with him to that house, later that night, and said, "If you don't come with me, my life is over," but would not explain what he meant by that.

The prosecutor says that another witness will testify that the defendant had behaved menacingly to the victim previously, and that the victim had been afraid of a physical attack.

That's Mona. She's going to testify.

For months, now, she has been mentioning here and there how conflicted she is about it: having to appear against a black guy. I don't get that. If he's guilty, he's guilty. Mona thinks Watkins is being railroaded because he's black, or maybe she doesn't truly think that, but she has to pretend to think it because otherwise she can't call herself a good person.

And she's afraid of what her friends will say about her if she testifies, but she has to. She's been telling me that she hopes she can get through it without saying anything that would hurt Watkins, but I don't see how she's going to do that, unless she lies.

Mrs. Solymossy says she will produce several witnesses who will place the defendant's movements on that night and suggest that he was trying to be seen.

This afternoon, Lieutenant Stamp testifies to the discovery of the body, following the phone call from the defendant. He tells the jury that he had been greeted, at the front door of the building to which he had been called, by the defendant and a female who identified herself as Cindy Phillips. They had led him inside, to where the body lay. He tells the jury that the victim's torso was still warm to the touch, but her extremities were cold. The defendant seemed agitated but was under control and coherent. The defendant had claimed he had returned to the house to retrieve his hat, and had discovered the body.

Stamp gives accounts of the defendant's interrogations. He explains in detail how the police had come to regard Charles Watkins as a prime suspect, thanks not only to the physical evidence, but to the evidence of witnesses who came forward later to implicate him. He says that according to their testimony, the defendant could have been at the scene, and would have had motive for killing the victim.

Watkins' lawyer, Mr. Pickens, objects that this is hearsay, but Judge Oliver rules that Stamp hasn't actually told the jury what anyone else said.

Mrs. Solymossy presents the vodka bottle with which the victim was allegedly beaten, as an exhibit. She also presents reproductions of the fingerprints that were found on it: they are the defendant's. Then she introduces photos of the bathroom sink, with bloody water in it, and close-ups of the fingerprint on it.

"The pattern of the fingerprints on the bottle," Stamp testifies, "is consistent with someone gripping the bottle by the neck and using it as a bludgeon."

Then Stamp testifies about the bloody water found in the bathroom sink: blood belonging to the victim. He testifies about the bloody fingerprint on the edge of the sink: the defendant's.

Mr. Pickens asks Stamp, "Would that fingerprint pattern on the bottle not also be consistent with someone simply picking up the bottle, maybe to examine it?"

"That is possible," Stamp concedes.

"Were the fingerprints on that bottle bloody?"

"No. There were blood traces on the bottle but the fingerprints were not made with a bloody hand."

"Is there anything to indicate that any specific person, to the elimination of anyone else, used that bottle as a clubbing tool?"

"No."

"And did you find the fingerprints of several other people on that bottle?"

"Yes. We found the deceased's prints. The pattern of those prints were as though to pick up the bottle and drink or pour from it. Not gripping it upside down by the neck. We found other unidentified prints on the bottle—but none that would be consistent with gripping it upside down, except the defendant's."

"Did you interrogate anyone else whose fingerprints were on that bottle?"

"We were unable to match the fingerprints to any other individual, besides the victim and the defendant, although there were prints that belonged to neither of them. Conceivably the liquor store employee who sold the bottle."

"Or another visitor to the apartment?"

"Conceivably."

Not likely, though. I knew Vicki could put away a bottle a day without any help.

"Did you seek those people out, and interrogate them?"

"We didn't identify the owner of every fingerprint on the bottle, and without knowing who they belonged to, we had no probable cause to interrogate these persons unknown."

"I see. Now, as to the fingerprint on the sink: Do you have any evidence as to when that print got there?"

"No."

"Could it have been made—if in fact it is the defendant's fingerprint—could it have been made when the victim had already been dead for some hours, and my client discovered her body? Could he perhaps, in the course of investigating the situation, gotten blood on his finger, which he then transferred to the sink in the course of washing it off?"

"That is possible."

Stamp's partner, Detective McCarney, testifies. He corroborates Stamp's account. He notes that the defendant had been concerned that he might be framed for the crime, and wanted it noted, during the initial questioning, that he was cooperating.

Mrs. Solymossy introduces the autopsy report. It describes the victim as "a well-developed, well-nourished Caucasian female, age 23, 71 inches tall and 161 lbs. Hair light brown; eyes grey. Marked *rigor mortis* of facial muscles and limbs. Hands are slightly clenched. No evidence of fibers or human tissue under the fingernails. Face shows red-blue cyanosis, with laceration of the left eyebrow area. Lips are cyanotic with tongue protruding.

"No evidence of struggle aside from bruising of the elbows, possibly caused by the decedent falling to the floor. No evidence of sexual assault. No sperm in the vagina or rectum, or the contents of the stomach.

"Cause of death: asphyxiation, caused by manual strangulation. Severe head trauma, caused by blunt instrument found on the scene, was inflicted prior, and would not have been sufficient to induce death."

The medical examiner testifies as to the condition of the body. He describes the head trauma and the damage to the neck.

The prosecution shows photographs of the crime scene to the jury, over Mr. Pickens's objections that they're inflammatory. I have not seen them, and they will not be released to us, but the expressions on the jurors' faces, as they pass around the photos, scare me so: they look appalled.

My imagination of those pictures will probably give me nightmares for the rest of my life. Vicki's eyes wide open and staring, as though she's pleading with someone; her tongue lolling out; the marks on her neck. It's like she's looking at me, almost reproaching me. Like I should have saved her. Like I could have saved her but chose not to. Which I know isn't true, and maybe the photos don't show anything like that, but I'm thinking it.

Watkins has been looking so intently at Mrs. Solymossy and the witnesses whenever they speak, but he's staring at the floor now. More photos are being handed to the jurors.

Wednesday. Cindy Phillips, who was with Watkins when they discovered the body, is testifying. She could be good-looking— she's got nice long dark wavy hair and a good figure, thin—but she looks old. She's only in her 30s but she's got deep lines in her face, and no lips. It's a face that's seen too many good times.

She explains that Watkins showed up at her apartment after midnight, maybe half-past, on the Saturday night/Sunday morning of the murder, and told her she had to go with him to a certain house, "or my life is over."

He told her they had to go to that house to get his hat.

"He said there were lots of people went in and out of that house, and if he left his hat there for long someone was sure to steal it," Miss Phillips explains. "He said it was expensive and he didn't want to lose it, so he had to go back there right then.

"But then he said he wanted to get a beer first, and I thought that was a little strange because he was so worried about getting his hat, so I said maybe we should do that first, but he said, 'It's almost one o'clock, and the bars close at two. We better stop in for a quick one.' He wanted to go to Topsy's, which is about a block from where I was living at the time, so we went there and we each ordered a beer but he hardly drank any of his. He was walking around, talking to people. He talked with Mr. Garthwaite, the owner, and with a few other people.

"Then when Mr. Garthwaite said, 'Last call,' he sat back down in our booth and he still was hardly touching his beer. He looked kind of worried and he hardly said anything to me. Then when Mr. Garthwaite said everybody had to leave, we got up, and Charles went over and talked with Mr. Garthwaite for another few seconds. Then we walked from Topsy's to that house, and I asked Charles what was wrong, and why he needed me to come with him. He said, 'I just have a real bad feeling tonight, and you cheer me up.'

"I thought maybe we were going somewhere to get marijuana, or maybe he owed somebody some money. Like maybe he was afraid there might be trouble and maybe if he had a woman with him that would keep a situation from happening."

"Did you think it was unusual to be visiting someone's house at that hour?"

"Maybe a little, but not very. I've done it before."

"What time did you arrive at that house?"

"Maybe 2:30. We left Topsy's a couple minutes after 2:00, and we were walking pretty slow."

When they arrived at the house, they spotted lights on inside. They got no answer at the front door, so they just walked in.

"Charles didn't act like he thought anything was up. He was laughing; I forget now what he was laughing about but I thought it was funny, I mean funny-strange, not funny-funny, that he'd been so quiet on the way over there, like he was worried about something, and then he was talking kind of loud about something—something that couldn't have been important, or I'd remember it now—and he was laughing, then we were inside the entranceway of the house and I couldn't hear anything except him laughing. Like no sound of anybody else being in the house.

"Then Charles went quieter, like maybe he thought it was strange, too, that we didn't hear anything. Then we go in, then he's going through the doorway into the front room, then into the bedroom when he reaches out one arm behind him, like to stop me, you know." Miss Phillips demonstrates by extending her left hand over her right shoulder, palm out.

Miss Phillips describes finding the body. She testifies that contrary to the original story, they found the body already covered with a sheet, and there was blood seeping through where the person's head was covered.

"You could see the bottoms of her legs, and her feet, and there was one arm sticking out from under the sheet. Charles said 'Oh, my God,' and I wanted to uncover her and make sure she was dead, but Charles said, 'No, don't touch anything. Obviously she's dead.'

"Then he picked up a bottle from the floor and held it up to me and said, 'He must have used this.' I thought that was strange since he'd just got done telling me not to touch anything."

"Objection," says Pickens. "Witness's opinion as to what's strange and what isn't is not evidence."

"Sustained," says Judge Oliver.

"Do you recall how the defendant held the bottle?" Mrs. Solymossy asks.

"Upside down. Like a club. He was, like, almost waving it."

Oh, this is starting to sound really bad for Watkins.

"I said, 'We have to call an ambulance, where's the phone?' Charles said he didn't know where the phone was, or couldn't remember, or whatever."

Miss Phillips testifies that she never saw Watkins go anywhere near the kitchen or bathroom sink. She says she did not see Watkins try to uncover the body.

"He sort of sagged, he looked like he wanted to sit down but then he stopped himself like he didn't want to disturb the room, and he stood there shaking his head for a minute or so, and then he said, 'We're going to have to report this. People know I've been here before and they'll try to pin it on me. My only chance is if I report it.'

"Then he said he had to get out of that room and have a cigarette. So we went into the front room and we each had a smoke, and he was freaking out; he said this was going to ruin his football career even though he hadn't done anything wrong.

"I asked him why not just take his hat and get out of there, and he repeated that people knew that he was in and out of that house; the cops were going to find that out and come looking for him; he said his fingerprints were all over the house. And then he said to me, 'I came by your house about ten, right?' And that surprised me, because I knew it was later than that, like, after midnight, and I told him that. But then he said, "No, don't you remember? I came over before that and you were acting kind of out of it.'

"I wasn't sure what to believe, when Charles said that, because I knew I hadn't been drunk or high or anything; I knew I'd been in bed asleep when he knocked on the door, but then I remembered that he said, 'You've got to come with me or my life is over.'

"And now here I was, sitting in this apartment, and in the room next door is this dead girl, and I was thinking, you know, maybe I better go along with whatever he wants me to say, or I might end up in the same situation. Anyway, that was when Charles saw the phone, in the corner of the room..."

Miss Phillips testifies that she did not know the victim, had never known of her. She had not been familiar with that house. At the time of the incident, she had known the defendant for "maybe a year."

"We were friends. I guess you could say we dated."

The prosecutor then reads aloud Miss Phillips' deposition that she gave immediately after the discovery of the crime, which had a different timeline from the one she was testifying to in court. Probably, Mrs. Solymossy anticipates that Mr. Pickens will bring it up on cross-examination. Miss Phillips admits that she had been lying, the first time, but it had occurred to her that Watkins might have asked her to do this because he had had a hand in the murder. This has been on her conscience, she says.

The prosecutor asks Miss Phillips if she has any charges pending against her—again, probably anticipating a point the defense will make. Miss Phillips admits that she has, that she is awaiting disposition of her case. No, she has not been offered immunity. No, there was nothing to tie her to the murder; no indication that she might be charged as an accessory so long as she tells the truth and disowns her original testimony. Yes, she had been told that she risked perjury charges if she lied to save the defendant.

"How do we know that you're telling the truth now," the prosecutor asks, "and not testifying against the defendant simply to avoid being prosecuted as an accessory?"

"People lie when they're scared or confused sometimes," Miss Phillips replies. "That's why I told a different story before. But this is the truth, now."

Mr. Pickens focuses on Miss Phillips' original story. He keeps implying, as best he can, that her original statement was the truth, and this new version is a lie that she has been pressured into inventing, to avoid prosecution, because the police and prosecutor are so eager to convict Watkins. He also asks Miss Phillips about her criminal record, which consists of a couple of misdemeanors plus the charges pending against her. He asks her if she has ever been charged with perjury or fraud. She said she has not been, and of course Mr. Pickens knows this, but he asked the question to put doubt in the jury's mind.

On re-direct, the prosecutor is able to get Miss Phillips to re-iterate that she had never seen the defendant go near a sink before he called the police, or after for that matter.

Dubose Garthwaite, the owner of Topsy's, testifies next. He's a tall, husky, black man; he looks prosperous and maybe ex-military, age about 50. I don't know him personally, but I think my parents have done Democrat stuff with him.

He's wearing a navy-blue suit, white shirt, and red-and-blue tie. He says he remembers seeing Watkins and Miss Phillips in his bar on the night of the murder, and talking with Watkins shortly before last call and again when the bar was closing. No, he did not see Watkins earlier that evening. Watkins often came into the bar for a beer, or more usually a Coke or orange juice, but Mr. Garthwaite has never seen him drink heavily or become disorderly. Pickens was able to get Garthwaite to concede it was possible that Watkins had been there earlier, and Garthwaite just hadn't seen him.

"But that's not likely," Garthwaite says. "It's part of my job to know who's in my bar and what they're up to, at all times."

Then Mona testifies. When I hear her name called, I turn around in my seat to see her coming in, at the back of the courtroom. She's awfully pale in the face. She's holding her head almost unnaturally erect. Mike comes in the door with her, holding her hand—her right hand. I can see that her left hand is rigid, the fingers bent in a way that's not natural.

I can't invite Mike to sit with me, since I'm in the press section, but I catch Mona's eye, first, and smile as much as I dare to. She gives me a nod. Then I catch Mike's eye, and he gives me a tiny bit of a smile. Someone in the back row slides over, and Mike barely has enough room to sit down. Mona doesn't look at Watkins or at Mr. Pickens.

Mona doesn't tell about that perversion that Watkins performed on Vicki. Maybe if Mrs. Solymossy lets her do that, Mr. Pickens could move for a mistrial. Maybe if Mona knew the law, she could bring it up on her own, so that Pickens could do exactly that, but I'm sure she doesn't have the criminal mind that I have. But she testifies that she had seen Vicki with the defendant, at least once.

Mrs. Solymossy asks Mona if she can identify the man she saw Vicki with, in this room. Mona, speaking so that I can barely hear her, and without looking at the defense table, says, "He's sitting next to Mr. Pickens."

Looking mostly at her lap, Mona testifies that Vicki had been telling her about a man named Charles—and that Charles had been threatening her in ways that made Vicki afraid for her life.

"Did she describe this man?"

"Well, that he was big. How big, I don't know."

"Did she mention his race?"

Oh, God. I can tell Mona doesn't want to admit this, but I'm sure she remembers that she gave that information to Lieutenant Stamp, and she can be sure Mrs. Solymossy has seen it.

Very softly, she says, "She mentioned that he was a black man."

"A little louder, please," says Judge Oliver. Mona repeats it. She's looking down, as though she has just said something horribly shameful.

"No more questions at this time," says Mrs. Solymossy.

Mr. Pickens is trying to take it easy on Mona, I can tell: possibly because he knows she doesn't want to be there. He asks her if she is positive that the defendant is the man named Charles that Vicki was talking about.

I'm telling myself, "Oh, Judas, you might have ruined your whole case!" I read that in *To Kill A Mockingbird*, when I was in eighth grade: Never, on cross-examination, ask a question that you don't know the answer to!

But Mona says, "I don't know for sure that the Charles that Vicki was talking about, was *this* Charles, no."

Mr. Pickens obviously he thinks he has scored a point. I can see that Mona looks a little healthier, more confident—like maybe she thinks she has somehow made the case against Watkins slightly weaker—and she catches my eye and gives me a little glint: an eyes-only smile.

Then Pickens asks, "Ms. DeGroot had recently given birth, had she not?"

(Funny, I say to myself, that he uses "Ms." What, is he showing off how progressive he is?)

"Yes, a few months before… before this." Mona looks so sad, and Pickens looks almost as sad.

"We understand that you and your husband are fostering the baby, are you not?"

"Yes." Mona still looks sad, but she smiles a little.

"Do you know the father of the child?"

Mona looks surprised.

"No."

"Did Ms. DeGroot know who had fathered this child?"

How would Pickens know to ask this? Had his client heard it from Vicki herself, at some point? Where else could he have found this out? And why is he asking this? He's only building sympathy for Vicki, isn't he? And why would he want to do that?

"She didn't, as far as I know," Mona says. "She named him Richard, after a man she had been living with—I'm not sure whether they were married—but she told me she was sure he wasn't the father."

Or did Pickens hear this from Mona? Was she acting, when she looked surprised at his question?

"So sad," Pickens almost murmurs, and shakes his head. "But it's great that you and your husband are looking after the child. Did Ms. DeGroot have a lot of company in her apartment?"

Mona looks shocked for an instant, and I feel pretty shocked, too, because I can see now where Pickens is going with this. He's going to try to make a slut out of Vicki, so that the jury will think that any of the guys who were in and out of her apartment could have killed her. For just that second, Mona looks at Pickens like he's betraying her, and betraying Vicki's memory—and then I guess she realizes that Pickens is offering her a lifeline that she had better grab ahold of if she doesn't want to contribute to this young man going to prison.

On the other hand, she doesn't want to smear Vicki. She tells Pickens that Vicki liked company; she was lonely a lot; she had been starting to date again, once she had had her baby, but "I don't know too much about it."

That's enough to satisfy Pickens, but when she leaves the stand and walks past where I'm sitting, Mona looks shamefaced at me, as much as to say, "I did the best I could."

§

I'm all antsy for the rest of the afternoon, because it's taken up mostly with procedural stuff that won't be relevant to any story

313

I could write—but at least I get a full draft of the story written, in longhand, while the session plays out. When I come out of the courtroom, I go over to the *Statesman* to type a clean copy and file it, and I stop by the sports desk to see that in Thursday morning's paper, we're going to report:

> The Board in Control of Athletics has accepted the report of its policy review committee, and unanimously voted to retain Leo Feldevert and Tobias Timmerman for the remainder of their contracts, either or both of which could, of course, be renewed. Feldevert's contract will expire on May 31, 1974, and Timmerman's on December 31, 1973.
>
> Feldevert has assured the policy review committee that he has no desire to coach the State University football team and does not wish to usurp the authority of the football coach. Therefore, the policy review committee expects that both men, and their staffs, will work together cooperatively and perform their respective duties as assigned functions in compliance with the established policies and directives of the Board in Control of Athletics.

That's what Feldy has been telling me all along. Why would he want to coach now? But why would we want to keep Timmerman in there? I suppose we have to—but if he messes up again this fall, people will find a way to blame Feldy.

§

It's Thursday afternoon. Judge Oliver had to take care of another case, this morning, so the trial didn't resume till after lunch. The prosecution called one more witness and rested. Then Pickens made his opening statement, which was short—and now he has called Charles Watkins to the stand.

Probably some lawyers would say that's a tremendous gamble, putting him on the stand. But if he doesn't testify, the prosecution evidence will be all the jury has to remember. And then, somehow, those fingerprints have to be explained away.

Watkins looks more relaxed than he did when I was interviewing him a few months ago. He sits easy; he smiles now and then. He says he has no idea who could have killed Vicki. He had merely been talking about his emotional state when he had told Miss Phillips, "You've got to go with me or my life is over."

"I was upset. I was under a lot of stress; I'd been walking around alone, wondering what I was going to do, how I was going to sort my life out, asking myself, you know, existential questions. I'm an emotional person, I worry. When I said all that, to her, I was speaking figuratively. Just meant that I needed her to come with me and cheer me up, or keep me company."

"I never said I wasn't in that house before," he tells the jury. "I have been, a lot."

Watkins' fingerprints had got on the bottle when he discovered the body, because he had lost his composure and wasn't thinking. As for that fingerprint in the sink, "That must have happened when I first saw her. I touched her, to see if she was alive, but she was cold, so I knew she was deceased.

"The blood in the sink probably happened when I went to wash it off. I was very upset, but I do remember washing my hands. I remember thinking that I might be compromising the crime scene, but I had to get the blood off me—and as far as I could tell there was nothing in the bathroom that would have been part of the crime. I know I shouldn't have washed my hands, but how would it have looked if the police had shown up and I had blood on me?"

On cross-examination, Mrs. Solymossy reminds Watkins that Miss Phillips said he had not gone near the sink. Watkins rolls his eyes the least bit, and exhales.

"Maybe she didn't see me go near the sink. Or maybe she's choosing not to remember that she saw it. She might have her reasons for testifying in a certain way."

Watkins has a similar response to the discrepancies between his timeline and Miss Phillips'. He insists that he showed up at her apartment two hours before she said he had.

"It's my word against hers, and she's told several stories. She's testified that she's been under pressure to change her story."

Watkins completes his testimony late in the afternoon, and court adjourns.

Nobody has testified that Watkins had blood on his person or his clothes at the time the police arrived. But he wouldn't have to have had. Maybe none got on his clothes. Or he could have gone home, changed clothes, and got rid of the bloody ones. Maybe that's when he realized he had left his hat behind.

I'm telling myself that Watkins gave the impression of an innocent man telling his story as plainly as he could. But that's it: an impression. I'm talking with a few of the other reporters, and I have to agree with them that his story isn't convincing. It relies on too many coincidences, and it contradicts the prosecution's witnesses—not that we can be sure they're all telling the truth.

As soon as court starts on Friday morning, Pickens says, "The defense rests." This surprises me, because I had heard that the defense was going to call people to testify that Watkins is a nice guy and would never do a thing like that. I look over at the man next to me, who's a middle-aged, fat guy, a reporter for the *Register*.

He knows what I'm thinking, because he mutters to me, "Pickens probably wanted overnight to think about those other witnesses. See, if he calls character witnesses, the prosecution can call other witnesses to say he's *not* a nice guy. But they can't do that, if he doesn't call character witnesses."

"Oh," I mutter back. "Thanks."

Now there's a sidebar, with prosecution and defense attorneys up at the bench, whispering with Judge Oliver.

"That fouls things up," the *Register* guy tells me. "See, if the defense calls any witnesses other than Watkins, then the prosecution gets to call rebuttal witnesses, and make its summation last. But if Watkins is the only witness, then the defense has the last word to the jury, and the prosecution has to sum up first. Which is another reason why Pickens didn't call any other witnesses. Now, prosecution probably wants some time to re-work their summation."

This reporter must be right, because when the lawyers step back, Judge Oliver announces that court is adjourned for the day, and summations will happen on Monday. I get to go to classes after all, which is great because it means less work that I would have had to make up later. And I don't have to file a story.

Mona told me, the last time I was visiting at her place—this was a few weeks ago—that the demonstrations last spring, in reaction to the shootings at Kent State and Jackson State, had disappointed the people she works with politically. They hadn't been able to get organized, so they hadn't raised as big of a stink as they had wanted to. They hadn't caused any serious disruption. She told me that May of 1971 is going to atone for that. They're going to shut down the campus entirely, is what she told me.

"I know you're not as political as we are," she said. "I don't want to force you into something you're not comfortable with, but we need all the bodies we can get, if you want to participate."

I wasn't sure then and I'm not sure now. I made noncommittal noises and tried to change the subject.

I was asleep, at Iota, at 3:00 on Saturday morning, when a bomb went off in the Rhetoric Building, which is an office building that stands—or stood—opposite the University library. Office space for Rhetoric professors, mainly, as the name implies. According to my sisters, at breakfast, all the fire department could do was contain it, keep the fire from spreading. Lefty, who usually gets up with the chickens, had been down there early in the morning to see, and she reported that Rhetoric was a shell. We could smell it, all the way over here at Iota. The fire. That awful electrical fire stench. God knows how many professors lost the work of their lifetimes, in just a couple of hours.

VERDICT

Now here I am, way early on Monday morning, walking by Territorial, and University Common, on the way to the KSCR studio to do my broadcast, and from there I'll go to the courthouse. Not much is happening yet. I see a few young men setting up a

317

temporary rostrum, at the top of the steps of Territorial, right in front of the main entrance.

When I get to the courthouse, the area for spectators is already packed. About a dozen young black men are sitting in a group. I recognize Abiatha Turner, and Isaiah Monroe. Monroe and some of the other men—not Turner—are wearing Black Panther regalia or insignia; at least, they're wearing combat fatigues with black berets, and sunglasses. I sit in the press section, as usual, listening to the prosecution and defense summations.

Mrs. Solymossy's speech seems routine: going over the evidence; pointing out the holes in Watkins' testimony. Then Pickens sounds pretty reasonable at first, pointing out places where the jury might find doubt. Reasonable, till he says, "And bear in mind, ladies and gentlemen, that this young woman whelped a pup by an unknown father..." he pauses a few seconds, then says it again, "an unknown father, just a few months prior to her unfortunate death—which might give you an idea of the kind of traffic that might have gone in and out of that apartment. Can we be certain, that out of all her gentlemen callers—which apparently were legion—that we have got the right one? Can we be certain of that?"

Mrs. Solymossy doesn't object. Judge Oliver doesn't react at all. This guy, this Pickens, who everyone says is such a social crusader, saying that about Vicki: I almost want to jump up and tell him he should beg forgiveness from the whole room, and maybe from God.

Then I tell myself, he's doing his job, he's defending his client—but how evil does he have to be, "doing his job"? I can understand, maybe, some corrupt prosecutor making a speech like that—but this guy, whom Mona always spoke so well of?

Did he have to do that? Would other lawyers have done it? I don't know.

From about 11:00 to 11:30, Judge Oliver charges the jury, then they file out to deliberate—and, presumably, to get lunch. Which I don't do, because if I leave my seat, I might miss the verdict, although the jury is not likely to be back immediately. I'm kicking myself that I haven't at least brought an apple or something. I sit there in the courtroom, writing as much as I can of the article I'll have to file tonight—about the summations, and the verdict if there is one.

Some of the spectators did leave, and they all were able to reclaim their seats. The spectators' area is only about three-quarters full, now. Not much is going on at the front of the room. Two assistant counsel are sitting at the prosecution table; Pickens' assistant is at the defense table; Deputy Sheriffs and other court officers are walking in and out. A few minutes after 3:00, I feel a sort of shock wave of energy going through me before I see or hear any change; I can see that other people in the room are feeling it too. Then more people are passing into the room, and I hear several people whispering, "Verdict."

Ten minutes later, a Deputy Sheriff escorts Watkins into the courtroom by a side door; the rest of counsel comes in; the jury files in and sits in the box; the court rises for the judge's entry.

Watkins has his back to me; I can only see his face in partial profile. He's looking away from the jury; the jury is not looking at him; once again, I think of *To Kill A Mockingbird*.

Judge Oliver goes through the formal language; the foreman of the jury hands the sealed verdict to a bailiff, who walks it over to the judge's bench. The judge rather dramatically (I think) puts on his glasses and reads it, nods slightly, and passes it down to the clerk—Mrs. Worthington, her name-plate says—who is seated beside him on a lower desk.

"The clerk will publish the verdict," says the judge.

Mrs. Worthington reads, "On the charge of which the defendant Charles Egbert Watkins has been indicted, the jury finds the defendant Charles Egbert Watkins guilty" [I hear a collective gasp and see Watkins' shoulders sag slightly, although that latter could have been my imagination] "of murder in the second degree."

"So say you all?" says the judge.

"We do," comes the murmured chorus: some of them in full voice, but most of them mumbling.

The defense asks for a poll; this is done, with two of the women barely whispering "guilty." Then the judge dismisses the jurors ("The court thanks you for your service and your citizenship"), who file out by their private door. The judge then sets a tentative sentencing date—for July—and re-sets Watkins' bond to $500,000. Then two Deputies handcuff Watkins and lead him out. He doesn't look back.

I hear sobs; I crane around and see two older black women crying, and an older black man, sitting between them, putting one arm around each of their shoulders. The judge adjourns the court. A bailiff re-emerges from the jury room to announce that the jurors have agreed not to speak to the press, that they are each being driven home or wherever else they want to go, so there's no need for the press to hang around hoping for an interview.

Several reporters approach the defense table, but Pickens says, "We have no comment at this time, other than we are disappointed and we certainly intend to appeal the verdict." Mrs. Solymossy says she'll have a brief statement in the main hallway.

There, TV cameras and microphones are set up; I can hardly see Mrs. Solymossy for the crush.

"We believe the jury reached a correct verdict," she says. "We had hoped to establish first-degree murder but evidently the jury did not feel that we met the burden of proof for premeditation. Our hearts go out to the family of the victim, and to the family of the defendant. That's all we have at this time."

It's just after 4:00. Those same cameras, microphones, and reporters are re-assembling outside, on the lawn of the courthouse, where three young black women and those 12 young black men are standing in a tight group.

"Today we have seen the age-old tale repeated," Monroe says into the microphones. "The quasi-legal lynching of a young and accomplished black man who is being punished for threatening the status quo, on trumped-up charges and falsified evidence— by an all-white jury. We had anticipated this verdict all along, so we are dismayed but we are not surprised. We are also not defeated. We will see this unlawful conviction overturned, and Brother Watkins released, by any means necessary."

"Does that include violent means?" The guy from the *Register*.

"We are not ruling out any possibility. As of right now, we need to assess the situation and plan our strategy. Our immediate plans are to march directly on Territorial and demand that the University stand bail for Brother Watkins."

320

"Right on!" shout several members of the group, as well as several young white people who are hanging on the periphery, looking more than slightly sheepish, like they're not sure whether they ought to be taking any part.

"Black power!" shouts Monroe.

"Right on!"

This group is now forming up in ranks of three, which is the width of the paved path that leads down the courthouse lawn to the sidewalk. I'm tagging behind them; so are a couple of the other reporters. We're marching, rather than walking, almost in step with each other. As though these would-be Panthers had practiced for it, and maybe they have.

It's a quiet procession, so far. Almost eerily quiet, and I feel like it wouldn't be right to talk to anyone. No slogan-shouting, no singing, no chanting. It's a four-block walk to Territorial, and when we get close to it, we can see that the crowd on the Common has gotten bigger. I'd say it's more than 300 people, mostly students but obviously not all. Some are carrying the predictable signs: "Remember Kent State," "Get Out Of Vietnam," "ROTC Off Our Campus."

I can hear Monroe groan, "Oh, shit." I can't tell if that's gratification or frustration. We keep marching. The Panthers apparently mean to keep to the sidewalks, which are fairly clear, then march up the walkway that divides University Common, to the front steps of Territorial. But the nearer we get, the plainer it is that it might be hard for them to get there—or maybe not. Maybe this is more than they had hoped for: all these people on the Common, a built-in audience. I only see three cops, and they don't look at all worried.

The rostrum is still standing, in front of the entrance to Territorial. Some guy in his mid-20s with collar-length hair and a Fu Manchu moustache is finishing his speech. The Panthers approach the steps while this speaker is yielding the microphone to Cornell Cohen, the President of the Student Senate—who's a well-known leftist agitator, so it figures he would be master of ceremonies—just as Monroe and his phalanx get to the bottom of the steps.

"Brother Cornell," Monroe calls, "we need the mike for a minute." He skips up the steps and he's standing next to Cohen, not quite physically elbowing Cohen aside, but herding him out of the way without touching him.

"Brothers and sisters! We've come from the courthouse, where Brother Charles Watkins has just been wrongfully convicted. We need to stand together in this time of crisis and respond with outrage to this lynching!"

The crowd doesn't react with any great energy: kind of a collective groan and murmur. I guess you could call it "hubbub." Lots of low talking. "Wait, what happened?" Cohen says. The mike picks his voice up.

"The racist, all-white jury found Brother Charles guilty of murder," Monroe says to the crowd. "This means life in prison, for a crime he did not commit." More hubbub. Monroe looks disappointed. Probably he expected more outrage.

I bet I know what's going on. The popular story, in some circles, is that Watkins is being railroaded on account of his race—but I'm pretty sure that even among the most radical of these demonstrators, quite a few of them secretly believe that Watkins is guilty, guilty, guilty. At any rate, they don't believe he's being discriminated against. It's for sure that some of the people in this crowd knew Vicki. They liked her, and I'm sure they want whoever killed her to get what he deserves, even if he does happen to be black.

Monroe might have lost this crowd—it's overwhelmingly white—if Cohen doesn't take back the microphone and shout, "We need to show our solidarity with Charles Watkins and with our comrades the Black Panthers!" Cohen starts trying to sing, "We shall over-co-o-ome…"

Why can't any of these people ever carry a tune?

A few voices join in, each in a different key, and after a verse or so, some of the demonstrators start chanting, "Stop the war! Stop the war!" as if to remind everyone of what they're there for.

Cohen, still at the microphone: "We need to regard this event as a teach-in. We're protesting several issues: the war, social injustice, and the here-and-now crisis that Isaiah has communicated. Isaiah, do you have anything more you want to share?"

It's looking, at this point, like the pitch of agitation is not going to get too high, because now they can't just focus on one thing. I have a feeling this demonstration will last into the night, and then it'll peter out. I need to get over to the Engineering Building and write my story.

I'm about to walk there from the Common, when a nondescript guy a few years older than I am—completely forgettable-looking, just a stereotypical demonstrator with bushy black hair—hands me this leaflet. No doubt it has been available since this morning—before the verdict, anyway:

SHUT DOWN STATE UNIVERSITY

Our demands to abolish ROTC have been ignored. Our demands that our troops be immediately withdrawn from Vietnam have been ignored. Our demands for a more just society, in State City and elsewhere, have been ignored. This morning a brother, Charles Watkins, stands falsely accused of murder. Therefore be it resolved:

WE WILL SHUT DOWN STATE UNIVERSITY. We call on all students to boycott classes on Tuesday, May 4, and Wednesday, May 5, and indefinitely thereafter, and assemble on campus to ensure that our voices are heard.

WE DEMAND

• One hundred percent divestment, by the State Educational Workers Pension Fund, in any companies involved in providing war materiel.
• Abolition of ROTC and any other military training programs, at all of Iowa's state-run colleges and universities.
• All textbooks, in all courses, to be subject to approval by a Student Committee for Social Justice.
• All textbooks to be free.
• Sliding scale of tuition, based on financial need.
• Official resolution by the administration and faculty,

demanding immediate unilateral withdrawal of Amerikan troops from Vietnam.

The flyer doesn't elaborate on what the boycott will look like, or how anybody will "shut down the University."

I get a couple of burgers and some fries from the Burger Shef on the corner of DeWitt and Lincoln Avenue, and take them to the Engineering Building—it's the first food I've had since about 6:00 this morning—and sit in the office of the *Statesman* writing a report of the summations, the verdict, the reactions of the defendant, counsel, and spectators, and the statements of counsel afterwards. I'll include Monroe's statement, then describe the Black Panthers' march and what I saw on the Common.

The *Statesman* already has another reporter covering the demonstration. That is Mike Kane, a grad student who thinks he's Hildy Johnson or Lincoln Steffens or some other type of hot stuff. I don't like him much—he takes himself way too seriously—but he knows his business. He has just come into the office to file his story, when I'm about to leave.

"It's getting pretty hairy out there," he says to the whole newsroom—which at this point is me, Lisa Quackenbush (our editor), and three or four others. "No violence yet, that I can see, but I have a feeling they're working up to it. Count on the real craziness tomorrow. Tonight, you probably want to get home as soon as you can—unless you're going to participate."

I have to walk north along DeWitt, in front of Territorial and the Common, to get back to Iota, and so far, DeWitt Street seems to be where most of the action is. Vehicular and pedestrian traffic is going slower because people are milling around, getting in the way, and I see, still, a few hundred people congregated on the Common. I'm some distance away, trying to walk away from this scene as fast as I can, but they've set up some sort of primitive floodlighting, so I can see President Nash at the rostrum, on the steps of Territorial, talking. They don't seem to have a very good public address system: I can only faintly hear him. I stop, and listen, straining.

"I understand your feelings," he's saying, "but an eviction of the R.O.T.C. just can't happen overnight."

Boos and catcalls.

"We'll be glad to work with you in a legal manner to make sure that your concerns are addressed," he says, "but I urge you to let the business of the university go forward."

More boos, and I'm walking back to Iota. Nothing much is going to happen tonight.

LOOKS LIKE A RIOT BREWING

The situation is still fairly quiet this morning, but the crowd is way, way bigger. I don't notice it in the neighborhood of Iota Delta Theta, but walking toward the main campus for my first class, I see the sidewalks are more crowded, the closer I get to University Common. I'm within 20 yards of the Old Biology building—which flanks Territorial to the North, as the Liberal Arts building flanks it to the South—and I'm having to thread my way through a real mob.

Ordinarily, I'd walk around the front of Old Bio and across the Common to get to Liberal Arts, but I can see it'll take me a while to thread through all these people. So I just walk into Old Bio, and through it—but then I come out on the other end and find myself in the midst of a total mob on the Common: some thousands of people, more than I can estimate, in front of the Territorial Steps.

I'm remarking how easy it is to identify people "not from around these parts," by the look of them. I can tell—at least by intuition—that a lot of these demonstrators are not locals. They must have been brought in from somewhere else. For one thing, I see a lot more Jewish-looking people than you could expect a State City crowd to have. Maybe I'm not supposed to notice stuff like that, and maybe I'm not even supposed to think "Jewish-looking," but I do, and I do. The average age might be older than our student body, too, like mid to late 20s.

I'm trying to skirt the throng, not walking across the Common to the Liberal Arts building, because that way isn't passable. I have to walk away from the Common, and cross to the other side of DeWitt Street, which is storefronts, and which is less clogged with people. Then I walk toward Lincoln Avenue, where I hope I can enter the Liberal Arts building at the far end.

Two Highway Patrol cars are parked along DeWitt, with State Troopers standing near them in their grey uniforms and Smokey Bear hats. Probably the city cops are deployed elsewhere. But I wonder if the State City police and the Highway Patrol combined will be enough, if it gets violent. I'm getting a strong feeling—from the general vibe—that that might happen. Not this morning, but by later in the day, or tonight, almost for sure.

Right now, it looks like it's orderly enough. I can see a few people in the crowd wearing white armbands that say PEACE MONITOR in black letters, although I have no idea how effective they might be, later. I can't see Mona and Mike, but I'd bet anything they're nearby—maybe with Little Red.

I look as far down DeWitt Street as I can see, and coming toward us, a couple of blocks away, I see a procession of maybe 50 black people—mostly men, most of them wearing that Black Panther-style gear. I'm pretty sure they're hoping to join the other demonstrators on the Common.

I'm standing right near one of the Highway Patrolmen, who's not much older than I am.

"This looks pretty ugly," I say. "What's going to happen?"

"It's going to get uglier." The trooper is raising his voice above the chanting and the other pandemonium. "Pretty fast, when it does. Really ugly. The local cops are actually getting death threats. On the phone. In the middle of the night. The guys who work the night shift are getting it the worst: The calls come when they're on duty, people telling these officers' wives and kids that The Pig is going to get killed that night. Looks like whoever's doing it has a list of all the cops, their home phone numbers—plus the hours they work. My house hasn't gotten any calls yet, but my wife is halfway round the bend from worrying about me."

I take a roundabout route to the Music Building, this after-noon—the most direct route is too crowded—and while I'm walking, I'm playing the Glad Game: thinking I'm glad that Mike Kane is such a hotshot (or thinks he is) and would not dream of letting me horn in on his story. The real craziness won't happen till late tonight.

All I've got is a follow-up story on the Charles Watkins case, for which I've only had to make a couple of phone calls. I was hoping to get comments from Isaiah Monroe, and maybe Abi-atha Turner, plus Mike or Mona, but I can't reach any of them. Not surprising. I'm going to fight my way back to the Engineer-ing Building to file my story.

It's about 8:30 at night; I'm about to head back to Iota from the Engineering building when Lisa Quackenbush looks out of a window in the newsroom and says, "Looks like it's rolling." I look out, too: we can see the intersection of DeWitt Street and Lincoln Avenue, where people are milling around a panel truck that has been set on fire in the middle of the street. It looks like a movie about a campus riot.

"Better not go out there," Lisa says.

"I'm sure not going to stay in *here* overnight," I say. "I'll just get out of the area as fast as I can. I'm Feldy's Girl. I'm invinci-ble."

Lisa laughs, but she doesn't leave with me.

In a strange way, that burning truck, down there in the street, reassures me. It looks like if there's any violence, it's going to be against property, not people. The fire seems to be having the effect of splitting the crowd in two. Some of them are moving south, toward Bancroft Street, which is State City's main east-west artery, and another section is moving north, in the general direction of Iota. Probably if I join that latter group of marchers, they'll serve as an escort to see me safe back to the house.

Speaking of property, those poor shop windows along DeWitt Street, facing the campus, never had a chance. Most of the windows up to the third floor of that block of buildings are broken out—some of them are windows of residential apartments—and it looks like some small-scale looting of the shops is going on, although I'm not close enough to swear to that. At the intersection of Lincoln and DeWitt, the fire from that burning panel truck is under control now, but it smells like I imagine Hell might smell.

I don't understand how shutting down the university—or the city—is going to end the war. Invading President Esterhart's office, a couple years ago: that was about the draft records. I could understand that, even if I wasn't sure they were doing the right thing. The Battle of the Union Steps was about Dow Chemical being on campus—so, same thing. But I don't get how anyone could think that this—realistically—is about Vietnam. Or about getting Charles Watkins out of jail. By the way, when I was doing my research for that follow-up article on the trial, I learned that Watkins has been moved to the Cerro Gordo County jail—about 100 miles north of State City—to reduce the chance of a mob trying to break him out.

It feels like I'm not experiencing events in sequence. Like everything is happening in flashes; everyone is running, nobody is walking. It's nighttime, of course, but I'm seeing light, pulsing: a strobe effect, so that everyone and everything seems to be moving jerkily, like in an old movie.

Some guy bumps into me, going past me in the opposite direction. He stumbles and grabs my arm to steady himself.

"Sorry!" He has to shout. He looks like David Crosby.

"It's okay," I say. "What's up? What's the story?"

"Gonna shut down Highway 6." He still is yelling. It seems like all of downtown is gibbering like a monkey cage. "We're gonna walk down to the State River, and across the bridge; then we're gonna set up barricades on Highway 6. Cut the city in half. Nobody gets in or out." He runs off; obviously he has ants in his pants to get where he's going.

I remember Feldy telling me, years ago, that he had learned in one of his psychology classes that all mobs are pretty much alike, in terms of how they work. They have a collective mind, a hive consciousness that moves them instinctively to burn down a building, or trash a store, or lynch someone. They hardly ever have a chain of command. For example, there's no General giving the order, "We're going to march to Highway 6, and shut it down."

But what do I know? This could all have been planned in advance, at least in a broad way.

I'm still trying to get to Iota, so I'm walking with another clump of people, in the other direction, away from where that guy was headed. I'm alongside a short girl about my age. Her hair is cut shorter than most boys'; she's wearing a floppy flannel shirt.

"Where are we going?"

"We're walking to I-80." She laughs, like this is the most bestest thing ever. "If we can form a chain across the eastbound and the westbound, we could shut down the whole state."

Do they really have enough people to close both Highway 6 and the Interstate? I'm walking along with this girl. For the time being, I'm pretending to be a demonstrator. We pass along DeWitt in front of the Common—and on the steps of Territorial, about 150 yards off, I can see ten or so people, holding candles. The last stubborn holdouts for peaceful protest, and I can't see what they're accomplishing, either—unless maybe standing there with their silly candles is their way of reminding themselves that they are Good.

Ten minutes later, and we're about 200 strong, now, proceeding still along DeWitt, in the general direction of the Interstate. But we've come abreast of Iota. I thread my way out of the parade and go up the front walk. I can see the lights are on, inside, and nobody seems to have damaged the building.

"Sellout!" that girl with the short hair calls after me. I turn around and give her the finger before going in the front door. I have never done that to anybody before in my life. She probably didn't see me do it.

Then, I find that I *can't* go in the front door. It's locked. I try my key, which works, but I can't get in the front door because it's barricaded, apparently. Or something is rigged up to it that prevents me from pulling it open. I try pounding on the door; I try hollering; I try rapping on the glass windows on either side of the door-frame. After about 20 seconds, a couple of my sisters show up at the other side of the door and remove the pennies that they've used to jam the door shut, and they let me in.

Actually, they *pull* me in, quick slam the door after me, and replace the pennies.

"Thank God," Janet Fletcher cries. "We were afraid you had got caught up in that, and you were killed or thrown in jail or something!"

I roll my eyes.

"We're watching it on TV," Chris Smith says. "They interrupted programming for it. It looks like the world's ending."

"No, it's just people being awful," I say. "Nobody's getting hurt yet, anyway."

Chris and Janet walk with me across the front room and into the TV room, and sure enough, on the screen, it looks worse than it looked to me, outside, when I was in the midst of it. Several of the girls look up from the TV screen and gasp at the sight of me. I give the TV a little dismissive gesture.

"It's ugly but it'll burn itself out," I say.

"We're not taking any chances," says Chris. "You never know if a bunch of them are going to decide to come in here… I mean, let's face it: a house full of good-looking girls, just the kind of girls they would hate, to begin with…"

I'm about to say, "Oh, please," but then I realize: Okay, that won't happen, but it's not so crazy for Chris and some of the other sisters to think it might. Whether they meant to or not, the demonstrators have created the impression that all they want is destruction. No reason why that shouldn't include raping sorority girls.

"They've got other fish to fry," I say. "They're going to try to shut down the Interstate. As if."

I've missed dinner, so I'll have to raid the fridge. Then, I've got practicing and studying to do. Time to lock myself in my room and hope nobody tries to blow us up.

I am furious at myself. I have no idea what part of the demonstration Mike Kane is covering. And I have deserted. I have run away from a story. For the second time in my career on the *Statesman*, I have run away from a story. How can I call myself a journalist, sitting here in my room at Iota Delta Theta, very softly practicing my cello, when I could be part of history? I'm not being sarcastic.

§

That, in a nutshell, is how I have apparently missed most of the Great State University Riot of 1971. By all accounts, it was a humdinger. When I came down to breakfast the next morning, the WMT Morning News was showing footage of the night before, when Territorial finally had been invaded, with quite a lot of damage, but no major fires set. Not there, but farther down North Marquette Street—about halfway between where I had dropped out of the demonstration, and the Interstate—the State Troopers managed to prevent the marchers from occupying the highway. But someone had thrown a Molotov cocktail that caught the gas tank of a car parked in front of the Omega Kappa Gamma fraternity house. The house caught fire, and they're saying the building is a total loss. Nobody hurt, thank God.

The reporter is saying that Highway 6 is still shut down at the Bancroft Street bridge, and people are advised to stay off of North Marquette Street, especially near the Park Road bridge. Highway 6 and Bancroft is a key intersection in State City, in terms of getting people into town and out of it, and it's blockaded.

Up the hill—overlooking the west side of Highway 6, on the roof of the Coffin, where Win lives—demonstrators set up a catapult of some kind, last night. They fired bricks, and cinderblocks—whatever they could find that was hard and heavy—which landed on the cars that were stuck on Highway 6 on the north side of Bancroft with cannonball force.

It's amazing that they didn't kill anyone. A few cars got hit, destroyed. If any of them had been hit in such a way as to ignite a gas tank—all those vehicles packed together, people stuck inside them—there would have been a chain reaction of car explosions and maybe dozens or even hundreds of people burned to death in the street. The people firing the catapult didn't think about that, though—or, what's even worse, maybe they did think about it, then went ahead and did what they did anyway.

Broadcasting live, now, on the TV screen, a reporter—a man with black hair, in his 30s, wearing a tan trench coat—is standing on the Bancroft Street bridge, which is covered with debris: paper, bricks, bottles, pieces of cloth. Behind him, demonstrators are waving and chanting—and still blocking the highway.

"Meanwhile," the reporter is saying, "a few blocks north of this intersection, up that hill that runs around behind Riverview," [he points behind him, in that direction] "a group of people got hold of some concrete construction pipes—culverts, five feet or so in diameter—and rolled them down that hill onto Highway 6 where it meets the western extension of Iowa Boulevard.

"The pipes reportedly did not hit any vehicles or people, but they temporarily blocked Highway 6 at the Iowa Boulevard extension, trapping motorists in their cars in a stretch of road that runs about 300 yards."

Once again: can you imagine what would have happened if one of those gas tanks had gone up? You have to wonder: Are any of the people who did what they did, last night—no matter what side of the dispute they're on—ever going to look back on it, and realize how lucky they were?

Now they're back to showing recorded footage of people who were there, last night, being interviewed.

An oldish fat man, dressed in work clothes, standing by his pickup truck: "Some of us who are stuck here in our vehicles nearest the demonstrators, we got out and tried to reason with 'em, askin' 'em to disperse so that traffic could pass. But, y'know, a few people, tryin' to reason with a mob, they never get far."

Now the reporter again, live: "It took several hours—well past midnight—to re-route the traffic that was stuck to the south of the Bancroft Street Bridge. The vehicles at the back of the jam finally started reversing—very slowly—and dispersing into side streets. The demonstrators continue to occupy the area.

"Motorists were able to get out of their cars and move the construction culverts to where there was enough room for those trapped cars to the north of here to slowly back out of that area, one vehicle at a time, and turn themselves around—but Highway 6 remains impassable here at the Bancroft Street bridge. This is Bob Beck, reporting from State City."

§

Approximately 400 people got arrested, on Tuesday night and into Wednesday and Thursday. I didn't miss any classes, despite all the confusion, the demonstrating on the Common and other places. No classes were cancelled, although none of them were very heavily attended. The demonstrators didn't reach their goal of shutting down State University—but they came close.

Wednesday night was when most of the physical injuries happened. The vigil on the Common started breaking up at nightfall. A lot of the demonstrators roamed the downtown in smaller groups, most of them looking for some variety of trouble.

Some of them, here and there, got into brawls—with farm boys, local high-school kids, and older blue-collar types who had come into the downtown area to beat up on the "peace freaks." A couple of gangs of black guys apparently were hunting for vulnerable-looking white guys. Probably there was enough bad behavior, and enough blame, to go around to all sides. I was safe back at Iota, by then, locked in my room studying, but I understand Wednesday night was—if violent—pretty anticlimactic.

At noon Thursday, President Nash gave a speech from the steps of Territorial—using that temporary rostrum—to which he had invited the press and as many students and University personnel who cared to show up. The situation had calmed down some, by then, but he announced that he was offering students the option of going home, with the grades they currently had in their classes, and considering their semester completed.

He added, "Anything that may have been admirable, at one time, has gone out of these demonstrations. They are no longer even political. It's time for this to end."

I don't know how many of them accepted Nash's offer, but I believe it was more than half the student body. By Thursday afternoon, the riots had all but burned themselves out, and by Friday the campus was almost deserted.

It's mean of me, but I suspect that a few kids, at least, were angling for that outcome all along: evading Finals Week. I continue to go to my near-empty classes, and I'll take my exams.

MONA AND MIKE TO THE RESCUE

I redeemed myself somewhat, over the weekend, for having run away from the demonstration on Tuesday night. It turned out that while I had been cowering in Iota, Mona and Mike had had a little adventure.

I was concerned that they might have been arrested again. I phoned their house on Wednesday, and got a recording: "The number you have dialed is not in service." That worried me, of course, and then just an hour or so later, that afternoon's *Examiner* reported that several houses on Kirk Street had been destroyed by fire on Tuesday night—including number 419. But the article didn't mention any injuries, so at least I could be pretty sure they were alive, somewhere.

The next morning, Thursday, I hunted down Professor Meregaglia at the Music Building, since I know he's friendly with Mona. He said he was wondering too, and he would let me know if he heard anything. When I got back to Iota that evening, there was a message from him that I should call Professor Lekberg, who teaches composition. I called Dr. Lekberg at his home— he's got a cattle farm about ten miles northeast of State City— and he told me that Mona and Mike were staying temporarily at Henry Fennelon's sheep farm, next to his.

I know Henry Fennelon by sight, although I don't know him personally. He one of those people who everybody in town sort-of-kind-of knows, or they know who you're talking about if you describe him to them. I'm pretty sure Feldy and Birdy would know him. He's about 45, big, rugged-looking. I see him sometimes in local theatre productions and in peace demonstrations.

Dr. Lekberg gave me Mr. Fennelon's number, so I called there on Thursday night and got Mona. She confirmed that she and Mike been burned out of their apartment, Tuesday night;

they had also been arrested again, the next day, while they were demonstrating—and released on desk appearance tickets.

When Mona started telling me all that, I said to myself, "There's your story for the *Statesman*." Mona and Mike Shapen, Two Leaders in the Local Peace Movement. The Riot Through Their Eyes.

As soon as I'd gotten done talking with Mona, I got on the phone to Birdy, and asked her (adding the sob story about how Mona and Mike were now temporarily of no fixed abode) whether I could invite the Shapens for dinner on Saturday night if I did all the shopping, cooking, and everything else.

I thought there was a good chance that Birdy and Feldy would be out that evening—Saturday is sometimes their "date night" in the off-season—but Birdy said, "I'd love to meet them; you've told us so much about them."

I'm at our house on Saturday afternoon to make the *chile con carne*. Birdy offers to help but I won't let her. Feldy passes through the kitchen and looks in on what I'm doing.

"Smells good," he says. "Doesn't surprise me that your friends are staying with Fennelon. He's a fairly interesting guy. A horse's ass, but an interesting guy."

"Oh, Feldy!" Birdy says. "Come on, he's nice."

"Oh, yeah, he is," Feldy allows. "He means well. The Fennelons of the world all mean well. He's interesting because he's such a stereotype. In his way. I don't mean there are a lot of Fennelons around, but you know them when you see them."

We're all standing around the stove. I'm stirring the pot—literally—and Birdy is having a smoke while we listen to Feldy.

"I call them 'muscular leftists,'" Feldy says. "Guys like Fennelon. They're posers. Oh, they're sincere. They mean what they say. But every damn thing they say or do, they're stroking themselves, and they're posing for everyone else. I knew a few of that kind in the Navy. Then after the war, they were the types you'd see at Paul Robeson or Burl Ives concerts, wearing their Henry Wallace buttons. They would root for the Dodgers, because Jackie Robinson. Not for any other reason."

I hope Feldy behaves around Mona and Mike.

§

Sander is out with friends, so it's me, Feldy, Birdy, Mike, and Mona, and Little Red/Hank, and they've brought Mr. Fennelon.

Mr. Fennelon is wearing a tweed jacket and a tie like he's not used to them. He's very polite. He and Feldy and Birdy talk a little about the football team, and about who might run for what office in 1972, while we're all having drinks in the den—and Birdy is being all sweet and fussy about the baby—then Mona and Mike start talking about what happened.

"Our objective was to take over the campus—peacefully—then shut down all of State City so that nobody could get in or out of it," Mike says. "After that, the ongoing strategy would have been to keep together, keep from dispersing, basically hold the university and the city hostage till Tricky Dick agreed to get us out of the war."

I'm trying to take accurate notes and enjoy my drink at the same time. Feldy and Birdy are having Scotch; so is Mr. Fennelon. Mike is having beer; Mona asked Birdy if we had any red Cinzano, and we did, so she and I are both drinking Cinzano on the rocks, even though I would have preferred some of that Scotch. For some reason I would have felt funny drinking hard liquor in front of Mona.

Feldy and Birdy are listening, not saying a thing. Feldy is nodding, looking really interested, although I can tell that he's internally shaking his head and rolling his eyes even if he's not actually doing it. I don't even have to ask any questions, hardly. Feldy can flatter Mona and Mike with just a nod or a look here and there. They keep talking and I keep taking notes.

Then, Mike starts talking about their house burning down.

"See, we'd been up on the Common, with the demonstrators, but then it was getting later and we're talking about shutting down the whole city, which, okay, I'm down with that, right? But Mona and I had this little fella with us, in the stroller, since at first we thought, well, we were just going to stand vigil till dark and then come home, but when it looked like there was going to be more than that going on, hey, groovy as far as I was concerned, but we had to get home and put the baby in his crib before we could do anything else.

"Okay, maybe we shouldn't have done it, it's not like I'm proud of it, but we thought we'd just be gone for a few hours, and we didn't want to get a baby involved when it looked like things might get dangerous. So, we thought: go home, put the kid down, then go shut down the Interstate. We figured our comrades weren't going to miss us much if we dropped out for 20 minutes."

Feldy and Birdy are paying attention, but not reacting.

"This house we live in... lived in ... it's a really crummy house. A duplex that should have been a single-fam—I was going to say it should have been a single-family home, but really it should have been demolished. It was substandard in all kinds of ways. I think it was only standing from force of habit.

"Well, as soon as we got within half a block of that house, Mona and I could see smoke coming out of it, out of the other apartment. I could see that smoke was coming out of the house next to ours, too. That was when Mona started running—I never had any idea she could run so fast—and I left the stroller there on the sidewalk and ran after her. I was right behind her, yelling at her to not go into the damn house, and I had to physically stop her and wrestle her away from the door so that I could be the one to go in. I told her to go back and look after Hank."

Mike glances over at Mona, like he's hoping for some display of admiration, and he gets one, in the form of a lowered-eyes gaze, and a simper.

"So I ran into our apartment. There was already a little smoke coming into our unit, but nothing seemed to be on fire yet, so I grabbed some diapers out of the bathroom, got Mona's cello and some other stuff. I brought it out and passed it to Mona; she tried to stop me from going back in. But, no, I had to do it. The smoke was starting to get pretty bad, but I got some of Mona's and my sheet music, and a lot of my research materials that were absolutely irreplaceable, for a project I'm working on for Professor Lekberg—I don't know if you know him."

Feldy and Birdy shake their heads.

"Heard the name," Feldy says.

"So, it looked like two buildings on fire, and a fire truck was pulling up, and one of the firemen hollered down to us from the truck, 'Stay right where you are, God damn it! The police want to talk to you people!' Which is crazy, because why would any of us want to set fire to the building? Sure, they would want to blame us, but that was our stuff that was going up in flames: our clothes and books and records and pots and pans. Everything we owned, and not just us: our neighbors too. The only person who could get anything out of burning those buildings would be the guy who owns them. I don't know, maybe one of the tenants wasn't paying the rent and he figured it would be easier to torch the building and collect the insurance, because he'd still own the land, right?"

Feldy looks skeptical.

"You suppose maybe someone started the fire to keep the fire department occupied?" Feldy says. "I mean, so that they'd be busy while other fires were being started? We saw on TV that buildings were going up all over town."

"I wouldn't be surprised if people were setting those fires because they knew our side would get blamed for it," Mike says. "Anyway, when that fireman said that, I figured I'd better get out of there, so I ran not toward Mona, but across the street, behind a neighboring house, and when I got behind that house I took the lid off a garbage can and threw it off in another direction, to maybe make them think I'd gone off that way."

Feldy glances over at Mona.

"Evidently you didn't get arrested," he says to her.

"Oh, I don't think the fireman even noticed me," Mona says. Her voice is barely above a whisper. "I was standing off to the side; I probably wasn't even in his field of vision. He was looking right at Mike. Probably if he said, 'you people,' it was, like, general, like 'you scabby hippies,' or whatever." Mona giggles a little.

"That's lucky," Feldy says. "Would have been a shame if you'd gotten arrested with that baby of yours." Feldy glances over at Mike—just a flicker—then looks back at Mona. "Have you got the kid playing football yet?"

Of course, Hank can barely toddle. Mona smiles.

"So, you two found each other again," Feldy says.

338

"I wandered off across the street and down the alley," Mona says, "and even if they'd wanted to, I guess they were too busy to try and stop me. I didn't see any police there yet. So I went in the direction Mike had gone, and we caught up."

"Probably there weren't any Blue Knights to spare, at that point," Mike says. "We could hear them, though. Sirens. All over, all kinds. Like they were coming from everywhere. Ghosts wailing, frogs croaking, donkeys braying, maybe some crazy giant gargling, any kind of siren you can imagine. Because you had local cops, state troopers, fire trucks, and whatever else, all going at the same time. We were off at a distance by then, but we could see that the house was going to go up before the firemen could get it under control."

"And no place to sleep," Mona says. "We could have found a phone booth and called around till we ran out of dimes, to see if any of our friends had a bed for us, or even a floor, but most of them would have been out, you know, participating."

"So we walked over to that elementary school, about half a mile from our house," Mike says.

"Horace Greeley?" I ask.

"That's the one," says Mona. "And we just slept on the ground there. Then in the morning we walked to the A&P, to get something Hank could eat, then we walked to the Music Building to see if anybody knew of a place where we could crash. And Dr. Lekberg was nice enough to call Henry, here..."

Mr. Fennelon shrugs, and looks humble.

"So we'll be farm hands for a few days, to work off our rent," Mike says. "Looks like everything has quieted down, now, but maybe we got some people's attention."

"You did what you could," says Mr. Fennelon.

"Yeah," says Mike. "Maybe we saved this ugly country after all. What concerns me is that most of the press is going to focus on the few bad apples who made the rest of us look like hoodlums. With the violence and all."

"You were trying to shut down the city, you say?" Feldy's voice is quiet, and kind, as though he were talking to me when I was a little girl. "Well, that's violence, isn't it?"

Mona looks shocked.

"If you're using force, to get people to do or not to do something, violence is implicit, it seems to me." Feldy is using the same tone. "If you're trying to stop me from going where I want to go, what else would you call it?"

"I would call it the people reacting to violence," says Mike.

Feldy looks over to me for not even a tenth of a second. Just a flicker of his eyes. He says all kinds of stuff, in that little look.

At this point, we move to the dining room. The *chile* I've made is sort of a cross between a pot roast, a stew, and barbecue; at any rate it can go onto a plate, without running all over everything, instead of a bowl. And I've got collard greens, white beans, and cornbread. With lemon meringue pie for after, just like Amelia Bedelia. A decent meal if I say so myself. If I were cut out for it, I'd probably make a pretty good housewife.

Mike, and occasionally Mona, tell us about how they were briefly arrested, then released, on Wednesday.

"We decided to go and join the crowd on the Bancroft Street bridge," Mona says, "but as soon as we got there—this would have been late Wednesday morning—the National Guard was moving in from River Drive and lobbing cans of tear gas at us—it looked like they were actually kicking them at us, like soccer balls—and at first we all lay flat on the asphalt, covering our heads, so that the gas wouldn't get to us.

"We thought the gas would dissipate, since we were on a bridge, and no buildings, right? But it did start getting to us, and then the guardsmen came in and made their arrests, which wasn't hard, since we weren't exactly in condition to resist and maybe most of us were happy to get away from the gas.

"The county jail had been full since the night before; they were going to transfer prisoners to jails in other counties, but in the meantime the National Guard—I assume it was the National Guard—had put up this temporary fence, in the Courthouse parking lot..."

"It was just a wood and wire snow-fence, at first," Mike says, "and the first few prisoners broke that down in a jiffy. But then they built a second one around us—we weren't going to move, because we had Hank with us and we could have been clubbed or shot—and this time it was barbed wire fencing that could be electrified. So we were in this big holding pen. They had several hundred prisoners in there. Most of us weren't held for even two hours, but Mona and I were already on the pigs' radar, because of other incidents, so we didn't get bailed out till Wednesday night and by then we were exhausted. I used my one phone call to see if Henry, here, could come get us, and he did."

"Lucky for you that he could get into town," Feldy says, and Mike doesn't know what to say to that.

With Mike, Mona, and Mr. Fennelon all telling their stories, I have plenty of material. Plus, I'm so proud of myself that I'm able to listen, dish food up for the guests, eat, take notes, and remember whatever I can't write down immediately.

"That Mona's a pretty girl, all right," Feldy says to me and Birdy, now that the company has left. "Maybe a little too earnest. Him too. Him, I didn't care for, frankly. They might outgrow it. Sometimes they do. But I have to worry about how they're going to bring their kids up."

Birdy sighs. "Oh, Feldy."

"Look, I don't blame them for being upset about the war," Feldy says. "I actually agree with them on that. It's their whole set of values that I can't get along with. This sort of vague Marxism. They don't know what kind of fire they're playing with."

Feldy pauses, shakes his head. Then he adds, "Plus, they are just... so... *stupid.*"

I'm shocked, to hear Feldy say this. He reads my reaction.

"Oh, they might have the type of intelligence that makes them good at music, or lets them score high on an IQ test," he says. "But you can be intelligent in that way, and still be dumb as a brick. Lots and lots of people are like that."

"They got me off the hook, anyway," I say. "I can write the story tonight, and tomorrow afternoon, and it gets me out of trying to write an 'I was there for the riot' story."

"That's not your specialty, anyway," Feldy says. "Your best articles, almost always, are your interviews and profiles. You're not Dickey Chapelle."

"You're not even Rosalie Simms-Pibity," says Birdy, "and that's a good thing. You write about people's personalities and values—not about their adventures, or yours."

Personalities and values. I'm thinking: In a way, Birdy is right about me—and Feldy might be right about Mona and Mike.

MAKING MORE TROUBLE

Meanwhile, Gary and his sidekick Gruber are still free agents, so to speak. Plus, while Gary's brother got that new job without much trouble—got it with Feldy's help, most likely—it's still just a scouting job, which he must have considered a big step down from assistant coach for a major college team. I guess Paul has convinced himself—and maybe Gary has, too—that Feldy somehow used the two of them, then let them take the fall. I don't believe that for a second.

This didn't come up on Saturday, when we were entertaining Mona and Mike. I didn't hear about this, at all, till Sunday after Mass, after lunch at the Coffin Corner—when I got back to Iota and finally got a chance to read *The Des Moines Sunday Register*.

Somebody—it could be Paul Schoyer, but I have no evidence that it was—has gone to the Iowa State Auditor with the story that certain employees of the State University Athletic Department were padding their expenses, especially on recruiting trips.

Feldy was quoted in the *Register* as saying, "My background isn't accounting. There have been enough stories already about bad feelings between me and Timmerman. We've been trying to patch things up, and I'm not aware of any such shenanigans."

This can't be any big thing, since Feldy never mentioned it to me this morning. Timmerman had been conducting the last day of spring drills, on Saturday, and the *Sunday Register* quoted him saying, "I know nothing about it and I have no comment."

By Monday, when the bones of contention became clearer, Timmerman—at least, this is what the *Examiner* reported that afternoon—told the press that Feldy had not only approved the extra expenditures (which were mainly for food and alcohol at restaurants out of town), but had urged him and his assistant coaches to "spend what you need to spend" to aid recruiting.

I don't know about this. Feldy and I have never discussed his work in as much depth as that. But it's interesting. Back when Brosnan was coaching, Feldy was accused—and I can't prove that this is *not* true, but I refuse to believe it, because it makes no sense—of being stingy with funds for recruiting to the point where he was suspected of sabotaging Brosnan.

I didn't believe that, back then, and why should I believe it now? It sounds, now, like Feldy has been trying to help Timmerman to recruit, or at least encouraging him to spend money on recruitment. I am fed up with the way the press keeps looking and looking for ways to stick it to Feldy.

§

Wednesdays are pretty busy for me, but at least I don't owe the *Statesman* an article. I've gotten through today's classes, and I'll have most of this evening to get myself set for Finals Week, which is always such a delight.

I'm coming out of my 4:00 Intermediate German class in the Liberal Arts building (one class I'm pretty sure to get an A in, anyway), heading for the building's north exit, intending to walk back to Iota. My eye catches the three newspaper vending machines that stand against the inside wall, next to the doors. They hold the *Register*, the *Statesman*—both morning papers that I've already seen—and the evening's *Examiner*, which I haven't seen yet. The front-page headline reads:

FELDY RESIGNS, TIMMERMAN FIRED

I stand dead still for about five seconds, then dig into my purse for a dime. There isn't one in my coin purse. I would have sworn from frustration (I might have taken the Lord's name in vain) but I don't, because I then spy a dime at the bottom of my bag. I have to use my fingernails to get it out. My head is about to explode, as though I'm afraid the vending machine will grow legs and run away before I can buy the paper.

> The State University Board in Control of Athletics announced this noon that it has accepted the resignation of Athletic Director Leo Feldevert, and revoked for cause the contract of head football coach Tobias Timmerman, both decisions effective on May 31. The announcement came on the heels of yesterday's report from the Iowa State Auditor's office that Timmerman had padded his recruiting expense accounts, and allowed his assistant coaches to do the same, on Feldevert's instructions.
>
> The Board said "Athletic Director Feldevert's resignation was accepted with reluctance. It had been brought to our attention when he renewed his contract in 1969 that Feldy was wishful to seek other options. He was persuaded at that time to stay on."

That, I am dead certain, is not the truth. Feldy has been talking—now and then, for years—about looking for something else, but he has never said a word about leaving without having another job lined up. He would never do that. "Accepted with reluctance," my eye. If in fact Feldy has resigned, I'll bet it was one of those "Do you want to resign, or be fired?" situations. Certain members of the Board have been gunning for Feldy for a long time, and they finally found a clear shot at him.

I bet they also advised Timmerman to resign, but he refused.

Now that this information is sinking in, I feel all empty inside. I'm seeing this blue patina over everything, not a Catholic blue: a cloudy blue, not dark and not light.

> No further elaboration was given with regard to the dismissal of Timmerman, and a spokesman for the Board said, "We will have no further comment at this time, except that we thank both men for their services and wish them both the best in the future."
>
> Contacted at his office, Feldevert told the *Examiner* that in the interests of general harmony, in view of the recent

unrest in the Department of Athletics, he believed that he would serve the school best by leaving.

"For 15 years I have given my best to State University athletics, and the programs I have run have always been in accordance with Big Ten and NCAA rules," Feldevert said. "I have never tolerated any practice that was contrary to University policy or procedure—let alone been a party to it. My conscience is absolutely clear.

"However, I cannot go on subjecting my family to the treatment that they've received over several years—the rumors, the abusive press coverage, the obscene phone calls. In particular, it will be impossible for my family to forget these past months, but I hope that in the long run the pain will be eased by memories of happier years.

"Finally, I felt that since the Board took the decision to remove Coach Timmerman, it was time for me to go, too. I don't want to be the Athletic Director who outlasted two coaches: that wouldn't speak well of my own performance. Given that, and other factors, I felt that resigning was the only honorable choice."

Coach Timmerman, however, told the *Examiner* that he had not finalized his plans but does not intend to accept the Board's decision.

"The reason given to me for my dismissal was the general disharmony within the athletic department during the past four months, as well as discrepancies with expense accounts," Timmerman said. "I cannot be satisfied with these reasons, since if there has been any disharmony within the athletic department I have always done my best to either quell it or distance myself from it. As for the reporting of expenses on recruiting trips, my assistants and I filled out and filed our reports precisely as we had been instructed to do by the Athletic Director."

My first impulse is to run back down the hall to a phone booth, and call home. But when I get to the phone booth, I think, why? Just go home. I look at my watch: the next bus on the route I want won't be leaving downtown for 20 minutes. I can walk it in less than that time. Or maybe I should first walk over to the Engineering Building, instead, to see if anyone at the *Statesman* knows any more about this. I stand where I've been standing, thinking, for a few seconds. My family has first priority and I still have all night to get to the Engineering Building.

I'm walking east on Lincoln Avenue, through the main business district. I feel the vibration first, then I hear the sound, of the five o'clock whistle from the State City power plant behind me and to my right, down by the Bancroft Street bridge. The blast startles me, for not even a tenth of a second—but then it comforts me, grounds me. The sound gives me comforting colors, light ones: blue, pink, grey, white.

The five o'clock whistle has always made me feel safe, happy. Like I'm in the right place. It has always done that, whenever I've heard it, for the nearly 15 years I've lived in State City. It tells me, "This is my home."

So, home I walk.

Now that the sound has faded, I'm not feeling comforted anymore. I feel like I've taken a bullet or a piece of shrapnel. I don't really know what that's like, obviously, but I imagine it must feel something like this—plus the physical pain, which I'm sure feels a lot worse than this dull ache in my insides. But when you've received that sudden shock, I suppose you have to start asking yourself: Where am I hit? How bad is it? What do I do now?

I know our family has plenty of money. Feldy will find some way to make a living. This doesn't need to affect me, personally, very much. That's something. But that's the end of any political career for Feldy. He might even decide to move us out of State City… which would mean losing the house.

Oh, Judas. The house.

I'm noticing familiar landmarks as I walk home along Lincoln Avenue: that gas station; that café; that little corner park. They comfort me. I turn right, onto Hilltop Street.

I remark, one by one, on the houses that I have hardly ever thought much about, since my first few years in State City. I barely notice the sky, till I do: it's brilliant blue. The temperature is at that perfect point between warm and cool. Such a beautiful, *amazingly* beautiful afternoon. I wish I could slow down, enjoy the walk, but I have to get home. I walk faster, and faster yet.

Feldy's car is in the garage, next to the Suburban. Win's Rambler is parked in the driveway, so he's here. Lights are on inside the house; the front door is unlocked. I don't announce myself, when I walk in, but just listen. My ears point me to the kitchen.

As best I can recall, this is the first crisis in the Feldevert family that has called for a conference around the kitchen table. That's a phenomenon I've only ever heard about, in novels and memoirs: when a family is having a catastrophe, they'll gravitate to the kitchen table. We have never done it, though, before now.

Birdy, Feldy, and Sander are sitting in the chairs of vinyl-wrapped metal tubing that go with the kitchen table. Win sits in a wooden chair that he brought in from the dining room. They all look stunned. Do I look that way too? Probably I do. I notice that the kitchen phone is off the hook.

"Get another chair if you want to join us," Birdy says. I have never before heard her speak in such a dull tone.

I do. Birdy slides hers over, to make room. Since one side of the table is against a window, it's a tight fit. Birdy and I are sitting with our backs to the foyer; Feldy on our right, with his back to the door that leads to the dining room; Win and Sander across from us, with their backs to the sink, the dishwasher, and a shelf of cookbooks.

A copy of the *Examiner* lies on the table. The main and the sports sections have been separated.

Feldy looks done for. Drained. He's still wearing his camel-hair jacket, white shirt, and black tie, which usually make him look so imposing, but now he looks crumpled; his jacket seems to sag on him. I have never seen him like this. Not even after a disastrous football game. Not even when his father died, a few years ago, and then his mother a year later. I would never have imagined him looking this way: like all the vitality, all the energy, have been taken out of him and he barely has enough left to stay sentient and moving.

"What are we going to do?" I ask.

"I've got several options in mind," Feldy says. He seems to have a little more energy, now that he's talking. He leans forward in his chair. "Don't worry, Terri. I've just been telling everybody else here, I'm not going to have any trouble supporting this family. But Birdy and I will have to think for a few days about what direction we're going to take. This is pretty sudden, but it's something I've been anticipating for a while."

"What happened?"

"The rest of the family knows the story. I held off calling you last night, because I was pretty sure this would be the outcome, when the report was made public, but I wasn't *sure*-sure, and I didn't want to get anyone alarmed for no reason.

"I was told there would be a meeting this morning, and that Timmerman and I were both supposed to be there. I thought about calling Mr. Barclay," [William Barclay, our family's lawyer] "but I didn't think it would come to that, yet. I thought the meeting would be to discuss the report—but there wasn't any discussion. Almost as soon as we sat down, they told me and Timmerman that as a result of the Auditor's report, they had decided that we had to go, and did we prefer to resign or be fired?"

Feldy leans back in his chair now, and smiles a little.

"At that point—it's funny, but it really did happen in a second—you could say I had a revelation. I no longer gave a damn about that job, or about this university. It doesn't make sense for me to keep smashing my head against a wall."

"Are we staying here?" I ask.

"I don't see why we would want to. There's nothing here that interests me or Birdy. Sander's got another year of high school, which is a consideration…"

"I don't care if I finish up here or someplace else," Sander says. Feldy winks at him.

I want to say, "No, don't leave; don't sell this house!" but I don't want to sound selfish at a time like this.

"Feldy, you have to know there are thousands of people out there who can see through this and know you didn't do anything wrong," I say. "All over the state. Gosh, hundreds of thousands of people support you. You've got to stay here."

Feldy casts his eyes down at the table and shakes his head.

"No, it's time to move on," he says, and he shrugs. "Birdy and I were thinking we could go up to Wisconsin for the weekend, and think things over just the two of us. Sander, you can hold the fort here. Win and Terri can look in on you—or maybe one of you could stay here with Sander while we're gone."

Win shifts in his chair and looks, suddenly, angry. I can't remember ever seeing Win looking angry. Never once, before this. That's so strange. To have never seen him angry before. But I don't think I have. I can tell because a vertical line has appeared between his eyebrows, and this is the first time in my life that I have seen that line.

"They haven't beaten you yet, though, if you don't let them," Win says. "Even if you decide to leave here, don't let anybody think they've beaten you."

"I've lost this battle, anyway," Feldy says. "But it's just a battle. We all have to remember that. It's on to the next one. And it'll be best for all of us if the next one happens somewhere else."

Feldy motions to the table, to the sports section of the *Examiner*.

"Terri, if you haven't seen it yet, take a look in there. At Jack Brady's column."

A FOOTBALL PROGRAM IN A SEWER
By Jack Brady

The decision by the Board in Control of Athletics to accept Athletic Director Leo Feldevert's resignation and dismiss Head Coach Toby Timmerman rids us of two of the most prominent players in this sordid drama, played out in the dysfunctional sewer that the State University football program has become. It's anybody's guess as to whether or not this development will reduce the stink and the infection, which will probably take years to clean out.

Very simply, someone informed the Iowa State Auditor's office that there was maybe a whole sub-department called "Padded Expense Accounts." Coach Timmerman's defense is that Feldy personally showed him how to falsify those expense account forms. Feldy denies it. The Board has finally decided to flush them both.

As one does, after a good… flush… I feel relief, more than anything else.

That doesn't mean that it was a fair call.

Coaches at State University are state employees. When they're recruiting, they have to pick up the tab for prospective players, parents, alumni, and other interested parties.

Practically and morally speaking, they can't go out of pocket for this. They need reimbursement somehow. I'm not up on all the details, but I understand it's pretty easy to cook up phony receipts for room service, or rooms not paid for.

There's no doubt in my mind that officials in the State Auditor's office have been shutting their eyes to this for some time. So has the Board in Control of Athletics. But now, it seems, an informer has forced the Auditor's hand; the Auditor in turn forced the Board's hand. Who knows? Maybe the Board was happy enough to be forced.

I can't doubt that the knives were out for both Feldy and Timmerman already, and this was the provocation that the Board had been looking for.

We can't blame them. The atmosphere here has been poisonous for too long. However, the Board overreacted, in my opinion. It has been an open secret, for years, that Feldy is over-involved with the football program and has not been an inspiring influence in the Athletics Department as a whole. He was a great football coach—and has been a disaster as Athletic Director. State University has to send him on his way. Not for having shown his coaches how to falsify expense reports (if that's what he did), but for creating, almost single-handedly, an intolerable situation at State University. A situation that makes it impossible for the Rivercats to field a winning football team as long as he remains in office.

But they didn't have to fire Toby Timmerman, or ask him to resign. Timmerman is actually a good coach; he just wasn't mean enough to stand up to Feldy. Not many coaches would be. He doesn't deserve to lose his job because he didn't use his own money to recruit football players. The Board asked him to commit *hara-kiri* for the greater good. He refused to, so the Board chose to execute him. That's inexcusable.

I roll my eyes to the ceiling. "Oh, for God's sake."

"Yeah, that puts the cherry on the sundae, right there," Feldy says. "Of all the… Brady's an ingrate, that's all I can tell you. I've done a lot for that guy, ever since I came here. But he's staying and I'm going, so knifing me in the back would naturally have struck him as the best option."

I can't hold it back any longer.

"But we can't give up this house! This is ours. This house. They can't run us out of town. You can't let them!"

"Honey, if we leave town, it'll be because Birdy and I believe it's best for the family. It's conceivable that something could happen to keep us here, but I can't think what it would be. I know you love this house; we all do. But it wasn't like we were going to stay here forever. We were always going to move on, one day."

"I always hoped this house would stay in the family, somehow," I say. I'm immediately sorry I said that, because I don't want to imply that I wouldn't have been happy if Feldy had moved on to coaching in the NFL, or been elected Governor.

"Well, I'm not going to give Brady or anybody else the satisfaction," Feldy says. "If anybody else feels hungry, I'm going to call the Nightingale right now and see if they have a table for us."

The Nightingale is a steakhouse/supper club that passes for the height of elegance in the State City area. It's not even in State City. It's in a tiny farming community about ten miles west of town limits, called Odgrove. It stands a few hundred yards away from a grain elevator. It's a low, squat, wood-frame building that doesn't look like much from the outside, but on the inside it's real Midwestern swank: dark, with a small bar and a good-sized dining room with leather-upholstered banquettes and flocked wallpaper. People sit at their tables happily smoking, working on elaborate cocktails like a pink lady or a Singapore sling, waiting for their 16-ounce steaks, massive baked potatoes, salads with homemade dressing, onion rings, Texas toast.

This is where you go for dinner when you're in the mood to celebrate. It's always packed following a football game, or on either side of a basketball game. Back when Feldy was Head Coach, he and other coaches would entertain recruits and their families here. Feldy and Birdy sometimes dine at The Nightingale, just the two of them, but us kids only get to go with them on special occasions, maybe once a year on average.

I'm not very enthusiastic about going there tonight, and I'm not so sure about Birdy either, but it's what Feldy wants to do. I guess out of defiance. I can understand that. As far as Win and Sander are concerned, they're getting Nightingale steaks, so what's not to like?

We hardly say anything on the drive to Odgrove. At the Nightingale, the hostess doesn't act any differently than she ever does. She just smiles and says to Feldy, "Brought the crew tonight, huh?" then leads us to a table in the middle of the dining room. Other people turn their heads as we pass through, but they always do, because Feldy is Feldy.

When we're working on our salads, Feldy asks Win, jocularly, "What's the Church's perspective on all the demonstrations last week?" which allows Win to tell us all about his plans (still tentative, but he's pretty certain) to attend St. Pius V Seminary in Davenport in the fall.

Sander has his junior-senior prom coming up, and Feldy kids him about it—tries to get him to talk about his date—but Sander is blushing and pretending it's no big thing.

"She's just a friend," he says. "We both wanted to go; there's nothing more to it than that."

"If you say so," says Feldy, very fake-solemn.

Birdy hardly says anything, all evening. Feldy tries a couple of times to bring her in, but she just gives this sorrowful smile and replies with only a few words, and one of us has to pick up the thread. At least she's eating.

Jake and Silda Rosen are leaving, while we're about halfway through our meal, and they stop by our table. Mr. Rosen is the Mayor of State City, now, and Rosen's is the biggest men's store in town. It's where the athletes all get their team blazers and slacks. He's a middle-sized, middle-aged man with curly greying dark hair and a Clark Gable-style moustache. He always wears a plain grey or blue suit, or a blue blazer on weekends. Mrs. Rosen is on the tall side, though not as tall as I am, and she must have been a knockout when she was younger, with black hair and very dark eyes. Mr. Rosen shakes Feldy's hand and says, "Good to see you. We heard the news. We feel terrible about it."

"Don't," Feldy tells him. "I don't."

Mrs. Rosen says to Birdy, "Are you okay? I feel silly asking if there's anything we can do, but is there anything we can do?"

She's obviously having a hard time thinking of what to say, and this forces Birdy to smile and laugh. She squeezes Mrs. Rosen's hands in both of hers, and says, "We're fine. Just trying to figure things out. This is nothing at all." Which I know isn't true, but not even Birdy has the right words for this situation.

Two more couples whom I don't recognize, but they're about my parents' age, stop by our table when they're leaving the dining room. One of the men just says, "Hey, Feldy, how's it going?" and shakes Feldy's hand. The other couple both shake hands with both my parents, and the man says, "It's a damn shame." Feldy says, "Thanks for noticing. But it'll work out."

The waitress knows us; she probably knows what's up, too—but she acts the same as always, all through the meal.

Now that we're headed home in the Suburban, we're still not talking. When we're getting near the State City limits, Feldy asks, "Everybody satisfied? I mean, with the meal?"

"It was great," I say. "Thank you. It was wonderful. Thanks for taking us."

"Yes, thank you, Dear," says Birdy. Win and Sander echo.

"Glad to hear it," says Feldy. "Might be a while before we're all back there again. But it was nice to do it one more time."

We drive to the Engineering Building, since I fibbed and told Feldy I still owe the *Statesman* an article. In fact, I just want to find out the latest. I lean forward in my seat to give Feldy a hug; he pats my arm. Birdy turns in her seat as best she can, and I give her one.

"Expect me back home tonight, if that's okay," I say. "I'd rather not deal with my sisters right now, and I don't want to be anywhere near Gail Timmerman, in these circumstances."

"Understandable," Birdy says. "Be quiet if you get in late."

I know Sander doesn't like being hugged, so I muss his hair—which he *really* doesn't like—before I get out of the Suburban.

HARRY CARAY

I sit in the press room half-heartedly working on an analysis of the Student Senate election that took place on Tuesday: a story that I don't have to turn in till tomorrow night. My mind's not on it—hardly anyone voted, anyway—but I'm forcing myself. Ben Bailey, the sports editor, stops by my desk and asks, "You okay?"

"Yeah, as okay as I can be. Nothing I can do about it."

"Did you hear about Timmerman? We're trying to track it down, but they say he killed himself. Literally committed Harry Caray. Cut himself open. We're trying to confirm it, but the line is busy at his house. We sent someone over there."

I just stare at Ben. I'm about to say, instinctively, "May God have mercy on him," but before I can say it, I remind myself that a suicide has placed himself outside God's mercy; it is futile, blasphemous, to pray for such a one.

Still, I have to feel guilty that I have just been eating a big steak and enjoying myself as best I could in the circumstances, while Timmerman—and, really? He never seemed like a suicidal type at all, to me—was literally killing himself. Doing it in such a horrible way, at that, if this story is to be believed.

Before I leave the newsroom, I check what the *Statesman*'s front page is going to look like in the morning. The top story is Feldy resigning and Timmerman getting fired, of course, and the secondary story's headline is TIMMERMAN SUICIDE RUMORS PERSIST.

354

It's close to midnight; I'm walking home. I can't get the thought out of my head: Timmerman killed himself? Over a job? I suppose I ought to feel sorry for him—I do feel awful for his family—but I can't feel sorry for him, because to kill himself for such a reason, he would have to be crazy, and I mean crazy like someone who isn't connected to reality. Completely and helplessly crazy—in which case, God will take that into account, and have mercy on him. Or maybe not. Or maybe it really is only a rumor. I can hope, yet; I can still have faith.

Everyone's in bed when I let myself into our house. The phone in the kitchen is still off the hook. This would indicate that the rest of the family hasn't heard that rumor. Anyway, it's not a sure thing, so I can pray for Coach Timmerman tonight, and I will.

§

I'm up in the morning before Birdy is, for once, and as soon as I'm dressed, I'm downstairs to turn on the TV and find out what's going on. *WMT Morning News* isn't saying anything about any suicide: they're reporting on Mick Jagger's wedding. *The Des Moines Register* didn't hear the rumor last night, obviously. Feldy and Timmerman are the main headline on the front page—the front page of the main section, not the Big Peach. But no mention of any suicide. George Conroy's column reads, in part:

> Want to know how it feels to get a knife in the back? Ask Toby Timmerman. He got one right between the shoulder blades, when the Board in Control of Athletics decided that the best way to clean house in the football program was to get both Leo Feldevert and Toby Timmerman to resign, or fire them if they refused to go quietly. Feldy, in effect, said he had been intending to leave anyway, and a year more or less would make no difference to him—so he resigned, maybe or maybe not with an upraised middle finger. Timmerman, like Bob Brosnan before him, said, "You'll have to fire me." I'm astonished that he didn't have a stronger reaction than that. Maybe he did.

As a State University alumnus, as a lifelong fan of all the Rivercat sports teams, and as a sportswriter who tries to be objective but is nevertheless an unabashed "homer," I am disgusted by the Board's decision to fire Timmerman. It's like punishing both the bully and his victim, when everyone on the playground could see that the bully started it. What sort of justice is this?

What crimes has Timmerman committed? 1. He handled his expense accounts the way anyone in his situation would have, with Feldy's instruction and blessing. 2. He had a horrible season in 1970—which everybody knows was due largely to circumstances beyond his control—after a surprisingly good one in 1969. 3. He didn't get along with Feldy. If you fired every member of the Athletic Department who has had problems with Feldy, maybe a couple of janitors would be left. I wouldn't even count on that.

Knives, knives. Oh, aha. Now the TV is showing live footage of Timmerman being interviewed in front of the Fieldhouse. He's saying that he's still entitled to the use of his office, and "I'm going to take full advantage. I'll have a statement for you later today." He definitely does not look dead.

I bet I know what happened. Probably the rumor about suicide got started when someone saw Brady's *hara-kiri* reference, last night, and it turned into a game of "telephone."

I hear Birdy coming downstairs. I fold my hands and thank God it didn't happen. Silently. No need for me to tell Birdy or Feldy about it, if it was no more than a rumor all along.

§

I have not been able to play the Glad Game about this; I haven't even thought about trying to. That statement from Timmerman, that was released around noon that day, ran like this:

I asked for a reason for my dismissal and I was told it was because of the disharmony in the athletic department. My question is this: has there not been noticeable disharmony for the past 15 years, since Leo Feldevert first set foot on this campus? Has Leo Feldevert not been famous for his feuds, all these years: first with Vic Enslowe, then with Bob Brosnan, and lately with me? What, or who, seems to be the common thread that has consistently woven itself into this "disharmony in the athletic department"?

I felt it was my obligation to get along with Leo Feldevert. I tried my best to do so. However, Feldy made it a habit to harass me during weekly staff meetings, and told members of the community that I was a poor coach who couldn't handle the team—despite the fact that in my first year, I improved the team's record from 1-9 to 5-5.

Then he went on to gripe about how the football program got a smaller expense account than the basketball program; that the football players weren't given access to free parking near the stadium; how the expense vouchers had been an excuse to find other reasons to fire him.

That same morning, Thursday, State Senator Rollo Scaff of Des Moines—Republican and long-time vocal critic of Feldy—took the Senate floor and asserted, "Leo Feldevert's conduct in his entire time as Athletic Director has been ruthless, and the firing of Toby Timmerman by the Board was gutless. If this is State University's concept of justice, and if the Chairman of the Board in Control of Athletics is a professor in the College of Law at State University, maybe we had better take a look at the law school as well. Timmerman has done nothing that any other athletics coach at a state-run university would not have done, and if there's to be any justice, he should have his job back."

Joe Bergman, a well-known attorney in Cedar Rapids (and a Democrat), was the Rivercats' quarterback during Feldy's first and second years at State, and now he sits on the Board of Regents. He issued a statement, that same morning, calling the Board in Control of Athletics' decision "the worst I've ever heard of. Coach Timmerman has at least been trying to turn the football program around, whereas Leo Feldevert has spent the past six years doing his best to destroy it. Feldy, in effect, is a firestarter: someone who deliberately causes a crisis in the hope

357

that he'll be called on to heroically quell it. Finally, he's been caught with the rags and the gasoline can in his hand."

Rivercat Booster Clubs in Fort Dodge, Sioux City, and Muscatine all issued statements of support for Timmerman. So did the Iowa High School Football Coaches Association.

The Rivercat varsity football squad released a statement, read by the defensive captain, Bruno Grozniac, in front of the athletic building. I wasn't there, but it must have looked impressive, since Grozniac is about six-foot-eight and weighs maybe 290. I know his nickname is "David" because of his physique.

He's also crazy. Not in a good way. He's our goon. If someone on the other team is playing a little too rough—or a little too well—Grozniac is in charge of correcting him. I wouldn't have guessed he could read, though.

The statement said, in part: "The football squad does not feel that the decision to fire Coach Timmerman at this time is justified. It is not fair to him or to the assistant coaches and players, who have just finished working with Coach Timmerman on our spring drills, and, most of all, it is not in the best interests of State University, Rivercat fans, and alumni. We strongly recommend that Coach Timmerman be reinstated."

I'm sure the Board in Control of Athletics never expected to get that kind of backlash. At around noon of that day, they announced that Timmerman would be given the opportunity to go before the Board at its regularly scheduled meeting the following Tuesday evening, for a second hearing.

Also at noon—in time to make the *Examiner*'s deadline and to get on the 6:00 news that night—Feldy held a press conference in the usual room. He was wearing not his Rivercat-colored ensemble, but a plain grey suit and blue foulard tie. I saw clips of it on TV, but I was able to hear the whole tape of it, later that night, in the newsroom of the *Statesman*, thanks to Ben Bailey.

Feldy talked for almost 20 minutes. He started by saying, "It's about time we close the books on my career at State University—and on the various disagreements, which I have to admit have come close to destroying the State University Athletic Department in the past few months.

"With regard to my own situation, I've been thinking of re-signing and moving on for at least three years, maybe more, but I felt I had a commitment to State University, plus a love and respect for State University that would have prevented me from resigning with a clear conscience.

"Today, however, I have to admit that I've lost the support I've enjoyed over the years from the Board and from the fans and supporters of Rivercat sports. The athletic program at State University has been badly damaged by a number of factors, and at this point, it's impossible for the program to be repaired by me. In fact, it can only be repaired if I'm not part of it.

"I'm recommending to the Board in Control of Athletics that they offer both the Athletic Directorship and the job of Head Football Coach to Oramel C. Hardin, who is currently the Head Coach at the University of Southern Louisiana in New Orleans. I've known Butterball Hardin for many years. You'll recall that he was one of my assistants in my last two years as Head Coach. I know him to be level-headed and a first-rate coach who gets the most out of his players.

"O.C. also has a personality that will help to heal the breach between the various factions here at State U. He would be a uni-fying force, and would be the best person imaginable to give us the athletic program we deserve. He would also be the first black head football coach in the Big Ten.

"I've also called this conference to answer some of the charges that have been brought against me, one by one…"

Feldy then went on to say that he approved of the Board's decision to fire Timmerman. He denied that he had been party to any fraud with regard to the expense accounts.

"I'm particularly hurt by the apparent efforts of certain peo-ple, formerly associated with the football program, to smear the department. I was disappointed in Coach Timmerman's decision to fire assistant coach Paul Schoyer, and I made my displeasure known at the time. However, it now appears that somehow, some people have convinced themselves that I'm responsible for Paul's removal.

"I've had to draw the conclusion that no controversies re-garding expense accounts would have arisen at all, had it not been for certain people's apparent desire for revenge, first against former coach Timmerman, and then against myself. Perhaps it's a blessing in disguise, though, since that incident also got rid of two malcontent players on the football squad.

"I have no immediate plans for the future, but my family and I are not worried about finding other ways to occupy ourselves. I hope that this is the beginning of the end of the tragedy that State University Athletics have gone through in this academic year. If I've had to be one of the people sacrificed in the course of ending it, so be it. On the whole, I've had a heck of a fine ride here at State University. Now I look forward to the next phase of my life, and more time with my family. Thank you all."

Then he left the room without taking questions.

That afternoon, Wayne Pulliam of the *Gazette* wrote:

> Leo Feldevert walked out of this noon's press conference, and out of State University Athletics, bloodied but unbowed—and unlamented. Nobody disputes that Feldy was a great coach, the greatest that Rivercat football has ever seen or is likely to see.
>
> The attributes that served him so well as a coach betrayed him as Athletic Director. We saw that from Day One. At first, we only heard whispers to the effect that as A.D., he would ruin State University athletics (especially the football team). After a year or two, that likelihood was acknowledged as a certainty. Since 1968 at the latest, Rivercat fans have been screaming at the Board in Control of Athletics to please acknowledge the presence of this elephant in the room, while the Board calmly kept replying, "What elephant?" It seems that they finally had to admit that the elephant was there, and had to be dealt with.
>
> Fair enough. However, the firing of Toby Timmerman has not met with favorable reviews. No wonder. That reaction could be a matter of the old American sympathy for the underdog. But I prefer to think that it was the peculiarly "Iowish" insistence on fair play—and the general agreement that fair play wasn't what Coach Timmerman

was getting. A contract is a contract, most Iowans believe, and Timmerman still has three years to go on his.

Many of us are not convinced that Timmerman is any great shakes as a coach. His first year looked good mainly because it was so much better than Bob Brosnan's performance the year before. The 1970 season was a disaster by anyone's measure, although not all Timmerman's fault. But any coach who takes over a horrible program is going to need several years to bring that program up to scratch, and some of us would like to see Timmerman have the chance to do it without Feldy barking at him every time Timmerman so much as coughs.

Now, though, Toby Timmerman has been tossed into the fire by the Board in Control of Athletics, presumably with the approval of the University President—I suppose because they felt that if Feldy had to be punished, it would only be fair to punish Timmerman too.

Only, no, it wasn't, and no, it ain't.

We don't know if we can get the Board to reverse its decision, but we can try, between now and next Tuesday. We have no doubt that the Board will go into that meeting with their collective mind made up, so let's help them to make their minds up now, before it's too late. We urge our readers to make phone calls, write letters (hand-deliver them if you can, because time is short), send telegrams, sign petitions, and march in the streets if you have to, to help Timmerman get his job back. It may be a lost cause, but it may not be, and at least we can say we tried to see the right thing done.

That same evening, a full-page ad appeared in the *Examiner* with 550 signatures, including Mayor Rosen and the other members of the State City Council and several other well-known members of the community—some of them large contributors to the University—under a letter that said, simply, "We, the undersigned, feel Coach Tobias Timmerman should be allowed to continue in his current position for the remainder of his contract." Mark you:

361

that petition must have been circulated and signed, the ad bought and paid for, in just a few hours.

On Friday morning, the *Register* ran an editorial—on the editorial page, not the sports page—that was basically a paraphrase of the *Gazette*'s.

Then came the *coup de grâce*.

As always happens in situations like this, nobody had the definitive story. I believe what Feldy has told me, obviously. Then there were the versions told by Paul Schoyer, Timmerman, and others. The State Auditor's office had forwarded all the information they had gathered both to President Nash, and to the Attorney General of the State of Iowa—saying, in effect, "This is your mess: deal with it."

Nash announced that he was appointing a special counsel to investigate the whole mess and determine whether any further action was warranted. The counsel promised a report by the end of the following week—but by that time, any report he could have made would have been redundant.

The Iowa Attorney General—a Republican, by the way, so he wasn't going to miss an opportunity to take a whack at Feldy—issued a statement on Friday morning.

> The attitude that Mr. Feldevert has carried toward the football program at State University (and perhaps to a lesser extent to other athletic programs within his department) is made absolutely pellucid by the evidence gathered by the State Auditor's office. Mr. Feldevert's actions—in contradiction of his recent statements—tend to support the contention of Coach Tobias Timmerman and four of his assistants that Mr. Feldevert has been covertly, indeed almost overtly, working against them.
>
> These coaches have admitted turning in falsified expense vouchers, and have said, credibly, that this was common practice among the entire athletic staff at State University. However, they say they were under both the orders and the instructions of Mr. Feldevert. Only Mr. Feldevert denies having told them to submit falsified accounts or showing them how to do it.

Nobody denies the existence of a two-year feud between Mr. Feldevert and Coach Timmerman. Based on present available evidence, I do not believe Mr. Feldevert, and I am convinced that a jury would not, if this matter had risen to a level that required criminal prosecution.

However, the Attorney General's office recommends against that course. The falsifying of expense vouchers was unofficially part of State University Athletic Department policy. Although wrong, it does not come up to the level of a crime.

If Mr. Feldevert had been aware of the expense account padding—and he must have been, since he approved the vouchers—it is strange indeed that he did not question Coach Timmerman or any other coach or assistant coach about them, unless Mr. Feldevert had been encouraging or even advising this conduct all along.

Then there is the matter of the 90-day recruiting suspension that the Big Ten issued against Coach Timmerman, which grew out of a photograph taken the previous fall that exposed a violation of recruiting regulations. In a telephone interview with the Attorney General, personally, on Thursday, May 13, a person whose name is currently withheld revealed that this person called the Big Ten's attention to the photograph, having first shown it to Mr. Feldevert—who advised this person to pass the photo along in the interests of "honesty," "integrity," and "making a clean breast of a serious matter."

While it was, indeed, a recruiting violation to invite a high school student to sit on the team's bench during a game, the fact remains that this would never have been noticed, let alone led to disciplinary action, had not Mr. Feldevert (according to this witness) advised this witness to inform on Coach Timmerman.

It appears more than coincidence that this matter was brought to the Big Ten's attention during the recruiting season, on the eve of spring football practice, and only a few days before the first day on which high school athletes could file letters of intent. It is hard to imagine any other time that could have been better calculated to do more damage to the State University Rivercats football program and to reduce the sale of tickets to games next fall.

This program is State University's program. Damage to the program is damage to State University.

And what if Mr. Feldevert had been aware of this recruiting violation earlier, and held it back as a weapon to be deployed at the proper time, waiting for this worst possible moment to reveal it?

In one way or in several, Mr. Feldevert has in effect betrayed, or given the appearance of betraying, State University and the people of Iowa—many of whom have for years regarded him as a hero and a treasure.

However, I do not believe that the facts justify the discharge of Coach Timmerman.

The disharmony in the athletic department can and should be traced to a source. The blame can and should be placed where it belongs. Nobody has presented credible evidence that Coach Timmerman was responsible for that disharmony, or even that he contributed to it in any significant way. His selection by a major news bureau as 1969 Coach of the Year makes it clear that he is a creditable football coach. Therefore, the only moral and legal conclusion must be that he is entitled to reinstatement.

The Attorney General is satisfied that Coach Timmerman and his assistants will atone for any errors they may have committed, and will make a good-faith effort to disinfect the toxic atmosphere that has long plagued the State University football program.

I'd love to know who that anonymous source was, or whether he even exists. Anyway, that report was published at 9:30 on Friday morning. Less than two hours later, the Board in Control of Athletics announced that they would convene an emergency meeting at 2:00 that afternoon. About three hours after that—not in time to make the evening papers, but in plenty of time for word to get around on the radio, and to make the 6:00 TV news—the Board's Chairman announced that upon further consideration, Tobias J. Timmerman would be retained as Head Coach for the length of his contract. So would his assistants, with the exception of Paul Schoyer, who was long gone.

"Leo Feldevert's resignation as Athletic Director has been accepted and is not a matter of contention."

As far as I know, Feldy didn't hear about any of this while it was taking place. He and Birdy were in their car all day, on the way to Wisconsin. They would not have been invited to the impromptu celebration that started early on Friday evening at the Timmerman home on Hutchinson Road, where—according to newspaper accounts and the gossip that I heard here and there—Timmerman fired up his barbecue grill for his assistant coaches and their families, plus various friends, neighbors, and sympathizers, who stopped by throughout that evening and past midnight, into the wee hours, bringing beer and casseroles.

The press was there too: probably not invited, but they showed up and nobody kept them away. George Conroy wrote in the *Register*, the next morning:

> This week saw one of the biggest reversals of fortune since January 1, 1960, when Leo Feldevert took the Rivercats to their first Rose Bowl in 18 years—only this reversal happened in less than a week. The events of the past months have been shocking, embarrassing, and hugely disappointing—but what happened in the past three days was heartening. Toby Timmerman hasn't achieved the folk hero status that Feldy once had, and he may never. But he showed us that a stubborn and basically honest man can be rewarded for his tenacity when the chips are down, rewarded by more friends than he probably thought he had, standing up for him and refusing to let him be mistreated.
>
> Not everyone is convinced that Timmerman is, or will be, a good coach. But there's general agreement that he hasn't had a fair chance and that he was blatantly sabotaged by the same people on whom he had to rely if he were to do his job.
>
> The people of Iowa are fair and sportsmanlike. While the original decision of the Board in Control of Athletics

365

was wrong, they're to be commended for their sense of fair play in reversing it. They had to eat crow, and it could not have been a tasty dish for them—but they ate it. Thus ends—or so we hope—one of the craziest episodes in the history of Rivercat athletics, which has had its share of crazy over the years. At this point, anyone who wants to heave a sigh of relief is entitled to do so.

In the *Gazette*, that evening, Wayne Pulliam had this:

> This is not a happy outcome. It comes with the departure of a man who arrived here 15 years ago as our champion; who left his position as Head Football Coach as a conquering hero; who for the next several years kept trying to convince us—in the face of growing evidence to the contrary—that he was looking out for the Athletic Department's best interests.

> *A glooming peace this morning with it brings;*
> *The sun, for sorrow, will not show his head:*
> *Go hence, to have more talk of these sad things;*
> *Some shall be pardon'd, and some punishèd:*
> *For never was a story of more woe*
> *Than this: when Feldy had to go.*

HOME AGAIN FOR NOW

Okay, then Feldy and Birdy stayed up in Wisconsin for almost a week, and returned last night, Thursday, while I was taking my last exam of the semester. Feldy drove the Suburban up to the Coffin this morning, to help Win move his stuff out of the dorm; now they're both at Iota, helping me. I almost told them not to come by Iota, in case Gail Timmerman were still here, but she has moved out already, thank God.

I ask Feldy, while we're packing my stuff into the back of the Suburban, if anything had been decided, and he says, "We'll tell all of you when we're at the table."

Birdy has a pot of spaghetti with clam sauce ready for us. She dishes up and we say Grace. I can't speak for Win and Sander, but I'm on edge and not much interested in eating till I know what's what. Birdy, Feldy, and Sander are starting in: only Win and I are holding back, till we both decide to stop just sitting there like a couple of dolts. After I've had a bite or two, Birdy makes the announcement:

"So. Feldy and I are just staying here another few days. We'll see Win graduate tomorrow, then we'll put this house on the market on Monday. We're going to move up to Door County for the summer. Then... well, Feldy has gotten an offer to be Chairman of the Board of The Kinsman Companies. That's a real estate investment company in New York City, and Grandpa Duffy is one of their biggest shareholders. Plus, Lou is there, so that's where we'll move at the end of the summer.

"We might get an apartment in the city, or we might buy a house in Westchester County, or in Connecticut. But we're getting out of the Midwest. Out of football, out of academia—and Feldy's going to have a new career. Sander, we're thinking that if you want to finish high school here, we could arrange for you to do that..."

"Not me," says Sander, with his mouth full. "I want out of here as bad as you do. After what they did to you and Feldy. They've got good schools back East."

"Teresa, since you're signed up for summer classes here anyway, maybe you could live here till it's sold and we have to get all our stuff out," Birdy says. "And, Win, of course."

It's only at this point that my comprehension is catching up with Birdy's words. We've lost everything. It's gone. All of it. Or will be, before the summer's over. I can't get any words out. I can't eat. I just sit. There's no way we would hang onto this house, no reason to do so—and maybe I shouldn't say anything at all if I can't say anything to change the outcome.

Obviously Birdy can read the look on my face.

"I know," she says. "But it would be crazy for us to stay here."

"It would be masochism," Feldy says. "I may look crazy, but I'm not that kind of crazy."

"We could stay in Wisconsin and wait for my parents to die," Birdy says, "but that would be pretty awful too."

"Plus," Feldy says, "I don't want to spend the rest of my life in Door County, a few miles from Green Bay, and from Madison, like I'm waiting to pounce."

I feel so empty. Like there's a big hole in my insides, just below my heart. I see a sickly greyish-green shade over everything, for a second or two.

"You'll be with us in New York before long," Feldy tells me. "You'll be working for CBS: you'll have Summerall's job."

I force myself to smile.

"I know it's tough," Feldy says. "But God gives you things you love, all your life long. Then, one by one, He takes them away. That's how He prepares you for death."

"Oh, Feldy," Birdy says.

Feldy shrugs. "We all have plenty of time left to find other stuff to love."

"It's the right thing to do," Win says. For a second, I think he's addressing me; then I see that he's looking at Feldy and Birdy. His face is hard: that's the only word that comes to mind.

"I'm disgusted," Win says. "For you guys' sake." He looks right at Feldy. "Just disgusted with how you've been made the scapegoat. I shouldn't, but I hate Iowa right now. Well, not really, but I'm… I haven't got the words for it. Okay, I've committed to St. Pius, so I'm stuck in Iowa for a while, but I'm going to go so far underground, there. If a seminarian can be cloistered, that's what I'll be."

Feldy chuckles. "That seems to be the consensus. We talked to Lou on the phone, the other night when we were making our decision, and he says he'll never set foot in Iowa again. Oh, he was steamed. He's taking it harder than I am."

I always knew—it stands to reason—that this house was never going to be forever, that one day the last of us would be gone from State City. At the same time, for years now, I have fantasized—if vaguely—that wherever I go in the world, this house on Hilltop Street will always be mine to come back to. Not just the house, either. Somehow, I have always believed that State City, and State University, and the football team, would always stay in the family. Now it's all gone. Like that.

I have never felt *beaten* before in my life. Till now. Sure, I have lost, here and there. Competitions: games and such. I have felt loss. When Feldy's parents died. When Feldy stepped down as Head Coach of the Rivercats. But how lucky I have been, all my life long. How amazingly, incredibly lucky. To have come all this way, and this is the first time I can remember where I feel—I imagine—the way you might feel if you got the living tar stomped out of you in a brawl.

But I play the Glad Game. I don't believe what I'm telling myself, but saying it out loud, to the rest of the family, makes me feel less awful.

"It's a blessing in disguise," I tell them. "We should be glad that we got the push we needed. This whole family is ready to move on. All of us. We have been, for a while now. We got all the good out of State City long ago."

"That's my girl," says Feldy. "I couldn't agree with you more. This family always comes out on top—all of us—and we will this time too."

BOOK V

SENIOR YEAR AT STATE

Our house only stayed on the market for a few days. I've taken a room in downtown State City for the last part of June, July, and into August. Win and Sander went up to Door County with Feldy and Birdy—who came back to State City when the house was ready to be turned over, to supervise the packing and removal. I was pretty involved in that process, but I asked Birdy, a couple of days before we were to vacate, if I might be excused on the actual moving day.

On the night I left the house for good—the night before my parents did—I forced myself to not look back, to not even think about it, when Feldy pulled the Suburban out of the driveway. We went to the Coffin Corner for dinner. Feldy and Birdy dropped me off at my room, after the meal, then drove back to their last night at Hilltop Street. They'll head back to New York in the morning.

I'm just a few weeks from being old enough to drink in a bar legally, and I'm sure no bartender would challenge me, so I thought about having a few, somewhere. Then I decided that would be ridiculous, sitting in a bar on a school night—and word would get around that Feldy's Girl was turning tricks.

I'm in bed early, and I'm not crying. I can't bring it.

§

Summer semester is almost over. I'll spend August in Door County with the family, then move back into Iota when the fall semester begins. Last night, I phoned Joe Barnett to discuss the upcoming football season and maybe ask him for a bigger role in the Saturday afternoon broadcasts—plus a longer weekly show. Joe asked if we could meet for coffee at the Rivercat Grille, this afternoon, "to talk about your future in broadcasting."

So here I am, sitting opposite Joe in a booth toward the back.

"I invited you to meet with me because I felt I ought to tell you face to face," Joe says. "Teresa, it just wouldn't make sense to have you back in the broadcast booth this fall, or for you to resume your show on Monday mornings. For any number of reasons. The events of this past spring were so controversial, and I know none of it had anything to do with you... well, except that you reported on the Watkins case... but there's a feeling here that people want the slate wiped clean, as far as the football program is concerned. I think a lot of people wish that Timmerman had agreed to step down, too, instead of coaching for the rest of his contract, but some people think that he might do better now that the controversy has quieted down, and..."

"And you don't want to remind people of what happened, by letting Feldy's Girl contaminate your radio station?"

"Oh, Terri, please don't take it that way."

"That is the only way it can be taken. I won't give you any trouble about it—but only because I know it wouldn't do any good to give you trouble. I would like to." I haven't touched my coffee, and I'm getting up to leave.

"Terri, wait a minute. I hope we can still be friends. It's nothing personal between me and you."

"Oh, no, of course it isn't." I'm standing, about to walk out. "I'm so disappointed in you."

"Just a minute, please," Joe says. "Sit, please. This doesn't have to be the end of your career."

"I'm too upset to talk about it now. Maybe another time. Right now I had better go."

Joe gets to his feet, too, and offers his hand.

My impulse is to refuse to shake, turn on my heel, and sweep out. But that would be burning a bridge. If I do that, I won't be able to use Joe as a resource, down the line, if I want to go further as a sportscaster. Not that I was ever in a position to count on that kind of career, beyond KSCR. But I should at least not be the person to destroy any chance I might have.

I barely give Joe's hand a touch with fingers and thumb, not my whole hand, and leave without any drama.

§

I was in Door County when Gary and Gruber came back to State City for the August training camp. Timmerman must have been feeling generous, on account of his reinstatement. Or more likely, he's feeling desperate. Now that Ted Blaha has graduated, he has nobody who could begin to play quarterback at the level that the Big Ten requires—except Gary.

From what I've been able to gather, now that I've moved back to Iota and the fall semester is about to start, Gary and Max approached Timmerman through emissaries, a few days after Timmerman had been re-hired. Then another of the assistants, Neil Schnelker, with whom Gary was friendly, made the case to Timmerman that the Rivercats couldn't count on winning any games at all, this year, if Gary and Max aren't on the squad. A couple of the offensive starters made the same case.

According to what I have heard, Timmerman told Schnelker that he would consider meeting with Gary and Max—but they would have to do some public penance first.

In June—and this, I did see, because I was in town—Schoyer and Gruber published a statement in several Iowa newspapers:

> We want to apologize to State University, to the Athletic Department, to Coach Timmerman and his staff, to all our teammates, and to all the other loyal supporters of Rivercat football. When we announced our intention to leave the team, this past spring, our decision was based on various misunderstandings and misinformation, and it was due in

part to our immaturity. We did a wrong and stupid thing, and we ask pardon.

We believed various false accusations against Coach Timmerman. We now know that those accusations were not true. We were badly advised and we acted hastily. In all humbleness, we ask that we be reinstated on the River-cat football squad for the coming season.

That, apparently, was dirt-eating enough to at least persuade Timmerman to talk with Gary and Gruber, in his office, a few days later. He told them (this was not made public, but I have reliable sources) that he would allow the team to vote on reinstating them.

I suppose Gary and Max figured that was better than nothing. I hear through the grapevine that they contacted as many of their teammates as they could, to campaign for their votes—and quite a few of those guys gave non-committal responses. I understand that Timmerman asked each team member to come to the meeting with a ballot prepared, to be turned in as they entered the room. Timmerman didn't announce the totals: only that Gary and Max were back on the team.

I'm forcing myself to live at Iota, for this last year, because I don't care to live alone in an apartment. I don't have any friends I feel close enough to, to share a place with. Above all, I don't want to give anyone the idea that I'm embarrassed to live there, or that I was asked not to. But aside from being physically in the space, I might as well not be an Iota sister.

Gail Timmerman won't even look at me, not that I care. Most of the sisters I was real friends with, graduated last spring. Lefty is gone. Janet Fletcher is still here, and we're still friendly, but the rest of the girls who lived here last year are no more than polite to me. I've always been a workaholic; I've never spent as much time with Greek activities as most of my sisters—so if I'm more detached than usual, in my senior year, it won't be noticed.

I'm no longer writing for the *Statesman*. I have enough newspaper credit to fulfill the requirements for my major—and it might be uncomfortable to have my by-line in the State University newspaper this year. My plan, this fall, is to finish whatever requirements in my Journalism major are outstanding, and get my senior recital out of the way—then in the spring semester, I'll tie up all the loose ends for both my majors.

I am also going to complete my plans to get out of State City, permanently.

I have a car. I bought an old light-blue Buick Skylark this summer—it's got some rust and a few dings but it's still pretty impressive—and come spring, I'm going to drive it out of here. Once State City has faded from my rear-view mirror, I hope I can never think of it again.

§

I haven't seen Mona in months. The day before classes started, Mona phoned me at Iota to see if we'll still be working together. We're sitting in Hamburgher's, now, discussing what I might like to play for my senior recital, but that subject only takes a few minutes. I'm going to play the Handel C Major sonata for cello and piano (if I have to play something baroque, to show I can do it, I way prefer Handel to Bach); Suite No. 2 for Solo Cello, by Ernst Bloch; and Maurice Ravel's sonata for violin and cello. It'll be no problem to line up a pianist and a violinist, and Mona says Professor Meregaglia is sure to approve that program.

Mona tells me about the apartment that she had Mike have moved to. It's over on the south side, in a fairly new building.

"It's owned by some real estate company," she says, "so at least the building is pretty well-managed, although I hate that we have to give our money to a corporation."

Mona has her Master's degree, now. She's doing well in her doctoral studies, and reasonably happy, so it's possible that she'll have a musical career after all.

"I haven't played anything but open notes in more than two years," she says. "Maybe I never will really play again, but I keep working with the Silly Putty and hoping for the best. At least you don't need much digital agility to conduct an orchestra."

It occurs to me, all of a sudden, that I have never seen or heard of a left-handed cellist. I ask Mona if there is such a thing.

"A cello could be set up backwards," Mona says, "but you'd have to custom-make it from scratch. The fingerboard would need to be mirrored; you'd have to move the bass bar and sound-post to the other side—and I have no idea whether the scalloping on the front face would have to be different. I'd never be able to play anyone else's instrument. Plus, I would have to re-train my right hand to do the fingering, which would take years, and teach myself to bow with a hand that hardly works."

Then she sighs, and says, "I can't help thinking that I can blame America's involvement in Vietnam for taking the cello away from me. I wouldn't have gotten my hand stepped on. I think, now, that it was that incident that truly radicalized me. I'm trying not to be bitter about it."

"You're going to be a great conductor," I say. "That's something you can be glad about. When you're conducting the New York Philharmonic in a few years. If you hadn't gotten your hand stepped on, you wouldn't be there."

Mona tries to smile—I can see that—but she can't.

"I might have been there as a soloist," she says.

I could kick myself for having said something so stupid.

"You know, they're building that new Music Building and auditorium over on the other side of the river," Mona goes on, "and it's supposed to open a year from now. For the time being I should just hope I get to conduct there.

"Mike and I are adopting Hank, so that's another complication that won't make it any easier to get my degree. But we're glad to do it. Vicki's parents agreed to it, and we don't hear from Red at all—haven't, since before Hank was born. So, that's one kid who's going to be raised right, we hope. Plus whatever children Mike and I eventually have of our own."

I know Mona means well—she would never intentionally bring children up badly—but I remember what Feldy said.

"Good luck," I tell her. "I should come visit him soon. You know, I'd like to help you out. If I can. Help you look after him."

MORE BRATWURST

The Rivercat Booster Brat Brekker is scheduled for the morning of September 11, one week before the first game of the season. I'm going, out of defiance. Nobody is going to think that the Feldeverts have been driven away. People are going to know that one of them, at least, is still here and still involved—if only to this poor extent, and if only for this one last year.

That enormous canvas canopy has been set up as usual, on the practice field near the stadium. Walking toward it, I can see that it's already getting full of people. The marching band is standing outside it.

About 200 yards away from the gathering, there's a huge canyon recently dug into the ground. It looks like a bomb crater. That's where the foundation will be laid for a new indoor arena: the future venue for Rivercat basketball, gymnastics, wrestling, and other sports events. It will take two years to build. But it was Feldy who masterminded the plan. It was Feldy who turned State University into a real power in college sports: all sports, not just football. It will be Feldy's building—but I bet he gets zero recognition for it.

Come to think of it, it's possible that that new Music Building that Mona is looking forward to would not be getting built, either, if Feldy hadn't raised State University's profile the way he did, and brought in so much more revenue.

I'm wearing a chocolate brown skirt, white blouse, and bright red sweater. It's too warm for the sweater, so I'm wearing it with the sleeves tied round my neck. But I have to have the red. I want people to see me.

A few of the people walking near me, heading for the tent, are nodding or saying "hi"; a few others look startled, surprised to see me. Others pay me no attention.

I don't go near the food right away. I have to mingle first, and not be shy about it. I know most of the people under this canopy, at least by sight. In any year up to now, dozens of people would be coming up to me, greeting me. This year, I have to do the approaching. I knew, going in, that I would have to.

I see Dr. and Mrs. Ingram, who come here every year. I give them my biggest smile, hold my hand out.

"Rex, Lydia. So nice to see you two again. Ready for another season?"

The Ingrams look surprised to see me, and not particularly pleased. Not dismayed, not hostile, but nonplussed. They might have been less shocked to see Feldy himself.

"So glad you could come," I say. I shake hands with them as though I'm hosting this event and they're my guests. "I'm so excited about our team. I have a feeling we're going to bounce back this fall. We're going to contend."

Almost in chorus, the Ingrams say, "Let's hope so. Good to see you," and move on.

I have several similar encounters in the next few minutes. Some are friendlier than others. Some act more surprised to see me than the Ingrams had acted, and some less so, but the conversations are almost exactly the same, each time. At least nobody snubs me, once I've taken the initiative, and now that I've had a few of these conversations, people are starting to come up to me, telling me they're glad to see me.

Jake Rosen asks me about Feldy. He's dressed more formally than most of the other men here—in a navy blue blazer, grey slacks, and a rep tie—but I wouldn't have expected anything else from him.

"Feldy's great. He and Birdy are in New York, in Bronxville, just north of the city. He's got several business opportunities that he's working on. Really exciting."

"I'm so glad to hear he's landed on his feet," Mr. Rosen says. "I felt awful about how that whole thing shook out. It's a shame the situation couldn't have been resolved somehow without so many people getting hurt, but... gosh, academia, it's crazy. I'm glad to see you back here. This is your last year, isn't it? I hope this won't be your last year broadcasting the football games."

This is the first time today that anyone has alluded to hearing me on the radio. I have to bite back the reflexive response, which would be to tell Mr. Rosen that I've already had my last year calling Rivercat games, because I've been assassinated just as surely as Feldy was. In a fraction of a second, I decide to not mention that situation at all, and let Mr. Rosen be surprised when he fails to hear my voice on the airwaves next Saturday.

Football players are mingling, greeting guests. I see Gary at the far end of the canopy, with a few people grouped around him.

I've done enough for a start. I get a bun and a bratwurst from the steam table; I pile on the sauerkraut, fried onions, and mustard; I take a Coke from the oversized garbage can full of ice. I sit down at one of the long tables, near the speakers' dais, where Mr. Rosen will be starting things off any minute.

Across the table, and several people down from me, is Ted Blaha. He's still in good shape. He's wearing a tight blue and white striped polo shirt. I wave; he smiles and waves back.

A drum roll, from the marching band outside, and a flourish from the trumpets, followed by the "Rivercat Rouser." Everyone is clapping in time, of course. Then the other fight song, "Go, You Rivercats, Go!" with more clapping, and applause at the end. Then Mr. Rosen steps to the microphone.

"Thank you all for coming here this morning. This is going to be a great year for all the Rivercat teams: can you feel it?"

The crowd rumbles rather than cheers: a lot of them have their mouths full.

Mr. Rosen speaks for an uninspiring minute or so about his high hopes for the football team in the fall, "And let's have another championship season in basketball, okay?" This, too, gets a pretty limp cheer from the crowd.

"And now, some of you have been waiting a while to get your first look at the guy who'll be leading our Athletic Department this year, and he's a hard guy to miss, too. You folks didn't come here to hear me; I'm pretty sure you'd rather hear from our new Athletic Director, O.C. Hardin!"

Hardin is 45—I saw it in the papers—but looks younger. He's got this very round, smooth, shining, dark brown face: almost as dark as Rivercat uniforms. His head looks almost the size and shape of a bowling ball, only with bright white eyes, and a cream-colored high-crowned cowboy hat perched on it. He's got an enormous smile, with some gold inlays in his teeth. He's wearing the standard brown slacks and camel blazer—the jacket must be at least a size 60—with a red pocket square.

Hardin is immense. I'm guessing he weighs 100 pounds more than any of the football players—except maybe just 75 more than Bruno Grozniac.

He steps forward, shakes hands with Rosen, and takes over the microphone. He's got a big, deep, hearty voice with a timbre similar to Feldy's, only Southern and black.

"Well, Jake, Ah don't know that Ah have a whole lot to say to these good folks this mornin', aside from givin' 'em a big hearty 'thank you,' just as you did, for comin' out here today. Ahma warn y'all, right up front: My job, here at State University, will be to stay out of the way. Ah hope to do my job as best Ah can, let the coaches and the ath-a-letes do *their* jobs as best *they* can, and let ever'body's woik speak for itself. Ahma keep as low of a profile as Ah know how to, which in my case might be kinda difficult."

This gets light laughter from the audience. Someone, from the outskirts of the tent, sings to the tune of the National Anthem, "O-oh, Cee, can you see... ?"

Hardin grins.

"Yeah, Ah can see. Ah can see you a knucklehead!"

The whole tentful of people, it seems, is falling apart laughing. Hardin stands there, obviously enjoying it, for a good 20 seconds before he goes on. I bet that singer was a plant.

"Y'all have been through some rough times," Hardin says. "We've maybe just woken up from a nightmare, but keep that in mind: we done woken up now. This here's morning, here at State University, and it's a beautiful day a-dawning."

Applause and some cheers, more enthusiastic than any response to any of Rosen's remarks. Hardin refers to the new arena that will go into "that big ol' hole in the ground that y'all see over there." He praises State University's baseball team (which did have a better summer than expected), and the basketball team. He talks about the warm welcome the state of Iowa has given him and his family.

"The Ath-a-letics Department is a team, and our team is gonna make a positive impact during our time at State University. Ah realize that Ah have a giant pair of boots to fill. Ah'm replacin' a legend, and that's a lot to live up to."

I hear a murmur from the crowd and I can't tell if it's approving or not.

"There ain't nothin' fancy or... what's the word? Mack-a-villain about me. Ah'm plain ol' Butterball Hardin, and Ah reckon the best way to do my job here, is to let the coaches coach, and the players play. On that note, Ahma invite our head football coach, Toby Timmerman, to step up here and tell us somethin' good about the football team."

I have to force myself not to scoff at anything Timmerman might say. I'm sure, now that I've thought about it, that he didn't lie about Feldy showing him how to fill out expense vouchers. That's done all over the United States. Still, it infuriates me that there was such an outcry for Timmerman's reinstatement, while almost every one of the creeps sitting under this canopy was happy and relieved to see the back end of my father.

My anger, as it develops over the next few seconds, is directing itself far more at those people than at Timmerman. I'm not paying attention to what he's saying about the football team. I have this bright yellowish-orange glow in front of my face for a second or two while I think about how I would love to go among this crowd with a baseball bat, breaking heads.

"All in all," Timmerman is concluding, "we've got a fine football team on our hands this year. I hope I can coach them as well as I saw them perform during the August training camp. We're going to win some football games. Now, to tell you a little more about how we might do that, I'd like to bring up our starting quarterback, Gary Schoyer."

The applause for Gary is pretty limp. I guess a lot of people aren't ready to forget his attitude last fall, and his shenanigans this past spring. Oh, sure, I understand why the organizers would want him to speak at this breakfast—to show unity, to show that the dissension is history—but they might have known that people are still plenty mad at Gary.

Gary looks more than slightly shamefaced when he steps up to the mike, but maybe that's my imagination. Now he's standing next to Timmerman, and the two of them shake hands an instant longer than they might have, ordinarily. It looks like they're gripping harder than usual, to drive home the point. But Gary seems pretty poised, when he starts to talk.

"Thank you, Coach. I want to express to all the fans—here and in the rest of Iowa—how glad I am to be playing for Coach Timmerman this fall. There was a lot of misunderstandings between a lot of people, last season and last spring, and I have to take my share of the responsibility for the confusion. But we've all worked out our differences, and we had a great training camp, the best one I've seen in all my time here. Coach has us all pulling together and he's really bringing out the best in all of us; I can't imagine that we won't have a strong football team this year."

I look away from Gary, and Ted Blaha catches my eye. He smirks at me the least bit, and rolls his eyes for an nth of a second. I have to clap both hands over my mouth to pretend I'm sneezing. Then I give him an eye-smile.

The speeches end; the band reprises the "Rouser" and "Go, You Rivercats!" while the crowd claps along; now the show's over and we break up a lot faster than we came in.

A few folks are staying behind to eat more, or to chat with the coaches, players, and other celebrities. Ted catches my eye again, and smiles more of a smile this time. I give him one back, and get up from my place to dump my empty plate and Coke can. Across the table, Ted has the same idea, although he's closer to the trash can than I am, so he waits there for me.

"So good to see you," he says. "I felt so bad about how that whole business worked out. I'm glad you're back. Your parents left town, right?"

I have no idea what Ted is doing, now. I know he hasn't been drafted by the NFL. (I read the lists in the paper, last winter.)

"I guess you didn't sign on anywhere as a free agent," I say.

Ted laughs. "No, I didn't try to. I never expected to get drafted, and free agency would have been a real long shot. I'm working in our store downtown, for now. Are you and Gary getting ready to pick out a ring?"

Now I laugh.

"No way. I haven't been with Gary since… gosh, February."

"That shows how out of touch I am. Gary and I were always pretty friendly, but we never talked about personal stuff, and we never saw each other much in the off-season. I'm glad he's back, for the team's sake—but, gosh, that whole thing was so weird."

"Yeah, it's not something I like to talk about."

Ted and I are walking toward the parking lot.

"Can't blame you," he says. "I'm glad to be out of it. Not that I'd trade the experience. It was amazing: being the starting QB on a Big Ten team. I can hardly believe I did that. But, time to move on. I was always thinking I would go into my dad's business. You know, a lot of the jocks major in Business Administration because, face it, they didn't go to college to be doctors or engineers or whatever. But I majored in Business because, okay, our operation is small, now, but it's gonna get bigger in the next few years. I've been brainstorming with Dad about how we can make that happen."

"I remember that car." I point to Ted's Oldsmobile 88. "Two years ago, remember? I was interviewing you and Gary."

"That was like just yesterday. I suppose you're still doing the radio thing again, this season."

I was still hoping to keep it to myself, but now I feel like I have to tell Ted, so I give him the short version of why I won't be on the air anymore. Ted looks gobsmacked.

"You're kidding. Oh, that's bullshit. Excuse the French, but it is. I never got to hear you, obviously, but I heard you were doing it. That's bad. That really stinks."

"Well, you can imagine I wasn't happy about it."

"Are you going to any of the games this year? As a fan?" Ted laughs—self-consciously, it seems to me. "I wouldn't blame you if you showed up to root for the other teams, considering."

"I'll go to a game or two. If I can get a ticket."

"Why don't you come with me next week? Our family has a whole block of seats, season tickets, and Dad bought two more for this fall so I could bring friends. What do you say?"

I laugh. "That'll be too funny of a combination: you and Feldy's Girl at the first game of the season. Sure, I'd love to."

TAILGATING

It's funny: I have never been to a tailgate party; never even seen one except at a distance. I barely remember attending any games at Winnemucca—and at State, I've only ever sat in the V.I.P. area, or in the press box. I've never been one of the crowd.

I only know Mr. and Mrs. Blaha from hearing Feldy and Birdy mention them off-hand once or twice, over the years. Now here I am in the back of their Chevrolet Kingswood, next to their eldest son. In my lap I've got a chocolate cake that I bought from a bakery downtown this morning, as my contribution, because I'm too lazy to bake a cake myself.

Well, and because I don't want to occupy the Iota kitchen and have to take questions from the sisterhood. I didn't tell any of them where I'm going with it: just "to a party." If they see who's picking me up, in front of Iota, I'll deal with the questions later.

I can smell all kinds of food-smells coming from the rear of the station wagon. Mr. Blaha is driving. He looks younger than Feldy and Birdy; well-built, not fat, but what Feldy calls "prosperous"—so far as I can tell, which isn't much since I'm sitting in the back. Mrs. Blaha has greying blonde hair and light blue eyes. She's on the plump side, but not so you'd remark on it. She gives me such a pretty smile when she turns around in her seat to shake hands.

"So, you're Feldy's Girl," she says. "We've heard so much about you, about what a great job you did on the radio, but we never got to hear you. Because we've always been in the stadium."

I'm embarrassed to tell Mrs. Blaha that this is going to be a new experience for me. I never thought about how being the coach's daughter isolates you from the fans, but it does.

"How does it work?" I ask Mrs. Blaha. "Tailgating, I mean?"

"Well, you have to pay through the nose to get into the stadium parking lot," she says. "If you want to tailgate, you have to reserve two spaces. You drive into your space, set up your table, set up your grill if you have one, or whatever. Some of the people we party with, we only ever see during the football season. Your crowd always runs into the parties on either side of you. The food's always great. Everybody brings something different. That's the main thing. The food and the fellowship."

Mrs. Blaha thinks for a moment. "I guess 'everybody brings something different' can be taken in lots of different ways, not just the food. There'll be a few Oregon State fans there, I expect. It's funny: we didn't always see much fraternizing, years ago— back when your father was coaching and we were winning." She laughs. "The other teams' fans like us a lot better now that we're not so likely to beat them."

When we get to the stadium parking lot, Ted and his father set up the folding table that had been riding on the roof of the Kingswood; Mrs. Blaha and I start getting covered dishes out of the back of the vehicle. A few of their friends are already there, waiting for us; the table is full of food in no time; there's a cooler of beer iced down—no, two of them. I've got a paper plate filled with potato salad, deviled eggs, little smokies wrapped in bacon, and a fried chicken thigh. I'll allow myself one can of Hamm's.

I would never have guessed how crazy the conversation is, at one of these parties. People predicting that this or that player will be the surprise of the day (or of the season), or saying that if the Rivercats would only run this or that play…

I'm fighting back the urge to intervene, and correct this person or that one who obviously doesn't know diddly about football tactics or strategy. I give myself an assignment: observe, don't talk. Don't do a darn thing to attract any attention.

I've always known, intellectually, that most people go to football games as a special treat, but for me it has always been just part of the routine of life. I've always enjoyed it—well, loved it, more than almost anything aside from my family and God—but I've never experienced this atmosphere. It's so loose, so friendly. I get the feeling that hardly anybody is here because they live and die with the Rivercats. They're just here for the fun. This is only now sinking in.

At the other parties near ours, I see people playing cornhole, plus a few kids throwing a football around, weaving and running between vehicles and getting in everyone's way. Most of the people wearing Rivercat t-shirts and sweatshirts are wearing the white or camel-colored versions, since the weather is still pretty warm. Quite a few people wearing Oregon State's black and orange are being entertained at one gathering or another. I've got the Rivercat Brown skirt I wore last week for the Brat Brekker, but no sweater. Ted is wearing jeans and a plain white shirt. It's too hot for him to wear his letter jacket.

Ted is doing a lot of hand-shaking. Plenty of fans want to pay their respects to last year's QB, even if he never was a star. I'm keeping a distance from him, mostly talking with Mrs. Blaha about the team. Mrs. Blaha never mentions Feldy or Coach Timmerman: I sense she's being careful not to touch any wounds.

Kickoff is scheduled for 1:30. Mr. Blaha suggests that we all go into the stadium about half an hour before. "We don't want to miss The Gong," he says. He turns to me, and adds, "Ted never got to see The Gong, all the time he was playing. He was always in the locker room, you know."

For the past three seasons, I've been too busy with the radio broadcasts to notice much about the pre-game stuff. It was the same when I was going to games when I was younger. I would have been busy bickering with my brothers or chatting with this or that fan who wanted to hobnob with Feldy's Girl. I'm aware of The Gong, but I've never really paid attention to it.

"It's my favorite part of the experience," Mr. Blaha says. I'm walking into the stadium between Ted and his father; Mrs. Blaha is on her husband's left. "We don't always have the best team, but the band's always great. It's like going to the horse races. I don't know if that interests you, but I always thought, when I went to the races, that the race itself was anticlimax. It was all the stuff that went before it that interested me. The 'riders up'; the post parade; especially the load-in."

I laugh. "That's great. I never thought of that. I can see it."

The Blahas' seats are near mid-field, about 30 rows up: practically ideal. They must have paid a bundle for them.

The Rivercats and the Beavers are trotting off the field, where they have been warming up. They're going into the tunnels at the south end zone that lead to their locker rooms. They'll officially take the field a few minutes from now. In the north end zone, the Rivercat Marching Band—in their chocolate-brown jackets, camel trousers, and black bell-top shakos with red plumes—are crowded together in tight ranks and files. The drummers and sousaphone players stand along the sidelines. At the back of the end zone, one of the bandsmen is waiting next to a huge brass gong, like that one you see at the beginning of old British movies.

I know it sounds sacrilegious, but it occurs to me: this feels like the moment at the beginning of a high Mass. Only here, instead of tingling at the mystery, I'm tingling at how much fun this will be.

"Good afternoon, Rivercat fans, and welcome to another season of Rivercat football," intones the public address guy, all bright and breezy. "It's a beautiful day in State City, Iowa, and it's time to get ready for… *The Gong!*"

BONGGGGGGG.

The Lady in Red, in her spangled leotard, soars out onto the field, leaping like a ballerina, twirling her baton into the air and catching it as she proceeds most of the length of the field.

"State University proudly presents… the State University Rivercat Marching Band! With our Lady in Red, Miss Kelly Colfax! Our Drum Major, Joseph Pulaski!"

The Drum Major, wearing an enormously tall busby and flourishing a staff longer than himself, high-steps onto the field, following Miss Colfax.

"Our drum line and sousaphone section!"

The drums and cymbals play an elaborate ruffle while the drumline and sousaphones quick-march onto the field with their knees pumping high, to form a square between the 15- and 25-yard-lines.

"And two hundred and forty marching Rivercats!"

The drumming continues as the rest of the band marches on, in formation. Another ruffle, and a flourish, then the entire band strikes up the "Rivercat Rouser" as they form the shape of a giant catfish that stretches the length of the field.

I feel myself grinning like my face might break when the Lady In Red dances across the field; I feel the fine hairs rising on the back of my neck as the drums get going; I leap to my feet when the brass begins its flourish; now I and the rest of the fans are clapping along with the "Rouser." The whole stadium. I glance over at Ted, and he grins at me.

The song concludes with the band re-forming into ranks and files; the crowd cheers.

"And now," says the P.A., "our greetings to the Beavers of Oregon State University!"

The band plays "Hail to Old OSU," then salutes the visitors' cheering section. Light applause, and a few boos, from the crowd. The band strikes up, "Go, You Rivercats, Go!" and we do the rhythmic clap-along, again. The band plays State University's third fight song, "Swim Along, Rivercats," as they march to the south end zone, then into the bandstand, where they'll sit till halftime.

"And now, for the 64th consecutive year, it's time to welcome Muddy the Rivercat into the stadium! Ladies and gentlemen, here's Mud in your eye!"

Muddy is standing on a pallet carried by four male cheerleaders who bring him from the tunnel onto the field, waving his Rivercat banner. It makes me think of Groucho Marx, as Captain Spaulding, being carried into that drawing room by "native bearers." The cheerleaders set him down at midfield; he capers for a few seconds before defiantly stabbing the flag-stick into the turf and standing with fist on hip.

From their places in the bandstand, the band starts playing "Mars, the Bringer of War" from Gustav Holst's *The Planets*. Again, the crowd comes to its feet, cheering, because that music is the signal for the entire Rivercat team, coaches, and auxiliary personnel to swarm out of the tunnel and onto the field.

"You like it from up here?" Ted shouts to me. "Now if only the team can live up to all that ceremony."

The Beavers run out of the visitors' tunnel, much less ostentatiously—wearing their road uniforms, white with black and orange trim—to light booing from the stands. The P.A. tells us to rise for the National Anthem. Ted sings it, good and loud—and on key. I sing softer because I'm not confident of my voice.

Then, because it's the first game of the season, the P.A. introduces our starting offensive and defensive units, plus the kicker and punter, each of whom trots from the bench to midfield. Coach Timmerman joins them, shakes hands with each of them, and they all return to the bench. The kickoff squads line up on the field; the Rivercats to receive. The kickoff goes into the end zone for a touchback; we're underway, starting at our 20.

Two running plays—a sweep to the weak side, and an off-tackle—gain a first down for the Rivercats on the 32. But the next play—another sweep—loses a yard, which brings up an obvious passing situation.

It's the quickest busted play I have ever seen. Two defenders—an end and a tackle—tear through the pocket without any opposition and slam Gary to the ground for a seven-yard loss.

"Who had those guys?" Ted hollers. I can see Coach Timmerman, down on the Rivercat sideline, presumably shouting words to the same effect.

"Nobody touched them!" Ted says to me. I can't figure out how that happened, either. I just shake my head and give Ted the "damfino" look.

On the next play, those two linemen are contained, but a defensive end on the other side of the line gets through—again, it looks like no blocker interferes with him at all—and drags Gary down for another loss. It's fourth and 24; we have to punt.

Oregon State scores a touchdown on its first possession; they kick off to us again. This time, our returner runs it back to the 25. We work the ball to midfield on a mixture of running plays and play-action passes—then we seem to stall there. It's third and ten from the 50: another passing situation.

Oh, Judas. They're sending everybody. An all-out blitz. The three linemen, four linebackers, even the free safety, all charging through at full speed before our blockers can even form a pocket, and Gary disappears.

I see Gary's helmet escaping from underneath the pile of white uniforms, and rolling away. A collective, accusatory "Ohhhhh!" comes from the stands, and the referee does throw a flag, but I hardly think of that.

It had simply been a question of which Beaver would get to Gary first. It's like they all got him all at once, and now it's taking them a while to get off of him.

Gary looks like he's unconscious or almost. He's barely moving. Ted puts his hand on my forearm; I reach across with my other hand and grip his. The trainer and a couple of assistants are kneeling over Gary; he's still barely moving. Oh, Judas...

He's moving a little now, but he's not getting up... Now the assistants are dragging him to his feet, holding him up... he's been down for a minute at least; can he even walk?

He can't get off the field by himself. The crowd is clapping like they always do when an injured player gets to his feet, since that means that at least he's not dead, but I can't clap. I'm still holding Ted's hand; I'm afraid I'll break it. They get Gary off the field and he's sort of walking, for the last few steps, but he has to be supported all the way to the bench. Now he's sitting, at least. Timmerman is talking to him.

The referee places the ball 15 yards ahead of the previous line of scrimmage, and arm-signals the penalty.

"Personal foul on the defense," says the PA announcer. "Fifteen-yard penalty; first and ten for the Rivercats on the Oregon State 35."

"Oh, no," Ted mutters. "I wonder..."

"What?"

"Tell you later."

Thanks to the penalty, we have good field position—but our second-string quarterback, Flick, is in for Gary. We can't gain another first down, and our kicker misses the field goal attempt.

Gary is on the bench for the rest of the half, which ends with Oregon State leading, 17-0. He's at least moving under his own power when the teams run off the field and into the tunnels.

"What were you going to tell me? That you were wondering about."

"That looked like a bootsie," says Ted. He's grim. "That play where they got Gary. If the team wants to punish one of its own guys, for whatever reason, the rest of the team plans when they're gonna do it, then at some point the offensive captain somehow gets word to the other team's defensive captain, and he lets the rest of his squad know about it in the next huddle. Then our guys step aside and let the other team throw everything they can at Gary. And they hope he doesn't get up for a while."

"Oh, Jesus Christ."

A Commandment bites the dust.

"I could be all wrong, but that's what it looked like to me. Gary has made a lot of enemies. With this and that."

"Ohhhhhh." I'm staring at Ted with my jaw hanging. If this is true—if the team set Gary up—well, it's awful, but I can see how they might feel that he had it coming. That article from last year; then he deserts the team and undermines the coach—not that I feel kindly toward Timmerman, but still…

But for all we know, Gary might be seriously hurt, even if he left the field without help at the end of the half.

"That's so irresponsible," is all I can think to say to Ted.

"You might say so," Ted says. "I can't feel a lot of sympathy for him. I hope they decide he's had enough."

Gary is back on the field for the second half, and his blockers seem to be doing their best to protect him. He only gets sacked once more—but his passing is way below par. He seems not to have any confidence whenever a passing situation comes up. Like a golfer with the yips. He does manage to put together two scoring drives in the second half—for a touchdown and a field goal—but it's not enough. Oregon State's offense is too strong. Flick takes over again at the end, when we're obviously beat. The final score: Beavers 34, Rivercats 10.

If a game is close, or if the Rivercats win when they were expected to lose, nobody leaves early, and it takes about ten minutes, at least, before it's worth even getting out of your seat. Then it takes another five minutes to get into the aisle, and it's very slow going as you walk up or down the steps to one of the vomitoria—after which, leaving the stadium is fairly easy. This time, people were starting to leave after three quarters, so now that the clock has almost run out, it looks like it'll be a pretty easy exit.

"Could be a brutal season," Ted says. We're on our feet, inching sideways, toward the aisle. "But, let me tell you, it's a relief to be watching it from up here. I never would have thought I would say that, but it's the truth."

"What's going to happen to Gary? Are they going to keep trying to get him hurt? Should you tell him what's going on?"

"He'll be told—if he hasn't figured it out. Want to come back home with us, have dinner at our place?"

We all return to our vehicle, stash what's left of the food, fold up the table, and take off—although it takes us almost 30 more minutes to get out of the parking area, once Mr. Blaha has started the engine. We spend that time re-hashing the game, but Ted doesn't say a word to his parents about what happened to Gary.

The Blahas live in a big Colonial-style white house, with a huge yard, in Ezekiel Heights, on the west side, on the same side of the State River as the stadium, less than a mile from it. Ezekiel Heights is a fancier neighborhood than Hilltop Street; most of the houses are newer. The Timmerman family lives a few blocks away, in just a slightly less-nice area than the Blahas. If you live in Ezekiel Heights, it's because you have Made It.

I ask Mrs. Blaha if I can help in the kitchen, but she says it'll be a while before we eat and it's nothing she needs help with, so Ted, his father, and I throw a football around in the front yard.

"Go out for one," Ted says. I run a post, about 45 feet. Ted lofts the ball to me.

"Come on! That one would have been picked off before it got halfway to me. What do you think I am: a girl?" I peg the ball good and hard to Mr. Blaha, to prove my point. He barely catches it, and lobs it underhanded to his son. I trot back to near where Ted is standing. "Try it again."

I run the same pattern. This time Ted throws it harder: not quite game-speed, probably because he can see I'm not a fast runner, but it's a real pass. He throws it ahead of me, like he's supposed to, so I'll run into it, instead of having to slow down and reach for it. My momentum carries me into the neighbors' yard. I spike the ball, and Mr. Blaha cheers.

It's past nine o'clock, now, and Ted is driving me back to Iota in his Oldsmobile.

"Ted, I had a wonderful time," I tell him, before we've gone a block from his parents' house. "If there's another game that you haven't promised yet, let me know."

"Actually, I was gonna suggest Ohio State, week after next."

"It's a date."

I should not have used that phrase. I truly did not accept Ted's original invitation with anything other than friendship in mind, but now all of a sudden... It's not anything romantic I'm feeling, I'm pretty sure of that. Just affinity.

"How is the rest of the team going to treat Gary now?" I ask. "Are they going to leave threatening notes in his locker written in blood, or something? Or beat him up in practice?"

"The note in blood might not be a bad idea. No, what they'll probably do is, they'll send Grozniac to see him, plus whoever is the offensive co-captain this year; I'm out of touch. I guess it's old 63, Vipulis. So, yeah, maybe Grozniac and Vipulis stop by his apartment, all casual-like, maybe tomorrow—well, here, I'll show how it might go."

Ted pulls over to the curb, on DeWitt Street, a couple blocks north of Iota.

"You be Gary," he says. "I'll be Grozniac." He raps on the dashboard. "Can we come in for a minute?"

I look at Ted like, "Huh?" He grins.

"Come on, play it with me," he says. "Can Vip and I come in for a minute?"

"Sure, okay, I guess."

"Won't take long. We just have some information you might want before we practice on Monday. Can we sit down?"

"Okay, sure," I say. I don't know if I'm supposed to motion to an imaginary chair, or what.

"Think you'll be 100 percent, next Saturday?"

I think for a second about how Gary might reply to this.

"No reason why I shouldn't be," I say, as Gary. "I'm a little sore now, but nothing to complain about."

"That's good," says Ted/Grozniac. "Vip and I were talking with some of the other fellas, about what happened in that first quarter. They wanted us to tell you they hope nothing like that ever happens again this year."

I look perplexed, and wary.

"I think some of the fellas just wanted to get your attention. You know, you pissed a lot of people off last year. But the feeling is that as long as there isn't any more of that shit go on this year, that'll be the last of it."

I still don't say anything.

"The way it was told to me, nobody wants to fuck you up for permanent." Ted must be in character, now, what with the language and so on. "We need you in there at QB. The guys don't want to throw away the season on your account. But some of 'em did want to make a point. And they wanted to do it in public. Maybe if they had wanted to get you out of there for the season, it would have happened in practice. An accident, like. But like I said: I think everybody's willing to call it even, now. And maybe we can start over, on that basis. That how you see it?"

It takes me a few seconds to reply. Gary himself would have been thinking of various responses, weighing the wisdom of using any of them—which, again, would have taken a few seconds.

"I guess so."

"Good." Ted gives me a big smile. "Then our work here is done." He keeps that grin on his face and sticks his hand out to me. I shake hands with him.

"Get 'em next week, good buddy," he says. "C'mon, Vip."

I'm staring at Ted, for a few more seconds.

"You're a pretty good actor," I tell him.

"Nah, I can just do a good Grozniac."

"You didn't know about this, did you?"

"No. Who would tell me? But I wasn't surprised."

We're quiet for a few seconds more, then Ted pulls the car away from the curb.

"Another thing." Ted sounds hesitant. "You'll laugh, but I'd like to see *Shaft*. Maybe next weekend. Are you curious?"

There's no place for Ted to park, in front of Iota, so I say, "It's okay; just drop me here." I would like to give him just a tiny kiss goodnight, but I know it's best not to, so I say, "See you for *Shaft*," then I reach across to put my right hand on his right forearm, to signal that he shouldn't come closer for now, before I get out.

SHAFT? RIGHT ON

Well, we're 0-2, now. Lost to UCLA, on the road, this afternoon, 31-0. We had no business scheduling them. I heard it on the radio. Gary had a hard time finding receivers to throw to, but it doesn't sound like he got hurt, let alone intentionally.

It's about 9:30; Ted and I are coming out of the movie theatre, and I take the sleeve of his letter jacket. I'm holding onto it while we walk the couple of blocks to Hamel's. I hope I'm not giving him wrong ideas: maybe making him think I'm being too forward, or that I'm more interested in him than I am. Oh, I am interested, I admit that. I like Ted. I feel—for want of a better word—"chemistry." But I don't want to get involved with Ted, or with anyone, if I'm going to leave State City in the spring and have my career. At the same time, I don't want Ted to think I've already kicked him into the Friend Zone.

Hamel's is crowded and noisy, mostly with students. A bluegrass group is performing on the stage in the main dining room, so we sit in one of the side rooms where we can talk. While we're waiting for the pizza, I'm telling Ted about my senior recital, which I've scheduled for October 23.

"That's earlier than I had planned, but I'll have it done. I'll be practicing my butt off for the next few weeks. I'm not sorry I took the double major, but I'm finding it harder and harder to see myself with a career in music—teaching or performing."

I tell Ted about Mona, about how Mona's future as a cellist got ruined, and I have to tell him about Mona's connection to the Charles Watkins case.

(Watkins, by the way, was sentenced to 50 years, back in July. His supporters are still trying to raise that increased bail, and money for his appeal, but for now, he's in Fort Madison.)

"I still don't know what to think about that case," Ted says. "I have to assume he did it. From what I've read, the evidence

394

was there—but I would never have imagined it. *There* was the guy with the pro career. To screw up like that… I don't get it."

"People do all kinds of things that you don't understand how they could do them," I say. "I guess we all have it in us to do… well, *anything*, it seems like… and you wonder if maybe people who *don't* do awful things are just lucky that the wrong button never got pushed."

"Yeah, like what went on in May, with the riots," Ted says. "I don't fault the demonstrators as a group, so much. I mean, gosh, my lottery number was 356, so I was never in any danger of going, but otherwise, who knows what I would have done? Guys are being sent over there to die, for *nothing*. But the ones who started the fires downtown and all that: You wonder if any of them have asked themselves, 'What did I think I was accomplishing?' Only, I bet a lot of them still believe they did right."

By this time, the pizza has arrived.

"In a way, I'm still on their side," I say. "About the war, anyway. It's crazy. We have to get out of there, and you would think Nixon could do it a lot faster than he's doing it. But these demonstrations don't seem to be only about the war, now."

"Everybody likes power," says Ted. He detaches a slice of pizza and lifts it to his gaping maw—everybody looks ridiculous when they're eating pizza, don't they?—and he's about to bite into it when at the last instant he judges it too hot to start in on. He sets the slice back down in the pan.

"Everybody likes to be in charge, or at least feel that they can dominate other people," he says. "Probably a lot of them—like your friends, maybe—they don't realize that they're being used, by people who want to control *everything*. Even control what we think. Okay, there's stuff wrong with society, but not as much as they say there is. You're right: they have a bigger agenda. It's like these people want to destroy everything about society, almost like America is bad by definition and they want to destroy it so that they can rule over the destruction."

Ted suddenly looks more intense: almost angry.

"You know what that riot proved to me?" he asks. "It proved that *they* are the problem. There's nothing wrong with wanting to make the world better, making it fairer. That's not what these

395

people want. All these battles they say they're fighting? I wonder how sincere they are about 'the movement.' Some of them just want power." At last Ted takes a big bite of the pizza.

I wouldn't have guessed that Ted had any political views. I never thought about it. I wonder how Mona or Mike would have responded, if he said all that to them. Sure, I've heard people say something like what Ted is saying to me, but it's only ever been blue-collar types, on some TV documentary or sitcom that's supposed to illustrate how stupid and wrong those people are.

"But don't you think they want a fairer society?" I ask. "I mean, besides wanting the war to end. Maybe they're not quite sure how they're going to do it, but don't you think maybe they want to find a way to fix all the problems that they see?"

I start eating, to give Ted a chance to respond.

"I'm not sure they're *for* anything," he says. "It's all about what they're *against*. Well, okay, they're for Marxism, if they can define Marxism. I didn't major in history, but I took some, and it seems to me that this is how these people have seen themselves, since way before Marx. Since before the French Revolution. Since hundreds and hundreds of years ago, one way or another. They seem to have this idea that all of history has been a plot by powerful people to keep less powerful people down, keep them in a sort of permanent slavery.

"And you know what? They're right. What they miss, is that *they* want to be the powerful people who do the oppressing."

I hate hearing Mona and Mike being thrown in with the people Ted is talking about, but for the moment I can't think of any way to contradict him.

"I have some friends in the movement, like my cello teacher… well, she's not my cello teacher, exactly; I've told you a little about Mona. She's the very last person I'd call an oppressor. She's almost too sweet for this world."

"A utopian, I'll bet," Ted says.

"I guess maybe."

"The trouble with utopians is that they turn into totalitarians. Rousseau, and those guys. The French Revolution. And here in America, you had the transcendentalists: Thoreau, Emerson. Not that they went around guillotining people—but they had this idea that society could be perfected. If only we could have an all-powerful government run by totally benevolent people who could fix anything that needed fixing."

"Okay, I can see where Mona might be like that," I say. "And her husband."

"But man can't ever be perfect," Ted says, "which means society can't be, either."

"Man is sinful," I agree. "It's our nature. It's how God made us." I think for a couple of seconds; luckily Ted has his mouth full. "It seems to me that if you think that man can perfect society, you almost have to reject God."

"That's what these people do, most of them," Ted says. "They're mostly atheists, or they think religion is for ignorant people—I should say, *and* they think religion is for ignorant people—and it's those poor ignorant people that they have to save, otherwise they'd drown in a rainstorm because modern progressive people aren't there to tell them to lower their heads and shut their mouths."

I laugh.

"You remind me of my brother Win. Maybe you ought to go to seminary too. You'd give good sermons, anyway."

"I've got the wrong personality for the priesthood. I'm pretty introverted. No way could I be a priest, and anyway I've never thought of it. I like being a jeweler. Or the son of a jeweler, learning to be a real jeweler, I should say, at this point. It's fun. Some people might think it looks boring—but I guess you could say it's my kind of boring."

"What would you have done if some NFL team had picked you, last winter?"

Ted considers.

"I'd have gone to the training camp—there's no way in the world I could have said no to that—but you know what? I'd have done it just so I could say I did it. My heart wouldn't have been in it. I wouldn't have made the team, because deep down I wouldn't have wanted to. I got banged up pretty good, a few times in four years, and that's what I would have had to look forward to. Playing for the Cats was fun—but I'll leave the NFL to Gary."

"That'll depend on how Gary does this year," I say. "Whether he gets drafted, I mean. It sounds like he didn't do that well this afternoon. We couldn't establish the run—and if they know he has to pass on practically every down, he's not going to complete a lot of passes, is he?"

"Gary will be drafted," Ted says. "He's a real talent. Whether he plays in the NFL will depend on which team drafts him—you know, whether they really need a quarterback—and what his attitude is like when he shows up at their training camp. That's his big problem. No worries at all about his talent. He's potentially an NFL quarterback. I'm thinking he might mature this season. Then, who knows? He could be a real star."

Ted pauses for a moment.

"Are you still not seeing him?" he asks. "You might be missing an opportunity."

"Well, we're not enemies. We're just not dating. We're… you know, we're not right for each other. I still like him, but it wasn't going to work out."

I'm not sure whether I want to encourage Ted. I don't want to know whether he's involved—so I don't ask him. If he's taking me to football games, he isn't steady with anyone else. But that doesn't mean I want him getting ideas about me—especially not if he's going to spend his life as a jeweler in State City.

Still, I take Ted's sleeve again, when we walk to his Oldsmobile. There's no vacant parking place in front of Iota, but this time, Ted leaves his car idling and double-parked to see me to the front door. I give him a peck on the lips, and a giggle, before I go inside.

Gradually, some of my sorority sisters have started to relax around me, and they're acting friendlier. The two factions—the Brenda Starr camp and the Gail Timmerman camp—seem less distinct, now, than they did at the start of the semester, although Gail will still barely acknowledge me.

It's a funny thing, but the thaw seemed to start the other day, after I bought some new clothes. I was wearing this white dress—mostly white, with geometric turquoise designs on it, and a few smaller designs in bright red; I'll only be able to wear it for another month or so, before the weather turns. A couple of girls remarked on it. Nothing big, just "Hey, new dress! Very nice!" or words to that effect. It is splashier than what I usually wear, and the skirt is maybe shorter than what I've been wearing, although it's still pretty conservative. More formal than what most girls at State University wear for everyday.

Then the next day it was cooler, so I wore my other new outfit: a Donegal tweed skirt and jacket, mostly brown but with little flecks of green, yellow, and red. That evening at dinner, almost everybody at the table kind of went "oooh," when I came into the room; I hadn't known it was that special, but obviously they thought it was a different look for me.

Janet said, "She's got to look good for her new guy," and the others giggled. I forced myself to laugh along, because I have started to feel guilty about how I've been keeping to myself.

Plus, if my sisters have been less friendly to me, this fall, than before, it could be my fault. None of them have asked me anything, or said anything to me, about what happened to Feldy. Maybe I've been distancing myself from them because I was afraid that they would give me grief about it, one way or another—but so far, not a word. I don't care that Gail's not talking to me, but what does she have to complain about? Her father is still here. To the rest of my sisters, it's as though that business never happened. As though I were not Feldy's Girl at all.

They seem to know I'm spending time with Ted, although I don't think any of my sisters know him. I go to the Ohio State game with Ted and his family, like before, and it's even more fun because this time nobody gets hurt and Gary passes pretty well—although we lose, again, 28-14, so we're 0-3 on the year, with Homecoming Week coming up.

Gary must have heard something, because he phones me on Sunday, early in the afternoon, to ask if we could go for coffee, like we used to, maybe at Hamburgher's.

"I felt bad about how we just *stopped*, all of a sudden," he says. "I'd like to catch up, if that's okay."

I tell him I'll meet him there. Rather than being picked up in his Corvette.

I daresay I don't look friendly, because Gary looks uncomfortable when we sit down. I tell him I thought he did a good job yesterday, considering, and he says, "Thanks," with this grim expression on his face. Then, nothing, till after we've ordered.

"First of all," Gary says, while we're waiting for the pie, "I had nothing at all to do with getting your dad in trouble. I didn't know anything about that photo of the Indiana game. Maybe Paul knew something about that, but I didn't, I swear."

"Okay." I'm still not smiling, at all.

"I was pretty pissed off at the way the fans turned on me, last year, and I felt Coach wasn't supportive enough. Texas wanted me, and I thought it would be a lot healthier situation. And frankly—you might not like to hear this, but it's true—your dad said I should do it."

I just incline my head.

"But I'm trying to make up for it. It looks like Timmerman and I are okay. At least we're getting along."

"Too bad that hasn't translated into a winning season," I say. Gary looks offended. I shouldn't have said it, but I couldn't help it. Then the pie arrives, so we don't have to talk for a minute or two, and I can think about where to steer the conversation.

"So, you and Ted are a thing, now?"

That's kind of sudden. I want to stall by taking another bite, but that would be too obvious.

"Oh, gosh, no. Where did you hear that? No, his family and mine have always been friends." (Not true: his parents and mine were mere acquaintances.) "They're just who I tailgate with. Now that my career as a sportscaster has been derailed, which thanks very much for."

Gary claims he doesn't know what I'm talking about. I have to tell him the story.

"I'm done in this town," I tell him, when I've finished. "Socially and every other way."

"Look, I didn't mean anything to happen to you or your dad on account of anything I did. I never thought anything would."

I do the eyebrow raise again. Gary glances down at the table for a moment.

"It would be nice if we could spend some time together, again," he says. "I miss having my good angel around. Especially now, when we're having this crappy season. I've seen other girls but they're not you. I miss having someone looking out for me."

I try to smile at least a little.

"I'll always listen if you want to talk," I say. "I'll give you advice if you want it. I'll always be your friend, but it would be stupid to try to get back together."

Gary looks like he's trying hard to smile, too, and he's not quite making it.

"You might be missing out," he says. "I'm gonna be playing on Sunday, next year."

"That's what Ted said the other day. You probably will be, and I'll root for you, but maybe I don't want to end up married to a star. I've seen it. Oh, I shouldn't say that. It worked out for my mother. At least, she seems to have handled it pretty well, unless she's keeping some awful secret from me. But that's a tough assignment—and I'm not my mother."

This makes Gary chuckle, if bitterly.

"No. You're Feldy's Girl, all right."

§

In a way, I feel like I'm home, for the first time in months. I'm in Sister Timothy's classroom. I've stopped by to invite her to my senior recital. She's at her desk; I'm next to the desk in a wooden chair—like when we used to have our conversations most weekdays, when I was her student. Now it's late afternoon and classes have been let out.

Sister Timothy is concerned about how I'm getting along, "after what-all happened," so I have to bring her up to date on that: where Birdy and Feldy are; what I'm going to do next.

"You can't wait to graduate, can you? To get out of this town and get your career going. Are you still looking at journalism?"

"Well, my parents are in New York now, right near the city, so probably I'll go live with them for a few months after I graduate—while I'm looking for work. I'll start right at the top, with the major networks and newspapers. My father has some connections, and so do my mother's parents."

"I believe you'll get whatever you go after. You've always been that kind of girl. You'll end up a brighter star than your father."

Sister Timothy is giving me as big a smile as I've ever seen from her before.

"That's what your vocation is," she says. "To be a star. It doesn't matter so much which profession you choose, or how you get there, but you'll be a star. That's what God wants for you. Are your parents coming back here, for your recital?"

"Very quietly. They're flying in to hear me perform late that afternoon, then I guess we'll go out to dinner, then they're catching a red-eye back to New York that night. They're still pretty bitter about how things turned out. As I am too. And so is the rest of the family. Next spring, nevermore will the evil name of Feldevert blight this fair city."

"You're well rid of us," Sister Timothy says. "State City needs you more than you need it, maybe—but it doesn't deserve you."

RECITAL

I've been in the State University Orchestra all four years of my undergraduate career. In my junior and senior years, I've been part of the String Orchestra and the Chamber Orchestra; I've performed in various chamber ensembles. This will be my first opportunity, in my university career, to give a full-length recital of my own.

I'm practicing with Mona, with Professor Meregaglia, with my two accompanists, taking as much of their time as they can spare for me. I've mailed out invitations to as many people as I can think of to invite; I've put up notices on the Iota bulletin board—but I've decided against publicizing the event beyond that. And God forgive me for being so vain as to do that much.

I couldn't confess to Monsignor Koudelka. He might not have recognized my voice, but I wasn't going to chance it. I went to confession at St. Stephen, where I'm not known. The priest there said it was no sin and I shouldn't think anything of it, but it still bothers me a little. I have never heard of any other undergraduate student publicizing her recital like I have done.

I haven't been near the house on Hilltop Street since I left it a few months back. I've been avoiding the neighborhood, to the point of taking roundabout routes when I might otherwise have driven through it. But now it's a dull, rainy Monday afternoon five days before the recital, I'm in my old Skylark, running an errand to which the most direct route takes me past that house. I would have taken a different route if I had been thinking about it, but I have too much on my mind at the moment.

I just had a lousy rehearsal session during which Professor Meregaglia really seemed angry at me for a second or two about how I was controlling my bow. He can make you feel so worthless if you mess up. He uses terror as a teaching tool.

I hardly had any sleep over the weekend. I'm disappointed because Feldy and Birdy are only going to be in town for a few hours—grudgingly at that, I suspect—and they won't be here to help me with any of the preparation. I feel like I haven't been pulling my weight in all the activities Iota has been involved in. I'm barely skating by in my course work. I'm pretty certain that my recital is going to be a fiasco, with me probably making mistake after mistake and having to apologize to the audience and leave the stage in the middle of it...

I turn onto Hilltop Street automatically.

I realize my mistake at once, but I tell myself to be an adult. Driving past that house won't be the end of the world.

Then I do drive by it. I see a man I don't know, setting out the garbage cans at the curb for pickup the next day. Not Feldy doing it; not me or one of my brothers doing it. A stranger whose family now lives in that house.

Tears start running down my face. I never cry. Damn it, I never cry. I never curse either, except when I do. But I never cry. Not since I was very little, and even then I hardly ever did. For a few seconds I try to control myself, but I'm afraid I'm not driving safely, so I turn onto a side street, park, and cry—loudly enough that I'm feeling embarrassed, even though there's nobody who could see or hear me—for three or four minutes.

I have never felt so hopeless. I have never felt so certain that I have been fooling myself, all my life long, by ever thinking that I would amount to anything if only I work hard.

I'll never amount to squat. Even if I have a career of some kind—even a great career—I'll know deep down that I don't deserve it, that I'm a fraud. I won't even get married, I suppose, since I'll be so busy pursuing some career that won't satisfy me. The man I might want to marry probably doesn't even exist.

In my whole college career, I have dated four men. No, three. I had one date with Andy Palinkas that convinced me he wasn't worth a second one. I dated Gary, for a year and a half. Something may have happened in Boca Cerrada, to another girl who doesn't even exist—and if she did exist, she would not remember it. And now Ted, who doesn't make me feel that spark that supposedly I'm supposed to feel. In any case, Ted has his career, and it's going to keep him in State City, where I don't want to be.

I know I'm fairly attractive, but how long will it be before I start losing my looks? Plus, it's not every guy who won't mind my height.

I'll be a bitter, angry, lonely old maid, consumed by my career, and angrier still because my career will probably amount to being a secretary or office manager—because it will turn out that I can't cut it either as a musician or as a journalist—at some company where I'll see women with more talent, more smarts, more direction, actually going places.

§

The recital is over; it was not the disaster I had dreaded. We're in the "chamber auditorium" of the Music Building: a little theatre that seats maybe 150 people, although nowhere near that number are here. I'm my own worst critic, and I didn't notice any mistakes that anyone else would have noticed except maybe Mona and Professor Meregaglia—and my committee. But not many of those.

I felt like I lacked energy, during the first part of the Handel, but at least I played the notes. Then I started feeling more confident, and I took care of myself well enough the rest of the way. I communicated the music, more and more so as I went along.

I felt like it all really came together on the Ravel. I'm relieved, exhilarated at the end, when I take my curtain call. Only now do I allow myself to take note of who is in the audience.

Of course I knew Birdy and Feldy would be here. They're sitting toward the front—well, they *were* sitting toward the front: they're standing now, applauding, and I'm afraid that they might holler, but they don't. Win is down from Davenport and he's standing and clapping next to them; so is Sister Timothy. Ted and his parents are sitting a few rows back.

Gary isn't here, since the Rivercats are playing the Hoosiers, in Bloomington, this afternoon. (I don't know yet how that game came out.) The Shapens are here. They have Little Red, or Hank, with them; he stayed quiet all the way through. Only Janet is here from Iota. A few of the cello studio are here, plus a scattering of other music students who have to attend a minimum number of recitals per semester. I'd call it an average turnout, but smaller than I might have hoped for. Doesn't matter now.

Birdy, then Feldy, are the first to embrace me when I leave the stage and emerge into the seating area from a side door. Then Win. Then Mona.

"You really did it." Mona is laughing and crying at the same time. "You really, really did it." She wipes her eyes with a hankie. "I'm sorry; I'm so proud of you." I give Mona another big hug, then I give one to Mike, and one to Sister Timothy.

I've set out some cupcakes, at the back of the auditorium; Win brought cookies that he said he made in the kitchen of the seminary. Mona has brought honey-cakes. Sister Timothy takes a cupcake and carries it out the door of the recital hall; I suppose she's got stuff to attend to back at the convent.

Birdy and Feldy have a bouquet of white roses for me. Mrs. Blaha gives me a little box; in it is a gold and pearl pin in the shape of a treble clef: very modest and tasteful, but obviously not an inexpensive piece.

"It's from all of us," Mrs. Blaha says. She leans in, and whispers to me: "It's mostly from Ted, but he's shy. Comes out of store stock, so it didn't cost us a thing."

My parents know Ted's parents only a little, but they're cordial. Feldy says to the Blahas, and to the Shapens, "We're all going to dinner at The Nightingale. I reserved for four, but I bet they'd have room for nine. Or ten. The little fellow makes ten. Come along."

Mona and Mike say they have to take the baby home—but the Blahas accept. I feel put out, since this means I'll have no time for real conversation with Feldy and Birdy. This is my last opportunity till Christmastime.

Win drove from Davenport to Cedar Rapids to pick up Birdy and Feldy at the airport, so he now drives them to the Nightingale, with me following in my car, the Blahas behind me.

We're seated in the restaurant; we've all ordered cocktails; Feldy is the center of attention, as usual. The Blahas aren't all that musical, so they don't find much to discuss with me, about the recital, but they're interested to know what Feldy is up to.

"I've got several things going on," Feldy tells them. "I'm chairman of a real estate company; I'm also in talks with a consortium that's looking to expand cable television, which is a small market right now, but it's going to get big in the next few years: huge big. Which could come in handy one day soon if my daughter ends up as a sportscaster, like she's been talking about. I'm exploring some other opportunities that are classified for now, but I'm out of football entirely, and I couldn't be happier."

I usually read Feldy real well, but in this case I don't know whether he means what he has just said, or if he's faking.

Feldy turns the conversation to the Blahas' jewelry business; then to my various options: for graduate school, for seeking a journalism job in New York or elsewhere. Football, and the Rivercats, never come up. Nobody even asks the waitress who won today's game. She's new: she doesn't recognize us.

We break up at about 9:30 in the evening. The goodbyes in the parking lot take a couple of minutes. The Blahas—after more thanks to Feldy and Birdy, and more congratulations to me— finally get into their car and head back to State City.

Feldy and Birdy give me extra hugs, then Win gives me one, then they all drive off toward the Cedar Rapids airport.

I'm driving back to Iota, alone—feeling relieved and happy and full of great food, but still disappointed.

§

My recital got top marks from the committee. Professor Mereg-aglia told me I could probably have my pick of graduate pro-grams, if I want to go into music education. Then he said, "But a-to be frank with you, your a-future as a performer is a-limited. You are good, and you might get a-better, but you are not a Ca-sals, not a DuPré. You play accurately, pleasantly, with a-good control, but with a-no artistic fire. You are a-maybe too intelli-gent to be a brilliant musician. If you make a-music your career, it will have to be in teaching. If that's a-what you wanna do, I'll give a-you the highest recommendations."

Which is as nice a way to put it as he could have.

"Not that I ever seriously thought I would have a career as a concert cellist, but having it confirmed for me, like that... that sort of took it out of me," I'm telling Mona. It's Monday night. Mona, Mike, and I are sitting in their new apartment—which still does not look lived-in enough yet. Mona and Mike look like fish out of water. They need to make the place a little crummier.

"But that's not bad," Mona says. "It's not like I expect to be the next Nadia Boulanger, either. I'll end up teaching at some college and maybe conducting the orchestra there, if I'm lucky. Or maybe conducting an opera company, if Mike's career takes off before mine does, which it probably will."

"But whatever happens," Mike says, "whichever of us gets a break first, Mona and I will be able to help each other career-wise. Maybe you ought to find a musician to marry."

"Kind of late to start looking for one of those," I say.

"Go to a conservatory," says Mike. "Get your MFA and your MRS degree at the same time."

That's mildly funny, so I laugh to oblige him.

"It's more complicated than that," I tell him. "I don't want to get involved with anyone unless I'm pretty sure he's marriage material. Which means he can't just be going in the same direction as me. I have to marry someone who has my values, too."

"Well, sure," Mike says. "Mona and I couldn't have gotten married otherwise. Arguably, the point of marriage is to bring up children. Some people say that if you don't have children, there's no point in getting married at all. Well, a lot of people think marriage is a bourgeois construct that outlived its usefulness generations ago, if it ever did have any usefulness except to protect wealth, you know, to keep wealth concentrated among certain families. Mona and I got married to pacify our parents. Otherwise we wouldn't have bothered. We can bring up a family just as easily without the rings and the piece of paper."

§

The Rivercats' record, through October, was 1-6. In their three November games, they seemed to finally get it together. They won two in a row—one on the road and one at home. They finished the season by tying Michigan—the Big Ten champions— in Ann Arbor. Gary had three outstanding games at quarterback; I was happy to see him end on a high note.

A disappointing season, for sure, at 3-6-1, but nobody who took a realistic view had expected any more than that, considering what had gone on in the 18 months leading up to it.

Now that the recital is over, I have a bit more time, and I'm starting to spend more of it with Ted. We went to that last home football game together, and a few days later, he drove me up to Cedar Rapids, where his grandparents live, to have Thanksgiving Dinner with his family.

It was a huge do. Mr. Blaha's parents are retired; they have a big, rich-looking house. Mrs. Blaha's parents, the Kaderas, were there too, plus all kinds of cousins and in-laws. How Ted managed to squeeze me onto the guest-list is a mystery: I'm pretty sure I was the only outsider. I almost felt like I was taking advantage to get a free meal that I didn't deserve.

When we were all at the table, eating—they have a wonderful big dining room, probably bigger than the one on Hilltop Street—Ted's mother asked me whether Ted and I had known each other as children, since we were only a year apart scholastically. I explained that I went to Catholic schools, all along.

"Our kids didn't go to Catholic school, because their parents went to Catholic school," Mr. Blaha said—smiling as if to say, "See how clever I am?"

I wanted to tell him that my own experience had been pretty positive, but how could I know what it was like for him?

"I hope you weren't driven away from the Church," I said. "I know some people are. I take it you don't worship at Our Lady. I've never seen you there."

"No, we go to St. Loy," said Mrs. Blaha. "We like the atmosphere there: It's more tolerant, more... progressive. Not that Our Lady isn't a beautiful church, and I'm sure it's a nice congregation, but St. Loy is more our idea of what the Catholic Church should be."

In other words, you wish Catholics were more like Unitarians, I thought. I kept smiling, but it cost a little effort. If the Blahas worship at St. Loy, I count it against them. I can't help it.

"We all come to God in different ways," I said, and I felt like a simpering idiot. "I haven't been to Mass at St. Loy in a while. Maybe I'll give him another chance." When Hell freezes.

Ted drove me back to Iota, that night, and we kissed goodnight at the door a little more... affectionately? than we ever had before. There was no risk of our being seen, because I had Iota practically to myself, for Thanksgiving weekend.

I'm not letting it go any farther than that. I've reminded Ted, as nicely as I can, that when spring comes, I'll be gone, and who knows what could happen after that? Not to mention, if he's a heretic like his parents... Okay, that's a joke, but only partly.

Ted and I talk on the phone every day. I don't feel like spending time with any other guy. I never hear from Gary anymore. I'm sure he has found someone else, too.

Feldy and Birdy sent me photos of their house, months ago. It's about the same size as what we had in State City, somewhat similar architecturally, but it's white, wood-frame, rather than brick. Win and I are flying out there at Christmas for two weeks.

I'LL TAKE MANHATTAN

"I hope it gets easier," Win is saying. We're sitting side-by-side on the plane from O'Hare to LaGuardia. Since we're flying east, away from the sun, it's getting dark fast.

"This first year is kicking my butt," he says. "I had no idea it was going to be this hard. I'm going to stick with it as long as I can; I think it's important that I have that education. But I have to ask myself if this is truly what I've been called to. For one thing, I've met this girl…"

I want to laugh, so I do, but I control it.

"You were going to be so cloistered. You were going to go so far underground…"

"Yeah, it's easy to talk like that. Then you meet someone who makes you question it. We don't see much of each other, but we get together and talk sometimes. She's a waitress at this diner near the seminary; she's maybe 19, and she's… I don't know, she can come across as not too bright, but that might have more to do with her being so naïve. She's, what's the word?"

"She's not worldly?"

"That's it. She isn't going to college, doesn't read much. But she likes to hear me talk. For some reason. And I see her at Mass every Sunday. When she gets off work, she likes to sit with me in the diner while I study, which I shouldn't let her do, I feel guilty about it, but… I can't hurt her feelings by staying away from there."

"Win! You're in love!" I give Win an elbow. "Lucky you!"

Win smiles, but he doesn't look happy about it.

"Unlucky me. I shouldn't see her anymore. It's a temptation."

"Or maybe an indication. Maybe you think you have a vocation—gosh, vocation, temptation, indication, we're on vacation; at least we're not in Penn Station—but maybe it's not what God wants. Maybe it's what *you* want—I mean the priesthood—but maybe God dropped this girl in your lap to point you in another direction."

"Maybe." The drinks cart is coming down the aisle, and Win says, "I'm buying. If you've never had Chivas Regal, I highly recommend it. Ice, no water or soda."

"It's mixed up," Win tells me when we've got our drinks. "I'm not liking what I see. At seminary. Maybe the priesthood isn't what I thought it was, or maybe it's changed from what I saw when I was growing up—or maybe I didn't see enough of it. For one thing, just about all the men are homosexuals, and they seem to be encouraged to act on it. Not officially encouraged, but close. It's almost like if you aren't in that… community, they don't want to know you. If you're abstinent, it must be because there's something wrong with you. They brag about it. About what they do.

"It's grotesque sometimes. Like, the other night, one of the younger fathers said to a few of us, 'I was on my knees half the night, last night, and I sure wasn't praying.'"

"Oh, Judas."

"Yeah. Like that was a good thing. Like that wasn't breaking a commandment. And okay, this is a small thing compared to the sexual stuff, but the music. That 'guitar Mass' crap has even gotten into the seminary now."

Win shakes his head, and I can see he's organizing a mini-lecture in his mind.

"You can see how it happened," he says. "The folk revival of the past few years. Then Vatican II brought in the idea that maybe ecumenism is a good idea, that it doesn't matter what you believe, that we're all one under God. Then you've got these songs that you hear on the radio all the time, like "Spirit in the Sky" and "Get Together." And *Jesus Christ Superstar*, which basically popularizes blasphemy, although *Superstar* isn't as bad as some people think. Plus, some people think it's more fun to play that kind of music in church: certainly easier than traditional liturgical music."

"Uglier, too," I mutter.

"These are people who would be completely in the dark if they heard words like 'immanence' and 'transcendence,'" Win says. "They're so occupied with the concept of 'Jesus-among-us' that they can't begin to think about 'Jesus-beyond-us.' That's how concepts like 'God is Love' have been debased, and have lost their Biblical meaning—and can be used, you know, promiscuously. I used to love guitar music. I still do, I still play it, but guitars don't belong in the Mass."

"Maybe God is calling you to do what you can to correct all that," I say. "You've got a few years to go, before you take your vows, and I'm sure it'll get a lot worse in the meantime, so who knows how much you'll be able to do?"

I let Win think on this for a few seconds.

"There's another possibility," I say, then. "Maybe you could marry a nice Catholic girl—if not this one you're seeing now, then some other nice Catholic girl—then have as many children as you can, and teach *them* the true Catholic ways, at least. So they don't get wrong ideas from somebody else. At least, you'll know you're doing some good."

"That's a point," Win says. "I don't want to act like I know better than anybody else, let alone that I *am* better than anybody else, but like I say, some of the people I see in the priesthood, now that I've started working with them up close... A lot of them shouldn't be there. I might be one guy who can at least watch over one parish, and make sure that parish flies right."

"Assuming a whole lot of damage hasn't already been done by the time you get there," I say. "If you have kids, you'll be working with them from as soon as they're born. But, you're right, a parish is a lot more people than a family, and who knows? You might get your Bishop's hat eventually. That would be a lot of people, a lot of parishes. Besides, if you don't do it, how do you know what any other Bishop is going to do—any other Bishop who gets the diocese that you would have had?"

Win and I kick this around for another couple of minutes, then I say, "I've been having a hard time, too, thinking about my vocation. I'm pretty sure now that music isn't it. I don't regret the time I put into it, but I don't have the talent or the desire that you need to make a career of it. I guess it's journalism, then— only I wonder about that, too.

"I've had all these fantasies of being a sportscaster, but I'm not going to get a job like that overnight. I'll have to work my way up to it, probably as a TV reporter, which is a job I'm sure I could handle, only I wonder, would I be doing any good?"

Win chuckles. "I thought that's what all journalists signed up for, was to do good."

"Oh, yeah, they do." I say. "They think that's what they're doing, most of them. But the ones who are the most gung-ho about doing good, those are the ones who spend their time reporting bad. Like they have this idea that the more time they spend finding out bad stuff, and exposing it, the more good they're doing. And I wonder whether they're actually making society worse by giving more exposure to what's bad.

"Look at all the awful stuff that happened just in State City, in the last couple years. Feldy basically got assassinated by the newspapers. The riots. Vicki getting killed. All the violence, all the dishonesty. I'm not saying journalists shouldn't report that stuff. But how will I be helping anybody, if I spend my life looking for awfulness and exposing it?"

Win shrugs. "You become a sportscaster; you get really good at it; you make people feel happier by making the football games more interesting. There's all kinds of ways you can contribute to society. They don't have to all be serious and not fun."

§

This might be the nicest vacation I've ever had. I've seen a lot of Manhattan: more than I saw the last time we were here. The house in Bronxville is, in fact, about the same size as our old house in State City, and most of the family got here for Christmas Day. All of us—kids, in-laws, grandparents, and grandchildren— put in at least a few days here between mid-December and early January. At least Win and I—but usually some of the rest of us, too—have been taking the train down to the city almost every day.

Those few days before Christmas are the most exciting time to be in Manhattan. It's like magic. It gets dark earlier here than it does in Iowa, at this time of year, because it's right on the edge of the time zone, and I prefer that, because then you appreciate all the Christmas lights, all over Manhattan, and the energy, with the sidewalks and streets so packed with people and taxis, and

413

everybody getting in each other's way and having fun with it. The weather stinks, though. It's nicer up here in Bronxville, where it's not as slushy and foggy, but Manhattan is so awfully wet and disgusting in December.

I've seen two Broadway shows. I don't know how Feldy managed to get so many tickets, but the whole bunch of us saw *Follies*: me, Win, Feldy, Birdy, Lou and his wife Joan. Jack and Jerry and their families hadn't arrived here yet. Then Win and I saw *Superstar*, and Win is right: It's blasphemous, but it's entertaining, and not as awful as some people say it is.

The Met is overwhelming. You can't begin to see it all in one day. I'll go there every weekend, when I'm living here. The Museum of Modern Art is more manageable; so is the Guggenheim.

My interactions with my other brothers are about the same as they always have been, ever since I've known them. Lou is cheerful and friendly but doesn't have much to say to me; Jack and Jerry are too busy having fun with each other and with their families; Duffy and Sander are glad to talk sports with me, but they don't have much conversation beyond that. As for the nieces and nephews, I have never considered myself good with children—I have never had much liking for children, not even when I was one—but I'm doing my best.

Birdy loves being a grandmother. She's not happy unless she's fussing over one or another of the smalls. Feldy is doing his best with them, too—which is not a bad best, since he has plenty of experience—and he seems almost his old self. I notice, though, that he's hardly talking about sports at all. If anybody brings up football, he stays quiet.

A few days after Christmas, one afternoon, I finally caught Feldy alone, working in his study—which is a nice one, bigger than he had in State City, with a beautiful view of the snow and some pine trees, out the window—and I got him to talking about how I might proceed once I graduate. I asked about his involvement in the cable TV industry, and whether he might have some connections I could use, if I do try to re-start my sportscasting career. He said he would ask around.

"Hey, what were the opportunities in sports that you were so vaguely telling the Blahas about, after my recital?"

414

Feldy sort of smirked.

"It's very speculative," he said. "There's talk about forming a new football league. That's all it is, right now, is talk. There's this lawyer out in California who's behind it. He's calling it the World Football League. The idea is to maybe establish teams in Hawaii, the Pacific, maybe Europe eventually. I've seen his plans, and I'm skeptical. Also, he and his friends are trying to attract investors—and I'm not as dumb as I look."

"But it would be great for you, if you could make it work," I said. "Maybe you could even own a team, *and* coach."

Feldy shook his head.

"That is so tempting. I'm tasting it, believe you me. But I'm not going to ask Grandpa Duffy to risk his money on it, which is what I would have to do. And I'm realistic. It'll take at least two years, probably three or four, to get a venture like that off the ground, and no guarantee that it would fly at all. The up-front costs would be unimaginable. It would be a tremendous gamble.

"Plus… okay, I'm not all that experienced in the romance department. I only had a few girlfriends before I met your mother. But I do know this: If you try to re-kindle an old flame, it won't even last half as long as the first time, and it'll hurt twice as bad. Look at old Humphrey, now: running for President again. That would be me. Coaching a team of stumblebums who couldn't cut it in the NFL. Or, God knows, Japanese sumo wrestlers. And everybody shaking their heads and saying, 'Poor Feldy: he smelled the sawdust; he couldn't keep away.' Nuts to that."

That was so sad, to hear Feldy talk like that. It hurt me, inside. But he was right. I can't pretend he wasn't. He's done with football and that's how it's going to have to be.

"Are you liking what you're doing now?" I asked. Feldy shook his head again and looked down at his desk.

"God, no. I'm not cut out for this. Sure, I can call myself an executive, and the pay is great, but I am *So. Bored.* My heart's not in it. Not that I'm not grateful to Grandpa Duffy. I'll stick with it till something better comes along, and lump it if it kills me."

Feldy grinned at me, then, but it looked like he was forcing it.

"As for your situation," Feldy said, "you'll want to live in the City, if you want a career in broadcasting. Or stay here till you're self-supporting. Evidently Ted Blaha isn't exciting enough to keep you in State City, is he?"

It jarred me to hear Ted's name. I hadn't expected it.

"Oh, Ted." I sort of waved Ted out of the conversation. "I'm not that serious about him. I like him. He's going to be a great husband for somebody. But he's, you know, he's *State City*, through and through. That's where he's going to stay. Which means whoever he marries is going to stay there, too."

Feldy chuckled.

"It would be funny if you stayed," he said. "Just to annoy the bastards. But, no, you want a career. Whoever you marry, it's going to have to be a guy who's willing to go along with that. I don't even know if there's a man out there who could be a match for you. But New York's a big city; you're sure to find somebody. It just might take you a while."

We talked for a few minutes more about my career prospects, and I wondered why I wasn't feeling more enthusiastic about this discussion. I've gone through seven semesters of college, now, with one more to go, and I know less about what I want out of life than I did when I was in high school.

I didn't say that to Feldy, but I did say to him, finally, "It's funny, but I don't want to go out and change the world, like maybe I used to. I've gotten to know some of the people who do want to change it, and sometimes the changes they have in mind are pretty awful."

"Change is over-rated," Feldy said. "Change can come from good people sticking to what they're good at, and that kind of change is usually beneficial. Change that comes from people going out there determined to cause change, as though change was the objective... that is usually not good change. Even if they think they're on the side of the angels.

"Like your friend Mona, for example. Obviously, she means well. She might have a great heart, but it's absolutely in the wrong place. People like her and her husband tend to go around tearing down walls without finding out why the walls were built there."

"It's confusing," I said. "I just have this feeling that I ought to do whatever I can do, to make the world better, any way I can. God wants us all to do that."

"I like to think that maybe I made the world better by building some young men up, building their characters up, while I was
coaching them," Feldy said. "Birdy and I have made the world a
lot better by bringing up you and your brothers.

"That's my greatest accomplishment. Our teams won a lot of
games, and winning is fun, but that's incidental. Family is what
life is about. If you mess up your family, the rest doesn't matter."

It's harder to find any time to be alone with Birdy. In any case, I
don't know how to start a conversation with her about my vocation, without the risk of making her feel wistful, and maybe—I
can't know, but I sometimes wonder about this—a little regretful
of seven children, no career of her own, being so defined by the
man she married.

For days now, I've been trying to catch Birdy when nobody
else is around. I might as well try to catch her while she's walking
around on the Moon. Now it is happening, on New Year's Eve,
early in the evening, before dinner—because *she* wants to catch
me alone. Win and I have just ridden the train back from the City
and walked the few blocks from the station to the house. I go
into the kitchen to see if Birdy needs any help. She's already got
Jerry's wife, Stephanie, in there helping her.

"Come downstairs with me," she says to me. "I've got some
girl-talk for you while I put in another load. Steph, make sure
nothing explodes up here, okay?"

I don't know what to expect.

"Don't tell anybody this." We're in the basement and Birdy is
talking softly, like she thinks there might be spies down here,
maybe lurking behind the washer and dryer. She's taking clothes
out of the washer and tossing them into the dryer by the double-
handful. "I'm thinking about going back to school. Getting my
law degree. Maybe not even to practice. Just for the satisfaction.
What do you think? Is that too crazy? We can afford it, and I'll
have no more kids at home, starting next fall."

"Why, no, that's a great idea," I say. I'm also talking very
softly. I start re-loading the washing machine, from the hamper
that stands under the clothes chute. "It's what you've always
wanted, and it's about time."

417

"It was Feldy's idea. He brought it up a few days ago, before we got invaded. I don't know how hard he had thought about it. We didn't talk about it much. But he did say it. And he said the same thing you just did: 'It's what you've always wanted.'"

"Then that's that," I say. "It's great that you're finally going to do it. Maybe it wasn't your true vocation—what, 28 years ago?—but maybe it is now. I wish I were as sure of what I want as you are. Why are we whispering?"

Birdy laughs—loudly—and shakes her head.

"I'll be damned if I know," she replies, at a normal volume. "But what do you mean, you're not sure of what you want? When did that happen?"

And this is my chance. I tell Birdy substantially what I told Feldy, the other day.

"I'll do what I've been thinking about: move to Manhattan and get into broadcasting somehow. Maybe magazines or newspapers, but probably broadcasting. But I'm wondering if that would be a waste of my life; if that would just be something I was doing for vanity. Not something I'd be doing because it was what God wanted for me.

"I'm starting to worry that I've been thinking about what I *should* want, rather than what I *really* want—and, my gosh, I don't *know* what I really want. That's what's driving me nuts. I don't even know if I'm ever going to have a family. Do you know, I'm 21 and I've never truly fallen in love with anyone? Isn't that pathetic? Not even in a crush sort of way."

I start the washer. Birdy looks nonplussed.

"Not even with Gary? I thought you might end up marrying him, if you worked on him long enough."

"Oh, no." I laugh. "I mean, I thought I loved Gary, but I never came close to *being in love* with Gary. I was attracted to him, and you could say I felt love for him—but I never felt *in love*. I have no idea what it's like. To love somebody that way. I wonder if I'll ever know what that's like."

"Oh, I'm sure you will," Birdy says. "One day. Ted isn't the one, either, huh?"

"Ted? No, no way. He's nice, I like his company, his whole family is great, but I'm not in love with him, either. I've never felt at all romantic about him. I just *like* him."

Birdy thinks for a few seconds. She fishes in her apron pocket for her cigarette pack and lighter.

"I sometimes wonder if just liking a guy—or liking a girl, if you're a guy—might not be underrated," she says. "Romance is nice, but it's not the point of marriage. If you look at history, you find that marriage is usually about economics. About preserving whatever wealth you have, and keeping the family going."

It's like a physical jolt, almost, although of course it doesn't hurt. But it stuns me for a second, because this is just what Mike Shapen said to me, a couple of months ago.

"Marrying for love is a new idea—if you consider all of human history," Birdy says. "It used to be considered almost a lower-class idea, at that. People do marry for love, and sometimes they have great marriages, but romantic love doesn't last."

This is quite the conversation to be having in front of a washing machine.

"Didn't you love Feldy?"

"Yes, I did, and I do, but I didn't marry him because I loved him. I married him because it made sense to. I might have loved him, but not thought him a good man to have a family with—in which case, I'd not have married him."

"Okay, then what made you decide to marry him?"

"Oh, gosh. Well, I wanted children, obviously, and Feldy was the best possible specimen to breed from." Birdy giggles. "That was important. And my parents approved of him, even though there wasn't a lot of money in his family. We all knew he was going places; we all knew he'd be a good provider. It made sense. It would have been insane not to marry Feldy. I knew that, as soon as I knew he felt that way about me."

Birdy takes another drag, and has another little think.

"I don't know if I should be telling you this," she says. "I know it's not done, nowadays, because people have different attitudes. But in those days, people got married... so they could have sex. We didn't think of doing it outside of marriage, then. We knew that some girls did, but we also knew that no nice boy would marry them, unless the girl tricked the boy into *having* to marry her. Which happened. Because men have appetites."

"So you might get married because the sex was going to happen anyway?"

I'm not quite sure whether I feel shocked, or if I'm just telling myself I *should* feel shocked.

"You could almost say that," Birdy says. "Sex does play a part—and where I grew up, staying a virgin till you were married was important. Granted, that's not always the case today. I'm not sure I want to know how people behave themselves now, with regard to that sort of thing. But people do want to... *do it*... and the surest way to guarantee you'll have a sex life is to get married.

"Sure, if you want to go outside the teachings of the Church, you can... but the risks are pretty big. Disease, or you might get pregnant by someone who doesn't want to get married. And maybe it's outdated for me to think this way, but I have to believe that fooling around when you're single reduces your prospects for a strong marriage later."

I'm not sure I'm convinced of Birdy's last point or not, anymore. I was. Now I'm doubting. I've seen more of life, now.

"The point of marriage is to reproduce and bring up a family," Birdy says, "and make sure that the next generation flies right. If you're going to do that, it makes sense to marry the guy who will give you the best family, or looks like he will." Birdy stubs out her cigarette into an ashtray on top of the dryer, and starts toward the basement stairs. I follow. "But don't get married to anyone, unless you're sure. You're going to be married a long time."

§

It's the same flight number, same airline, same takeoff time that we took three years ago, coming home from New York after Lou's wedding. Only this time, it's only me and Win sitting together on the plane, looking into the sunset.

"Next time, you won't be coming back to Iowa, I guess," Win says. "A few months from now, your ticket's one-way."

A few months from now. That jars me. Win saying that. Makes it more real.

"You know what, though?" I say. "Now that I've been there a couple times, I don't feel so enthusiastic about living there."

Win raises an eyebrow.

"I'll have to, if I'm going to do the TV thing. But it must be tough for a single girl, living in that town. It seems like it would be the loneliest place in the world. And, gosh, I've been through four years of working my tail off and hardly having a social life. I don't know that I want more of that. Also, I hate where Birdy and Feldy live. The house is nice, but it's like they're on Elba."

"Feldy's still got plenty going on," Win says. "He's out of football, and that's a good thing."

"He's got plenty going on—and it's all stuff that doesn't interest him," I say. "I know I'm being obsessive, but it still sticks in my throat, the way he got run out of town. Feldy was a legend. A legend. Now he's an 'unperson,' you know, like they do in Russia. If somebody gets purged, they take him out of all the history books, pretend he never existed. That's what's going to happen to Feldy.

"In another semester, the last member of the family will be gone out of State City and…" (I give it a sing-song, trying to take the edge off it) "never a trace will survive."

Win laughs, and I remind myself that I said much the same thing to Sister Timothy, about three months ago. I've been thinking about it a lot.

"That's our heritage," I say. "Being flushed down the toilet."

Win looks more serious.

"I get it," he says. "Nothing is forever, but you hate to see it go. Anyway, there's nothing that says you have to end up in New York. You'll be able to go anywhere in the world and have a career. You can be a real cosmopolitan, if that's what you want."

"A citizen of the worrrrld," I'm drawing the words out, fake-dramatically. I'm about to add, "It might be fun," but I realize—all of a sudden—that I don't think it would be fun at all. I look out the window of the plane. Pennsylvania, I suppose, is below us; cirrus clouds are hovering between the plane and Earth.

I'm thinking about the way Feldy was treated. All the intrigue, the back-stabbing. How finally, Feldy had to be the scapegoat.

Not to mention the Watkins case and the sheer vileness of it. Watkins, who could have controlled himself and had a great career. How disgusted I felt with Vicki—may God forgive me—for letting herself in for all the horrible stuff that happened to her. The riots, which turned out to be for nothing. For *nothing*: I don't care what Mona and Mike say. The destruction; the ruthlessness. The not giving a crap for common morality—for the absolutely basic kind of morality that you're supposed to know by the time you're five years old.

It's not so much the *immorality*. It's the *amorality*. From people who think that they are so terribly moral.

I'm a long way from wisdom, still, and I always will be. But I'm telling myself, now, that I have had my eyes opened. That is what nearly four years at State University has done for me.

I'm fascinated by those wispy white clouds below us. For a few seconds, I can see nothing but white. I know this is one of my chromesthetic hallucinations. It doesn't disturb me. But it's so white. So blindingly, overwhelmingly white.

I'm enjoying it. This sensation. I'm feeling a tingle through my body, almost a mild, steady electrical shock—and now I feel such calm, such peace, like I can't remember ever having felt before.

God is Love. The Gospels say so. But God's love is not like human love. It's an entirely different concept that we can understand only vaguely, and maybe just intuitively. I've sometimes thought God's love might be best defined as Truth. Or maybe I should say that the bounty of God's love, is Truth.

I know, now. I am sure of myself. I don't say it aloud to Win, but I think, "What is happening to me?"—and then I know.

It takes me a few seconds to come back to myself. Then I tell Win: "That might have been my fantasy a year ago. It's clearer to me, now, what I need to do with my life. I haven't systematized it in my head yet, but I'll tell you all about it when I have."

Win chuckles.

"Can't wait."

Win and I split up when we get to O'Hare, early in the evening. I'm catching a connecting flight to Cedar Rapids, and he's taking a Greyhound to Davenport. We hug each other goodbye in the terminal. When I get to Cedar Rapids, I take the airport limousine back to Iota Delta Theta.

Most of my sisters are back from vacation, but I run up to my room without stopping to talk with any of them. First thing I do, even before I go to the ladies', I call Ted at his parents' house.

"I'm buying you lunch tomorrow," I tell him. "I've brought you something back from New York. And I've got some pretty important news for you. See you at the Mainliner at 12:30."

Ted sounds concerned. "Can you give me a hint?"

"Don't worry: It's good news. I just have to have overnight to get the whole story memorized."

I sit at my desk with a Bic and a yellow pad—I still haven't gone to the bathroom, I'm so jazzed—and I write and write.

THE MAINLINER

The Mainliner has been in downtown State City since the 1930s. It's a bar/restaurant that's decorated like a mixture of a club car and a dining car of a passenger train. It's a hangout for the older students in the evening, and a lot of downtown businesspeople and State University faculty have lunch there. I wish I could have prepared a meal myself, for Ted, but I have no private place to cook or serve it, so the restaurant will have to do.

I'm still not used to the way Ted looks on weekdays, now. For casual, he dresses the way he dressed when he was a student: jeans or chinos, plaid shirt, his Rivercats letter jacket. But on days when he's working at Blaha Jewelers, it's a sport jacket, white shirt, conservative tie. Seeing him dressed that way reassures me. It seems to me, though, when Ted arrives at the Mainliner, that he looks somber and tense, as though he's worrying.

We take a booth opposite the bar. I give Ted his present, which is a tie from Sulka that cost slightly more than I wanted to spend but it's so beautiful I hadn't been able to resist it. Subdued, though. Dark blue, of ribbed silk, with a rusty gold diagonal satin stripe, and lighter gold *fleurs-de-lys* alternating with the stripes.

"Wow." Ted says. "Perfect."

"Yeah, I'm proud of myself," I say.

"Well, I've got something for you, too," says Ted. He passes me a little box.

For a second, I'm thinking, "Oh, Judas, is this the ring?" But it can't be. He knew I wasn't planning to stay in State City, so he wouldn't have been foolish enough to propose to me—and he certainly would not do it in a booth in the Mainliner.

It's a very nice present, though. Gold filigree earrings, with teardrop-shaped opals. Small earrings, with small opals, but they're amazing quality, the opals. Dark.

"Oh, Ted. We both threw for touchdowns this time."

I am so impressed. Ted read me exactly. These are just what I might have chosen—if I had better taste. The waitress is here, so I can't gush.

We order, and then I do wax ecstatic just a tiny bit about the earrings, after all, before I start telling Ted about my time in New York. Ted doesn't have much news, since he would have been slammed with work over the holidays, but I go on for a while about the museums and the Broadway shows.

"But the greatest thing that happened to me in New York is the news I told you I was going to give you," I say.

Ted gives me a bit of a frown, and I see—I should have known he would—that he's assuming I'm going to tell him I got a great job in New York, or at least that I've firmed up my plans to move there, after graduation, and look for one.

The food arrives: ravioli and a salad for Ted; a tuna melt with fries for me. Ted still looks glum. Neither of us starts to eat.

"I came to a realization," I say. "Came to it early, since Epiphany isn't till Thursday."

Ted looks puzzled.

"Okay, Ted, here's the deal." I'm speaking only loudly enough for Ted to hear me. I'm looking right into his face. "You

424

and I are going to get married. We're going to do it this May or June, right after I graduate. We're going to get married at Our Lady, not at St. Loy. And we'll set up house here in State City."

I'm doing my best not to notice whether Ted is having any change of expression, which is tough since I'm also reminding myself to maintain eye contact. I keep going; I want to not give Ted a chance to talk till I've finished.

"It's not going to be a big wedding. Just a small one with our families and whichever of our friends want to show up. We're not going to invite half the town. Or, you can invite whoever you want, but *I'm* not going to invite a lot of people We're going to do it as soon after graduation as we can, because there's no sense in not getting started with our lives. We're not going to spend a year planning a big to-do and getting a thousand invitations out.

"And I do *not* want an engagement ring. I don't need portable property in case it doesn't work out, because I know it's going to work out. Plus, I don't need to show everybody that I was bought and paid for, or how much you paid for me. I know how much I'm worth to you, and that's all that concerns me."

Ted is staring, slack-jawed.

"I'm going to be your helpmeet. I'll work in the store if you and your father need me there, or I'll help you with your expansion plans. I've got room in my schedule to take a course or two in business or real estate this coming semester, so I'll be able to make myself useful somehow. We're going to find a house in the best neighborhood we can afford. Not an apartment. A real house. Something little and modest in a good neighborhood, rather than a fancier house in a worse neighborhood.

"We're going to have as many children as God gives us, and we're going to start early. It's going to be our job to bring up a decent family, because not very many people are going to.

"I'm choosing you because you're the best man I'm ever going to find, and I'm the best girl you're ever going to find, and we're perfect for each other. We both love this town—even if I've been trying to convince myself that I don't. And I've decided I don't want to do anything else *but* have a family—with you. I've had it with looking for something else because I wanted something else years ago, when I didn't know any better.

425

"What's important is that we both know where we're going. I want to bring up good Catholic children. But if I want a good environment for them to grow up in, I have to do what I can to create it. You're the guy I'm going to create it with."

I lock eyes on Ted and give him the slightest nod to indicate that I've made my statement. I take a bite of my sandwich, at last.

Ted continues to stare at me. He takes a slow deep breath, through his mouth, then leans back against the banquette and slowly lets it out through his nose. Then he leans forward again; he smiles on one side of his face, and gives his head a quick little shake, like he's recovering from a punch.

Now I'm scared that I've botched it. How could I have made that speech? Maybe I'm stupid, but I never imagined that I was capable of anything *this* stupid.

Ted takes another big inhale, and a slow exhale.

I'm despairing. Damn it all. Damn me for a damn idiot.

"Well." Ted chuckles. "That was easy. I thought you'd brought me in here to tell me you'd met a guy in New York."

I've never done anything so hard, I think, as keeping a straight face and not collapsing from relief.

"Eat before it gets cold," I say. I feed myself a French fry, to keep my face busy.

Ted does start to eat, like he's making himself do it. He looks like he's still processing.

"You'll still get to travel," he says, after a minute or so. "That's one of the great things about being a jeweler: you go on buying trips, so you get to see the world, but you go first-class all the way. Never a back-pack unless you want one."

"Don't think I didn't think of that."

Ted laughs, still nervous.

"I'm not believing this," he says. "I mean, it's great, but it's not what I expected."

I shrug, deadpan.

"I'm full of surprises."

I walk Ted back to Blaha Jewelers, after lunch. We're holding hands. Ted says, "Both my parents are in the store right now. Want to go in there and surprise them?"

"Better not. Tell them without me, so they have a fair chance to voice their objections."

"Not likely. They've been dropping hints since September."

When we get to the store, I grab Ted's face in my hands and give him a real kiss, right there on the street.

"Call me tonight," I tell him.

Less than five minutes later, I'm at the post office, and the letter I wrote last night goes from my purse into the mailbox. Then I walk back to Iota to phone Birdy and Feldy.

Dear Win:

I'm writing this because my thoughts were too complicated to tell you on the plane, and I hadn't sorted them out in my own head well enough to explain them to you. I am not going to mail this to you till I have closed the deal, because I am such a coward. But if it makes sense to send it to you then, I will.

It hit me when we were on the plane this afternoon, when you said that, about how I could have a career anywhere in the world. That was when it solidified in my mind, what God was saying to me. Right there. I know the career I want to have, and where I'm going to have it.

Being together with the whole family at Christmas was when I first heard the call, I believe, but talking with you was when I fully realized it: God was telling me I would be cheating myself, and cheating Him, if I didn't focus on having a family, having children, as many as I can handle—and bring them up to live the best lives they can, with Catholic values.

The more I've seen of life, especially in the past couple of years, the more hideous the world appears to me. But it won't go away, and it certainly won't get better if I don't do my duty to God—which is to have children and bring them up right, because who else will do it? If I don't do it, society goes on—minus the decent children that I didn't have. That would be letting God down, wouldn't it?

Another mission I have—this, you might consider mundane, but I feel that it's my duty nevertheless, and it will be a happy duty believe it or not—is to keep Feldy's name alive, here in State City. And get his reputation back for him, if I can. I am going to make sure that if ever a word is spoken in public against Feldy, Feldy's Girl will be there to contradict and correct.

Not only that. It's my duty to myself to stay a part of the fabric of State City, and State University. Who knows? Maybe one day I can buy our house back.

I'm going to use my education right here. I have the two majors. The music, I can pass along to my children. The journalism, I can use in any number of ways. I hope I'm not sounding vain when I say this, but my strategy involves eventually being a big wheel in this town.

My duty is here. Not just to preserve or restore Feldy's reputation, but to make State City and the university less bad than they have become. I know nothing will be as it was, but I have to fight for what I value, and bring up children who will do the same. That is doing God's work.

No matter what I do with my life, I realize that I can't have much impact on the whole world, not really. But I can at least do my best to improve and protect my corner of it. It occurred to me, when we were talking on the plane today, that I feel much more passionate about doing that—infinitely more—than about being a celebrity or a *citoyenne du monde*. Maybe I always have felt that way but never admitted it to myself. Or maybe I'm being smart in hindsight, now, telling myself I knew it all along.

I think about my friends Mona and Mike. They are not bad people. But they are in terrible error. There are thousands of others like that, just in this town, most of whom will reproduce.

I'm not sure I'm in love with Ted. I have no idea what "being in love" means. But Ted has everything I want: security, family, stability, values. How Catholic he is, I'm not certain—but I can work on that, incrementally, so that he'll not notice that I'm drawing him further into the Church.

Ted will be a great husband and father—and I love the type of husband and father I know he has the potential to be. That is close enough to "being in love" for me.

"Sandy, could you please get Birdy or Feldy, whoever's closer?"

I'm in my room at Iota. I've been intending to break the news in a level, calm tone, but when Sander brings Birdy to the phone, I can't keep my voice down: I'm finally letting myself be excited.

"Birdy, I've got news. Ted Blaha and I are getting married." That was that. Then the rest pours out, at a pretty fast pace, so that Birdy won't be able to interrupt. "We're going to do it right after I graduate. May or June. We've decided to settle down here in State City; Ted's staying in his father's business, and probably I will too, to start with…"

I can't guess how long I would have talked without running down, but when I have to pause at one point to take a breath, Birdy says, "Dear, stop." She has to say it a second time, louder: "Teresa, stop!"

I'm afraid Birdy is about to object.

"Let me get Feldy on the extension," Birdy says. She calls off, "Feldy, could you please go pick up the phone in your office? It's kind of important."

"Honey, I don't know what to say," Birdy says while we wait for Feldy to pick up. "When was all this settled?"

"You settled it for me. You and Feldy. Thank you, thanks to both of you."

"Hello?" comes Feldy's voice.

"Feldy, I'm getting married, and it's your fault. You and Birdy. You both gave me such good advice at Christmas, and I'm taking it." I start my story again, from the top. This time I go on for maybe two minutes before anybody else can get a word in.

"I just want to tell you again: I'm so grateful to both of you. You showed me the path. You've both been such wonderful parents to me, all my life long, and this proves it. Thank you, thank you both, so much!"

Now I'm asking myself: Did I, subconsciously, calculate this way of telling them? I mean, it felt, when I was saying it, like it was just spilling out, so I could hardly control myself—but could

I have been deliberately stifling any reservations that Feldy or Birdy might have expressed, before they had had a chance to? Or am I being too cynical about myself?

"Terri, you have my blessing," says Feldy, when I run down. He doesn't hesitate for even a moment. "Ted's a fine young man."

"I agree with everything Feldy said," Birdy says. "This is the best news I can think of."

"We don't want a big fancy wedding, but Ted and I agreed that we would like a Mass. Instead of just the ceremony. If you guys don't think that would be too extravagant. It would make it so much more special."

Gosh, I'm so smart: asking for something that will add to the expense—although it won't add much—having cast the leaven by reminding my parents that this was their idea, and an extremely good idea at that.

It works.

Ted and I have not discussed a Mass at all, but I'll inform him in good time.

§

I've never been in the rectory of Our Lady till this afternoon. It's nice. I could live here. From the outside, it's gorgeous. It's right next to the church, and you can't call a two-story house "neo-Romanesque," but the rectory's architecture compliments the church. It's a light red brick house with a nice big stone porch that must be wonderful for the priests to sit on, in the evening.

Monsignor Koudelka greets us at the door. Ted and I. Ted and me, I mean.

Past the entryway, there's a big living room with lots of comfy-looking chairs and dark woodwork: very masculine but nice. Old furniture. I approve. To the right, off the foyer, is what looks like a library, not a very big one—smaller than the den in our house on Hilltop Street—with a plain wooden rectangular table and lots of bookshelves. Tall upholstered armchairs in the corners, bulky carved wooden chairs around the table. The books are mostly old; lots of them are leather-bound. I bet you could lose yourself for years, in this room. It feels bigger, somehow, than it is. It's not well lit. Somehow the dimness makes it feel bigger, which is counter-intuitive, but there it is.

The front window gives out onto Jefferson Avenue. It's so comforting to see people casually walking past, all bundled up. It's cold out there, but we're in here and warm.

The three of us sit at that table. A sister whom I don't recognize comes in with a pot of coffee and a plate of chocolate chip cookies. They're still warm.

Monsignor Koudelka has already briefed us about the questions we should expect him to ask us. He seems satisfied that we mean business, that we know what we're getting into, that I'm not pregnant, that we're going to have at least a dozen good Catholic children. He's all jolly and he seems like he's really happy for us. I let Ted do most of the talking, which I admit isn't easy for me. Ted asks him for May 29—Memorial Day, a Monday, after the Pentecost octave—and thank God for minor miracles: it's open. Or, it was open. It ain't, now.

"I have one special request," I say. "Is it legal for you to celebrate the Tridentine Mass, for our wedding? It's not actually forbidden, is it? Or is it?"

Monsignor looks surprised, and interested. I'll bet he has never heard that request. He leans forward and gives me a big smile, like he's enthusiastic about explaining it.

"The Holy Father never specifically banned it," he says, in his Welk-ish accent. Monsignor Wunnerful.

"That's a rumor that the reformers have spread. First of all, following an appeal by Cardinal Heenan, in the United Kingdom, the Holy Father last year issued the so-called 'English Indult,' which makes clear that the Bishops of England and Wales may permit the use of the former Roman Missal..." (Monsignor pauses, trying to remember the exact words) "at the request of groups asking 'for reasons of genuine devotion.'"

He pauses, and nods, like he's deliberating on his words.

"You need the permission of the Bishop to celebrate the Tridentine Mass in a public setting," he says, "but I would argue that this is a private wedding, invitation-only. It's a lot easier to ask forgiveness than to ask permission, isn't it? In the circumstances, I can't imagine that the Bishop would object. He certainly won't object if he never hears about it."

Monsignor sighs, and looks at the ceiling for a moment, then he looks back at us.

"The Second Vatican Council declared that 'Latin is to be preserved in the Latin rite.' The Council also directed that the laity should be instructed so as to enable them to say or sing the parts of the Mass pertaining to them—in Latin—and that Bishops should consider the holding of Latin Masses, especially in the case of multi-lingual congregations."

He's looking at us so gravely now.

"It's my own belief that Latin is not merely a ceremonial language," he says. "It's the language that is in effect the lifeblood of the Church. It's through Latin that the truths of the Church remain universal and immutable. If we lose Latin, we create a modern Tower of Babel. No family can stay united if each member speaks a different language."

He smiles at us, and nods.

"You two are to be commended. You seem to understand that unity of language conduces to the unity of hearts—and certainly it is the role of the Church, and of the Sacrifice of the Mass, to make us one in the Spirit. It will be an honor to celebrate your wedding Mass for you—if you don't mind my nominating myself for the job."

§

The University Statesman, Wednesday, February 2, 1972

FALCONS CLAIM CLEMONS, EAGLES TO SIGN GROZNIAC

Schoyer Is A Colt; Chiefs Tap Vipulis

State University defensive back Clarence Clemons was the Atlanta Falcons' first-round choice yesterday, on the first day of the NFL draft, held at the Essex House Hotel in New York City. He was the 15th player selected overall. In the second round, the Philadelphia Eagles drafted Rivercat defensive lineman Bruno Grozniac.

A total of four State University Rivercats have been drafted so far. The Baltimore Colts selected quarterback Gary Schoyer in the eighth round, and the Kansas City Chiefs chose offensive guard Gundars Vipulis, also in the eighth round. The process resumes today, with several other Rivercats likely to be drafted.

Clemons, as a first-round pick, is the star of the article. Grozniac—since he's hard to miss on the field, and he's the defensive captain—gets almost as much space. Both of them have quotes in the opening paragraphs. Gary and Vipulis are quoted further down the article, with Gary saying, "This is an opportunity to learn from two of the masters: Johnny Unitas and Earl Morrall."

The *Register* is more generous to Gary. The main story, which headlines the day's Big Peach section, also focuses on Clemons and Grozniac, but a separate story, below the fold, is dedicated entirely to Gary, recalling his varied career at State: as the surprise star of 1969; as "Mr. Versatile" of the disastrous 1970 season; finally, as one of the few bright spots of 1971.

> "It's likely that I'll be the third-string quarterback in my rookie year, if I make the team," Schoyer told the *Register*. "Nobody can challenge Unitas, and Morrall has been one of the best backups in the NFL. It takes a few years to learn how to be a top pro quarterback, so Baltimore might be the best club I could have been drafted by, considering who-all I'll be working with.
>
> "My years here at State University were an amazing learning experience and I feel that I've grown up quite a bit during my time here. I'm grateful to Coach Timmerman and all my teammates, and I hope to see several of them on Sunday afternoons over the next ten to 15 years."

I knew better than to call Gary that day. He would be busy taking congratulations from plenty of other people. But I call him today—to ask if I can come over and congratulate him face to face.

"You better not," he says. "We partied kind of hearty, last night. You'd be so grossed out by the mess, you'd never speak to me again. How about we meet at Radcliffe, like we used to?"

That's where we are: in the Radcliffe Hall cafeteria, having coffee. The last time we'll do that together, I'm pretty sure. Even at that, it's one more time than I had expected.

"Gary, I'm so happy for you. You're right, Baltimore's the best place you could have ended up. McCafferty's a good coach, and Unitas and Morrall can't last much longer. You could be their starter by '73."

"If I make the team at all, which isn't any sure thing, but, yeah, I could have done a lot worse than the Colts. I just wish I'd been picked higher. I mean, eighth round. It's gonna be a pretty bare-bones contract. Like I told you before, they spend all their money on the top two or three draft picks; after that, you're supposed to just feel lucky that they picked you at all, and take whatever they offer you."

"The big money's still ahead of you," I say. "Make the team, prove your worth, and you'll be able to name your price."

"That's another thing," Gary says. "Making the team. The higher of a draft pick you are, the less likely you are to be cut, because they're already invested in you. If I'd gone in the first or second round, I'd have the team made right now, because this could be Unitas' last year, and Morrall didn't do much last fall. He might even retire before training camp starts. They'd be grooming me to take over."

"So you'll have to work harder than you would have, to make an impression. That's never a bad thing. They obviously drafted you for when Unitas is gone."

"Yeah. I'm optimistic. It's better than not getting drafted at all, which I did think was possible after that season we had. It's nice to know what I'm going to be doing this summer, anyway."

I think for a few seconds, before I decide to ask: "Are you going to marry this girl of yours, first? Before you're off to training camp?"

I take it for granted, that Gary has a steady girl. I don't know.

"This is real confidential." Gary leans in, across the little table, and lowers his voice. "Just between the two of us, okay? I think she would like that. But it's not going to happen. She's a sweet girl but she's not who I want to marry, and I don't think it would be good for her, either. I wouldn't be the right guy for her. It's just as well that I'm going to be gone this summer." Gary smiles on one side of his face. "It might have been different if it had been you. But that's water under the bridge."

I shrug, and look down; I feel like I'm blushing—and I know right now in the moment that I'm sending Gary the wrong signal.

"Or, I don't know, does it have to be?" Gary says. I straighten up and remind myself to look levelly at him.

"Gary, I'm marrying Ted. We haven't made a big announcement, but it's going to happen right after graduation."

Gary all of a sudden looks like I slapped him or something. Completely taken aback. He gives a little start, then sags in his chair slightly, just enough that I notice.

"When did you decide this?"

I tell Gary how the relationship developed, and how I proposed to Ted instead of vice versa.

"Which isn't traditional, the girl proposing to the boy, but I was going to make sure it happened, and it might not have, if I had waited for him to pop the question."

Gary has been sitting with his mouth half open, listening. Now he looks offended.

"So you weren't being quite honest with me, about how serious you were with him."

"No, at the time, that was the situation. I was telling you the truth. We were friends; then it evolved. I guess I didn't think it was important to tell you anything else, after Ted and I had gotten more... romantic. But, yeah, we're sending out invitations in a couple of weeks, and you're a friend of both of us, so you'll certainly get one. No, two."

Gary still looks stunned. I have to laugh.

"Look at you! You poor thing, you look like somebody shot your dog. Speaking of dogs, you're the proverbial dog in the manger, aren't you? Oh, Gary, come on, you and I would never have worked out. You want somebody more glamourous than I am. A *Playboy* model, maybe. And you're going to be in a position to get one or two of those, pretty soon."

Gary makes a neutral noise that I can't quite describe. He's trying for a smile, but he can't quite work one up.

"Well congratulations," he says, finally.

If he can't smile, I'll give him a big one.

"Best wishes," I say. Partly I'm smiling to show that I'm not just correcting him to be bitchy. "Groom gets congratulations, bride gets best wishes."

"Best wishes." His voice is all dull. "Ted's a good guy. But are you going to be okay with settling down here? That wasn't what you had in mind, last time we talked about it."

"No, it wasn't. My priorities changed."

"Somehow I can't see you as a good little housewife. Like… well, like your mother. Isn't that what you were always trying to get away from being? No offense, your mother's great."

"No, that's a fair question. Well, for one thing, the guy I'm going to marry is in a different position from you. He's not a star. He's not trying to be one. I don't have to tag along behind him. For another thing, he knows I have my plans too. They're compatible with his plans, but they're completely mine. You know, independent of what Ted or his father are doing." I smile again. "And they wouldn't be compatible with living in Baltimore. Apparently I've found my vocation—and it's here in State City."

"Is that so?"

"One of these days, maybe I'll get my radio show back, but on a bigger scale than before. Maybe I'll even buy KSCR, and use it to say whatever the heck I feel like saying. Then if I want to announce the football games, I will. Gary, I'm going to conquer this town, somehow. And maybe the university, for good measure. This might be fun."

Finally, Gary laughs with me, although he still looks a little bit sick. Our conversation doesn't last much longer.

§

Saturday afternoon. It's rainy and gloomy; the rain will melt most of the snow. Ted and I are sitting across the dining table from each other in his parents' house, to draw up our guest lists. Ted asks me if it would cause trouble if he invited the Timmermans.

"He was good to me; I looked up to him. I'd like to have him and Mrs. Timmerman there."

I hadn't even thought of this. That Ted would want to invite them. I'm deliberately not inviting any of my sorority sisters except for Janet and Lefty, so that I won't have to invite Gail Timmerman. I bet Ted can hear the wheels clicking in my head while I'm turning the thought over. I tell myself, "Pick your battles; you're going to be married for a long time."

I'm about to say, "Oh, why not? Ask the whole family. Just make sure they stay on your side of the church."

Instead, I say, "Keep in mind who's sending out the invitations. I could ask Feldy and Birdy, or you could send the Timmermans a letter on your own, though that might look odd…"

"Oh, right. I hadn't thought of that. The invitations. No, forget it. It wouldn't be right."

"You know, my folks would probably do it," I say. "Invite the Timmermans, I mean. They would do it for your sake. They wouldn't like it, though."

"No, you're right, they wouldn't like it," Ted says. "Forget it. If I have to do any explaining later, I'll think of something."

"Thank you."

I stand, walk around the table, and give Ted a big hug and kiss.

Ted invited a few of his teammates who still live in the area, and a few fraternity brothers: more people, in all, than I'm inviting. Added up, for the two of us, the entire list of family and other invitees comes to 95 people. There will be no maid of honor, no bridesmaids, groomsmen, or ushers. Not at a nuptial Mass.

My whole family will be there: Feldy, Birdy, Lou (yes, he's setting foot in Iowa again), Jack, Jerry, Win, Duffy, Sander, sisters-in-law, nieces, nephews, Grandma and Grandpa Duffy, Feldy's sisters and their husbands. The whole Blaha family, including both sets of Ted's grandparents. I've invited Sister Timothy; Mona and Mike; a few old friends of Birdy and Feldy's; Professor Meregaglia and his wife; Gary and a date; Janet and a date; Lefty and a date. Nobody else. It brings me up short, when I look at the list, to realize how few friends I have accumulated in my life.

I didn't bother with the graduation ceremonies. I have my diploma, and it's over. I spent graduation weekend moving—with help from the Blahas—into a very plain three-bedroom wood-frame house in a quiet neighborhood, you might call it a "prosperous working-class" neighborhood, on Terrace Road, on the east side. It's a starter house; we're buying it with help from both sets of in-laws. I've lived in it alone, for these past few days, to get it prepared. Ted will move in after our honeymoon, which is going to be part business but mostly pleasure.

Right after the ceremony, we're flying from Cedar Rapids to Chicago, then getting on another plane for New York and spending our wedding night at the Plaza Hotel. The next day, we board the *S.S. Rotterdam*. We'll stay about a month in Europe, where Ted is going to visit some of the merchants his parents buy from, and maybe cut a few deals—but it'll be mainly just us. First Antwerp, then Frankfurt, Zürich, Milan, Florence, Rome, Paris, and finally London. I'd love to see Prague, but that's for the future.

I'll be seeing some more of the world—but then I'll be coming back here.

ET CLAMOR MEUS AD TE VENIAT

Outside, it's a bright late-spring morning in State City. I didn't pray for it, but sometimes God answers prayers that you never offered. Sunlight is coming in through the windows of the basement of Our Lady. Long tables have been set out. Caterers are loading them with *hors d'œuvres* for the reception, which will take place right after the ceremony. Other than them, it's just me and Birdy down here, getting ready to go upstairs. Birdy is wearing a tailored bright yellow summer suit with matching veiled pillbox hat: just the thing for the Mother of the Bride. Birdy does have nice taste. I hope I have inherited it from her at least a little.

I've chosen a slightly unconventional wedding costume: it's a simple 1950s-style white taffeta dress with a full three-quarter-length skirt, with built-in petticoat to give it extra fullness.

"This was a brilliant choice," Birdy says. She's straightening my veil; brushing off specks of dust that aren't there, to keep herself busy. "I bet you're the only girl in the U.S.A. who went for this design, this year. It's just like you. A tiny bit old-fashioned and very Catholic."

I barely hear. I can't imagine how it could have come to me, but an image pops into my head: that girl, Brenda's friend—what was her name?—in the kitchen of that house in Boca Cerrada more than a year ago. Naked, scooting along the floor on her hiney, with her legs wide open and some other girl's head between them. I can't help it: it's there, that memory. I shriek with laughter; I almost double over.

"What?" Birdy sounds alarmed. I recover.

"Oh, just an extremely lame joke I thought of. I just laughed because it's such a dumb joke, in such bad taste that I can't repeat it, and now all of a sudden it popped into my head. Did you have things like that happen to you, when you got married? Crazy random thoughts?"

"Why, I don't remember any." Birdy gives my veil another little adjustment. "I was so happy. And so proud of the man I was marrying." She pauses a moment. "And what an adventure it's been! Well. Ready?"

We go upstairs and meet the rest of the wedding party at the back of the church. I can hardly believe my eyes. Monsignor Koudelka is wearing the gold chasuble. For an ordinary mass, he would wear green; white is more usual for a nuptial mass; but he is wearing the gold. For me. I don't want to boast, but it's for me.

Feldy gives me a smile and a wink, then takes hold of my right hand with his left for just a second, but he says not a word. Which is fine. I'm pretty sure I know what he's thinking.

I chose Pachelbel's *Canon in D Major* for the organist to play when the procession walks up the aisle: two altar boys, followed by Monsignor, then me on Ted's right arm, my parents behind us, then Ted's parents, then two witnesses: Win, and Ted's sister Diana. We take our places in the front pew.

Most of the congregation might have been surprised, when they entered the church, to see that the altar-table, from which the priest ordinarily celebrates the mass facing the congregation, has been removed. It's replaced by a small rectangular wooden table that holds two flower vases, two candles, a crucifix, a Missal on a stand, and a small silver bucket of Holy Water, with a wand in it: these are called the aspersorium and the aspergillum.

I'll bet they're even more surprised to hear Monsignor Koudelka beginning the Mass in Latin: they will have heard nothing but English in this church for eight years or so. Monsignor obviously has stayed in practice: he never stumbles or hesitates.

The homily is in English, and at a Catholic nuptial Mass it doesn't vary much. According to The Order of Celebrating Matrimony, the priest "uses the sacred text to expound the mystery of Christian Marriage, the dignity of conjugal love, the Grace of the Sacrament and the responsibilities of married people, keeping in mind, however, the circumstances of this particular marriage."

That's what Monsignor does. Then he tells the congregation:

"When Ted and Teresa came to me to announce their engagement, and ask if I would preside over their wedding, I was surprised at how quickly they had come to their decision, and how soon they wanted the marriage to happen. But from the moment they walked together into the rectory, I could tell that they were right for each other: that it didn't make sense to do anything but encourage them to get married as soon as possible.

"These are two young people who have been well known to the public, here in State City, for many years. They're setting up their household here, where we can keep an eye on them—and they can keep an eye on us. On that note, I call upon the bride and the groom to come forward."

One of the altar boys opens the gate in the communion railing for us to step through. Ted and I kneel briefly outside the sanctuary, then stand before the priest: Ted on the Joseph/Epistle side of the church (the right from the point of view of the congregation) and I on the Mary/Gospel side.

"Theodore James Roch," says Monsignor, "wilt thou take Teresa, here present, for thy lawful wife, according to the rite of our holy Mother the Church?"

"I will." Ted's voice is low, but clear.

"Teresa Maeve Veronica, wilt thou take Theodore, here present, for thy lawful husband, according to the rite of our holy Mother the Church?"

"I will."

I meant to make it loud and strong, but my voice *would* let me down at the critical moment, for no reason that I can discern, so it comes out not much above a whisper.

Ted and I join hands, and Ted repeats, after Monsignor, "I, Theodore James Roch, take thee, Teresa Maeve Veronica, for my lawful wife, to have and to hold, from this day forward, for better, for worse, for richer, for poorer, in sickness and in health, until death do us part."

"I, Teresa Maeve Veronica, take thee, Theodore James Roch, for my lawful husband, to have and to hold, from this day forward, for better, for worse, for richer, for poorer, in sickness and in health, until death do us part."

"*Ego conjugo vos in matrimonium,*" says Monsignor, "*in nomine Patris, et Filii, et Spiritus Sancti. Amen.*" He takes up the aspergillum and sprinkles us with Holy Water, then blesses the bride's ring, saying, "*Adjutorium nostrum in nomine Domini.*"

Only a few in the congregation, and I, reply, "*Qui fecit cælum et terram.*"

"*Domine, exaudi orationem meam.*"

"*Et clamor meus ad te veniat.*"

I believe I have always loved that response, more dearly than I have ever loved any other words in the Mass. The line comes from a prayer of an afflicted, but in the context of the Mass, it's not always a cry of distress. Sometimes it's gratitude. Again, hardly anyone besides me knows to say it. But I hear Sister Timothy's voice, at least: coming from several rows back, but loud.

"*Dominus vobiscum,*" says Monsignor. He's smiling right at me, then briefly at Ted.

"*Et cum spiritu tuo.*" I smile back.

"Bless O Lord these rings," Monsignor says in English, and he makes the sign of the Cross, "which we bless" [the sign again] "in Thy name, that they who shall wear them, keeping true faith unto each other, may abide in Thy peace and in obedience to Thy will, and ever live in mutual love. Through Christ our Lord."

"Amen." This time the whole congregation knows what to say.

Monsignor sprinkles a ring with Holy Water and passes it to Ted, who places it on the third finger of my left hand, saying (with a couple of stumbles), "With this ring I thee wed; this gold and silver I thee give; with my body I thee worship; and with all my worldly goods I thee endow."

Monsignor sprinkles the other ring; I put it on Ted's finger.

"In nomine Patris, et Filii, et Spiritus Sancti," says Monsignor. *"Amen. Confirma hoc, Deus, quod operatus es in nobis."*

This is out of most of the congregation's depth. Only Sister Timothy and I respond: *"A templo sancto tuo quod est in Jerusalem."*

"Kyrie eleison."

"Christe eleison." A few of the congregation respond.

"Kyrie eleison."

Now Monsignor starts moving his lips to *"Pater noster,"* praying soundlessly.

"Et ne nos inducas in tentationem," he says aloud.

"Sed libera nos a malo." I say it; I can hear Sister Timothy, Win, Feldy, and Birdy.

"Salvos fac servos tuos."

"Deus meus, sperantes in te."

"Mitte eis, Domine, auxilium de sancto."

"Et de Sion tuere eos."

"Esto eis, Domine, turris fortitudinis."

"A facie inimici."

"Domine exaudi orationem meam," Monsignor says again.

"Et clamor meus ad te veniat." A few more in the congregation join in this time, since they now know what to expect. Tears are running down my face.

"Dominus vobiscum."

"Et cum spiritu tuo."

"Let us pray," says Monsignor. "Look down with favor, O Lord, we beseech Thee, upon these Thy servants, and graciously protect this, Thine ordinance, whereby Thou hast provided for the propagation of mankind; that they who are joined together by Thy authority may be preserved by Thy help; through Christ our Lord. Amen."

Ted and I turn; I put my hand through the crook of Ted's right elbow. Ted and Teresa Blaha, now man and wife, retire to their pew. Ted lets me into the pew first; I smile and wink at my parents before we sit. I take Ted's left hand—I grip it hard in both of mine—as Monsignor proceeds with the Offertory, then the Consecration.

When it's time to commune, Monsignor nods slightly to the two of us, so we get up again and go to the railing to receive Holy Communion before the rest of the congregation. My first Holy Communion as a married woman; Ted's and my first meal as a married couple. I want to give God and St. Teresa a silent prayer of Thanksgiving—but no words are coming to me. I *feel* the gratitude, at least, and I know that God knows I feel it.

This bright yellow-orange light surrounds me, with odd tinges of pink and blue. I have never seen colors so wonderful. I feel a warmth not of this world—like I'm embraced by the Holy Spirit. I feel unsteady as I get to my feet; Ted takes my elbow and guides me back to the pew.

That yellow-orange is changing, settling into a blue aura, now, as I kneel. I'm contemplating, rather than praying, and the aura slowly turns to a bright cool green.

"*Ite, missa est,*" says Monsignor—from nowhere, it seems to me, since apparently I just now blanked out for a minute or two, trying to process all that has happened.

"*Deo gratias,*" I respond, automatically—and I remember Sister Mary Jane Patricia, back in first grade, smiling when she told us, "That means 'Thank God for the Mass,' not 'Thank God it's over.'" Which makes me smile too, now.

I'm back to Earth. I'm seeing clearly, as clearly as I have ever seen the world and beyond it. The organist begins playing Schubert's *Ave Maria*. The servers and Monsignor descend from the altar. Monsignor nods to Ted and I—Ted and me—to follow him down the aisle. I take Ted's right arm once again.

This is Truth. This is the bounty of God's love: this good man God has given me, and the knowledge that together, we will have a life pleasing to God.

I look right into my husband's eyes; I know mine must be shining. I whisper, "Here we go."